SEEKERS
OF THE FOX

Also by Kevin Sands

CHILDREN OF THE FOX

SEEKERS

OF THE FOX

KEVIN SANDS

VIKING

VIKING

An imprint of Penguin Random House LLC, New York

First published in the United States of America by Viking,
an imprint of Penguin Random House LLC, 2022

Visit us online at penguinrandomhouse.com.

Library of Congress Cataloging-in-Publication Data is available.

Book manufactured in Canada

ISBN 9780593327548

1 3 5 7 9 10 8 6 4 2

FRI

Design by Lucia Baez • Text set in Rilke

SEEKERS
OF THE FOX

CHAPTER 1

LACHLAN WAS DYING.

We could hear it in the way he was breathing. Each gasp, ragged and agonizing, broke at the end, a slow *hhhhhh-uh.* We might have explained it away as pain. Except now, as we carried him through the brush, Lachlan paused between each breath, taking in no air at all. Every one of us knew what that meant.

I suppose it shouldn't have come as a surprise. We'd watched our friend get run through the gut by a burning sword. The blade had been wielded by the Lady in Red, a fire elemental—a construct made of living flame, bound through magic in the shape of a woman. Lachlan had been burned all over his back, too. When we'd killed the enchanted elemental, it had exploded in a blazing burst. It was a miracle Lachlan was still alive at all.

But now he was fading, and fast. What we needed, then, was a new miracle.

We needed to find something to save him.

The Old Man watched from inside my head. I could almost see him, lounging with his back to one of the trees, filling his pipe as I trudged past. *What are the odds of that?* he said.

Not good. *You think I'm a fool, don't you?* I said silently.

The Old Man sounded amused. *If you have to ask that question, then you already know the answer.*

I sighed. Because he wasn't wrong.

He rarely was. It was one of the things I'd always found so infuriating. The Old Man—he'd never told me his real name; I'd just called him "Old Man" from the start, and he'd seemed to like that—had raised me. He'd rescued me from the streets when I was six years old and taught me his trade: how to manipulate people. I'd learned to read their thoughts, their feelings, their hidden intentions, from the way they moved, from the words they said—or the words they didn't. The Old Man had turned me into a younger version of himself: a gaffer, a charmer, a silvertongue—or a con man, a swindler, and a dirty rotten cheat, depending on whom you asked.

The Old Man was gone now. He'd abandoned me half a year ago, after one too many fights between us, when I finally told him I wouldn't run any more gaffs that might snaffle decent people. But he wouldn't leave my head.

Good thing, too, boy, he said, puffing on his pipe. *You should have at least one person in this skull of yours talking sense.*

I don't need you to remind me, I grumbled. Trying to save Lachlan, with his injuries so severe; it *was* ridiculous.

And yet. I still led this band of misfit thieves into the trees, away from the smoking volcano Bolcanathair. Deep inside it, in the ancient Dragon Temple, we'd defeated Mr. Solomon, a powerful Weaver of magic, and his elemental. Now, bent over, my back aching, I followed a faintly glowing trail of red that cut through the grass underfoot.

The trail wasn't easy to see. Would have been impossible,

actually, if it wasn't for the artifact that had attached itself to my left eye socket. The Eye—the Dragon's Eye, to give it the full name the Weavers called it—was capable of seeing enchantments and the magical energy that powered them: life.

That was what I followed now. The glowing red trail was Lachlan's life energy, draining out as he died. It was leading us somewhere, to something, though none of us knew what.

On its own, the trail would have been no trouble to spot. The problem was that *everything* living, plant or animal, had a glow through the Eye, each with its own special color. The grass shimmered with a ghostly green light, and it was almost bright enough to obscure the red we needed to follow. Keeping sight of it took all my concentration.

And if that wasn't bad enough, I was getting dizzy. Seeing the ordinary world and the magical glow at the same time made my head spin. The longer I kept the Eye uncovered, the worse it got. Even now, I was stumbling.

I'd have gladly handed off the bloodhound duties, but the Eye wouldn't let go of me. After I'd stolen it from the High Weaver, Darragh VII, the greatest enchanter in the world, the Eye had bound itself to my socket by some strange magic I didn't understand. Sentient—and completely untrustworthy—the Eye actually talked to me in my head.

Or at least it used to. The Eye's voice had been silenced somehow by Mr. Solomon, the Weaver who'd hired us to steal the thing. I'd have asked him about it, if he wasn't already dead.

Meriel's voice came from behind me. She sounded out of

breath. "Could you move a little faster, Cal?"

She had every right to be tired. Meriel, Gareth, and Foxtail had been carrying Lachlan's unconscious body, trading him off amongst each other since we'd left the Dragon Temple. She shifted him over her shoulders. "He's heavier than he looks."

"Wish I could," I said. "But if you'd like to have your eye ripped out and the Dragon's Eye put in your skull instead, I'd be more than happy to trade places."

"Well, when you put it *that* way . . ."

She said it lightly, but underneath, I could hear her frustration, fear, and anger. Frustration at our slow pace. Fear for Lachlan. And anger—not at me, but at herself.

Like I said, the Old Man taught me how to look deeper into people, to see the hidden messages they gave away without even realizing it. It let me understand the real reason Meriel was mad. Mr. Solomon had hired the five of us because we made a well-rounded team. Foxtail was a second-story girl, a cat burglar, with an uncanny knack for getting in and out of places unseen. Gareth was a book boy, our head of intel, skilled at uncovering information and even more skilled at sleight of hand. Lachlan was a runner, a gopher, a former Breaker with an intimate knowledge of the city of Carlow's underworld. He knew where to get the tools to do the job.

And Meriel was an acrobat. She'd never told us where she'd come from, and I hadn't been able to figure it out. She had a subtle accent I couldn't place, which was odd, because the Old Man had taught me just about every accent in the empire. But wherever she'd come from, in addition to having an otherworldly grace, Meriel was an expert with throwing knives, which she kept hidden in secret pockets all over her dress. She'd clearly been trained to fight.

The rest of us weren't. Particularly Lachlan, who, at only ten years old, was small for his age, and as good-natured as any thief I'd ever met. So if anyone was going to get hurt, Meriel thought it should be her.

She wasn't being fair, of course. No one can stop every bad thing from happening. Besides, she was wrong. It wasn't her fault.

It was mine.

It had been my plan that had led us to rob the High Weaver. It was my foolishness that had lost us the Eye—and my own—when Mr. Solomon had the Lady in Red tear it from my head. And it had been my plan again to take the Eye back from him, then seal the crack in the earth he'd made to tap into the primeval magic under the ground and prevent our world, Ayreth, from splitting apart. So if anyone should be dying, it was me.

The Old Man rolled his eyes. *What a tedious thing a conscience is,* he said.

How would you know? I said. *It's not like you ever had one.*

And I'm happier for it. But go on, punish yourself if it makes you feel better.

Seeing Lachlan healed will make me feel better, I said.

You think that's what's at the end of this trail? Someone's become awfully trusting.

He had a point. I was only following this path because that

was where the Eye was leading me. I'd asked it to help save Lachlan, and the red glow trailing from his dying body was what it had showed me.

Before that, however, I'd made a different deal with the thing. The Eye had saved my life in the Dragon Temple, given me the knowledge needed to seal the rift in the world. In return, it had made me promise to, in the Eye's words, "come for it."

I hadn't the faintest idea what that meant. But now, deep inside my mind, I thought I could . . . *feel* something. A hint of an emotion, a vague sense of urging

(forward go forward follow follow follow)

and the only thing I knew was that this feeling wasn't coming from me. It was the Eye, trying to communicate past whatever binding Mr. Solomon had used to silence it. It *wanted* me to keep going.

That was what worried me. I didn't know what to make of the Eye. I didn't know where it had come from, I didn't know what its purpose was, and I didn't know why it was pushing me forward. The one thing I did understand was that the artifact didn't care a single sept for any of us. We were nothing but tools to it, pieces in some grand game, to be used—or sacrificed. So I was sure that whatever the Eye wanted, I wasn't going to like it one bit.

Anyway, all of this meant it was entirely possible that we'd find nothing when we reached the end of this trail. Assuming we even got there. My head was really spinning.

See? the Old Man said. *What did I tell you?*

I sighed and headed into the woods.

∩◡

I made it another ten minutes. Then the glow of the forest floor brightened beneath my feet.

I stared at it. The glow looked like it was coming closer—

WHUMP

—because it *was* coming closer. I planted my face in the ground. "Mmlffgh," I said.

Small fingers fumbled about my forehead, pushing my eye-patch down to cover the Eye. With the artifact hidden, the lifeglow of the forest vanished, so I could see nothing but the ordinary world. Strangely, the urging I'd been feeling

(follow follow follow)

faded, too. In its place came a vague sense of frustration, just for a moment. Then it vanished along with everything else.

I rolled over and spat dirt. The Eye's vision might have disappeared, but my dizziness hadn't. Overhead, the forest canopy whirled. And bizarrely, among the leaves, I saw my own face floating, oddly distorted.

I blinked. My mind was such a jumble that for a moment I thought I was seeing some new magical effect of the Eye. Then I realized what it was.

It was Foxtail. My "face" was just my reflection shining off the girl's mirrored mask. She kneeled over me, her reddish-brown ponytail hanging past her shoulder. Lantern in one hand, she used the hem of her skirt to wipe the dirt off my cheeks.

Of all the oddities I'd encountered since I'd come to Carlow, Foxtail's mask was the oddest. Her entire face was covered by a polished steel plate, riveted to her skull around the edge. There were no eye slits, no mouth hole, no nothing. Just smooth, featureless metal.

I had no idea what enchantment had pinned it there, or how she lived with it. We'd never seen her eat. If it wasn't for the rise and fall of her chest, I wouldn't have even thought she breathed. How she got air through that mask was a mystery.

The steel didn't let her speak, either. She communicated instead through gestures. She was trying to tell me something now, but I couldn't make it out. Her hands were whirling along with everything else.

Gareth hovered behind her shoulder. Tall and lanky, he clutched a long, undulating silver staff: Mr. Solomon's dragon staff. It was the only thing the Weaver had left behind. The primeval magic had disintegrated the rest of him.

"Lie still a m-moment," Gareth said. He had a bit of a stammer, which grew worse when he got stressed. "You lost your balance."

"Is that what happened?" I said. "I just figured the world decided to punch me in the face."

I could tell by the twinkle in Meriel's eyes that a joke hovered on the tip of her tongue. She decided not to say it. *Too worried about Lachlan*, I thought as she laid him gently on the grass and chewed her lip.

I knew as well as the others that we didn't have time for this. But I couldn't even stand up anymore. "Just give me a couple minutes," I said. I took a deep breath, trying to ignore the reek of sulfur wafting from the volcano behind us, and closed my eyes to stop the spinning. Foxtail rested her hand on my shoulder. "I've never stared through the Eye for so long before."

But then, I'd never had a reason to push on like this. How long did the Eye expect me to follow its path?

"Cal," Meriel said.

"That was not a couple minutes," I protested.

"Cal."

"Seriously, would you just let me rest—"

"*Cal.*"

The urgency in her voice made me open my eyes. The world had mostly stopped turning. "What . . . ?"

Meriel stared up into the trees. I followed her gaze.

And my blood ran cold.

CHAPTER 2

TWO EYES GLOWED red in the branches.

Something followed us down from the Dragon Temple, I thought in a panic. *One of Mr. Solomon's creations, come to finish us off.*

But as Foxtail brought the lantern up, I saw the rest of the beast overhead. It had a long, lithe body, with spotted fur—

A leopard.

There was a *leopard* in the tree.

It stood on a branch above us, tail flicking, watching.

It's been stalking us, I realized. We hadn't exactly been quiet—in our worry, we hadn't even considered it—but as my dizziness faded, I decided the leopard had been attracted by something other than branches rustling in the night.

It had come for Lachlan, dying. His blood, and the smell of burnt flesh.

Meriel stepped astride the boy's body, her throwing knives already slipping from beneath her sleeves. Slowly, carefully, I stood, my eye on the great cat. It took a step along the branch, muscles rippling.

"Nobody move," I said. As if I had any experience facing down leopards. Maybe we were supposed to move. Make noise, scare it off. "Gareth? What do we do?"

I figured that Gareth, the only one of us with any education, might know something. But he was paralyzed with fear—and confusion.

"This can't be," he whispered. He gripped the dragon staff so hard his knuckles turned white. "Leopards don't l-live near Carlow."

"Tell *it* that," Meriel said through gritted teeth.

I still had no idea what to do. I glanced toward Foxtail, but the girl remained perfectly still.

"Give me the staff," I said to Gareth.

I had to pry it from his fingers. I knew the thing had an extraordinary enchantment inside it; Mr. Solomon had blasted great bolts of air at us with the staff after using it to crack open the earth. But I had no idea how to bring out its magic. I gripped it low instead, ready to swing.

The leopard turned its head to stare at me.

I froze, just like Foxtail. What was it doing? It could clearly see we'd spotted it and were ready for a fight. I wondered what it thought of our chances.

The Old Man raised an eyebrow. *Not good, I'd imagine.*

I had to agree. Meriel had her knives, but I wasn't sure how deep those short blades would go into a leopard's hide. Maybe if she got it in the eye . . .

Better to try something else first. "See if you can scare it off," I said to Meriel.

She threw one dagger, aiming low. It thunked into the branch, just below the cat's front paws.

The beast barely glanced at it. Could a leopard look disdain-ful? This one sure did. Yet it didn't seem to be threatening us, exactly.

So what was it doing?

Holding your attention, for a start, the Old Man said.

My eyes went wide.

"Gareth?" I said. "Do leopards hunt in packs?"

The question surprised him. "They don't . . . I mean . . . no. They're s-solitary animals."

If Gareth said it, I believed it. Then again, according to him, leopards didn't live around here.

Still, nothing explained what it was doing. Was it setting some kind of trap?

I scanned the surrounding trees, as much as was lit by Foxtail's lantern. If only I could see beyond—

The Eye, I thought suddenly.

Of course. It could see life. If there were more leopards about, their bodies would shine like beacons. Hoping the artifact wouldn't make me dizzy again, I pushed the eyepatch up and scanned the woods behind us. The world became awash with color, a soft green suffusing the trunks and leaves.

I froze. There *was* something there, glowing purple-red . . .

No, I thought, feeling foolish as I made out its shape. *That's just an owl.* It wasn't the only creature around, either. There were insects glittering like violet fireflies, and a squirrel, and several other birds. But no leopards.

"Cal!"

I whirled at Meriel's voice, bringing the dragon staff up

defensively. But now the branch overhead only glowed with the green of the trees.

The leopard had vanished.

"Where'd it go?" I said.

"It r-ran off," Gareth said.

I scanned the forest, but the Eye couldn't see it through the foliage. For some reason, it had abandoned its hunt, and I didn't think we were the cause.

We couldn't possibly have scared it away, I thought. *It could be circling around to surprise us.*

Either way, we needed to get out of here. The lifeglow of Lachlan's trail had gotten much harder to see as we entered the thicker woods. I wouldn't be able to watch for leopards and follow the path the Eye was showing me at the same time. Meanwhile, the pauses in Lachlan's breathing had grown longer. He'd be dead within the hour. Stalked or not, it was time to run.

I handed the staff back to Gareth. "Let's move."

I was grateful once we finally broke free of the woods, and not only because it gave no more cover for that leopard to hide. Seeing the normal and enchanted worlds at the same time had made me dizzy once more. I couldn't keep this up much longer.

Out in the open, we could see Bolcanathair again. A dark plume rose from the volcano, blocking the light of Ayreth's twin moons, Mithil and Cairdwyn. Molten rock flowed from the broken ring of the caldera. The lava glowed in the night, a dusky red that cast an eerie light on the cloud overhead. Flakes of ash continued to fall, blanketing the fields in a layer of gray.

The air still stank of sulfur, and inhaling the ash made us cough and spit out little black bits we couldn't seem to keep from our mouths. Even so, I was glad for it. The lifeless ash covered the Eye-glow of the grass, letting me see Lachlan's trail without any strain. It pointed toward the road, some few hundred feet from the trees. Then it took a sharp turn toward Carlow, following the flagstones of the Emperor's Highway. Two miles away, braziers roared atop the towers of the city walls, their fires flickering against the sky.

Now I could keep the Eye covered, peeking out every few minutes to confirm we were still following the trail. Meriel groaned with relief as she handed Lachlan off to Foxtail. Though Foxtail was even shorter than the boy, she was remarkably strong and carried him with ease.

Picking up the pace, we passed a pair of farmhouses, cattle lowing nervously in the fields. As the farmers and their families tried to calm their anxious herds, they stared up at Bolcanathair with worries of their own, wondering if the smoke and ash were the worst of it, or whether a bigger cataclysm was yet to come. The only good news was that the lava was flowing east, toward Lake Galway. The city of Carlow would be spared. For now.

One of the farmers saw us along the road and called out. "Ho!"

I waved back but said nothing. We couldn't afford to stop.

He tried again. "Ho! Children! Are you all right?"

He'd spotted Lachlan, slung over Foxtail's shoulders. "Fine, Artha be praised," I called back. "Our brother's tired; he's fallen asleep. We're taking him home."

It wasn't the best lie I'd ever told, but there wasn't any good reason for a group of children to be running from an erupting volcano in the middle of the night, carrying an unconscious boy. The last thing we needed right now was a delay from a concerned bystander trying to help.

The farmer had a son around Lachlan's age. He spoke to his father, who nodded. The boy ran into the farmhouse to grab something, then began to jog after us, his heels kicking up clumps of ash.

I cursed. "Keep following the road," I said quietly. "I'll get rid of him."

The others hurried on ahead, Meriel and Gareth walking behind Foxtail to block Lachlan's wounds from view. I waited for the farm boy to arrive.

He ran up to me, holding what he was carrying aloft. "Thought you might need this," he said.

He'd brought us a wineskin. Surprised, I popped the top. There was water inside, and I took a swig. It wasn't cold, but my throat was parched. It was like drinking from a clear mountain stream.

"Thank you," I gasped, drawing a breath. "I have some money—"

The boy looked shocked I'd even suggested it. "I'm Donal."

"Callan," I said. "We're very grateful."

He smiled. "Spirits bless you," he said before running back to his family.

I'd almost forgotten what kindness felt like. I watched him go for a moment.

Then I chased after the others.

I took one more sip before passing the skin along. I'd have guzzled the whole thing, but my friends deserved it more. They'd been doing all the heavy lifting—literally.

As happy as I was to have the water, the encounter with Donal's family left me worried. Lachlan's lifetrail was aiming us toward Carlow. It was one thing to carry a dying child around in the dark. The second we entered the city, someone would see how badly hurt he was.

Even worse, the High Weaver already had both the Stickmen—the city watch—and the emperor's regiment of Pistoleers searching for the thief who'd stolen the Eye from his underground laboratory. Now, with Bolcanathair's eruption, *everyone* would be out of their homes, gawking. The streets would be nothing but trouble.

So I was relieved once again when the lifetrail didn't take us into Carlow. A half-mile south of Donal's home, I peeked out from under my eyepatch and saw the glow veer off to the east, onto another farm.

This one raised pigs. I smelled them before I saw them, the stinging scent of barnyard cutting through the rotten egg of volcanic fumes. Four dozen sows grunted outside the barn, corralled in well-trodden mud. Through the Eye, their life glowed an earthy sort of red, almost brown, as if reflecting the slop beneath them.

Lachlan's trail of lighter red wound past the pen. At first, I thought the path would lead us through the farm to the woods beyond. Instead, the glow ended right at the feet of a man sitting on a stool under a flickering torch, just beside the barn's open door.

The Eye had led us to . . . a pig farmer?

CHAPTER 3

A JOKE.

It had to be. A cruel, twisted joke. The Eye had toyed with me before. Cruelty would match its sense of humor well.

Except this didn't make any sense. Whatever the Eye thought of me, it still needed me. It had wormed its way into my mind once, raiding my most private memories. But it hadn't been able to control me after that, and now it couldn't even speak. If it were to make me angry enough that I rebelled against it, it would never get what it wanted.

What's more, as soon as I'd spied the pig farmer through the Eye, a new feeling

(there there go there)

had replaced the distant sense of urging me forward. This was clearly where the artifact meant to lead me.

In my mind, the Old Man shrugged. *Why second-guess what you can't know? The Eye sent you here for a reason. Go find out why. Unless you think Lachlan has time to waste.*

The boy's breathing had changed again, now a *huh-huh-huh*, followed by an agonizing pause. He had only minutes left to live. And we were out of options.

Putting my patch back over the Eye, I told the others what I'd seen. "This is it."

Foxtail passed Lachlan off to Meriel while I took the lantern. Though Foxtail's hat had a veil that covered her mask, there'd be no explaining why she was wearing it while wandering through the dark. She gestured at the fields around the farm, then disappeared into the night. Going to scout the surrounding area while we saved Lachlan, I guessed.

The rest of us made for the barn.

The farmer watched us as we came down the road. He was older, maybe in his fifties, with a craggy face and a wide, muscular frame. Wrangling pigs, willful animals that they are, had kept him in good shape.

There was something on his lap, but in the faint light of the torch, I couldn't see what it was. As we turned off the Emperor's Highway and onto his land, he leaned toward the open barn door and placed whatever he'd been holding just inside it.

The pigs greeted us in a friendly way as we passed, poking pink snouts through the slats in the pen and grunting. I couldn't help thinking that Lachlan would have loved this.

I gave the farmer a somewhat desperate smile. Whatever the Eye expected from the man, we needed it. "Spirits' blessing upon you."

The farmer nodded but didn't answer.

"I'm Callan," I said. "We're travelers from Redfairne."

This time, I waited for a response. Silence makes most people uncomfortable. If you don't say anything, they'll fill the emptiness with talk.

This man didn't seem to care. He sat there, unhurried, tracing a finger along a steel chain around his neck. When he did eventually speak, it was more out of a sense of curiosity.

"Bragan," he said.

I wasn't sure if that was his first or last name. May as well play it safe. "Sorry to trouble you, Mr. Bragan, but our friend is hurt."

Meriel laid Lachlan on the thin layer of ash that had piled up on the grass beside the pathway. The pigs shifted, trying to get a closer look. *They can smell his blood*, I thought.

Bragan glanced at Lachlan, uninterested—at least at first. But when he saw the wound in the boy's stomach, he frowned and sat up a little.

"What happened to him?"

I still wasn't sure what we were doing here, so I didn't tell the farmer the truth. Instead, I said, "We were passing Bolcanathair when it erupted. Lava fell from the sky and burned him."

Bragan studied Lachlan from the stool for a moment, then stood. He stepped closer, inspecting the body. Then he looked up at me.

I was a practiced liar, taught by the best. I knew how to control my voice, my expression, my body, all so I wouldn't give away any tells. This man was a pig farmer. He should have believed me.

But he didn't. I could see it in his eyes.

"So what do you want from me?" he said.

"We were hoping you could save his life," I said.

"Boy needs a physick, not a farmer."

Lachlan's injuries were far too severe for simple physickry. "He'll be dead before we reach Carlow," I said. "A friend told me you could help."

Bragan studied me with interest. "Now, who would tell you something like that?"

From the tone of his voice, I didn't think he expected an answer. I didn't really have one to give him, anyway.

Bragan looked down at Lachlan again. As he did, I glanced past the man, toward the barn, where Bragan had placed something behind the open door. From the way he'd moved, it was clear he didn't want us to see it.

But since his eyes had been on us when he put the thing away, he hadn't hidden it completely. A bit of it stuck out from behind the painted wood. It was hard to tell in the torchlight, but it looked like a book.

What kind of farmer sat out on a night like this, in falling ash, a volcano erupting a few miles away, to have a read?

When I met Bragan's eyes again, he smiled slightly. He'd caught me looking. It didn't worry him. If anything, he seemed amused.

He took a good look at the others then. He only glanced at Meriel, dismissing her immediately. But when his eyes fell upon Gareth, standing farther behind us, his breath caught in his throat.

"Where did you get that?" he said.

He was staring at the dragon staff.

"From my father," I lied. "It's a family heirloom."

The man twirled his finger around the steel chain hanging from his neck. It slipped out from under his collar. There was a pendant attached to it: a single stone of onyx, with black and orange bands.

He'd meant the action to look casual. I knew better.

"What family would that be?" Bragan said.

I took a step back. This was not going well at all. "Solomon."

That was a gamble. I used Mr. Solomon's name only to see if the man recognized it. I don't think he did.

He held out his right hand, his left still fingering his onyx pendant. "Let me see it."

"If we do," I said, "will you heal our friend?"

"No."

"Then you're not getting the staff."

He smiled without humor. "I apologize," he said, "if I made you think I was asking your permission."

Then the man unleashed his power.

CHAPTER 4

Bragan gripped the pendant at the end of his chain. He whispered a word I didn't understand. I heard a roaring sound, like I'd been caught in a heavy wind. Then he stretched his hand out toward Gareth.

And the wind became real.

It rushed inward, whipping up dirt and ash. The force blasted Gareth from behind, tearing at the dragon staff he was holding.

Gareth's grip was tight enough to yank him off his feet. He fell, the staff dragging him through the dirt before he finally let go. The staff flew through the air to land with a smack in Bragan's open palm.

Meriel's knives were already out. She flung them at Bragan's chest. They tumbled, but before the blades could reach him, a tug of wind deflected them, sending them thudding into the barn instead.

Meriel tried again, finding two more knives among the folds of her dress. But now Bragan had the staff. He slammed the butt of it into the ground—*Just like Mr. Solomon*, I thought—and then a cyclone blew outward, whipping Meriel's knives off into the night.

The twister spun, catching the rest of us in its wake. The barn rattled, and the pigpen shook in the howling air. The pigs, squealing in fright, were bowled over in the wind, bumping each other as they scrambled to flee.

The cyclone shoved me backward, too. I teetered, arms windmilling. Gareth, already on the ground, covered his head as ash and dust whipped around him, face buried in the earth. Meriel slid backward, heels dragging grooves in the mud, the wind plastering her dress to her body.

Somehow, she managed to stay on her feet as the twister washed over her. She pulled two more knives from Shuna knows where and sent those at Bragan, too.

They did no better than the others. Three feet from the man's chest, the blades hit a swirling wall of wind. One went spinning to bounce off the pigpen. The other sailed back in her direction.

Eyes wide, Meriel cartwheeled out of the way just in time, so the dagger ripped her skirt instead of her flesh. Grinning, Bragan punched the staff twice in her direction.

The air rippled as blasts of wind chased after her. She managed to tumble out of the path of the first one, but the second caught her by the legs. With a cry of pain and surprise, Meriel was flung like a rag doll, spinning across the Emperor's Highway and into the field beyond. Part of the blast caught Lachlan, too, unconscious on the trail. He rolled a few times before sliding into the gutter beside the road.

My heart sank. I had no idea if Meriel was alive or dead. And Lachlan, poor Lachlan; surely his body couldn't take any more punishment. But I didn't have time for grief. Bragan had turned his grin on me.

He drew back his staff.

The pigs, the Old Man whispered

and then I was leaping over the fence into the pen, sprinting toward the animals huddling against the far side.

It was a gamble. I was betting Bragan wouldn't hurt his pigs. Not because of any sort of humanity; it was obvious his role as a farmer was merely a cover. I was wagering that cover meant he wouldn't be willing to damage his livestock.

I guessed right. As I dove between the squealing sows, Bragan checked his attack. He turned his gaze toward Gareth instead, who cowered on the path from the road.

Then a figure darted across the roof of the barn. It leapt from the edge, arcing downward toward Bragan.

It was Foxtail. The light of the torch reflected from her mask, and her ponytail fluttered behind her as she fell. With Bragan turned our way, he never saw her coming.

He didn't need to. Three feet above him, Foxtail's surprise attack was foiled. She hit that whirling wall of wind, and it blew her away as easily as it had Meriel's knives. Foxtail sailed backward through the air, limbs flailing, before clipping a shoulder against the edge of the barn and tumbling out of view.

Bragan spotted her just as she disappeared. He laughed, wagging a finger in her direction. Then he laughed harder at me as I scrambled in the mud with his livestock.

"Here, little piggy," he said.

I cast my mind out for help. *What do I do?*

The Old Man answered, *The Eye made a deal with you.*

So what?

So it may not care about you, he said, *but would it send you here just to die?*

No, I thought. *It needs me.*

"Won't come out, piglet?" Bragan taunted. "Then I'll play with this one instead."

He held his hand toward Gareth, who'd finally started to crawl to safety. Gareth cried out in alarm as the wind lifted him from the ground and slammed him back into the dirt.

Dust swirled around him. Bragan raised his hand again, and once more Gareth rose, high this time, spinning, caught in a twister.

"Come, then, pig," Bragan said. "Come to your slaughter."

The Eye needs me, I thought again. *But how does that help me fight this man?*

You can't, the Old Man said. *You don't have the power.*

Then what did I have? Nothing.

Hardly nothing, the Old Man said.

But what—

Oh—of course. He meant the Eye. But how was that supposed to . . . ?

Gareth spun in the air, too scared now even to scream. Bragan whistled a merry tune, making Gareth's body dance in the air with the beat.

No time to question it. Peering over the pigs, I raised my patch and looked at the man through the Eye.

And the artifact's sight left me stunned.

Bragan was surrounded by a sphere of translucent violet: the enchanted wall of air that protected him. His flesh glowed red behind it, with its own hint of purple. Like I'd seen on Mr. Solomon, there were runes shining all over his skin like tattoos. Weaver runes.

Except . . . not quite. These runes looked different from any I'd seen before. They were . . . simpler. Less swirly, less intricate. Nothing but straight lines and angles.

And those runes weren't the only source of magic I could see. The dragon staff blazed in his hands, a deep royal purple, almost as bright as the stream of primeval magic that had shot from the earth back in the Dragon Temple. A sparkling stream of that purple spiraled down Bragan's arm, wound across his chest, and arced from his outstretched hand toward Gareth. The shine surrounded my friend, an indigo whirlwind keeping him aloft.

I stared at the magic in wonder and horror. I could see it now, yes. But I still didn't know what to do.

Then something stirred deep inside. An emotion. Not mine. And this one didn't stay buried.

I felt a sudden, vicious contempt. And outrage. Furious, murderous outrage.

It was the Eye. The *Eye* was enraged.

Why?

It brought you here, the Old Man said.

Yes, I thought. It brought me here to get help. Instead, Bragan had attacked us. And that infuriated the Eye.

So maybe this outrage was the only power I had.

Bragan lifted Gareth higher. The wind whipped at his clothes, threatening to tear him apart.

I stood.

"You *dare*," I said.

Still whistling, Bragan turned my way.

"*You DARE*," I roared, feeling every ounce of the Eye's fury. "*You dare to defy ME?*"

Bragan drew back the dragon staff, ready to punch it out to send me to oblivion.

Then his whistling faded.

And he stared in utter shock.

CHAPTER 5

I STORMED TOWARD him. If he wanted, he could have killed me in a heartbeat.

Instead, all his magic winked out. The purple whirlwind that held Gareth aloft vanished, leaving the boy to crumple in the dirt. The sphere that surrounded Bragan wavered, thinned, then disappeared, violet tendrils curling away like smoke.

He still gripped the dragon staff, which hadn't lost its light; it blazed like the sun in my Eye-sight. But he didn't punch it out at me. He lowered it, mouth open.

"You," he whispered. "It's really you."

I kicked open the gate to the pigpen. Bragan stepped back, alarmed. I marched toward him, glaring at him through the Eye.

He couldn't stop staring at it. Fear lined his face, but also wonder—and joy.

Good thing for him he didn't know what *I* was feeling at the moment. The outrage had swelled within me. This worm had denied me the help I needed. He'd hurt my friends. More important, he'd tried to hurt *me*. He'd *laughed* at me. Called me a *pig*. Let's see if he laughed when I grabbed him by the neck and strangled him. How I would *love* that, to squeeze his *throat*, feel his *bones* snap, watch the life *drain* from his *eyes*—

Well, the Old Man said, *someone's feeling grumpy*.

His voice cut through the rage. The fury that burned inside cracked, suddenly distant. I stopped, confused.

Strangle the man? Watch the life drain . . . ?

What in Shuna's name was I thinking?

Then it occurred to me: *I* wasn't thinking at all. Those feelings weren't mine.

Hurriedly, I pulled the patch down to cover the Eye. And as the Eye-vision of Bragan's glow vanished, so did the feelings of outrage and contempt. They lingered, vague and distant, but only for a moment. Then they disappeared, too, leaving only a brief lashing of frustration from deep within.

I took a breath. Bragan still looked uncertain, but with the Eye tucked away, he regained his composure. He bowed.

"Forgive me, blessed one," he said. "I didn't know who you were."

That begged a question: Exactly who did he think I was?

Someone important, the Old Man said. *So play it out, boy.*

The way to pull a gaff like this was to give Bragan what he expected. I didn't know what that was. But I knew what *he* was: powerful, cruel—and cowed by the Eye, subservient.

So I shoved my own instincts down. What I wanted to do was run to my friends, see that they were all right. Most of all, to run to Lachlan. Was he even still alive?

But that wasn't the role. Bragan expected cruel indifference. So indifferent was what I would be.

I said nothing to the man. Instead, I glared at him like a wolf facing down an upstart cub. Meriel returned to the light, limping. Her dress was a mess, and her left leg was obviously sore, but other than some scrapes on her fingers, she didn't seem much worse for wear.

She was, however, looking decidedly murderous. I needed to cut off any thoughts of revenge. If Bragan started with his magic again, we were finished.

"Take the staff," I commanded her.

She turned her anger on me. "*What* did you—"

I whirled on her. "Take. The staff."

My sudden hostility surprised her—which was exactly what I'd hoped. Her surprise disarmed her, and in the cooling of her blood, she understood. I was playing a role. And she needed to play along.

She yanked the dragon staff from Bragan's hand, then helped Gareth up. He stood, shaken but unhurt except for a few scrapes. Meriel shoved the staff into his arms, then hurried to Lachlan, who was lying alone in the ditch. Foxtail joined us, too, rubbing her shoulder where she'd hit the edge of the barn. There was a tear in her dress, marked with blood.

Bragan was still watching me. I hadn't responded to the last thing he'd said.

"Who did you imagine I'd be," I snapped, "walking onto your farm with a staff like that?"

"I assumed you were thieves," he said. And, well, he wasn't wrong. "The patch you wear keeps your gift well hidden."

Gift. The Eye had once said the same thing. this is my gift to you. do you like it?

Remembering it made me shiver. Still, I needed to keep playing my role. "It is not yet time," I said angrily, "to reveal the truth to the world."

Bragan bowed again, palms out in supplication. "Of course not, blessed one. My apologies. I hadn't expected the Emissary to be so young."

The Emissary? So that's who he imagined I was. Whatever that meant.

"I've kept watch," he said, clearly expecting me to understand that, too. "Again, I beg your forgiveness. I should have seen the signs. The eruption in Garman. Now Bolcanathair's rumblings, on the very night of the syzygy."

He was talking about the alignment of the sun, our planet Ayreth, and our twin moons. That's what had drawn the primeval magic to the surface, close enough for Mr. Solomon to tap into.

"And the dreams . . ." Bragan continued. Here, his face lit up with joy again.

I had no idea what he was talking about, and while something in the back of my mind told me what he was saying was important, we didn't have time to explore it. "Enough," I said. "We came here for a reason. I need you to heal my companion."

I almost said "friend" again. But Bragan believed I was the Eye's Emissary, and I was pretty sure anyone serving that artifact wouldn't have friends. Just tools.

"Of course," Bragan said, and he turned to Meriel, who carried Lachlan toward us.

But her head was bowed. My heart sank, because I already knew what that meant.

"It's too late," she said, sad, bitter, and full of rage. "Lachlan's dead."

CHAPTER 6

Despair.

I'd failed. I was supposed to keep Lachlan safe. Keep them all safe. Everything we'd done had been my plan. Always mine.

And I'd failed.

Bragan's whirlwind had blown most of the ash from his property. Meriel laid Lachlan on the grass. She kneeled beside him, her hands gentle on his chest. Gareth looked pale, stricken. Foxtail stood at a distance, staring off at the smoking volcano, not even willing to look at the body.

I'd have liked to say Lachlan looked peaceful, but he didn't. His clothes were filthy and charred. His eyes looked empty, like he'd never been that friendly, kind-hearted child.

Guilt gnawed at my gut. Guilt and grief. I'd seen plenty of dead before, but never anyone I'd cared about. Never a friend.

After the rage I'd felt when the Eye had seen Bragan, I was scared to lift my patch and unleash those emotions again. But I had to. I had to see the truth.

I peeked under it, just to look at Lachlan, and nothing else. My heart sank even further when I did.

His light was all but gone. The cheerful red that had suffused his body had faded, dimmer now than the light from the grass. And even that remnant of his soul had started to vanish.

"This is your fault," Meriel said through clenched teeth.

I thought she was talking to me. But it was Bragan she was staring daggers into.

As for the man himself . . . I didn't know what he was. No farmer, certainly. But not a Weaver, either, not exactly. Not part of their guild. Something separate. I knew almost nothing of Weavers and their enchantments, but there was something different about his magic. Something less refined. More brutal.

Either way, Bragan looked unperturbed. "The child was alive when you brought him to me?"

"Yes," I said, trying to hide my sorrow.

"Then there's still time." He strode toward the farmhouse. "Bring the body inside."

Meriel carried Lachlan into the house. Though she was limping, she pulled away when Foxtail moved to help. She wouldn't let anyone else hold him.

As for me, I barely dared to hope. Bragan's home looked pretty much like any farmhouse: simple, functional furniture; ordinary, well-used tools. Nothing obvious that might break his cover, indicate whatever the man's true purpose here was. The only thing that stood out as odd was that Bragan had no family, and no sign of hired help. For a farmer, that was practically unheard of.

He stopped in the dining room at a broad table of worn oak, the varnish rubbed away in spots. He removed the candleholder in the center and motioned for Meriel to lay Lachlan down.

"Remove his shirt," Bragan said before heading upstairs.

There wasn't much shirt left. The explosion of the Lady in Red had burned away the back, and in the struggle outside, one sleeve had torn all the way to the cuff. Still, Meriel unbuttoned it, took it off, then folded it neatly, as if it were ready to tuck away in the closet.

Bragan returned, his own shirt gone. His muscled torso was marked with a long, thick scar that led from his upper ribs to his sternum—the handiwork of someone's blade in a distant past. He carried a canvas cloth rolled into a tube, which he untied and let flop open.

Inside was a toolkit, though not one belonging to any farmer. There was an assortment of knives, a charcoal stick, paint-brushes, a row of needles, and a collection of tiny jars of colored inks, all sealed with wax.

I assumed he'd take out the tools and get to work, starting whatever preparations he needed to make. Instead, he just stood there staring at Lachlan's chest. His lips moved, though only barely.

One of the skills the Old Man had taught me was lipreading. I'd never gotten very good at it, but I could usually catch the gist of a conversation. Here, I couldn't understand a single word Bragan was mouthing. I didn't think it was even our language.

His eyes moved as well. Watching the eyes was something I *was* good at, because where a person looked usually told you what they wanted, where they were going, or what they planned to do. In Bragan's case, his eyes shifted around Lachlan's chest, here and there, in a distinct but unrecognizable pattern. He was visualizing something.

Then, without warning, he removed a thin, short-bladed knife from his toolkit—and he plunged it into Lachlan's chest.

Foxtail started. Gareth looked shocked. Meriel gasped, then reached out and grabbed Bragan's wrist. "What are you doing?" she cried, horrified.

Bragan looked over at me, his expression neutral. He said nothing.

Inside, I was just as horrified as Meriel. But the Old Man had taught me to remain in character—at least outwardly—always seemingly in control. It took all my will to do it.

"Meriel," I said.

"I'm not letting him desecrate Lachlan's body!"

"If this works, it won't *be* Lachlan's body. It'll be Lachlan. Let him do his job."

Frustrated, Meriel released Bragan's wrist.

He kept his eyes on me. "I realize she's in service to you," he said calmly, "but if she touches me again, I will kill her."

Her eyes narrowed. "You'll *what*?"

This was getting out of hand. "Foxtail," I began, but she was already on it. She grabbed Meriel by the arm and tugged her out of the room.

Meriel protested. Still playing my role, I glared at her. She caught my eye and clamped her mouth shut, even though she was clearly still fuming.

Bragan watched them go—well, not *them* so much as Foxtail. Her veil had come off in the fight, and she hadn't bothered to put it back on. Bragan's eyes lingered on her mask. It seemed he couldn't quite decide what to make of her, which was interesting. This was the second time I'd seen a Weaver—or whatever Bragan was—be surprised by Foxtail's mask. Once again, it made me wonder about what was underneath.

But we had more important things to deal with at the moment. Bragan returned to his knife and began cutting.

It was sickening to watch. Gareth turned pale, and it was all I could do not to cry out for Bragan to stop. But I stayed silent, and not just because the person I was pretending to be wouldn't be squeamish. As Bragan worked, I realized what he was doing.

He was carving a rune into Lachlan's flesh.

I would have said a Weaver rune, but again, this symbol looked less like the glyphs I'd seen Mr. Solomon use and more like the enchanted tattoos on Bragan's skin. No elegant loops or swirls, just straight lines and angles; once again, the word *brutal* came to mind. Though as awful as it was to see him cut into Lachlan, what he did next made me go as pale as Gareth.

Bragan carved the same symbol on *himself.*

I could barely watch as he stuck the knife in his own chest. Bragan gritted his teeth in pain as he worked, ignoring the blood that ran down to stain his trousers. Gareth covered his face, peeking through his fingers, transfixed with horror.

It was a blessing when Bragan finally finished. He took a deep breath. "I'm ready. Whom do you choose?"

"Choose?" I said. "For what?"

"You must decide," he said. "Which of your companions will be the sacrifice?"

CHAPTER 7

I SPOKE SLOWLY. "What do you mean . . . sacrifice?"

Bragan paused. "You do understand how bindings work? The energy of the enchantment—"

"Comes from living things," I finished. "I know. But—"

"The nature of the life source matters," Bragan said.

I'd forgotten. Mr. Solomon had told us the same thing. *The nature of the enchantment determines the life you need to use.*

Horror grew inside me. "You're saying to give Lachlan his life back . . . one of us has to *die*?"

Again, he paused. "Apologies, blessed one. I presumed you understood that."

I looked at Gareth, feeling nauseous. He looked pretty ill himself. "There must be another option," I said.

"There's a boy who lives on a farm up the road," Bragan said. "He would be suitable."

"Donal?" The boy who ran to give us water? "You want me to go kill Donal?"

"No. He has to be alive when the binding begins. Just bring him here. I'll do it."

This was madness. "I'm not murdering *anybody*."

Bragan frowned. That was the wrong thing to say, and I knew it. The Eye's Emissary shouldn't care a whit for some random child's life any more than Bragan did.

Quickly, I covered my mistake. "My path requires secrecy," I said, as if that should have been obvious. "I can't leave a trail of dead children behind me. There must be another way."

Bragan saw the sense in that. Still, he said, "I know of no other."

Gareth spoke. "Isn't it . . . I mean . . . couldn't you s-substitute energy from another source?"

"In theory?" Bragan said. "Yes. But the energy would need to be converted. You'd require much more life to start with."

"We're surrounded by life," I pointed out. "The trees, the grass. Artha's eyes, the pigs. Use a pig."

He looked at me like I was a fool—and I was pretty sure only my status as Emissary prevented him from calling me one. "I can't use a pig. Their energy doesn't begin to compare. I'd need a dozen to do the conversion. Maybe more."

"So use them all."

"I can't. Not at the same time."

Now I frowned at him. "Why not? I knew this Weaver once who had a poison dagger. It was imbued with the souls of seven thousand snakes."

"No doubt," Bragan said impatiently. "But that would have taken *years* to bind. Each soul extracted one by one, then held in a soulstone, until all the life energy was ready. Then, and only then, could it be transferred.

"With a pig," he continued, "I could do a few at a time, at most. Then I'd need to rest. What's more, I would need a soulstone, which I don't have."

"We'll steal you one," I said.

"There isn't time. I can revive the child the way he was only as long as the echo of his soul lingers in his body. That gives me a few hours. Three, four at the most."

I didn't doubt him. I'd seen Lachlan's soul fading when I looked at him through the Eye. "Is there nothing else that could work?" I said, desperate.

"You'd need a single—" he paused for a moment—"a single source of energy. Like a soulstone."

There.

He'd hesitated. He'd started to say something, then caught himself, changed it before he continued. That meant he *had* thought of something. He just didn't want to tell us what.

Why not?

Has to be something that matters to him, the Old Man said. *Something he wouldn't want to give up, but thinks you would. He doesn't want to lose it. But he also can't deny the will of the Eye's Emissary. If he can hide the truth from you* . . .

I racked my brain, trying to think of what Bragan could possibly value. Then I realized: I'd already seen it. The thing he wanted when we'd first come to his farm. The thing he'd taken when we'd denied him.

Glowing with magical energy, bright as the sun.

"The dragon staff," I said.

Bragan winced. I'd guessed right.

I took the staff from Gareth and placed it on the table. "The Eye showed me its light," I said. "Use it."

"Emissary . . . blessed one . . . you can't," Bragan said.

"Why not?"

"This staff, it's ancient. It was made four thousand years ago by the Dragon's Light himself. He imbued it with air magic, molded directly from the primeval—the raw, untamed energy from which the world and its life were created. Its power is immense. It'll serve you much better than this child ever could."

I had no idea who the Dragon's Light was, and I really didn't care. "I've had enough of your blathering. Do as you're told."

Still, Bragan hesitated. "If you do this, there may be consequences."

I glared at him. "Are you threatening me?"

"Of course not, blessed one," he said through gritted teeth. "What I mean is that the primeval is chaotic. Unpredictable, dangerous. Using the staff may have unknown effects."

"You said it yourself: there are no other options." And to give him that final push, I removed the patch to let him gaze upon the Eye.

Worried only about Lachlan, I hadn't considered the Eye might still be furious at Bragan for attacking us. And when the artifact saw Bragan again, I did feel its outrage at the man's defiance. But this time, it was faint, as if the stone held only the barest grudge. Instead, what I felt from it most was *satisfaction*. That *this* was as it was supposed to be.

With Bragan's shirt off, I saw more than before, too. Through the Eye, the runes ran all down his shoulders, his arms, his stomach. But there was one thing that wasn't a rune at all.

On his chest, underneath the cuts he'd made in himself, the

outline of a creature glowed, a strange shade of off-white. It had a thick body, a long neck, a crested head, two wings, and a tail.

A dragon. His entire chest was covered by a glowing dragon.

Bragan surrendered, humbled but frustrated. "As you wish."

I almost covered the Eye again, but I didn't. Partly because I wanted Bragan to know it was watching him, so he wouldn't try to sabotage the binding to save the staff. But I also wanted to see what was happening—what was *really* happening.

Gareth watched from the corner, wary but fascinated, as Bragan leaned over Lachlan's body. In his right hand, Bragan held the staff. With his left, he covered Lachlan's eyes. Then he closed his own.

He began to murmur. The staff glowed as bright as ever— and then even brighter. The violet energy swelled, as if sloshing around inside the artifact.

Then it began to drain away. The energy ran into Bragan's hand, down his arm. When it reached his chest, it found the cuts he'd made in himself. It flowed along them like quicksilver through a maze.

Bragan gasped.

His skin flared brighter red, then dimmed. *Pain*, I thought. *I'm seeing his pain.*

Then, slowly, Lachlan, too, began to glow. The alien, angular design Bragan had carved in the boy began to shine purple, a mirror of the symbol on the man standing over him.

And the faded red inside Lachlan joined the dance. It swirled like ink in water. Faint red tendrils spiraled up in whorls to touch the glowing glyph on his chest, as if tasting it.

Then the two began to mix.

At first, it was a violent tumble. The red and purple sloshed together, clashing, then recoiling, a maelstrom of fighting colors. Then they started to blend, and where the red touched the violet, the violet changed.

Inside my mind, the Eye was a whirl of its own emotions

(yes yes yes)

as the red grew inside Lachlan. More light flowed from the staff. Its brilliance faded, the violet thrashing as it disappeared, as if fighting its own death. Bragan's chest shone with it. So did Lachlan's, as more energy left the man to fill the boy's body. That, too, was consumed by the red, growing broader and brighter, until there was almost nothing of the staff's energy still inside him.

Then Bragan collapsed.

He crumpled in a heap. The dragon staff fell from his fingers, clattering on the floorboards. The staff had warped; now it was nothing but a twisted snake of silver, no glow within, devoid of any enchantment at all.

I looked at Lachlan. He just lay there.

Then his chest heaved. He gasped. He opened his eyes, sat up, and stared back at me in wonder—and horror.

"Artha's bulging bum, guv," he said. "Let's not do that again, eh?"

CHAPTER 8

IT WAS AN almost joyous reunion.

I covered the Eye so I could see Lachlan with nothing but my own sight. He looked completely healed. The charred hole in his stomach from the Lady in Red's flame sword had closed, the burns on his back gone, as if they'd never been there at all. The rune Bragan had carved into Lachlan's chest had disappeared, too, without even a hint of a scar.

I barely had time to wrap him in a hug before, lured by the sound of Lachlan's voice, Meriel and Foxtail ran into the room. They stared along with Gareth, stunned, then grabbed Lachlan in hugs of their own, holding him tight in amazement, joy, and awe.

"Shuna's twitchy nose," Lachlan said. "You'd think I died or something—ow!"

Meriel whapped him for that joke, even as she laughed along with everyone else.

Lachlan grinned and patted at his trousers. Then worry crossed his face. "Where's Galawan?"

Gareth reached into his pocket and pulled out the little metal sparrow. Lent to us by Mr. Solomon—well, given to us now, I guess, since he clearly wasn't getting it back—Galawan was a construct, an artificial bird made of hammered steel and gears, powered by an enchantment. Lachlan had claimed him as his pet.

The bird tweeted a happy melody as Gareth handed him over. He was a tough little creature. Even with all the knocking about Bragan had done to us, the sparrow didn't have a single dent.

Lachlan's grin returned as he hugged Galawan to his chest. All was fine in his world now. So, too, with the others, who still regarded him with wonder. Yet though I was overjoyed to see him alive, a pit gnawed at my gut.

Because I knew—*only* I knew—something hadn't gone quite right.

Bragan remained on the floor, his breathing ragged. I helped him up and into the front room, seating him on a bench near the window. I could see the pigs from here. They rooted in the mud, the magic that had terrified them already forgotten.

"Are you all right?" I said.

Bragan nodded. "I'll need to eat, and then to sleep." He heard the happy voices in the back room. "So it worked?"

"Sort of."

He looked up at me.

"Lachlan's alive," I said. "But before I hid the Eye away, it saw his essence. Lachlan's soul energy is back to the same red it was before. But there's something else inside him now. Something that *isn't* Lachlan."

"What?" Bragan said intently.

"It looks like . . . a stain." I couldn't think of a better word for it. "A stain on his soul. It's violet, the exact same color as the dragon staff's enchantment used to be. It's small, but it's there, and it's moving around inside him, like a worm. Almost like it has a mind of its own."

Bragan shrugged. "I warned you."

"That's . . . primeval magic? From the staff?"

He nodded. "I tried to convert it all. But the primeval is . . . willful. I didn't have the strength. And so the fragment I couldn't change now lives within the boy."

"What does that mean?"

"Nothing good."

I was getting tired of the way he danced around every issue. "Explain yourself."

"I can't," he said. "I have no answer for what might occur. The primeval is pure chaos. As far as I know, no one anywhere can predict what it will do."

I bit my lip. "Is it possible it won't do anything at all?"

Bragan shook his head. "That's the one thing I can say with certainty. Primeval magic is not content to remain confined. Whether it will create any visible effects cannot be said. But now that it's inside him, it will find some way to grow. Eventually, once it grows large enough, it will consume his soul. When it does . . ."

"What?"

"The child will no longer be the child. The boy will die."

My heart sank. "There's nothing you can do?"

"I have neither the knowledge nor the skill to extract primeval magic from within a person. I've never even heard of such a thing being done. Most likely," he said with a pointed look, "because no one has ever been reckless enough to infuse a soul in this way."

"So that's it," I said. "It was all for nothing."

Bragan looked pensive. "Perhaps not."

"I thought you said there was nothing you could do."

"Not I, no. But if our master has a purpose for the child, then there may be a way to remove the primeval and save him."

Our master. It gave me a chill to hear Bragan describe the Eye that way. "What do I need to do?"

The man's eyes became slightly glazed, as if recalling something. "Follow the path."

His words made me remember the urging I'd felt from the Eye

(follow follow follow)

in the forest around Bolcanathair. But that path had ended here. Unless . . .

Quickly, I pushed up my patch. I looked at the floor, outside the window, searching for any glowing trail the Eye might reveal. "I see nothing."

"Because our master didn't show you the path." Bragan spoke with increasing excitement, as if finally understanding something that had eluded him. "He showed it to *me.*"

"Where?"

"Yes. *Yes. That's* what it meant." Eyes wild, he tried to rise. He stumbled and fell back on the bench.

I steadied him. "What *what* meant? What are you talking about?"

He gripped my sleeve. "You must go to the lakeshore."

"Why? What will we find there?"

He looked at me intently. "The truth."

CHAPTER 9

A VOICE SPOKE from the doorway.

"The truth about what?"

We turned. Meriel stood there, arms folded. Gareth watched from behind.

Bragan answered her question, though he spoke only to me. "I don't know. I only know you will regain the path you seek at the lakeshore."

My arms prickled with goose bumps. The lakeshore was where the Eye had wanted to go right after we'd escaped from the High Weaver's laboratory. I'd refused—all I'd wanted then was to be rid of the thing—but now Bragan was telling me to go to the same place.

"How do you know about the lakeshore?" I said.

"I dreamed it."

Meriel snorted.

Bragan finally addressed her. "You sneer because you are ignorant. For those of us with understanding, dreams are precious. They allow us to walk through Shadow, the realm of secrets, where extraordinary, magical creatures, beings of unimaginable power, to whom we are nothing more than specks of dust, may speak with us, and endow us with blessed wisdom."

Meriel rolled her eyes. A week ago, I'd have done the same. But I'd seen too many strange things since then to dismiss what the man was saying. The fact that he'd already echoed the Eye's instructions meant, dream or not, I needed to hear it. "Tell me what you saw."

He stared into the distance, remembering. "I stood at the edge of Lake Galway. I was in Carlow—at least, where Carlow would one day be, for there was nothing in my dream but untamed wilderness."

I was surprised when Gareth interrupted. He usually stayed quiet when strangers were speaking. "How do you kn-know?" he said. "I mean . . . that it was Carlow. How do you know it was here?"

"Bolcanathair was to the north," Bragan said. "Its shape was unmistakable."

"Go on," I said.

"The volcano was smoking. Ash was falling. A chunk of its side had blown off, lava flowing into the water."

I shivered. "Like tonight."

"*Exactly* like tonight."

"When did you have this d-dream?" Gareth asked.

"The first time was three nights ago."

"The *first* time?" I said.

"I've had it every night since."

Three nights ago. That meant Bragan started having the dream before the volcano blew—but only *after* we'd stolen the Eye. He'd seen the future.

Bragan continued. "I stood on the shore. Across the lake, in the distance, I saw a shining white light. I wanted to cross the water, to reach the beacon, but there was no boat. I searched the sand but found nothing to help. Then I heard a voice whisper."

He turned to me, eyes blazing. "It was *his* voice."

Another chill. He was talking about the Eye—talking as if the thing was a god. "What did—" Playing a role or not, I couldn't bring myself to say "he." "What did it say?"

"'Follow.'"

"That's it?" Meriel said.

"No," Bragan said. "I called back and asked, 'Follow where?' I heard no answer. But the air beside me began to glow.

"I looked to my left. The light twisted, taking shape. Floating just above my head was a pair of words, but they were blurred, and wavering. I could only make out one of them: 'gate.'"

"What happened next?" I said, breathless.

"Nothing." Bragan's eyes focused as the memory faded. "The dream ended there, every time. But that is the beginning of your path; I'm certain of it. Find this gate, and you will find what you seek."

CHAPTER 10

BRAGAN STUMBLED FROM the bench to raid his pantry. He wolfed down two pounds of salted ham and a basket of fruit before finally passing out from exhaustion, half an apple still in his mouth.

We left him there, slumped over the dining room table. In a fit of conscience, I removed the apple so he wouldn't choke. We then took turns using Bragan's water barrels and bath to wash off the ash, the stink, and the blood from the fights we'd gotten into that night.

The scars that covered my back, my sides, and my stomach hurt—they always hurt—but they stung worse when I soaked them in water. This time, I was so banged up—and so dazed by everything we'd witnessed tonight—I barely noticed. I ran my fingers over the knotted flesh, Lachlan's resurrection playing over and over in my mind.

I kept seeing his wounds close before my eyes. I'd once hoped to hire a Weaver to heal my scars, give me a normal life. *Would it have been like that?* I wondered. The magic repairing my body, the pain fading as the marks of the Stickmen's punishment were smoothed away?

Except in Lachlan's case, it really hadn't gone as planned, had it? I could hear the Old Man in my head again, the same refrain as always. *Told you, boy.*

I know, I know, I sighed. *Fiddling with nature is for fools.*

I finished with the tub and got dressed. Putting on my dirty clothes reminded me that Lachlan's shirt was destroyed, so I took one of Bragan's to replace it. If there were any privileges to being the Eye's Emissary, surely free shirts was one of them.

It was absurdly big on Lachlan's small frame. We had to tuck half of it inside his pants and roll up the sleeves to even see his hands. He looked ridiculous, but it was better than him running around half naked. Finally, before we left for Lake Galway, Meriel swiped a handful of crowns she found in a jar in the pantry.

She counted out the bills happily. "When it comes down to it," she said, "Bragan isn't such a bad fellow after all, is he?"

She rifled through his pockets, smiling.

The full magnitude of what had happened in Bragan's home didn't really hit the others until we were outside. Even then, the impossibility of Lachlan's resurrection, the miracle of seeing the dead returned to life . . . it wasn't something any of us had words to express.

Lachlan walked ahead of us as we passed from the farmland that straddled the Emperor's Highway into the woods, skirting the city walls. His eyes were alight with newfound wonder, staring around him like a small child who'd never seen a tree before.

"Shuna's sneezing snout," he said. "Was everything always this beautiful?"

I guess there's nothing like dying to make you appreciate

being alive. We stared back at him, still barely able to believe he was all right. Foxtail romped beside him, basking in his happy glow. Meriel hovered protectively behind them, like a big sister afraid her crazy younger brother would run off and tumble under a carriage wheel. Even Galawan seemed to keep watch over him, flying away and back again as if to check the boy was still there.

Head in the clouds, Lachlan stumbled a lot on the roots of the trees we passed. Every time, Meriel was there to catch his sleeve. "Will you watch where you're going?" she said, exasperated.

"Sorry, luv. Artha's ears, you're pretty. Was she always this pretty, Cal?"

Meriel looked flustered at that—and even more flustered when I said, "An absolute vision." I nudged Gareth and said, "A vision of *what* is the question."

"I heard that," Meriel said.

"You were supposed to."

A pinecone bonked off my head.

"You're pretty, too, Foxy," Lachlan said. "Or at least I bet you are under that mask. You ever going to show us yer face?"

Foxtail turned to us and spread her hands, bemused.

"Did you give him wine?" Meriel asked me and Gareth. "You know you're not supposed to do that."

"Nah, luv," Lachlan said. "It's just—a *mouse!*" he shouted, pointing. "*Look!* A *mouse!*"

"You've seen mice before, Lachlan."

"Yeah, but them were *city* mouses. This is a *country* mouse! Let's catch him, Foxy!"

He chased it through the fallen leaves. To Meriel's dismay,

Foxtail joined in the fun, pouncing after the little creature in the dirt.

Meriel threw her arms in the air. "I give up. Why are we going this way, anyway?"

"It's not a good idea to go through Carlow tonight," I said. "With the eruption, the Stickmen will be out in full force."

"I'm saying why go to the lakeshore at all?"

"Bragan's dream told us to."

"Who cares?"

"The Eye does," I said. "I made a deal with it, remember? It saves me, seals the rift, and heals Lachlan. In return, I go where it leads me. But you bring up a good point. *I* made the deal. None of you did. You don't have to come with me if you don't want to."

"I didn't mean *that*," Meriel protested.

Lachlan halted his chase a moment. "Course we're coming, guv. Can't leave you all alone. What would you do without us?— *There he is! Get him!*"

"Right," I said to no one in particular. "I'll be lost without a proper mouse catcher."

Gareth smiled, watching Lachlan and Foxtail as they sprang after the fleeing rodent. Meriel followed, as exasperated as before.

"He seems back to n-normal," Gareth said quietly.

"Uh-huh." I didn't say anything more than that. I'd told them we were following Bragan's vision because the Eye wanted me to, and of course that was true. But it wasn't what *I* cared about.

What Gareth couldn't see was that stain inside Lachlan, that purple worm wriggling around the boy's soul. I hadn't yet told the others about it. I wasn't sure why.

Yes, you are, the Old Man said.

I sighed. Yes, I was. I hadn't told them about the stain because if I had, they'd ask me what to do to fix it. And I had no idea at all.

Bragan had insisted we would find something to help Lachlan at the lakeshore. That Lachlan's fate and my deal with the Eye were somehow intertwined. But Bragan *served* the Eye. And I had no illusion that the artifact cared even the tiniest bit about Lachlan's fate—except as a way to get what it needed. Which prompted a very big question.

What, exactly, did it need?

I knew why *we* were going to the lakeshore. But why did the *Eye* want to go there? come for me, it had made me promise. The Eye had never told me what that meant, and Bragan's vision hadn't made its goal any clearer. I was starting to wish I'd stayed a little longer at his farm, to interrogate him some more when he woke up. Who *was* Bragan? And what was his relationship to the Eye?

He'd said he "kept watch," looking for "signs." I'd gleaned that meant watching for signs of the Eye's return to the world above. But for what purpose? Why would anyone want to serve an artifact?

What's more, from that Fox and Bear story Shuna had sent me to find in Carlow's library, it sounded like the Eye had been locked away in the cave below the High Weaver's mansion for thousands of years. What legacy would Bragan be part of, to wait around for anywhere near that long?

I asked Gareth what he thought.

He mulled it over, frowning. "Did Bragan say anything else? I mean . . . while you were alone with him?"

Keeping the stain inside Lachlan a secret for the moment, I said, "Nothing about the Eye. Though . . ." I told him about the enchanted tattoos on Bragan's skin. "The runes looked simpler than Weaver runes."

"Like . . . precursors?"

"I don't know what that means."

"Things that came before," Gareth said. "I mean . . . the runes on Bragan's skin could be early versions of Weaver runes."

The more I thought about it, the more that felt right. Early, primitive runes, which the Weavers refined over millennia. "Could be," I said. "It wasn't just the runes, though. There was a dragon on his chest, too."

Gareth drew a breath.

"What is it?" I said.

"I was thinking . . . I mean . . . you remember that book about the dragon cult?"

"The one you found in the library? With all the pages blank?"

He nodded. "I thought maybe . . . The full name for the"—he waved awkwardly at my patch—"is the *Dragon's* Eye. Mr. Solomon took it down to the Dragon Temple. And then Bragan said the staff—the *dragon* staff—was made by someone called the Dragon's Light. And he has a dragon on his chest. So m-maybe . . . I mean . . . Bragan is one of them."

"A dragon cultist," I said, surprised.

Gareth nodded.

That explained something—and at the same time, nothing. There was a certain logic to the fact that a dragon cultist would consider a "Dragon's Eye" to be a holy relic—and me, bound to it, the Eye's Emissary. The problem was that we had no idea what a dragon cultist actually *was*.

I shook my head. I really should have pressed Bragan more about it. And I would have, if I hadn't been so worried about Lachlan. Bragan had said the stain would grow until it killed the boy. He just didn't know how long it would take. That told me nothing—except that we couldn't afford to waste any time.

My worry kept me peeking at Lachlan with the Eye. I felt like a man condemned to hang, checking his pocket watch every minute, dreading when the dawning hour would arrive. Unfortunately, just as the watch wouldn't change the condemned man's fate, the Eye couldn't make the stain disappear. There it was, worming around inside Lachlan as he chased that mouse— actually, he was chasing a squirrel now—the stain a violet evil in a sea of innocent red.

Meriel, resigned, had stopped trying to catch the two of them. Instead she just herded them in the general direction of Lake Galway. It occurred to me then that, besides Lachlan, I hadn't really examined my other friends with the Eye before. After we'd left the Dragon Temple, I'd been focused solely on the lifetrail on the ground.

Now I studied Meriel. It was fascinating to see how everyone's soul was slightly different, in a way that the color seemed to match who they were. Lachlan's was bright and cheerful. Meriel's was a swirly, fiery sort of red—hot-blooded and mercurial, just like the girl herself.

I glanced at Gareth next, when he wasn't looking. His red was a little cooler, almost with a slight blue tinge. As for Foxtail—

"Hey," I said. "What happened to—"

I broke off, confused.

"What happened to what?" Meriel said.

I covered the Eye. In my normal vision, Foxtail was straight ahead of me, next to Lachlan. They'd returned to chasing the mouse, and with one great pounce, Foxtail actually caught the thing. She held it by the tail, its little feet wriggling, trying to escape.

But...

"Well?" Meriel said.

"Forget it," I said.

She looked at me funny but shrugged and returned to the others. When she turned her back, I tested my view of Foxtail through the Eye again.

And I saw nothing.

CHAPTER 11

FOXTAIL WASN'T THERE.

Or rather, she *was* there—but not when I looked through the Eye.

Foxtail gave off no glow at all. If I covered my own eye, then all I could see around me was the shining light of life: the trees; the mouse, glowing an earthy red; Lachlan; Meriel trailing him; Gareth trudging along beside me.

But no Foxtail.

Yet when I covered the Eye and looked through my real eye, Foxtail walked ahead of us, just as one would expect. She'd stopped playing with Lachlan and released the mouse back into the woods. Now she made her way through the trees. And the thing was, from how she moved—a little too casual, yet never turning my way—I was pretty sure she'd stopped horsing around because she knew I was staring at her.

Maybe, I thought, *she even realizes why.*

Foxtail knows the Eye can't see her? the Old Man said. *Interesting.*

"Is something wrong?" Gareth asked.

Normally, he'd be the one I talked to about this sort of thing. But since I wasn't sure what it meant, and I didn't want to have that conversation within earshot of the others, I said, "It's nothing."

We walked on east, toward the lake.

The docks were absolutely jam-packed.

It was nearly two in the morning by the time we reached Lake Galway. No docks ever really slept in any city; sailors frequently kept odd hours since ships didn't run by the clock, and the taverns were always open to travelers landing in the dark of night. But I'd never seen anything like this.

I probably shouldn't have been surprised. Bolcanathair's eruption pretty much guaranteed a sleepless night for anyone in Carlow, and not just because of the lava glowing on the mountainside. The Seven Sisters volcano Bolcanoig had blown only four weeks ago, devastating the province of Garman in Ayreth's far east. People had to be wondering if this was the start of something just as bad.

Some were already taking no chances. Night launches were usually rare, but we saw five boats set sail within the first few minutes of our glimpse of the water. Other sailors stood around, lounging against stacked shipping crates and gossiping about the smoking plume over a shared bottle. The taverns were just as alive, pipe music and raucous laughter spilling out of doors propped open to let cool air inside. I told Lachlan to keep Galawan tucked away. The construct was certain to attract attention.

"So what is it we're actually looking for?" Meriel said.

Good question. "Hey, Lachlan? You used to be a runner for the Carlow Breakers. You know the docks, too?"

"Course, guv," he said. "What d'you need?"

"Is there a gate somewhere around here?"

"Sure. Galway Gate. Just down the way."

He pointed us along the boardwalk to where the ground sloped up from the water's edge. Set into the city walls were four wide gates. The portcullis was down in three of them, the northernmost gate still open. A pair of Stickmen stood there, checking the stock of every merchant sailor who passed through.

In ordinary times, the two of them might have been the only guards. Tonight, they were backed by a pair of Pistoleers. The soldiers stood nearby, watching the lava flow to the north and brushing ash off their sharp red uniforms.

"Is there something unusual about these gates?" I asked Lachlan.

"Nothing special I know of," he said. "Other'n it's the only gate with more than one pass."

That wasn't strange. Carlow was the empire's capital. A staggering number of people lived here—nearly three million, it was said—including countless nobles, traders, and others with a high demand for luxury goods. To say nothing of the need for food, clothing, and the like. A single gate in the wall would have ground the shipping trade to a halt.

"Maybe the Eye will see something," Meriel said.

I wasn't keen to remove my patch with all these people around. I managed to look somewhat normal by pushing it up and rubbing the socket underneath as if it were bothering me, all the while peeking through my fingers. I saw the usual glow of life through the Eye, and nothing else.

I shook my head, frustrated. "I don't understand this stupid thing. It gave us a clear trail to get help for Lachlan. Why won't it point the way anymore?"

I wondered if it was annoyed with me. It hadn't given me any strong emotions since we'd left Bragan's house. If anything, when I'd used it to study my friends, the only thing I'd felt from it was a vague sense of boredom. Even so, every time I put it away, I always got that fleeting wave of frustration. It really didn't like being behind the eyepatch. Was it possible the thing was sulking, and that was why there wasn't any path to follow?

"It might . . . I mean . . . maybe it doesn't know the way," Gareth said. "The exact way, I mean."

That was an interesting idea. The Eye's power had kind of left me thinking of it as some sort of all-seeing intelligence. Maybe it didn't actually know as much as it wanted me to believe.

"It must know *something* about this place, though," I said. "It wanted me to come here after we stole it. And it gave Bragan that dream."

"Assuming . . . I mean . . . we don't know that dream came from the Eye."

True. And there was a different possibility, too. Back when it could talk, the Eye said a lot of things I didn't understand. It even mocked me for it. In the Eye's mind, it might be giving me perfectly clear directions, and I was the stupid one for not following.

"Could there be a secret gate?" Meriel said. "Something underground, like the Dragon Temple?"

Another interesting idea. "Lachlan?"

"Can't think of anything." He scratched his cheek. "Did used to be a smuggler's tunnel."

"Where?"

"'Bout a mile south, under the wall. Gone now, though, guv. Got blown up when the Stickmen hauled in the Breakers."

One of the Pistoleers was eyeing us. We were starting to look like pickpockets, standing there in ragged clothes, scoping out our surroundings. I moved us away, closer to the water. Lachlan got distracted again, wandering off to chase a flock of seagulls. Foxtail trailed him, keeping watch. Gareth stared up at the ships.

"Where else would there be a gate?" Meriel said.

"Around here? I don't know." There were other city gates where the main roads left Carlow, but I didn't think those were near the docks.

"I told you that dream stuff was nonsense," she said. "If this isn't the right gate, why would Bragan say he saw it?"

Suddenly, Gareth stiffened. "He didn't."

"Sure he did. You were there, you heard him."

"But that's not . . . I mean . . . it's *not* what he said. Bragan didn't see *a* gate. He saw—"

"The *word* 'gate,'" I said, voice rising. "Floating in the air."

Gareth nodded. Then he pointed up at the hull of the ship beside us. Its name was painted just under the rail, near the prow: WANDERING WHALE.

"A *ship's* name," I said.

"It's p-possible," Gareth said.

My excitement faded a bit as we looked across the docks. There were hundreds of ships here, from iron-hulled cargo steamers to quad-masted galleons to private skiffs and fishing boats.

"It'll take us forever to search all these," Meriel complained.

It would be easy to miss one, too, especially as some were casting off even as we spoke. But maybe we could find a shortcut.

"Lachlan. Lachlan!" I called, and Foxtail dragged the boy away from the seagulls. "Where's the harbormaster?"

Lachlan jerked his thumb toward a two-story stone building near one of the larger docks. "Right there. Why?"

"We need to see his ledger. The one that says where each ship is docked."

"Ooh, I wouldn't do that, guv. He ain't our man."

"Every harbormaster in the world takes bribes," I protested.

"Not anymore. Last bloke soaked his beak till it was dripping. Good one, he was, easiest man ever to slip a crown. But he got tossed—"

"When the Stickmen cracked the Breakers," I guessed glumly.

"Righto. We try and grease the new one, he'll knock our heads, sure as Shuna's a fox. What d'you want with him, anyway? Thought we were looking for a gate."

"No. We're looking for a name with 'gate' in it."

"A name . . . Well, why didn't you say so? No one ever tells me nothing."

"You know of something?" Meriel said.

"Course I do." Grumbling, he led us back toward where the sailors clustered, near a row of lodgings and alehouses. "Right there."

He pointed us toward a tavern. It was one of the rattier inns on the wharf, and that was saying something. The grimy, once-white paint had worn off the outer shingles, peeling in long strips, an ugly sea-foam green underneath. In front of its crooked door were a pair of stones shaped into rough obelisks. I knew what they were supposed to represent: the stone pillars where Lake Galway emptied into the Spiritsblood River, its waters flowing toward the sea.

The door banged open. A sailor stumbled out, blood pouring from his nose. A second man with meaty hands planted a boot on the bleeding man's backside and sent him sprawling into the mud.

"Don't come back tonight, Sheehan," the bouncer warned.

He wiped his hands on his shirt and went back in. The door slammed behind him, making the board above it rattle. On it was the name of the tavern: GALWAY'S GATE.

Meriel stared at it incredulously. "Our 'path forward' is through a sailors' tavern?"

I looked at Gareth. He shrugged.

Guess we were going inside.

CHAPTER 12

Foxtail tugged at my shirt.

She pointed to the ground. *I'll stay out here.*

That was probably a good idea. Wearing a veil in this kind of tavern would put every pair of eyes on her the moment she stepped inside. In fact . . . "You should stay, too, Meriel."

"Why?"

"Like you said, it's a sailors' tavern." I motioned to the man bleeding in the mud.

She seemed amused. "You think I can't handle myself?"

"I know you can. But sea dogs are superstitious."

Most sailors thought women on boats were bad luck. It wasn't so bad that they wouldn't take female passengers, but you could probably count on one hand the number of ships that would accept a girl on their crew. And they viewed their taverns as extensions of their boats. We might be in for more of a scrap with her around.

"It's funny," Meriel said, "that you imagine anything you say will stop me from going in there."

"Miracles do happen."

"We've used up our miracles tonight, sweetheart."

Lachlan elbowed me, eyes wide. "She called you sweetheart!"

I opened the door. "I'm pretty sure she didn't mean it."

Galway's Gate was hot, sticky, and it stank: stale sweat and staler beer. Which made it pretty much everything I expected.

The crowd was roaring tonight. No one knew what omen Bolcanathair's eruption was forecasting, but everyone believed it meant danger—and danger, for some reason, made sailors happy. Probably because it made them feel at home. Every time they set out on the water, they risked their lives against thundering storms, rogue waves, or murderous pirates.

Whatever the cause, the din was loud enough to bust eardrums. There were no musicians in here, just men shouting at each other so they could be heard over everyone else. There was a fight going on in the far corner; men nearby threw coins into a pot on the table, placing wagers on who would win.

Lachlan grinned at the chaos. Gareth looked like he'd rather be anywhere else. I was sure he was remembering how the Westport Breakers he grew up with used to bully him. But no one was interested in Gareth. It was Meriel who got all the attention.

Like I'd warned her, it wasn't often a girl graced the air of this kind of establishment. Especially not a beauty like Meriel. We were barely a step inside before the men at the nearby tables gave each other *hey look at that* slaps and turned our way. One of the men catcalled her and shouted.

"Ooh, lookee-look! The entertainment has arrived! Come here, lassie, and sit—"

A throwing knife slammed into the man's pewter mug. Ale glugged through the hole onto his lap.

He stood, cursing. His friends laughed at him. So did the table across the way. A giant of a man leaning against the wall lifted his own mug high overhead.

"Do mine next, girl!" the giant shouted, then tilted his head back, opened his mouth, and waited for her to throw another blade.

That got even more laughter, and when Meriel blew the giant a kiss, everyone cheered. It also started a contest where people began to throw things at the giant's tankard to make it spill. When a chair tumbled past, the meaty-handed bouncer stepped in, and we hurried farther inside.

Meriel gave me a look that was somewhat smug. "Just how many of those knives do you have left, anyway?" I said, somewhat sourly.

She thought about it for a moment. "Seven," she said finally. "No, six. No, wait . . . you know what? I'm not sure. You're right, I should probably get more—hey!"

Lachlan had drifted away from the rest of us, beckoned over by a man sitting alone at a table by the fire. Meriel stomped toward him and put a hand on Lachlan's arm.

"What do you want, old man?" she said.

"I mean no trouble," the man said. Three of his front teeth were black, and he was missing his right arm. His sleeve hung down, a knot at the end. "Was just asking my young friend if he'd like a story."

"Why would he?" Meriel said, still suspicious.

The man seemed surprised by that. "Why, everyone likes stories."

"Sure. But what do you care?"

"Stories are my trade. Used to be a ship's mate. Traveled all over the world, saw all manner of amazing things, till a great white whale took my arm. Now I tell of adventures to earn my keep." He shook his mug; it was nearly empty. "For a cup of ale and a few septs, I'll give talk of whatever you like. Tales of the high seas? Fox and Bear?"

Lachlan's eyes were alight. "Can we, Cal?"

"We don't really have the time," I began.

Gareth grabbed my arm. He looked at the storyteller, then at me.

I paused. Was this what we were supposed to find in here? A story? "What's your name, old man?"

"Fergal at your service, lad."

"Do you happen to know a story about the Dragon's Eye?" I said.

He thought about it. "Can't say as I do. But I can make one up. I'm good at that. You'll like it, I promise."

I shook my head. "Sorry, friend. We're only looking for the truth." Meriel began to usher a disappointed Lachlan away from the table.

"Wait a minute," Fergal said. "Wait, now, hold your sails. I don't know no tale about no Dragon's Eye, it's true. But if it's dragons you like, how about the story of the Dragon's Teeth?"

I stopped. "The Dragon's . . . Teeth?"

"Oh, yes. A sordid tale it is, too. Of emperors and High Weavers, magic blades and murderous betrayal."

I looked over at Gareth. His eyes were wide.

"Barman," I called. "Bring us a pitcher."

Fergal smiled.

CHAPTER 13

THE FOUR OF us pulled up chairs around the table as Fergal poured himself an ale.

"Our story begins," he said, "nearly four thousand years ago. It was the Age of Discovery, when our ancestors had not yet spread across this world, which the Spirits, Artha the Bear and Shuna the Fox, built for us.

"Look around and understand, children: None of this was here. There was no Carlow, no empire. All was yet-untamed wilderness, ready to be claimed by the first band of explorers brave enough to find this shore.

"Well, come people did. But no ordinary explorers. These were Weavers, the very first of their kind. And they were drawn here, not by lush lands and pleasant waters, but by some great magical artifact buried deep in a cave below the surface. No one knows what that artifact was . . ."

I almost said *I do, it's under my eyepatch.*

"But the Weavers came and built their first Enclave directly above the enchantment below."

Fergal sipped at his ale. "Now, even then, there was no city to speak of. Remember, this was in ages past, and binding was still thought of as witchcraft. So the land remained a wilderness, with just a tiny town of merchants brave enough to set up shop and bring in goods to sell to the Weavers. That was how it stayed for five hundred years.

"Then a warlord rose in the south. A barbarian, a chieftain of one of the horse tribes of the Plains of Torgal."

Meriel sat up in her chair. Something about what the man had said surprised her.

"This chieftain was a genius tactician," Fergal said. "Though his tribe was small, he conquered his brethren, adding the strength of their tribes to his own, until all of Torgal was his. With his rivals defeated, and a now-massive force behind him, he set his sights on other lands. The kingdom of Sligach was directly to the north, a plum, ripe and ready to be plucked.

"Well, march north he did—but not to Sligach. Instead, he bypassed the mountains and brought his troops here, to the shores of Lake Galway. To conquer? No, for there was no country here to conquer. He came, instead, to destroy."

The old man swirled his ale in his tankard. "Like all barbarians, he held his people's superstitions against enchanters. The secrets of magic, he believed, belonged only to the Spirits. What the Weavers were doing was blasphemy.

"When he reached the Weaver Enclave, his force was unlike any Ayreth had ever seen. Nine hundred thousand was the number of his army. And the Weavers, do you know how many there were?"

We shook our heads.

"Fifty." Fergal grinned a black-toothed smile. "Only fifty

enchanters against the horde. The chieftain attacked immedi-ately, intending to raze their tower to the ground. But the Weavers met him with magic. The chieftain's army fell back—burned by fire, frozen by ice, swallowed by earth—while the Enclave was completely untouched."

Lachlan listened, enraptured, as Fergal continued. "It was clear now to the warlord that he would not succeed so easily. He lay siege to the tower, hoping to strain the Weavers' defenses. For two full years, he remained, waiting, attacking, then waiting again.

"The chieftain's losses were immense. Ten thousand men died for every enchanter that fell. But even with such a ratio in their favor, the Weavers were destined to lose. Do you know why?"

"Life," Gareth said suddenly. "They ran out of life to power their m-magic."

Fergal raised his mug in salute. "Exactly so, my young friend. The bindings in the Weavers' artifacts could protect them only as long as the energy that powered them held out. Magic rods, staffs, rings, and brooches, all began to fail. Until only seven Weavers remained.

"Six accepted the inevitable. With defeat looming, they began to weave one final, terrible enchantment. They planned to destroy their own tower in a grand magical explosion, erasing their enemy from the face of the world—and themselves, with their Weaver secrets, as well.

"But the seventh, the youngest of the Weavers, rejected this suicidal plan. Instead, he ventured from the tower to parley with the chieftain and offer him a truce.

"If the chieftain would make peace, the young Weaver promised, the seven remaining enchanters would bind themselves to the chieftain as his advisors. And to sweeten the pot, they would provide him with artifacts of unrivaled power. A pair of swords: the Dragon's Teeth.

"These swords, twins in every way except for the gems that fashioned their pommels, were made of no metal known to man. Some say the blades were made of skystone; others say ancient bone. Some even say the blades were fashioned by Artha herself, drawn from the primeval magic she and Shuna used to create the world. Whatever the truth, they had extraordinary powers.

"The first of the swords, Camuloth, was a soulstealer. Its pommel black as jet, the blade had the power to drain the life of any enemy with a single cut. Its sister, Belenoth, was a healer."

A healer?

I sat completely still, listening.

"Pommel white as the sun," Fergal continued, "Belenoth could draw the stolen energy of Camuloth and heal the wounds of its owner. When used together to cut down enemies and restore one's injuries . . ." Fergal's voice trailed off.

"Whoever held them would be nearly invincible," Gareth said, amazed.

"So it was," Fergal said. "Which might explain why our chieftain cast aside his superstitions and accepted the deal. Dual-wielding the Teeth, he led his armies across the world. Kingdom after kingdom fell to those blades, until none anywhere opposed him. And thus a lowly chieftain of the Torgal horse plains became Aeric, first emperor of Ayreth."

Fergal refilled his mug with ale.

"What happened then?" Lachlan asked, breathless.

"For all his skill at war, Aeric proved to be equally great in peace. He returned to the site of the Weaver siege and built himself a capital city, which he named Carlow. But what interests you, I believe, is the fate of the Dragon's Teeth."

I nodded, as riveted as Lachlan—but for a very different reason.

"You would think," Fergal said, "that Aeric would find a place of pride for the weapons that won him an empire. Not so. Instead, he commanded the blades be locked inside the treasure room of his newly constructed palace. And he drew up a law, unbreakable even by emperor's decree: No man would ever touch those blades again, on pain of death. Not even his own descendants."

Meriel frowned. "Why would he do that?"

Fergal leaned toward her. "Most scholars claim it was so no other man could ever reach the heights of Aeric's greatness. But the truth is simpler, and more alarming: Despite all they had done for him, Aeric was *afraid* of the Dragon's Teeth. He said the swords *whispered* to him, promised to tell him terrible secrets that no man should ever know."

A chill ran down my spine. Whispered to him . . . like the Eye?

"Where are these blades now?" I said.

"Ah," Fergal said. "That's where the story turns. For a thousand years after Aeric's death, the Dragon's Teeth remained untouched. Barely anyone even remembered they were there. But then a boy became ruler of the empire when his father died of the weeping sickness. He was Galdron III, child emperor, only nine years old. And he would be the last of Aeric's blessed line.

"By this time, the Weavers were well ingrained as advisors to Aeric's descendants. Galdron had the misfortune of having as his tutor the High Weaver Veran IX. Veran was a schemer, chafing at his subservience to emperors who, unlike him, had no special talents of their own. When the young boy took the Ruby Throne, Veran set his mind to gathering power, hoping to overthrow his liege and rule Ayreth himself.

"If that was all there was to it, perhaps our history would have taken a different path. But Veran's scheming was not entirely a product of his own will. For he, like Aeric before him, heard whispers in his ear. Whatever dark power had spoken to our first emperor began to speak to the High Weaver as well.

"Insidious words in his head, Veran sought to steal the Dragon's Teeth. But how? To even touch those blades brought a sentence of death. For months, the High Weaver resisted that voice. Until one fateful night, he snuck down to the treasure room, used his enchantments to dispel the magic lock on the chest, and freed the swords from their confinement.

"That was a terrible crime in itself. But much worse was about to come. For young Galdron, who had no knowledge of Veran's dark desires, loved his old advisor. Curious about what Veran was doing, the child snuck after the High Weaver. When he saw Veran take the Dragon's Teeth, Galdron was horrified. The boy begged his beloved tutor to return the blades. It would be their secret, he promised. No one else needed to know.

"But Veran would not give up the Teeth. He struck his emperor, and Camuloth drained Galdron's life.

"It was then, standing over Galdron's body, that Veran realized the magnitude of what he'd done. He had murdered the emperor, a child—the first regicide in a thousand years. Horror broke his mind free of the whispers that had confounded it, and his dreams of ruling shattered. There was no power for him, and no future. His fellow Weavers would disown him for what he'd done. And when the Emperor's Guard caught him, he would be tried and executed as a traitor.

"With no other course of action, Veran took the Dragon's Teeth and fled. He boarded the emperor's personal warship, the *Silver Star*, and commanded its crew to set sail. A pursuit followed him not long after, but Veran had already crossed Lake Galway. He disembarked at Redfairne, little more than a tiny fishing village at the time."

"What happened then?" I said.

Fergal shrugged. "None can say. Galdron's death and the resulting scramble for the Ruby Throne brought forth the First Civil War, which plunged the empire into the Age of Chaos. Most of the records of the time are lost. Some say Veran continued east, across the plains, all the way to the other side of the world. Others say he went north and hid in the mountains. Either way, he was never heard from again."

"So . . . the Dragon's Teeth are lost? Gone forever?"

"No," Fergal said. "For artifacts as powerful as the Dragon's Teeth cannot rest quietly. Legend has it that the swords will be found again. And the path to their discovery will shine from the Blade of Heaven."

CHAPTER 14

"The Blade of Heaven," Lachlan said, enraptured. "What's that?"

Fergal drained the rest of his mug and wiped his mouth. "That's the curious part. No one really knows. Best guess is the Blade of Heaven is some sort of geological marker."

I looked over at Gareth. "Like a rock formation," he murmured.

Fergal nodded. "Aye. Like Galway's Gate, the stone pillars at the mouth of the Spiritsblood. Or the arrow in the rock of Bolcanashach, the Seven Sisters volcano near Sligach."

He leaned in. "Thing is, friends, I've traveled all over the world. And outside of the legend of the Dragon's Teeth, I've never heard of the Blade of Heaven."

My mind was racing.

Twin swords. Camuloth, a soulstealer. And Belenoth . . . a *healer*.

Such incredible magic . . . Could it heal the stain in Lachlan's soul?

You will regain the path you seek at the lakeshore, Bragan had said.

And then I remembered something Mr. Solomon had told me, right before he'd taken the Eye. *The Eye is not the only artifact of its kind. There's a . . . let's call it a set. The Eye, no doubt, wanted to join with its brethren.*

Dragon's Teeth . . . Dragon's Eye. The names couldn't possibly be a coincidence.

This tale was why the Eye sent us here. To learn about the Dragon's Teeth. It wanted me to find these swords.

But why? What had Mr. Solomon meant when he said the Eye wanted to join with its brethren? What would happen then?

Nothing good, the Old Man said.

Still, I said. *If they could fix Lachlan . . .*

Can they? Or is that just what the Eye wants you to think?

I knew what he was getting at. *Need, greed, and speed*, he'd once told me. *These, boy, are the three pillars of a most effective gaff.*

Here I was again, right in the thick of one. We needed a way to heal Lachlan. The Dragon's Teeth might offer that power—and more. And we had to find them before the stain grew inside our friend and killed him.

Need, greed, and speed. I sighed. Once again, the Eye was setting me up to get snaffled. "Is there anything else you can tell us about—"

My question was interrupted by the tavern door banging open. A boy of sixteen shouted over the din. "They're searching the ships!"

Chairs clattered to the floor as every patron but Fergal leapt from their tables and rushed outside. Confused, we followed. And there we saw what the boy meant.

The Stickmen were raiding the docks.

An entire company of the city watch—there had to be sixty, seventy men at least—fanned across the wharf, halting cargo loaders, blocking gangways, shoving furious sailors away from their crafts. And they weren't alone. Backing the Stickmen was a company of Pistoleers, lending the emperor's authority to the raid—and staving off the likelihood of violence, too. A sailor would happily get in a punch-up with a Stickman; all it would cost him was a few days in jail. Try that with a Pistoleer and he'd hang.

"Look at that," one of the sailors said.

On Lake Galway, four of the emperor's dreadnoughts sailed in a line, forming a blockade, turning all ships back toward port. It wasn't much of a wall, really. Though the warships were huge, the fact that there were only four left giant gaps that would have been easy to sail through.

But there were very few who'd defy the will of the emperor. Especially after a sloop tried to run the blockade without being searched and got its sails shredded by chained shot. I wouldn't like to be on that crew when the navy boarded them.

"Artha's blistered backside," Lachlan said in surprise. "Why're they closing the port?"

A passing man with a scar on his cheek heard the question and answered. "They're searching for something."

"For what?" Meriel called after him.

Running backward, he spread his arms—*who knows?* But I think we could guess well enough what they wanted. It was nestled in my left eye socket.

"We need to leave," I said, scanning the crowd. "Where's—"

Something light and spiny bounced off the top of my head. I looked up to see Foxtail sitting on the tavern's roof, beside the chimney. She waved.

"Can everyone please stop hitting me with pinecones?" I said.

Foxtail motioned toward the trees behind her. *Head for the woods.*

That did seem the best way to avoid the search. Several of the sailors had already figured that out and made for the trees. Foxtail disappeared over the roof.

We ran around to the back of the tavern to join her. She leapt down nimbly from the gutters, then led us into the brush. We ran a good half mile before stopping to catch our breath. This far out, we could just hear the shouting on the docks. Another cannon boomed in the distance.

Lachlan was confused. "Shuna's snout. Never seen nothing like that. Why's the emperor's pants in such a bunch?"

I was pretty sure it wasn't the emperor who was angry. "It has to be the High Weaver," I said. "Darragh is searching for the Eye."

"He's been searching for the Eye for three days now," Meriel protested. "Why blockade the port tonight?"

"That," Gareth said quietly, nodding toward the smoking volcano.

I agreed. "We steal the Eye, then three days later, Bolcanathair blows? Darragh would realize that's not a coincidence." He'd also realize the Eye was still in Carlow. "We have to get out of here—now."

"I know plenty of spots to lay low," Lachlan offered.

Under normal circumstances, I'd have taken him up on that. But the stain on Lachlan's soul had put us on a clock.

"We don't know what Darragh's plans are for searching the

city," I said. "He might be working up a binding that will help him locate the Eye. If he does, he's going to come for it. And if you'll excuse the pun, I've kind of become attached to the thing. Until we find a safe way of making the Eye let go of me, I'd rather he didn't try to take it back."

"So where do we go, then?" Meriel said.

"Where the Eye wants us to go. After the Dragon's Teeth."

Meriel frowned. "Fergal said no one knows where they are."

"But he did give us a place to start looking."

"Where?" Lachlan said.

Gareth answered. "Redfairne."

I nodded. "That's where Veran disembarked with the swords. If there's a trail to the Blade of Heaven, that's where we'll find it."

"How?" Meriel said.

"I don't know yet. Maybe the Eye will show me something. Even if not, I know Redfairne. The Old Man and I more or less lived there when we weren't on a job. I have contacts in the city. Maybe they can help us find the way."

Foxtail spread her hands, then gestured in the direction of Lake Galway. *Sure, but how will we get there? We going to swim across?*

Considering the other side was ninety miles away, no. But she did bring up a real problem. With the blockade, taking a boat was out of the question. So was a stagecoach. It was only a two-day ride around Lake Galway, but given how many people wanted out of Carlow right now, we'd be lucky to find one in a week. Given the stain inside Lachlan, we couldn't afford to waste that kind of time.

So. We couldn't sail out. Couldn't swim out. Couldn't ride out. Couldn't walk out. That left us only one path.

The Old Man laughed. *That's so crazy*, he said, *it just might work.*

First, we'd need to collect our things from the rooms in Carlow where we'd been staying. I turned to the girls. "Do you think you two could sneak back to the Tiger Arms Hotel without being seen?"

Foxtail put her hands on her hips, offended I'd suggest otherwise. Meriel was a little miffed herself. "We'll take the Thieves' Highway," she said, referring to the city's rooftops. "But why?"

"If we're going to leave the city, we'll need our stuff. Don't bother with all our disguises; we can get new togs in Redfairne. Just grab our wallets and satchels, a couple of valises, and a decent change of clothes for all of us. Make mine the finest we've got."

"And bring them here?"

"No," I said. I had somewhere very different in mind.

CHAPTER 15

THE HELIOPORT WAS packed.

With all other routes out of Carlow bottlenecked by the Stickmen, those who wanted to flee in case the smoldering volcano finally blew were looking for any way out, provided they could afford it—airship tickets weren't cheap. Nonetheless, the size of the crowd was a good thing. The chaos would work in our favor. It usually did when playing a gaff.

As for the others, they didn't understand why we were here. It was late morning by the time Meriel and Foxtail had joined us with our things from the hotel. Hidden in a copse near the helioport, we'd changed from our torn, dirty clothes into fresh, clean outfits. Now we looked respectable again. Me in particular, dressed in the best finery Lachlan had scrounged up for us last week.

Lachlan wasn't much worried about anything. He stared up at the massive airship—the *Malley*, the same ship I'd come in on last week—utterly fascinated. "Shuna's bouncing baubles," he breathed.

But Meriel, in particular, looked confused. "Didn't you say the Weavers ran the airships?"

"They do," I said.

"Ain't this the most dangerous way out, then?" Lachlan asked.

"Exactly the opposite. It's the *least* dangerous *because* it's run by the Weavers."

They all looked puzzled at that, so I explained. "It's something the Old Man taught me. *The things people trust the most are what they defend the least.* It's like, if you're going to war, where do you mass your troops? On a border with an ally? No. You station them where your enemy will invade."

I motioned to the airship tethered to the landing pad, its great helion floating overhead. "This is the same thing. The Weavers don't control the roads, and they don't control the ports. So that's where they'll look most keenly. They'll never expect the thieves to be foolish enough to walk through their own front door."

Meriel turned to Foxtail. "Do you think he knows he just called himself a fool?"

Foxtail spread her hands. *Hard to tell.*

"I'm serious," I said. "Trust me, this will work."

That was sort of a lie. An airship *was* our best chance of getting out of Carlow without getting caught. But I couldn't guarantee it would work. I just didn't want to tell them that. The more they thought about failure, the more nervous they'd get. Especially Gareth. And that would only tip off the Weavers. My friends weren't gaffers; they weren't used to playing the odds.

Even now, Gareth didn't like this. "What if they search the p-passengers?"

"I expect them to," I said. "At least, they'll search *most* of the passengers. There's one class they won't lay a hand on. Which is why I needed my things from the hotel."

I opened my valise and pulled out a gold-embossed ticket. "I'm going first class," I said.

"Where'd you steal that from?" Meriel said, surprised.

"I didn't steal it. The Weavers gave it to the passengers you, uh, *inconvenienced* when you pickpocketed them on our way to Carlow. So . . . thanks for that."

Meriel looked put out, as if the joke was somehow on her. "Well . . . fine. What about our tickets?"

"Oh, you're not going first class."

"What? Why not?"

"Because to get any more of these," I said, "we *would* need to steal them. And if a first-class passenger complains, the Weavers will listen. Fourth class, on the other hand, well, no one cares about them."

"They'll search us, then?" Lachlan said.

I shrugged. "So what if they do? You're not carrying anything bad. I'm the one with the Eye."

Meriel couldn't believe I was sticking her in fourth class while I got to ride in style. I ignored her sputtering. "Gareth," I said, "we've all seen your card tricks. I assume you're as good a pickpocket, too?"

Gareth looked embarrassed, but also proud I thought well of him. "I . . . no. I mean . . . yes. I can do it. Just not as . . . um . . ."

As usual, he was being self-deprecating. My guess was that if he'd wanted, everything in our pockets would already be in his. "See that man over there?"

Gareth nodded.

"He has a fourth-class ticket, right side, back of his trousers," I said. "The man next to him with the spectacles has one in his vest, left breast. And the lady in the tall hat has two in her purse."

"How d'you know that?" Lachlan said.

"I've been watching them," I said, annoyed. "This is what— Are you lot ever going to trust I know what I'm doing?"

"Sorry, guv."

"He's so touchy," Meriel said to Foxtail.

Foxtail nodded. *I know.*

"Snaffle the tickets," I said to Gareth. "And leave them each fifty crowns for their trouble, if you can."

Gareth went to work. Meriel was near outraged. "Fifty crowns! You're getting soft."

To my dismay, I thought I was. I could practically see the Old Man shaking his head.

Either way, I had my ticket. Gareth was getting the others. That still left us with one big problem.

Foxtail.

She'd covered her mask as usual. But when the Weavers searched the lower-class passengers, they'd demand to look under her veil. Getting her on board was a huge gamble—one I was certain I'd lose.

"I'm not sure what to do about you," I admitted to her.

She waved my concern away, then pointed to the airship.

"You'll get on yourself?" I said.

She nodded.

"How?"

She just patted my cheek and walked away.

"Wait, Gareth still has to give you your . . ." I trailed off as she disappeared into the crowd.

"I will never figure out that girl," Meriel said.

She didn't even know the half of it.

Once Gareth returned with our tickets, we slipped into our roles. Using the same forged patents of nobility I had the last time I rode the *Malley*, I was once again Alastair Quinn, seventeenth earl of Garman Minor. Gareth, Meriel, and Lachlan were my servants.

Meriel grumbled as I made her carry a valise. Lachlan didn't mind. He just kept staring up at the *Malley*.

"The color," he said, awed. "It's so pretty."

"You think?" I didn't, myself. The airship was amazing, certainly, but the color was the plainest thing about it. Just an ordinary beige for the skin covering the massive helion, and the gray metal of the three windmill propellers at the back. Though the patterned walnut of the passenger tower hanging below the helion was nice.

First class, naturally, was given priority boarding, so I made a big show of sending Meriel, Lachlan, and Gareth off to stow my luggage. Then I strolled over to the stairs that led to the entrance to the *Malley*.

And there, to my dismay, I saw I'd got it terribly wrong.

The Weavers *were* searching first class. Not with a pat-down. Instead, there was an older Weaver standing at the foot of the stairs, his seven-pointed silver star pendant clearly visible around his neck. He held some sort of rod. It was around ten inches long and made of some odd metal, almost like bronze, but with a pinkish tinge. He gripped it at its center, the rod sticking out on either side of his hand, and waved it over each passenger before letting them through.

Behind the man stood three Pistoleers. They were far enough away not to intimidate the passengers, but close enough for me to know what they were there for.

There hadn't been any kind of search when I'd ridden the *Malley* to Carlow. I nodded toward the rod in the Weaver's hand. "What is that thing?" I asked the lady ahead of me.

"I have no idea," she said. "You there! What are you doing?"

"Just a precaution, my lady," the Weaver said. "This instrument detects enchantments. It's perfectly harmless."

"And what business is it of yours if I'm carrying an enchantment?"

"Ordinary bindings will be no problem," the man said smoothly. "We're only looking for one particular item. A thousand apologies, my lady. The search is commanded by order of His Imperial Majesty."

By order of Darragh VII, High Weaver, more like. Heart pounding, I looked around casually, as if curious about the helioport. In reality, I was searching for escape routes. *The Pistoleers are all on my left. If I could make it to the crowd without getting shot—*

And then there was no more time. I'd reached the front of the line. The Weaver smiled at me and said, "This will just take a moment, young master," and began his search.

He held the rod low, near my boots. Then, slowly, he brought it up. Past my legs, my belt, my stomach, my chest—

And the rod began to hum.

CHAPTER 16

THE WEAVER PAUSED.

The rod vibrated in his palm, a gentle *rrrrrrrr* sounding from the device.

The Pistoleers behind him perked up.

The Weaver was still smiling. "Are you carrying a binding, my lord?"

"I . . . yes," I said, and I slapped my forehead, as if I forgot. "I am."

And I drew Galawan from my inside coat pocket.

I'd borrowed him from Lachlan before we'd split. I hadn't taken the sparrow because I thought I'd get searched. I'd done it because I thought Lachlan would. Galawan wouldn't have fit the boy's disguise; it was far too fine, too valuable for a child in fourth class to carry. If he'd been caught with it, there'd have been questions.

As it was, there was nothing strange about an earl's son owning a construct. "This is my bird," I said to the Weaver. "I carry him everywhere. His name's Galawan."

Galawan tweeted a friendly melody. The Weaver took him from my hand, deeply impressed.

"Such extraordinary craftsmanship," the man said. "May I ask who made him?"

I wasn't about to tell him *Mr. Solomon*. "I really wouldn't know,"

I said, as if such matters were beneath me. "He was a gift from my father, when I reached the age of decision."

"Of course. Er . . . one moment, please." He handed the bird to a surprised Pistoleer.

"Pardon me," I said in protest.

"I'll return him, young master," the Weaver said, "once I've finished my search."

Before I could argue any further, he brought the rod near me again. I forced myself to appear calm, but in my mind, I was preparing to run. Lachlan would be so upset that I'd lost Galawan. Assuming I made it out of here alive.

But nothing happened.

The Weaver brought his rod up to my head, right in front of my eyepatch. Yet it gave off no hum as before. Instead, it remained completely still, no more sound than any inert bar of metal.

"All done, sir," the Weaver said. He handed Galawan back to me, offering one last look of admiration for the little sparrow. "Our apologies for the delay."

It took a second for me to realize I was free. I sniffed, as if this whole process was beneath me, then boarded the *Malley.*

A steward welcomed me with a glass of sparkling wine. I sipped at it absently, confused about what had just happened.

That rod didn't detect the Eye, I thought. Why not? Was it that the Eye was no ordinary enchantment? Or was something even stranger going on?

I stared at Galawan, wondering if I already knew the answer.

This time, I couldn't enjoy the *Malley*.

It wasn't so much that the ride had changed. The view was still as amazing, seeing the world from three thousand feet up. I watched the emperor's iron dreadnoughts, lined in their blockade near the port, as we rose high into the air. I watched the other boats on the water, too. And Carlow. The fields, the farms. Then the long expanse of Lake Galway. And Bolcanathair, which had nearly stopped smoking, just a few vapors rising now to join the thick cloud overhead. The airship was just as wondrous as before, too: the gentle hum of the engine, the soft *whoom-whoom-whoom* of the propellers, the rush of breeze through my hair when I stuck my head out the side.

No. What was different was me.

When I'd boarded the *Malley* a week ago—Shuna's teeth, had it really been that short a time?—everything had been so full of promise. I'd had Mr. Solomon's letter and the possibility of a payout that would heal the scars which forever marked me as a thief. And not just that. My cut of Mr. Solomon's job would have left me with more than enough crowns to buy an apprenticeship.

This, up here, was what I'd have chosen. Join the Airmen's Guild, ride the clouds. Spend the rest of my life in the sky.

That was over now. Our payout was up in smoke—literally burned by the Lady in Red. As for my scars . . . I didn't know anymore. We were chasing the Dragon's Teeth to save Lachlan, but Fergal's story made me wonder: Could Belenoth heal me, too? Could I end up on an airship someday, after all?

I didn't dare believe it. Too much would have to go my way

for that to happen. Because after what Mr. Solomon had done to me, not only would I have to now find the money for an apprenticeship somewhere else, the Dragon's Teeth would have to heal both my scars *and* my missing eye. The Airmen's Guild would never take a half-blind apprentice.

I shook my head, feeling like a mark. All hope had ever got me was pain. *You were right*, I said to the Old Man. *I was a fool to think I could have this.*

Maybe, he said. *But you're entitled to be a little foolish once in a while. Why not dream of better?*

That doesn't sound like you, Old Man.

Because it's not me, he said. *It's just your memory of me. I'm not actually here.*

"No," I sighed. "But I wish you were."

I'd said those same words on my way to Carlow. Back then, I'd been trying to mock him.

This time I meant it.

I stayed by the rail, watching the water pass below. It would take three hours to cross Lake Galway, so lunch was served, on silver trays carted around the deck by stewards. I accepted a plate of razor-sliced beef in oil and spices and leaned back over the side, staring down again.

Then a hand stuck a cracker in my face.

"Baked salmon, my lord?" a high voice said.

"No, thank y—" Then I turned and saw who it was. "*Meriel?*"

She was holding a pair of canapés, salmon and white sauce on a cracker. She smiled impishly.

"What are you doing here?" I said, alarmed.

"I was worried you might be lonely." She stuffed a cracker in her mouth. "Sure you don't want one? They're really good."

"Forget the fish. You're going to get us in trouble." I glanced back at the central cabin. A spiral staircase led to the upper decks, where the second-, third-, and fourth-class passenger areas were. An attendant stood at the foot of the stairs, keeping watch so the lower-class passengers couldn't come down. "How did you even get past the stewards?"

She wiggled her fingers. "Magic."

"Meriel..."

She laughed. "I climbed down the side."

I stared at her in horror. "The side...of the *airship*?"

"What else?"

"But...that's crazy. The wind...the height...What if you'd lost your footing and fallen?"

"Now you're just trying to hurt my feelings. Can I have some beef?" She took a piece off my plate.

"Artha's pounding paws," I cursed.

"Oh, don't be so serious," Meriel said. "No one saw me climb down, and I never fall. That's *my* job, remember?"

"And what if the crew recognizes you didn't come on with first class? What if they ask to see your ticket?"

"I'll show it to them." She pulled a stub of a gold-embossed ticket from her purse.

"Wha...where did you get that?"

"I stole it from that woman with the little dog. Well, don't look." She plucked another slice from my plate. "Will you relax already? I promise, I won't cause any more trouble. Besides, I didn't bring my parachute this time."

"I . . . you . . . fine. Stop stealing my beef."

She laughed again, then linked her arm in mine, leaning her head against my shoulder as she gazed over the side. The scent of her jasmine perfume left me a little distracted. And surprised, too. She'd never been so affectionate before.

Seeing Lachlan die and then come back to life has changed her, I thought.

It hasn't changed her, the Old Man said. *It's made her drop her walls. You've seen her playing with Lachlan before. This is the girl inside. The one she won't let herself be.*

He was right, as usual. As much as Meriel liked needling me, I remembered how upset she'd been when I got stuck behind that portcullis in the High Weaver's home, after I'd sprung the floor trap. How stricken she'd looked when I lost my eye. The Old Man would have me file this away, keep the knowledge close, in case I needed to use it against her later. Just like how our visit to the asylum had revealed her nervousness around the insane. But just like before, I didn't want to.

The girl's right, the Old Man said. *You are getting soft.*

Meriel rested against me, contented. "So beautiful, isn't it?"

I nodded.

She looked up at me. "Oh, come on. Are you still mad at me?"

"Of course not."

"Then why are you so glum?" She poked me lightly in the side. "Come on, tell me."

I really was getting soft. I'd never have let my mask slip like this when I was with the Old Man. "It's nothing. I just . . . I thought I might end up here. An apprentice with the Airmen. With the money we were supposed to get from Mr. Solomon's job."

"Oh." She looked around the deck, suddenly seeing the airship from a different perspective. Measuring it against a different life. She hugged my arm a little, understanding. "Would have been nice."

"Yeah."

"Is that all, though?"

"What do you mean?"

"Back in Carlow. You just seemed so . . . I don't know. Pushy. Like we had to race to get out of there."

"You'd rather the Stickmen were still on our heels?"

"No. But we probably could have spared a day or two in hiding until the search wasn't so hot. So what's really going on?"

Either she'd gotten more perceptive than when I'd first met her, or I really was letting down my guard. Still, there wasn't any point in hiding the truth now. If anything, it was a relief to actually tell someone.

"It's Lachlan," I said. She grew serious as I explained how using the dragon staff to revive him had left a stain on his soul. I told her about Bragan's warning, and his belief that following the path the Eye laid out for us might be able to cure him.

"The Dragon's Teeth," she said, surprised. "One of them . . . what's its name?"

"Belenoth."

"Right, that. Fergal said it's a healer."

"Yeah," I said. "So all Lachlan's life depends on is a trail left by a High Weaver who died two thousand years ago. Which we learned about in a sailors' tavern, told to us in a story which may not even be true."

Meriel chewed on a fingernail, one of her telltale signs she was worried. "Does Lachlan know?"

"No. And I don't want anyone to tell him. It'll just scare him, and there's nothing he can do about it anyway."

"What about the Eye? Have you seen anything with it yet?"

"Nothing. And believe me, I've tried."

It was strange how much I'd begun to rely on the thing. Part of me hated having it in my skull. I resented the way it had grabbed me and wouldn't let go. Even thinking about the time it had sifted through my memories made my guts twist. The Eye had made me relive in full detail the terror and the agony of the worst experience of my life: when the Stickmen had whipped six-year-old me for stealing an apple, leaving me marked forever with the constant pain of my scars.

Then there was how it spoke in my head—or used to. Feeling its emotions was almost worse, as if someone else was living inside me, a constant threat to take over my mind. I found myself wishing the thing would just talk again.

Even so, I had to admit there was a part of me that actually . . . I wasn't sure of the word. I didn't *like* having the Eye, exactly. But there was something about looking through it, seeing the magical world—what the Eye had called the *true* world—that was intoxicating. The beauty of the colors, the pulse of life within . . . there just wasn't anything ordinary that could compare. That part of me almost dreaded the day when the Eye would finally let me go, and I wouldn't see that beauty anymore. Assuming it *did* ever let me go.

Besides that, the Eye had been enormously useful. It had led us to Bragan, then made him surrender, and that had brought Lachlan back to life. Even now, though I knew it had its own secret purpose for wanting the Dragon's Teeth, I was hoping that it would help me find them. Then maybe we could heal Lachlan for good.

Thinking about that had kept me looking for some sign of the trail since the *Malley* took off. I'd got quite good at seeing through the Eye in public without anyone noticing I had a jewel in my head. I just pushed the patch up a little, rubbed my socket as if the eyepatch was making me itch, and peeked through my fingers.

If seeing the world from on high was amazing just with my own eyes, then looking through the Eye was really something else. The lifeglow wasn't as well defined up here, but I could see so much more of it. Before we'd got too far over Lake Galway, I saw the endless green covering the fields surrounding Carlow. Even the lake was its own spectacle, with little flashes of color as fish, birds, and other sea life darted along near the surface of the water.

I'd finally gotten an answer, too, as to whether the airship ran on magic. It did. I'd peeked at the engines and seen they glowed bright violet, the same color as Bragan's enchantments, and as in the dragon staff.

Which reminded me. "You and Foxtail made this eyepatch, right?"

"Why?" Meriel said. "Doesn't it fit?"

"It's fine. I was just wondering . . . how did you put it together?"

"There's a steel cup underneath. I wrapped it with soft leather to pad the edge, then sewed over that with the cloth from my dress."

I ran my fingers over the fabric. The dress she'd used, emerald in color, had had dragons printed on it in deeper green. Meriel had cut it so a single dragon adorned the patch. "You stitched it yourself?"

"Look, if something's wrong, just tell me. I can fix it—"

"No, really, it's great. Totally comfortable. I just meant, if that's what *you* did, what did Foxtail do?"

"She gave me the steel," Meriel said. "Actually, the whole thing was her idea. She brought me the cup and suggested you might like a patch instead of a bandage."

"I do. Maybe more than you'd think." When she looked at me quizzically, I said, "The patch blocks the Eye's sight. That's good, because otherwise, I'd be so dizzy, I wouldn't be able to stand. But I think the patch does *more* than block its sight. I think it blocks it out from the whole world. *Both* ways."

"What do you mean?"

"I told you the Eye can't talk anymore. But its presence is still there. Sometimes I can feel what it's feeling. But *only* when the Eye isn't behind the patch. Each time I put it away, I can sense its frustration with me, and then all its emotions are gone. If I had to guess, I'd say the Eye can't tell anything that's happening in this world unless I let it see for itself."

"That's a little creepy," Meriel said.

"Imagine how *I* feel. The thing is, though, I don't think that's all the patch does. When Bragan attacked us at his farm, it was because he didn't know who we were. He didn't realize I was carrying the Eye."

"Why would he? You can't see it when the patch is on."

"It's more than that. From what Bragan suggested, he couldn't even *feel* it. As if the patch had somehow blocked him from detecting it was there. And then to get onto the *Malley*—did you guys see that pink bronze or whatever rod?"

Meriel nodded.

"That rod detects enchantments," I said. "It found Galawan easily enough. But it completely missed the Eye."

"Because of the patch?"

"That's the only thing I can think of. I suppose it's possible the Eye's just a different kind of binding. But if Darragh told the other Weavers to use those rods, we have to assume they should be able to detect the Eye, even if it's hidden. Yet it didn't. It made me wonder if one of you did something to the patch."

"Not me," Meriel said. "Why don't you ask Foxtail about it?"

I said I would. But I didn't plan to. I knew very well she wouldn't answer me.

Still. That girl and I were going to have a long talk one of these days.

◠◡

Meriel and I spent the rest of the trip together, swiping food off the trays the stewards carted by and gazing over the side. As put out as I was with her recklessness in coming down to first class, I was glad she'd joined me. Thinking about Lachlan and the Eye was a constant weight on my shoulders. She helped take my mind off the gloom.

Her comment about the Eye picking up Veran's trail did keep me checking over the side, however. And as we approached Redfairne, I spotted something in the distance. I frowned.

"What is it?" Meriel said.

"I'm not sure," I said. "Block me from view."

She huddled close, opening her parasol to hide us from the other passengers. I tried not to think of her jasmine perfume as I took a good look with the Eye.

We were close enough now to see Redfairne. I hadn't got the chance to view it from the air on my last trip because we'd taken off before sunrise. Now the city was crystal clear. I'd lived there off and on for years, but I'd never seen it like this. It really was something to witness.

But the beauty of the view wasn't what caught my eye—or the Eye.

There was a light.

At first it was too dim to make out. But the closer we got, the more it looked like . . . yes. It was a beam. A beam of pure white light, shooting up from—

I grabbed Meriel. "Oh no."

"What's wrong?"

"We failed. We *failed*."

"Failed what?" she said, alarmed. "What's happening?"

"The primeval magic. It's burst through the surface. We didn't seal it up." The world . . . it was going to crack.

"Where?" Meriel said. "Where is it?"

"There." I pointed.

"Where?"

"Right *there*."

Meriel looked confused. "All I see is Redfairne."

"You can't see the light?"

She looked at me, puzzled. "No."

I blinked and covered the Eye. Sure enough, the beam of light disappeared.

Wait a minute. "Did you see the primeval magic back in the Dragon Temple?" I asked.

"Of course," Meriel said. "It was blinding."

"But you don't see any light now."

"Cal, I have absolutely no idea what you're talking about."

So only the Eye could see this. Had it found the trail again?

I looked once more through the artifact. Sure enough, the beam returned, clearer than ever. It rose from the surface all the way up into the sky. With the winds coming from the east, we'd finally got out from under the black veil Bolcanathair had spewed; it was just ordinary clouds and sunshine on the other side of Lake Galway. So from where we floated, it looked like the beam went directly into the sun. There was even a little glowing arc, curved crosswise, where the light passed through a wisp of condensation. In fact, it almost looked like—

My heart skipped a beat.

The sun . . . it looked like a pommel. The beam continued, like a grip, then passed through the cloud, where the arc made a crosspiece. The light then continued straight down . . . like a blade.

A sword.

It looked like a *sword*.

"The Blade of Heaven," I said. "It's there. It's right *there*."

Meriel was getting cross. "Will you *please* tell me what you're talking about?"

"The Eye. It's showing me the Blade of Heaven."

Legend has it, Fergal had said, *that the Dragon's Teeth will be found again. And the path to their discovery will shine from the Blade of Heaven.*

No wonder no one had ever found it. Fergal thought the Blade of Heaven was some kind of geological marker. What it really was, was a shining light—*and you needed the Eye to see it.*

"The path to find the Dragon's Teeth," I said. "I know where it is."

Meriel stared, wishing she could see it, too. "It's in Redfairne?"

"Not exactly," I said. "It looks more like it's . . ."

Then I realized exactly where the Blade was pointing.

Oh *no*.

CHAPTER 17

"It's *underwater*?" Lachlan said. "Shuna's snout."

We'd landed at Redfairne and disembarked. The helioport was right next to Lake Galway, so Meriel and I went to the overlook by the shore and waited for the others to join us. Lachlan was absolutely ecstatic about his balloon ride, practically jumping up and down when he and Gareth came to meet us. His enthusiasm tempered when I told them what I'd seen through the Eye.

The Blade of Heaven—which was supposed to lead us to the Dragon's Teeth—pointed directly *into* Lake Galway, some distance off the coast of Redfairne.

Now Lachlan stared out over the waves, as glum as Meriel and me.

"So Veran never even made it to Redfairne," Gareth said quietly.

"Doesn't look like it," I said. "Something sank his ship."

"H-how far out?"

"Five, six miles, maybe."

"Artha's fuzzy rump," Lachlan said. "I can't swim."

"No one's swimming out there, Lachlan," Meriel said.

"Aw." He looked dejected. "That mean it's over?"

"There might be a way," I said. "I have a contact; we'll see. For now, we should get out of here. But first, we need our luggage. And where's Foxtail?"

Everyone looked at each other.

"No one's seen her? Did she even get on the *Malley*?"

They all looked blank—and rather worried now. As for me, I felt sick. Foxtail had left us with a promise that she'd sneak on the airship herself. She was so good at prowling that it had never occurred to me that she might not succeed. Did we leave her behind?

The porter wheeled our luggage to us at the overlook. He read the name on the tag. "My lord Alastair Quinn?"

I nodded, trying to appear cool while frantically scanning the helioport for Foxtail. The porter removed the valises from the dolly with a grunt, and I tipped him a few septs. He'd already left by the time I realized he'd made a mistake.

"Wait," I called, but he was off in the crowd. I turned to Meriel. "Did you bring that case?"

Among our things was a larger valise I didn't remember. Meriel looked just as puzzled. "No," she said, and she leaned down to inspect it.

Then she stumbled back with a squeal. The valise was *moving*.

It began to unzip itself in the corner. A dusky little finger stuck out and waved at us.

"*Foxtail?*" Lachlan said, delighted. "You stuffed in there?"

"Lachlan." I pulled him up by the collar, glancing at the crowd. "Please don't talk to the luggage."

☾☽

I'd only been gone a week. Somehow, it felt like forever.

It wasn't that the clockmaker's shop had changed; it was empty of customers, as usual. Lachlan thought the place marvelous, all the hands ticking away, cuckoos popping out little birds. On the carriage ride here, I'd returned Galawan to him. Now he pulled the construct out, trying to show the sparrow all these potential playmates. Gareth, too, was fascinated by the machines. Even Meriel and Foxtail wandered the shelves, curious.

"You really lived here?" Meriel said.

"When we weren't on a job."

Seeing this place through my friends' eyes made me feel a little guilty, as I realized I'd been judging it too harshly. Grey's shop was actually kind of fun. I'd made a lot of good memories here over the last seven years: playing with gears and cogwheels under the tables, swapping rude jokes with the clockmaker, sitting by the fire with the Old Man. I guess I'd fallen into that trap of everyday sights losing their charm. Or maybe it was that staying here after the Old Man abandoned me had left a sour taste in my mouth.

"Oh! Oh!" Lachlan said. "Look, Galawan! A *cat!*"

Good old Lopsided had joined us. Lop wasn't a real cat, of course. He was a poorly made clay construct. His legs had sunk into his body, so he leaned to the left, giving him his name.

Lop came from behind the counter at the sound of my voice and rubbed his head on my leg. I picked him up. He purred and pawed gently at my cheek.

Lachlan brought Galawan close. The bird tweeted in alarm as

Lopsided stretched out to bat at him instead. "I'm not really sure they're going to be friends," I warned Lachlan.

"Give 'em time," Lachlan said. "He's got a pretty glow."

"A what?"

"The cat. He's all glowy. Just like the airship."

I looked at the others. They looked back, just as confused.

"Lopsided . . . is glowing?" I said.

"He's kinda faded and all, but yeah. Can't none of you see it?"

I stared at Lachlan for a moment, stomach fluttering. Then I looked at Lop with the Eye.

He *was* glowing.

Of course he was. Lop was a construct; he was enchanted. The Eye saw the glow of magic bound within him, as it always did. Lop's light was dim, as Lachlan had said, but it was clearly the same purple shine—

As the Malley's *engines*, I realized.

I finally grasped two more things then, as well. First, the glowing: the colors the Eye saw had a deeper meaning. Each color corresponded to the kind of magic inside. Red was life, at least in people and other mammals, the hue shaded by their own natures. Leaves and trees glowed green. And purple . . .

Purple was *air*. The same magic that Bragan had used against us, the magic inside the dragon staff, the *Malley*'s engines. In Lopsided, too, apparently.

And the same as the stain on Lachlan's soul.

Now I understood. When Lachlan had said the airship was a pretty color, it wasn't the ship he was talking about.

He could see *enchantments*.

CHAPTER 18

I KEPT VERY still. When I spoke, I did so casually, so as not to alarm him. "Lachlan? Are we glowing, too?"

He seemed puzzled. "Course not. Should you be?"

"No. It's . . . nothing."

The others were looking at me a little oddly. Gareth and Foxtail didn't know about the stain on Lachlan's soul. And I hadn't told Meriel about the different colors I could see through the Eye. So none of them could put it all together.

Nonetheless, it was clear now. Lachlan could see enchantments—but *only* those with the same violet color that was inside him. The stain had attuned him to air magic.

My heart sank. Bragan had warned me the primeval would start having effects. What alarmed me was how it had happened so soon. It hadn't even been a full day since the stain invaded his soul.

A quick peek inside Lachlan showed the primeval swimming inside him, bouncing off the edge of his Lachlan-red glow, as if trying to escape. It hadn't grown, at least. And as far as side effects went, seeing enchantments seemed harmless enough. But I didn't like what it forebode.

How fast were these changes going to come over him? How much time did we have left?

I didn't get the chance to mull it over. Grey clomped down from his private rooms upstairs, drawn by the sound of our voices. As he appeared in the doorway, it struck me as odd that he hadn't been here already. Even when there were no customers—which was pretty much all the time—he liked minding the shop, tinkering with his clocks.

When he appeared, I was surprised at how tired he looked. His clothes hung loose, and he had bags under his eyes. I think we'd just woke him.

He saw the girls first. "Welcome, young ladies!" he said amiably, not realizing they weren't customers. Then he spotted me standing among the displays.

He paused. He didn't say anything, not sure if I was on a gaff or not, and not wanting to snaffle the deal. But his gaze remained steady on my eyepatch, a question behind his eyes.

"Hey, Grey," I said, a little sadder than I'd intended.

He waited at the edge of the counter. I joined him. He glanced at the others in the shop, brow raised.

"They did the Solomon job with me," I said. "They're friends."

He was surprised to hear me call them that. But there was a softness in his expression when I used the word. The idea that I might have friends pleased him.

At any rate, he was used to the occasional colleague the Old Man had sometimes brought into the shop, so having the place full didn't faze him. "Come in, then, lads and lasses," he said in his thick brogue. "Have a look around."

He puffed up a bit with pride when he saw the others admiring his clocks. As they poked through the stock, Grey leaned over the counter and spoke quietly. "So, boyo, word is the Carlow Stickmen are losing their minds. Volcanoes exploding, High Weaver on a rampage. Somethin' 'bout Pistoleers, too?"

Grey had always had his ear to the ground. Though I suppose news of the chaos we'd left strewn behind us would have spread far and fast, regardless. "We might have had something to do with that," I admitted.

"And . . . ?" He nodded toward my patch. "You on a gaff?"

"Wish I were."

His face fell. "Ah, Cal."

"It's all right."

But he closed his eyes and shook his head. "Never should've given you that letter."

I shrugged. "Not your fault. Taking the job was my choice." Even though the Old Man taught me better. "Frankly, I'm beginning to think I couldn't have made any other decision."

"What's that mean?"

"That maybe things aren't as random as they seem," I said. "What's with you, though? You don't look so good."

He laughed. "Nice to see you, too, boyo. So tell me: If you're not on a gaff, what's with the merry band o' cutpurses?"

I made the introductions. Meriel joined us at the counter. Gareth nodded shyly from the shelves, then returned to studying one of Grey's glass-walled clocks, trying to work out how the cogs, springs, and gears meshed to make the thing run. Foxtail and Lachlan both waved, Lachlan with a disarming grin, as they sat on the floor, playing with Galawan and Lopsided. Feeling safe here, Foxtail lifted her veil.

Grey nearly choked when he saw her mirrored mask. "Artha's bleedin' eyes!"

Foxtail stood and gave a little curtsy, amused. I remembered, back in Mr. Solomon's parlor, she'd found my reaction to her mask funny, too. Made me glad she didn't go around showing everyone.

When Grey looked at me, I shrugged. He stared a moment longer, then left it alone. Whatever it was, he wanted no part of it. "And, uh . . . I suppose you'll be wantin' a place to stay?"

"We have a few crowns left," I said. "We'll get rooms down at the Mulberry."

"Ah, just stay here."

I paused. "Really?"

"'Less you have somewhere else you need to be."

This was very odd. The Old Man had brought plenty of strangers in our business to Grey's shop, but the clockmaker had never opened his home to them. And he didn't have a lot of space above. Yes, he'd let me live here after the Old Man abandoned me, but Grey had known me since I was seven. Even then, my room was basically a repurposed closet. What was he up to?

I was kind of curious to find out, so I said, "All right. In the meantime, there's no gaff, exactly, but we are on a job. It's a salvage. You know anything about deep-sea diving?"

"Do I look like a fish?" he said.

"An eel, I would think."

He swatted at me, a half-hearted swing I dodged easily. "Getting mouthy, ain't you, now you got troops to back you up."

I jerked a thumb at Meriel. "She's the one to watch out for."

She smiled. "Aw. Isn't he sweet?" Then she snapped her fingers. "That reminds me: Cal said you can get us stuff. Can you find me more knives like this?"

Meriel pulled one from the folds of her dress. Grey looked it over. "No worries. How many you need?"

"Say two . . . no, three dozen."

He blinked.

"Don't ask," I said. "Anyway, about that salvage. Didn't we know someone who arranged something like that a few years ago?"

"What's so important you want to go diving for?" he said.

I frowned. "It's a job. A lot safer than the last one, too. Why are you being so evasive?"

Grey tried to keep his face blank, but I'd spent way too much time around him, and the Old Man had taught me too well. In fact, remembering the Old Man made me think again of all the characters I'd met through him over the years.

And then I knew exactly why Grey was being cagey.

CHAPTER 19

"Daphna," I said as the memory returned. "It was Daphna who set up the dive."

"Who's Daphna?" Meriel said.

Grey made a sour face. "Told you to stay away from her. Look what she did to you."

"My eye is hardly Daphna's fault."

"Who's Daphna?" Meriel said again.

"She put *promises* into yer head, boyo," Grey said. "Promises she never should have made. Talking 'bout yer scars, 'Oh, I can get 'em fixed.' She knew you'd want the prize she offered, and sure enough, you chased it. Even when you knew the race was for fools."

He wasn't completely wrong, even though, as I'd said to Grey earlier, I was starting to think my getting offered the job to steal the Eye was no accident.

Meriel poked me repeatedly in the side. "Who. Is. Daphna? Who. Is. Daphna? Who. Is—"

"Would you—" I pulled away. "She's a broker. Of sorts."

"She's a snake," Grey said.

"She *is* a snake. But she can get just about anything. Deals mostly in enchantments. Anytime the Old Man needed something to do with bindings, we went to her."

Gareth, listening, joined us. "She's a W-Weaver?" he asked, worried.

"No. Just *very* well connected to the guild. She knows everybody. Even the High Weaver himself."

"Which should be warnin' enough," Grey said. "The Old Man dealt with her smooth, sure, but that's 'cause *no one* ever tried to snaffle the Architect."

The Architect was what everyone called the Old Man. It hadn't been until I'd spent a few years with him that I finally realized he was famous. "He did teach me a few things, Grey."

"So he did. But you ain't him, and Daphna knows it. Do a deal with that one, you best not forget every smile comes with a dagger up the sleeve."

"Sounds like my kind of girl," Meriel said.

Grey scowled. "It ain't something to be proud of."

"We'll be fine," I said. "Daphna likes me."

"Yeh, she does," he said. "And if you think that'll make a bit o' difference, you're dumber than I thought."

He wasn't wrong about that, either. Daphna's trustworthiness went only as far as her own self-interest. But I didn't see how I had any choice. If the Blade of Heaven pointed to Lake Galway, then according to Fergal's story, either the path to the Dragon's Teeth or the Dragon's Teeth themselves were lost below its waters. Even if I wanted to ignore the deal I'd made with the Eye, we needed those swords to heal Lachlan.

So. It was time to visit an old friend.

Only Meriel wanted to come. Daphna's connection to the High Weaver made Gareth nervous, Foxtail wasn't interested, and Lachlan was having too much fun playing with Galawan and Lopsided to bother.

Normally, I'd have balked at bringing someone to meet a contact like Daphna. People in our business didn't tend to be trusting around strangers. In this case, however, I thought the girl's presence might help. Daphna liked playing with new toys, and I suspected she'd find Meriel curious.

Besides, there was something I'd been meaning to ask Meriel. And this trip would give me the perfect chance to do it.

Daphna lived all the way across town, so we hired a carriage to take us. Meriel watched the city go by. Redfairne was a sleepier sort of place than Carlow, not nearly as grand as our empire's capital. But it had some nice areas with old stone shops and fountained gardens, and Meriel had never really seen it. Just that one time she passed through to take the *Malley* to meet Mr. Solomon.

"So who is this Daphna, really?" she asked as she gazed out the carriage window. "I mean, like, *who*."

"She's the daughter of a powerful Weaver," I said, "who himself was the son of a High Weaver. Not Darragh, this was a few High Weavers back."

"She didn't want to become a Weaver herself?"

"Oh, she's far too lazy for that. Lot of work, becoming a Weaver. The academy, the apprenticeship, the research. That's not for her. She just likes pretty things. And getting one up on you. If she can do that, it'll make her day. Anyway, she's traded on her family connections for years. Knows everyone who's anyone in the Enchanters' Guild."

"I thought Weavers didn't trust outsiders."

"Like I said, she's not really an outsider. She grew up with a lot of those people. She even knew Darragh when they were kids. According to the Old Man, Daphna used to be quite the beauty."

"So what's she doing slumming with the likes of you? No offense."

"She likes the thrill of it," I said, amused. "Hanging about with criminals, sticking her fingers in pies on the wrong side of the law. She tried for years to charm the Old Man. In the end, he snaffled way more from her than she ever got back."

She regarded me for a moment. "He sounds like something else, this Old Man of yours."

"He was."

She hesitated. I could tell she wanted to ask me more about him. I wasn't sure if I wanted her to or not.

In the end, she didn't. She returned to sightseeing out the window.

For my part, I wanted to ask her something, too. Before we stole the Eye back from Mr. Solomon, I'd seen a vision of Meriel in the future, shown to me by Shuna in that . . . vision pool, I guess. The Fox had called it a "junction," but I didn't know what that meant. In it, I'd seen Meriel's death. She'd been executed in some far-off land.

What I'd witnessed had been terribly personal. Before Meriel was led to the chopping block, she'd wept over the death of a man. Whoever he was, it was clear that he'd meant a lot to her. And I was sure their executions were connected intimately to wherever she came from.

Even though Meriel had started dropping the walls she kept around her, I doubted she'd tell me the truth if I asked. But Shuna had shown it to me. Which left me wondering if it was something I should know.

The Old Man had given me good techniques for drawing out information. So I didn't need to pry too hard. Instead, I glanced out the window of our carriage, then did a double take. I craned my head, as if watching something pass.

"Did you see that?" I said.

"What?"

"Nothing, I guess. Just some slogan painted on a wall. I saw the same thing back in Carlow, but I never figured out what it meant."

"What did it say?"

"Don't know. It's in some strange language." I opened my satchel. I'd made sure to bring a quill, ink, and paper along so I could write it out. "Do you know what this means?"

I showed her the paper.

feyc anrygán

In the vision Shuna had shown me, those words had been painted on Meriel's forehead. When Meriel saw them now, she stopped breathing, and the pupils of her eyes shrank.

"No idea," she said.

Even an amateur would have seen through that lie. It was kind of interesting how, even when people knew you could read them, they kept forgetting it.

"Where'd you see this?" she said, trying to sound casual. "On a wall?"

"Yeah."

"And in Carlow, too?"

Again, even if I hadn't been able to tell before that she was lying, I would have now. She was showing entirely too much interest in something that supposedly meant nothing to her.

I could have pressed her on it. I wanted to, and not just to be nosy. As much as she liked to aggravate me, she cared about me—and I cared about her, too. Watching her die in that vision had been terrible. Yet it was clear she didn't want to tell me. So I just shrugged and put the paper away, like it was of no importance.

Meriel tried to pretend the same. But she stopped asking questions about Daphna, and she stopped looking outside the carriage. She just sat there quietly, chewing her fingernails, lost in her own thoughts.

CHAPTER 20

DAPHNA'S VILLA WAS in the hills, a stone's throw outside the city proper. It had belonged to an earl, Daphna had once told me, who'd fallen into a bit of trouble with the Weavers. She'd got him out of it—at the price of taking his home.

It was easy to see why she'd wanted the place. The villa was stunning, with a brilliant view of both Redfairne and Lake Galway. A low stone wall surrounded the property, with a botanical garden, an aviary, and a pond filled with blue-and-green-striped fish, fed by a freshwater spring. I should have made Lachlan come with us; he'd have found dozens of new friends for his bird.

The stone benches by the pond were Daphna's favorite place to lounge. But the afternoon's sudden chill had driven her inside, it seemed, because the steward who greeted our carriage in the roundabout said his mistress was in the sunroom. He escorted us through a hall of marble supported by pillars wrapped with gilded thread, ceiling-high paintings on display. A pair of fountains burbled on either side, with two long channels of flowing water fed by the same underground spring.

Meriel stared at it all, mouth open. I understood exactly how she felt. The first time I'd seen the place, I was seven years old and had never been to Redfairne before. The Old Man had taken me to Grey's shop to meet the clockmaker, then across town so he could introduce me to Daphna.

I'd walked this hall just as awed as Meriel. The Old Man had flicked me on the back of the head. *Quit gawking, boy.*

I'd only been with the Old Man a year, but he'd taught me a lot in that time. *I'm supposed to gawk,* I'd said. *That's why she made us walk through here. It's meant to impress us.*

He'd laughed, pleased. It made me feel warm inside, proud. *So it is,* he said. *But since you know she's manipulating you, why let her do it?*

She'll like me better if I fall for it, I'd said.

He'd laughed again, even more delighted, and ruffled my hair. *So she will.*

And she *had* liked me. Every time we visited her, Daphna gave me sweets. She stopped when I turned twelve, at the age of decision. I'd been proud that she no longer considered me a little child—and yet also kind of disappointed. They were good sweets.

Daphna's sunroom was at the southern edge of her villa, facing away from the hills. Here the rays shone through the glass roof and walls unimpeded. And here we found Daphna, reclining on a lounge chair, soaking up the warmth.

I'd told Meriel that Daphna used to be a great beauty. Now in her sixties, she'd lost the glow of youth, though she still dressed like a woman forty years younger. She wore a long, flowing dress of folded gossamer and ankle-strap sandals that sparkled with silver studs. Her forearms were covered with shiny platinum bangle bracelets, her neck wrapped with thin chains of the same metal. Though wrinkles lined her face, she was still a handsome woman—if a little reliant on makeup.

She plucked a cherry from a bowl as we entered, dangling it over one finger by its stem. The way Daphna moved always reminded me of a cat. A lazy one, watching as if you were a mouse, trying to decide whether you were worth the effort of catching.

She smiled, genuinely pleased to see me. "Cal! Darling. How good of you to visit." I leaned down to let her kiss me on both cheeks. "And what have you brought me? A guest."

"This is Meriel. She's an associate of ours." I chose my words carefully. If I'd said she was an associate of *mine*, it would have meant I was on a gaff, and Meriel was my mark, and whatever I said, Daphna should play along. An associate of *ours* meant Meriel was in the business, a thief like me, and we could talk freely.

Daphna looked Meriel up and down. "Shuna's heart. Aren't you beautiful?"

I'd always had something of a hard time reading Daphna. The Old Man had never had any trouble—he'd played her like a lute—but the Old Man was at a level I'd never reach. Still, I detected a bit of sting in her words.

"And an acrobat, too," Daphna said. "How interesting."

Meriel stopped. That was the wrong thing to say to her. She didn't like to be shown up by strangers—or friends, for that matter. "How would you know that?"

"Why, dear, your elegance, your grace. It's written in every step you take. Just like your accent tells me you're from Torgal. I'd wager you have a little knife or three somewhere under that dress, too."

Uh-oh. Daphna's claws were out. Though everything she was saying was *technically* a compliment, she wasn't saying it to be nice—and Meriel knew it.

She doesn't like how pretty Meriel is, I realized.

How young *and pretty,* the Old Man emphasized. *Careful, now.*

As for Meriel, she remained absolutely still. I could see the walls she kept around her slamming back up. But Meriel's reaction meant something else, too.

What Daphna had just said was true.

Well, well. I'd known about the knives, of course, and Meriel being an acrobat, but I hadn't realized she was from Torgal. It finally explained why I hadn't been able to place her accent. The Old Man had taught me just about every speech pattern in the empire—but Torgal wasn't *in* the empire anymore. They'd broken free in the Second Civil War, six hundred years ago, abandoning for good the unity that had begun with their own native son Aeric, first emperor of the world.

The Tors, as they were called—not always kindly—had kept to themselves since their rebellion, barely even bothering to trade with the vast empire of Ayreth to their north. Though the Old Man had dragged me all over the place, I'd never even met someone from Torgal before. Guess now I had.

For all its warmth, Daphna's sunroom had suddenly turned cold. Meriel was furiously frosty—and though Daphna was still difficult for me to read, her smile told me she was enjoying playing with her prey. Maybe I really should have brought Lachlan. Then we'd have had sweets instead.

I was relieved—and a little bit surprised—when Meriel said nothing at all. Daphna bade us sit, then called for fresh cherries for everyone before turning to me. "If you're not on a gaff, why are you wearing that patch?"

"Better this than what's under it."

"You can't mean . . ." She sat up, upset. "What happened?"

"Got too clever for my own good," I sighed. "Doesn't really matter. We're on a new job now."

"Oh? Do tell."

"You ever heard of Veran IX?"

"Sounds vaguely familiar. A High Weaver?"

"A couple thousand years back."

"Well, now you've just ruined my day," she said, pouting. "You made me think of my old history master, Owain. Absolute bore of a man. Veran . . . oh! The Childkiller. Murdered the boy emperor, Galdron III."

"That's him."

"Why in Artha's name are you asking about that?"

"Do you know what happened to him? Veran, I mean."

She scrunched her forehead, thinking. "Stole the emperor's swords and ran away. Came to Redfairne. Then disappeared off east, or something."

"What if I were to tell you," I said, "that that's only half true? Veran stole the swords, but he never reached Redfairne. The ship he stole from Galdron, the *Silver Star*, was bound here, but it sank, deep in the waters of Lake Galway."

"I'd wonder why you'd think I care about ancient history," Daphna said, already losing interest.

"Because I know exactly where his ship sank."

That brought her back. "Are you serious?"

I nodded.

She looked from Meriel to me. "How do you know this?"

I obviously couldn't tell her the truth. So I said, "One of our team is a book boy. He found some old records hidden away in a library in Carlow."

"Carlow?" She frowned. "When were you in Carlow?"

"Last week. Just got back today."

She studied me, still frowning. "I thought I helped you with a job in Coulgen."

"I finished that one a month ago."

"So what were you doing in Carlow?"

She was being awfully aggressive about this. "Just pulling a small gaff."

"A small gaff? That ends with you losing an eye?"

Now Meriel was frowning, too. "What business is it of yours what he's doing?"

"It's my business, Tor-girl," Daphna said, claws out again, "because Cal and I have been working together for years." She turned back to me. "I know people in Carlow. I could have helped. Just because the Architect ran off on you doesn't mean we can't still do jobs. I could have stopped"—she waved at my patch—"whatever did that."

Meriel looked like she was ready to stick Daphna with one of her knives. But this was something I hadn't really considered—and I cursed myself for my mistake.

I shouldn't have told Daphna about Carlow. And not just

because the actual job involved ripping off her Weaver friends. If there was one thing Daphna hated, it was being left out of something big.

I did my best to mollify her. "I agree completely," I said. "That's why I'm here. Didn't you put together a salvage a few years ago?"

Daphna sat back slowly. "A cargo steamer went down in the coral off the coast. A friend wanted to jump the wreck before the owner could recover it."

"That's exactly what we need," I said. "A deep-water salvage. How fast can you make that happen?"

"How fast do you need it?"

"Today is good. Yesterday is better."

"Impossible."

"Redfairne's a harbor town. You can't find us a boat?"

"The boat's the easy part," Daphna said. "The rest of it's the problem. I'll have to call in a team of experienced divers—"

"No divers," I said. "We'll do that ourselves."

She looked at me like I'd lost my mind. "You can't."

"Why not?"

"Where do you think you're going to find a diving suit that fits you?"

I had no idea. Truth was, I didn't know anything about diving at all. "I assumed you could get us some kind of enchantment. Isn't there something that will let us breathe underwater?"

She stared at me. "Cal . . . what's really going on here?"

I sighed. Daphna was too clever not to recognize at least part of my story wasn't true. "The swords Veran stole were the same blades Aeric the First used to conquer Ayreth. How much do you think they'd be worth?"

"If they actually exist? Priceless. Beyond priceless."

"There's your answer," I said. "It's the haul of a lifetime."

"*If* they exist, Cal. *If.*"

"You think it's just a legend?"

"Most of those old tales are legends. Even if they aren't, and you're right about the *Silver Star*, those swords will have been underwater for two thousand years. They'll be nothing but rust."

I hadn't really considered that possibility. Still, I didn't think that was the case. The Eye wouldn't send me after something that didn't exist. "The Dragon's Teeth lasted over a thousand years in the emperor's treasure room without once being touched. They're enchanted. The binding will have protected them, right?"

That made her pause. "Possibly. But—"

I cut her off before she could object further. "Look, maybe we're wrong. Maybe the swords are long gone. Even so, the *Silver Star* was Galdron's ship. There had to be gold, silver, jewels aboard. Things that *don't* rust. If you don't want to help, we'll find someone else. But are you really willing to pass up a chance like this?"

Daphna considered it. There was no doubt it was a gamble. Still . . . "Where exactly is the wreck?" she asked.

I laughed. Like she thought I'd tell her.

She smirked. "All right. What are you offering?"

"You arrange the diving boat, and whatever enchantments we need to do the dive ourselves. In return, we get the swords, plus a half cut of everything else we find down there. The rest is yours."

Now it was her turn to laugh. "Even the Architect couldn't have snaffled me with that, darling. I'm backing everything, you're risking nothing. And the enchantments you need—on short notice, no less—will cost a fortune. So the deal is, *I* get everything else *and* a share of the swords."

"Not a chance," Meriel said.

I held up a hand. "Equal share of the swords when we sell them?"

"Cal," Meriel said, alarmed.

Daphna ignored her. "How many are you?"

"Five," I said. "Six, including you."

"Really." She gave me a speculative look. "I never thought I'd see you working with anybody but the Old Man."

"Things change, Daphna. And time is ticking. You in or out?"

She thought about it, eyes calculating.

"Oh, Cal." She smiled. "How could I say no to you?"

CHAPTER 21

Meriel was furious.

"How could you agree to that?" she snapped as our carriage drove away from Daphna's villa. "Why would you give her part of the swords?"

"I didn't," I said calmly.

"You . . . what?" She was confused. "You did. I heard you."

"What did I agree to?" I said. "An equal share of the Dragon's Teeth—*when we sell them*. But we're not planning on selling them, are we?"

That made her pause. "So we're just going to take off with them?"

"I don't know what we're going to do," I said truthfully. "But if we do take off, you got a problem with that?"

"No. Still, why did you deal away the rest of the loot?"

"Because of Lachlan," I said glumly. "That glow he saw in Lopsided? That's the primeval magic's doing. It hasn't even been twenty-four hours since he was brought back, and it's already affecting him. And I think that's only the beginning of what will happen. We don't have time to dance about with who gets what. Once Lachlan's healed, we can figure out something then. Besides, when we're in the shipwreck . . . well, you have pockets in that dress of yours, don't you?"

Slowly, Meriel brightened. "Why, yes. Yes, I do."

It was dark by the time the two of us returned to Grey's. Lachlan had made a little maze of clocks in the corner, urging a purring Lop to run the gauntlet. Gareth was sitting with the clockmaker at one of his tinker tables. Grey was showing him how the innards of a pocket watch worked, which I found a little surprising.

Even more surprising was Foxtail. She was crouched barefoot atop the shelves, springing from one to another, practicing her leaps.

That wasn't the odd part—at least, not odd for her. No, the strangest thing was Grey hadn't grabbed her by the ponytail and hauled her down. He didn't seem to mind Lachlan using his merchandise as maze walls, either, despite the fact that Lop kept knocking them over. Clearly, something had changed in Grey since I was gone, and I didn't know what.

Are you sure about that? the Old Man said.

What do you mean? I asked, but he wouldn't answer.

Grey looked up as we joined them. "Well?"

"Everything's set," I said. "Now we wait for Daphna."

Grey opened his mouth as if to argue. Then he just shook his head in resigned disappointment and returned to showing Gareth the pocket watch. Definitely something strange.

Well, whatever it was, I was too tired to care. None of us had slept yesterday, and it was all I could do to stay awake. "I'm off to bed. Goodnight."

Meriel followed me upstairs. She was surprised to see where I'd be sleeping, on my old cot in a closet. "Huh," she said. "For some reason I thought it'd be bigger."

"Welcome to the glorious world of Callan, master thief. Don't worry, I'm sure Grey has something equally grand cooked up for you."

In truth, I was so tired, that cot was looking really good right now. I flopped onto it, facedown.

"At least take off your boots," Meriel said.

"Mn."

I was beginning to drift away when I realized Meriel hadn't left yet. I kicked off my boots.

"There," I said. "Happy now?" When she didn't answer, I said, "What is it?"

"About Daphna," she said.

"What about her?"

"I realize you can practically read minds and all," Meriel said, "but just in case you missed it: I hate her."

It was well past daybreak when I woke. I nestled into my pillow, dozing on and off, before finally dragging myself from the cot. First thing I did was go to the tub, hoping against hope that Grey had fired up the forge this morning. If he had, there'd be hot water.

The familiar gurgle of the tap and the steam rising from the ceramic was almost too good to be true. I slipped in. The heat burned my scars, but I didn't care. The water soaked every other ache away.

I just kind of sat there, marveling. This was the first lazy day I'd had since . . . well, I couldn't remember. As worried as I was about Lachlan, there was nothing I could do until Daphna told us our salvage expedition was ready.

I pulled off my patch. As usual, the Eye-vision returned, though the only thing glowing in this room was me. I studied my carnelian skin; it seemed to shine brighter as I flushed with the warmth of the bath.

"How about you, Eye?" I said. "Still can't talk?"

A faint feeling of anger swelled inside. I didn't think it was directed at me. It felt more like an animal, furious at being trapped in a cage.

I supposed I couldn't blame it, even though I still couldn't decide whether I was glad it was cooped up in there or not. I wondered what would happen when it finally broke free.

Even soaking in the heat, the thought made me shiver.

Starving, I went downstairs to raid Grey's pantry. I could hear him in the back at the forge, working away.

Gareth was the only one in the shop. He sat at the tinker's table, reading instructions from one of Grey's old notebooks. He was putting some kind of contraption together with springs, gears, and box metal.

I watched him silently. After fitting the last piece, he wound a tiny crank on the side, and the device began to tick. The gears shifted, *whirr-click, whirr-click*, and a small brass arm on the front started moving. Gareth sat back, delighted.

"I spent half my life here," I said, "and I have no idea how you did that."

Gareth looked startled, almost ashamed at being caught having fun. Then he relaxed and gave me a small smile. Pleased, he showed off his contraption.

"What does it do?" I said.

"Just moves the arm," he said. "It's the basic mechanics of a clock."

It was probably a simple thing—really, what did I know about it?—but it was amazing to me how, after only one night under Grey's tutelage, Gareth had been able to make something like this on his own. I was proud of him—and a little sad for him, too. Like me, he'd been stuck in this life of ours, with no chance to be anything but a thief. What could he have been instead, given the opportunity? Something great, I bet.

I said as much. He smiled shyly, feeling his own sadness—but also the pride.

"Where is everybody?" I asked.

"Still asleep."

"Why aren't you?"

"I wanted to do this." He motioned to the clock. "I never sleep much, anyway."

Actually, I was glad no one else was around. I wanted to tell him something. "You all glow different colors."

He looked at me, puzzled.

"Through the Eye," I said. I knew he was curious, so I told him. "We all look red, but everyone's shade is different. Yours has the tiniest hint of blue. It suits you, I think."

He sat quietly for a while, as if he didn't know what to make of that. "What about the others?"

I told him about Meriel's, red, hot-tempered, and Lachlan's, bright and cheerful. Then I told him about the violet stain. Gareth's smile faded as I explained what Bragan had said.

"Is there . . . I mean . . . has the stain changed?" Gareth asked.

"Not yet. Why? Did something happen?"

"No. Well . . . I mean . . . no. Just . . . Lachlan kept getting up all night. I don't think he's feeling well."

I dreaded going to check on him. I put it off for the moment by telling Gareth the other secret I'd kept. "Foxtail has no glow at all."

He blinked. "Nothing?"

"Not even a hint of it. Not on her skin, her hair, or her mask. It's like she's not even there."

Gareth frowned, thinking.

"Is it possible," I said, "that Foxtail isn't . . . well, like us? That she's a construct?"

He mulled it over. "Does Galawan glow? Or Lopsided?"

"Both do. Galawan is a fiery sort of red." Probably, I suddenly realized, because Mr. Solomon was a fire enchanter. "And Lopsided is purple. Pretty much the same purple as the stain in Lachlan."

"Because they're . . . I mean . . . they're powered by enchantments."

Right. So if Foxtail was a construct, she'd have her own glow. Which she didn't.

Suddenly, Gareth sat up. "Her mask." He stared at me. "*That's* what it does. It doesn't just hide her face. *It hides her from magical detection.*"

I stared at him, realizing he just might have hit on the truth. Foxtail's mask disguised not only her, but any trace of her from magical scrying. And it occurred to me then that my eyepatch— for which Foxtail had provided the steel underneath—had a similar enchantment on it. It not only blocked the Eye's sight when I wore it, but it had hid the artifact from the Weaver's detection rod back at the helioport.

I ran my fingers over the cloth of my patch. *It's just like Foxtail's mask.* The thought was startling.

I had no idea where she'd got the steel—had she had it with her all this time, or had she got it somewhere else, after I'd lost my eye?—or how she'd known to give it to Meriel to use. I suppose it wasn't a stretch that she might imagine we'd want to hide the Eye from detection. The High Weaver had hunted relentlessly for it from the very moment we'd stolen it. And considering that patch had saved me at the helioport, I was grateful—even if wary—that she'd helped make it. But as for the girl herself . . .

"What would be the point of hiding Foxtail?" I said.

Gareth didn't have an answer.

I was sure there was something critically important here that we were missing. But we didn't have enough information to suss it out, and I could pretty much guarantee Foxtail wasn't going to tell us. So when neither of us could come up with something, I put the question aside and forced myself to do what I didn't want to do. I went upstairs to check on Lachlan.

He was sleeping on a blanket laid on the floor in one of Grey's storage rooms. Lopsided lay curled beside him, Galawan on the cat's back. The bird tweeted a hello upon seeing me, but softly, as if to not wake the others.

Lachlan's shirt was soaked at the collar. His pillow and blanket were damp, too. It looked like he had the night sweats, feverish. Yet when I placed my hand on his forehead, he wasn't burning. If anything, his skin was cool to the touch.

I couldn't put it off any longer. Hesitantly, I lifted the patch.

There was the stain, wriggling around his soul like a worm. It seemed even more agitated than yesterday, bouncing off the walls of its confinement, as if testing the boundaries of Lachlan's glow. But other than that, it looked the same as before: same color, same size, same shape. If there was anything wrong inside, I couldn't see it.

I sat back, wondering. It was possible Lachlan's troubles had nothing to do with the primeval magic. Maybe he was just having nightmares. I mean, he *had* died. I couldn't imagine what was going on inside his head.

I turned to go, then stopped, thinking about the conversation I'd just had with Gareth. I looked once more with the Eye, but this time at the constructs. As before, they both glowed: Galawan a bright orange and Lopsided that same violet as the stain.

I frowned. Lachlan had said yesterday that Lop was faded, and he had been. I couldn't be sure, but this morning, it seemed as if the cat's glow was even dimmer. Though it was hard to tell if that was because it had actually diminished, or whether it just looked that way in contrast to Galawan's blazing shine. It occurred to me that, over the years, Grey had already had to get Lop re-bound with enchantment three times, because the cat kept running out of juice. Maybe that fading light I was seeing meant the enchantment was dying once more.

Either way, both Galawan and Lopsided did glow. Which meant Foxtail was something else entirely. I let Lachlan sleep, shutting the door with more questions than answers.

"Anything?" Gareth said when I returned downstairs.

I shook my head. "You know what? I think I'm going to stuff my face with whatever Grey's got in the pantry. Then I'm going back to bed."

Gareth shifted, as if he'd been about to ask something, then changed his mind.

"What is it?" I said.

"Nothing."

"Gareth, don't make me do this dance, will you?"

He smiled, a little chastened. "Sorry. It's just . . . I . . . have you ever been to the university?"

"Here? In Redfairne?"

Gareth nodded.

"No," I said. "The Old Man never took me. Nothing for us to snaffle. 'Scholars talk too much and own too little,' as he put it. Why?"

"There's this . . . I mean . . . the university has an expert."

"In what?"

"Literature."

Sometimes getting information from Gareth was like pulling teeth. "What kind of literature?"

"Well . . . um . . . Fox and Bear," he said finally.

I knew then exactly why he was interested in this scholar. Before we'd stolen the Eye from Mr. Solomon, Gareth had told me about an old librarian he'd known back in Westport, where he grew up. The man had helped Gareth for years, practically trained him in research and languages, then vanished as if he'd never even existed. Gareth believed the man had actually been a

Spirit—a *different* Spirit than Fox or Bear, one we'd never heard of before.

I didn't understand how that could be. Then again, I didn't really know the first thing about Spirits—and I'd actually met one. Nonetheless, thinking of Gareth's missing librarian also made me think about a question that had burned in the back of my mind ever since I was nine.

It had first come up when I was riding beside the Old Man. We'd been heading down to Marsden to pull a gaff on some silk merchant. The Old Man passed the time on the road by telling me stories of Fox and Bear. I liked when he did that—and considering how many tales he knew, I think he liked telling them even more than I liked hearing them. Not that he'd ever admit it.

Anyway, that day, his story made me remember the time we'd hid from the Stickmen in the snakesroost, back in that home we broke into as we were fleeing Perith. When the snake threatened to bite me, I'd repeated Shuna's words from one of the tales—*Please, friend, don't hurt me*—and the snake had let me go. At six years old, I'd thought it was magic, or maybe even the real blessing of the Fox.

By the time I was nine, I'd learned enough about magic to know that was just the fantasy of a very young, very scared child. Of course I hadn't bound any enchantments. But as to Shuna's blessing...I'd wondered.

Are the Spirits real? I'd asked the Old Man.

He'd snorted, like it was a stupid question. *Of course.*

How do we know?

We drop a sept into a Fox shrine before every job, don't we? Be a terrible waste of money if she didn't exist.

That doesn't prove anything, I protested. *Asking for luck is what we do. It doesn't mean Shuna's actually helping— Where are you going?*

He'd steered his horse away from me. *I don't want to get hit by lightning,* he said.

Oh, ha-ha. Seriously, how do we know the Spirits are real? Do they have special powers? What have they actually done for us?

He sighed. *Is this just you being contrarian again?*

No. What do you mean?

The Old Man waved at the fields around us. *Where do you think all this came from? The Spirits made it.*

But why? I said. *Why bother? And how did they create the world, anyway? What did they create it from?*

Now you're making cracks about my age? he said.

What?

The Spirits created Ayreth forty-two hundred years ago, boy. How would I know how they did it?

It was strange. Deep down, I *did* believe in the Spirits. So I didn't know why I was filled with so many questions. Maybe I was just being contrarian, like he'd said. *I just want to know what their purpose is.*

Well, then, he'd said, *the next time you meet a Spirit, don't forget to ask.*

He'd ended the conversation by poking fun at me, as usual. Now, standing in the doorway of Grey's shop, I wondered what the Old Man would think if he came back and I told him I'd really met Shuna.

I'd wonder, he said in my head, *why you didn't pester her like you did me with those questions.*

I had other things on my mind at the time, I pointed out.

So does Gareth.

To be fair, he had good reason. That librarian . . . well, a man who's in your life every day for three years, then disappears with no one else even remembering he existed wasn't exactly something to overlook. Just as odd, the last thing the phantom librarian had done was give Gareth a book of Fox and Bear stories, with the hint that they were somehow important. Since then, Gareth had read every Fox and Bear tale he could get his hands on.

"You want to go to the university," I said, "and talk to this expert?"

He nodded.

I didn't really want to, myself. I was still tired, and we were supposed to wait for word from Daphna. On the other hand, an old Fox and Bear story *had* given us the clue as to where to find Mr. Solomon, and how to steal the Eye. So there was no doubt that there was truth hidden in those tales.

The Old Man had never valued research. But his voice in my head also reminded me that Gareth was smarter than the rest of us. I'd be wise to listen.

"All right," I said. "If you think we should go, then we go. Besides, there's a question I want to ask, too."

CHAPTER 22

I'D NEVER SEEN Gareth so happy.

He gazed across the grounds of Redfairne University as if we'd suddenly stumbled into paradise. There was no doubt it was a pretty campus—all manicured lawns, old stone buildings, and meandering pathways of pink clay brick. But it was more than that for him. As he watched the people going by—professors deep in conversation, students reading on the lawn—I knew from his far-off look and the way he hugged his satchel to his chest that he was imagining himself among them.

I understood that. He saw this place the same way I saw the *Malley. This is where I belong*, he thought, and I thought he belonged, too. I wondered if, when all this was over, we could find some way to get him in. He deserved it.

In the meantime, we had work to do. Gareth said we needed to find a Professor Whelan, so I asked passing students for directions until one pointed out a wide three-story building with a sharply sloped gray roof and a clock tower.

"How do you know this Professor Whelan?" I asked Gareth as we made our way there.

"I don't. I mean . . . I've never m-met him. He wrote a book. About Fox and Bear. I mean . . . not stories. *About* Fox and Bear stories."

Gareth's stammer had worsened, and he kept wiping his palms on his trousers. He was nervous to meet the professor. I guess I'd have to do most of the talking.

The building we entered was a quadrangle surrounding a little garden in the center. None of the offices were labeled, so I just knocked on the nearest open door and asked the woman inside where we might find Professor Whelan. She sent us up to the second floor on the north side, and there we found the man himself.

He was a short fellow, thin, with a long face and a sort of sad expression—reminded me of an older, miniature version of Gareth, actually. He sat behind the most cluttered desk I'd ever seen: papers, books, scrolls, and quills all over the place. The rest of his office was filled with the same chaos. His feet were up on the desk, angled away from us, and he was reading, a pair of half-moon glasses perched at the end of his nose.

"Professor Whelan?"

He looked up from his paper as I knocked. "Yes? May I help you?"

I'd asked Gareth earlier what kind of gaff I should play to get the professor to talk to us. Gareth had been amused that I'd even suggested it. *You won't need to snaffle him*, he'd said. *Scholars love to talk about their work.*

Fair enough. But we obviously couldn't tell the man the truth of why we'd come. So I said, "I'm Callan. This is Gareth. If you have some time, we'd like to ask you about Fox and Bear. You see—"

His eyes lit up. "Of course. Come in, come in."

I was a little put out by his agreeing so quickly. Gareth had said he would, but I'd still invented whole identities for the two of us. We were students visiting from Carlow with our master, who'd instructed us to come here because Professor Whelan was the best, and so on. Now I wouldn't even get to use them.

"Have a seat," he said, though the only two chairs in the room were both piled with papers. "Er . . . just move those. You can put them there—no, wait, over there . . . oh, never mind. Just dump them on the floor. I'll deal with them later." He leaned forward, removing his spectacles. "So . . . Fox and Bear."

"Yes," I said. "We were wondering—"

Professor Whelan didn't even notice I'd started to speak. "The best way to think about Fox and Bear is as the ultimate archetypes."

I wondered if Gareth knew what an archetype was. I sure didn't.

"The Fox, Shuna," Professor Whelan said, "represents cunning and good cheer. She's friendly and helpful, but mischievous. The Bear, Artha, represents power and confidence. She's strong and capable, but aloof. We, as people, and as organizations, then chose our patron Spirits according to what we ourselves wished to model. Weavers and soldiers, for example, took Artha as their patron. Whereas merchants, entertainers, and the like chose Shuna."

"Thieves, too," I said.

Gareth gave me a sharp glance.

"Er . . . yes," the professor said. "Very true. In fact, young man, you bring up a good point. That while we tend to think of the Spirits as the embodiment of *positive* values, they are not perfect beings. They themselves have their foibles and failings."

Didn't I know it. "Like what?"

"Well, Shuna's not merely mischievous. If you read the stories closely, she's very much a rule-breaker, and actually quite reckless. This frequently gets her into trouble, wherein she needs the help of her friend Artha to get her out of it."

"I know the feeling," I said.

"Indeed." Professor Whelan nodded. "Artha, on the other hand, has quite an ego, even to the point, dare I say, of arrogance. She's also incredibly hot-tempered. In the early stories, when Fox and Bear are still friends, this is what gets Artha into trouble. So Shuna has to come in and sweet-talk her out of it. In the later stories, once they've become enemies, Artha's temper proves to be a real liability. Shuna uses it against her, often provoking the Bear into a foolish rage, which lets Shuna win the day."

So far, I'd been having a bit of fun with the man. But the more I listened, the more interested I became in what he was saying. We'd seen Artha's arrogance—and her rage—in the story that had led us to Mr. Solomon. And in Mr. Solomon himself.

Gareth, his nerves calmed, finally spoke. "Professor . . . you said 'archetypes' before. But archetypes are fictional. Do you not think Fox and Bear are real?"

"The Spirits themselves, Shuna and Artha? Most certainly, I believe they're real. The stories? Mm . . . that's a little different. My guess is that the *essence* of the stories is real. That is, these events happened, at least in some way, sometime in the past. But you must remember, none of the stories we read today are the originals. They've been told and retold, copied and recopied over millennia. They've changed so much from what they once were that they're little more than fables now."

Gareth had made the same point back in Carlow. Still, I was glad to hear the professor believed in the Spirits. The question I'd planned to ask him depended on it.

"If the Spirits are real," I said, "then how come they never interact with people?"

"How do you mean?"

"Well, we ask them for help, right? And drop septs into their shrines for blessings or luck. So if they're real, why don't they ever come down from wherever they are and show up in person?"

It was a question I desperately wanted an answer to—and not just because it had burned in my mind since I was nine. When I'd met Shuna, and she'd told me what I needed to do to save my friends, I'd tried to get her to help. She'd said she wanted to, but she couldn't. It was against the rules.

I'd asked her, *Who makes rules for Spirits?* She'd refused to tell me.

Though I hoped for an answer today, I hadn't really expected the professor to have one. So I was absolutely shocked when he did.

"Oh, I see," Professor Whelan said. "You're talking about the Pact."

CHAPTER 23

M<small>Y HEART SKIPPED</small> a beat. "The . . . Pact?"

Whelan nodded. "It appears in one of the stories. Only one, in fact. 'The Fox, the Bear, and the Lake of Ice.'"

Gareth stiffened in his chair, and now my heart thumped even faster.

When Gareth had first gone to the library in Carlow, looking for information about the Eye, someone had secretly slipped a page in among his research. It was the first page of that very same story: The Fox, the Bear, and the Lake of Ice.

"I . . . don't think I've read that one," I said.

The professor leaned back in his chair. "It goes like this: A village is dying. The stream that once flowed through it has dried up. Desperate, they call to the Spirits for help.

"Artha and Shuna hear their plea and decide to help the villagers. They go to a river and divert it so it flows into the dried-up stream. The problem is, a different village lived downstream of *that* river. So now *their* water has dried up. They beg the Spirits to return the river to its original path.

"Fox and Bear realize there isn't enough water to feed both streams. So they go up the mountains to the source of the river, a melting lake of ice—what naturalists today would call a glacier.

They use their magic to melt part of the ice so that there's enough water for everybody. Unfortunately, their magic shatters the glacier, which then tumbles down the mountain, melts, and floods both villages.

"The moral of the story is obvious," the professor said. "All actions we take, even with good intentions, may have unintended consequences. Shuna and Artha only wanted to help the villagers. But it left them worse off than if Fox and Bear had never answered their prayers at all."

"What does that have to do with a pact?" I said.

"Ah. Well. I haven't yet told you the story's ending. In most versions, Fox and Bear come down the mountain, dig a giant pit between the villages, and scoop all the water inside. In this way, a new lake is made, and both villages are saved."

"There are other versions?" Gareth said, listening intently.

"Indeed. In a few versions of the story—and I believe these are the *older* versions—the villagers are *not* saved. Instead, Shuna and Artha understand they've made a terrible mistake. They realize their powers put us in danger. And so they make the Pact. They agree that they will no longer interfere with us or use their powers to influence us directly."

I sat frozen in my chair. Shuna had said practically the same thing. That she wasn't even supposed to be speaking to me. *There are rules, Cal.*

"What happens if they break the Pact?" I said, breathless.

"Again," Professor Whelan said, "it depends on the version of the story. In most of them, they never state any consequences.

They just say they won't do it. In a few versions, the Spirits go deeper. They actually put a binding on themselves that *prevents* them from interacting with us.

"But in one version—and I think this is the oldest, as close to the original as we can get—the binding Artha and Shuna place on themselves doesn't prevent them from doing anything. They can choose to interact if they like. But if they do, they'll be punished."

"Punished by whom?" I said.

"That's the key. They'll be punished *by each other.*"

"So . . . if Shuna were to break the rules . . ."

"Then Artha would decide her punishment," the professor finished. "And vice versa. Which makes the Pact all but literally binding. After all, how would you like your worst enemy deciding your fate?"

I could barely believe it. This explained *everything.*

You're a Spirit, I'd said to Shuna. *Who makes rules for you?*

You'd be surprised, she'd said.

If this was true, then I had my answer. Who made the rules? *They* did. And if either one broke those rules, *their enemy would get to punish them.*

I was so lost in my own thoughts, I barely heard Gareth ask the next question.

"You believe in Shuna and Artha," Gareth said, then hesitated, like he was afraid the man would think he was mad. "Do you think . . . is it p-possible . . . I mean . . . could there be *more* than two Spirits?"

Professor Whelan shook his head emphatically. "No."

Gareth looked disappointed. It didn't appear he was going to continue with his question, so I did. "Why not?"

"Why would there be? We have no evidence for more than two. There are no shrines except those to Artha or Shuna. No one reveres any others, nor do they have a different Spirit as a patron."

"Could they not be f-forgotten?" Gareth said.

"I find that hard to imagine. Even harder to imagine a Spirit letting itself be forgotten."

"But what about the Fox and Bear stories?" I said. "There are lots of other animals in them."

"Certainly," Professor Whelan said. "A crow shows up most often, but there's also a deer, a snake, a rabbit, mice; the list is endless. However, there are two reasons why this is irrelevant. First, note that none of those other animals are ever the hero of the story. It's always either Fox, or Bear, or the two of them together.

"But the second piece of evidence is more telling, I think. In none of the stories, not one, is a different animal ever given a name. This tells us plainly that they're simply there as foils. None of them are of any particular importance . . . What is it?"

He'd noticed Gareth and I looking at each other.

"In that case, Professor," I said, "we have something to show you."

CHAPTER 24

GARETH PULLED A book from his satchel and handed it over.

Professor Whelan examined it curiously. The book was bound with sheepskin, the leather yellowed with age. When he opened the cover, the pages beneath crackled, a musty smell filling the room. He read the title page: *Olde Tayles for Yong Childeren.*

"Where did you get this?" Whelan said, surprised.

"A l-library, in Carlow," Gareth said. "It was . . . we found it."

The professor turned the pages gingerly, reading. "This is in the Middle Tongue," he said, amazed.

"I think it might be five hundred years old," Gareth said.

"Older, I'd say. By at least a century or two."

"Look at page . . . what page was it?" I asked Gareth.

"Three hundred and nineteen," Gareth said.

When the professor reached the page we sent him to, his breath actually stopped. He stared at it, mouth open, for quite a while. Then he began to read.

"One fine summer day, Shuna the Fox was romping with . . ."

He blinked, as if he couldn't believe his own eyes.

"Fiona . . . the *Deer*?" He gasped. "Bran the *Crow*?" He read all the way to the end, then sat back in his chair, eyes shining. "Do you realize what you've discovered?" he said, dazed. "This is . . .

I have to . . . Can I keep this?" he asked hopefully.

Gareth wasn't sure what to say. "Um . . ."

"It belongs to the library in Carlow," I said. "We have to return it." Eventually.

"Of course, yes," Whelan said, crestfallen. Then his eyes lit up again. "I'll make a copy."

We sat there, growing restless as the man scratched the story out on some loose papers. When he finished, Whelan handed the book back to Gareth with some regret. But he shook our hands warmly.

"Boys," he said, "this is the greatest discovery of my career."

"So," I said, my patience fading, "given that tale, is it not possible there really are other Spirits besides Fox and Bear?"

"Well, I suppose . . . Hmm." The question left him stumped. "I don't . . . I wouldn't have . . . There's a man," he said finally. "I've never taken him seriously; always thought he was a crackpot. But this . . ."

He faded off again. I had to prod him. "Professor?"

"Yes, yes, sorry. His name is Keane. He claims we're all wrong about the Spirits. Says he knows the truth about them. You should speak to him. He works at the university in Sligach."

Gareth, who'd been pleased at how the professor was falling over himself about this discovery, deflated.

"Professor," I said, "Sligach is three thousand miles away."

"Oh. Yes, I suppose that's true. Well, you should write to him, then. I'm sure he'll answer."

Except we had no idea where we'd be tomorrow, let alone how

long it would take for a letter to arrive. I looked glumly at Gareth. He was so disappointed. It appeared the truth was well and truly out of reach.

∩∪

We rode the carriage back to Grey's, mostly in silence. I was going over what Professor Whelan had said about the Pact between the Spirits. I wished the Fox were here, so I could ask her if it was actually true. Not that she'd have answered.

Still, thinking of Shuna made me wonder where she was now. The last time I'd spoken to her was outside the Dragon Temple. As for Gareth, he was lost in his own thoughts. Some of which, no doubt, was him wondering if that librarian who'd disappeared really *was* a Spirit after all—an increasing possibility, it seemed. But he also kept glancing my way, and I could read what was on his mind.

He was wondering why I was so interested in the Pact.

He'd already seen enough strange behavior from me. I hadn't told him that the message which led us to the book we'd found had come from Shuna. I also hadn't told him—or anyone else, for that matter—why I'd stomped off into the woods alone as Lachlan lay dying.

I had no doubt that Gareth, clever as he was, had started to put the pieces together. Even if he couldn't quite believe what the puzzle would reveal. Still, he kept looking at me, and I found it distracting. So after his fifth glance in my direction, I said, "Sorry, Gareth. I can't talk about it."

One of the things I liked best about Gareth was how he didn't keep pestering you. Meriel and Lachlan would have hounded me to death over this. Gareth just nodded and said, "All right."

"It's not that I don't want to," I said. "But, well, like we just learned, apparently there are rules."

He considered that. "I . . . understand."

"In that case . . ." I pulled a paper from my satchel. "Do you know what this says?"

I handed him the paper. On it were the strange words I'd written out for Meriel, the ones I'd seen on her forehead in my vision of the future:

feyc anrygán

He frowned. "Where did you see this?"

Feeling guilty, I said, "I can't tell you that, either. But does it look at all familiar?"

"It looks . . . I mean . . . it looks a bit like the Old Tongue. But . . . not really. Maybe an offshoot? Or a different dialect."

"Suppose that's the case," I said. "What's the closest meaning in the Old Tongue?"

He mulled it over for a while. "I think . . . 'behold the queen.'"

"Behold the *queen*?"

"Does that not make sense?"

"No," I said. "She can't be . . . Are there still queens?"

"Not since Aeric conquered Ayreth," Gareth said. "Unless . . . I mean . . . there's the empress. She's a k-kind of queen."

Meriel was clearly not the empress. "That wouldn't fit."

"Maybe it's . . . I mean . . . it could be a metaphor," Gareth said. "I mean, using the word 'queen' to indicate some kind of ruler."

"I know what a metaphor is. I just don't see how that could be right."

"It's probably not. Small changes in a word could mean something wildly different."

"If it's not 'behold the queen,'" I said, "what's the next closest translation?"

Gareth thought about it again. "'Visit the paddock.'"

That made me burst out laughing. "Definitely not. It must be a different language."

I put the paper away as our carriage arrived at Grey's. We disembarked, paid the coachman, and made for the door. "We should tell the others what we learned," I said.

Then the clockmaker's shop exploded.

CHAPTER 25

THE WINDOWS BURST outward with a terrible *WHUMP*.

Shards of glass flew overhead as we dove for the cobblestones. Splinters peppered the grocer's across the street, shredding fruit in their bins, leaving pulp and juice dripping onto the road.

Our carriage had already pulled away. Lucky for the driver, because he'd have been killed. Nonetheless, the blast spooked the horses. They bolted, sending the carriage bouncing down the street. The driver tugged desperately on the reins as the vehicle disappeared round the bend.

I lay there, dazed, ears ringing, barely able to comprehend what had happened. Gareth was shaking his head, trying to clear it of the noise. Blood dripped from his left ear. A piece of glass had grazed him, slicing a thin line across his skin.

Dogs barked up and down the street. All along the road, shopkeepers and residents peeked their heads out, then tucked them back inside after they'd got a good look at the destruction. Grey's shop wasn't in a nice part of town. If the Stickmen came, no one wanted to be a witness.

I was so dazed by the explosion that it was a moment before it dawned on me what it meant. I stared at the broken windows, horror finally breaking through.

Grey.

My friends.

No.

I scrambled to my feet. Gareth followed, staggering, as I burst through the door and saw the wreckage.

The clockmaker's shop was a disaster. Shards of glass crunched underfoot, every timepiece shattered. The heaviest clocks were the only ones still standing, including the best piece in the doorway, the one Grey had bought to impress customers, with its face of Artha and Shuna chasing each other through day and night. The smaller ones had all toppled, lying on the floor in disarray.

But what I was seeing didn't make any sense. A blast that powerful could only have come from an explosion of gunpowder or oil barrels caught in a fire. Yet there was no sign of burns anywhere in Grey's shop. No twisted metal, no flames, not even scorch marks on the walls. Glass had shattered, everything was tossed. That was it.

Meriel stood in the doorway to the forge, shocked and stunned. Foxtail wormed her way past Meriel, alert for danger.

"What happened?" I said.

"I don't know," Meriel said, voice shaking. "Foxtail and I were upstairs. So was Grey. It was only . . . *Lachlan!*"

The girls stumbled into the shop, frantic. They got a few feet inside before they stopped.

Lachlan was sitting on the floor, cross-legged. Galawan stood on his shoulder, flapping his wings and tweeting. Lopsided padded around him in a circle, unconcerned.

As for Lachlan, he was as unharmed as the others, staring in bemusement at the destruction around him. And it *was* around him. From the way the broken glass had spread and the clocks had toppled, the blast had been centered on Lachlan. He looked at me, confused.

"Cal?" he said in a small voice.

Grey stepped into the room. He looked around at the shop— *his* shop—and slumped. He didn't seem angry or beside himself, just resigned.

This wasn't the Grey I knew. This was a man overcome. Defeated. I just didn't know by what.

Yes, you do, the Old Man said.

I didn't have time to think about that now. We went to Lachlan, helped him stand, looked him over. Foxtail ran her hands all over him, pushing clothes aside, searching for wounds. There wasn't a mark on him.

"Lachlan . . . what happened?" I said.

"I dunno." He sounded scared. "I was just sitting here playing with Lop, yeah? And I was sad, 'cause his light was fading, and I knew if it went out, he'd be gone. Then I had a thought. Maybe I could put the light back, eh? So I put me hands on him and pushed. And . . . did I do all that?"

My blood went cold.

The others looked puzzled at what he'd said. But I understood.

Lopsided padded over to me, purring. He weaved between my feet, rubbing his head against my legs. I pushed up the patch and looked down at the cat.

Lop was shining.

His violet light was brighter now, even more than Galawan's blazing red. Whether Lachlan knew it or not, whether he understood what had happened or why, he'd done this. He'd recharged the construct's enchantment.

Deep inside my head, the Eye stirred. A faint sense of interest

(yes)

and satisfaction. It made me shudder.

"It's all right, Lachlan," I said. "No one's hurt."

"So it *is* my fault." His lower lip trembled. "I'm really sorry, Mr. Grey."

Grey sighed. "Doesn't much matter, lad."

In the back of my mind, I knew the clockmaker's reaction was even stranger than when he'd first seen his shop destroyed

(you know why)

but I wasn't paying attention to that. Because spying Lop's new glow made me turn the Eye on Lachlan. And what I saw made my heart sink.

The stain in his soul had grown.

The worm was no longer a worm. Now it was a swirl the size of both my hands. It moved around within him, excited by what it had done.

The primeval will grow, Bragan had warned me.

And so its growth had begun.

Lachlan trembled, shaken, blinking away tears. The girls held him. Grey leaned against the counter, weary.

I almost didn't see it. I was so focused on the stain that I nearly missed the other terrible thing the Eye showed me. A different kind of stain. But this one wasn't in Lachlan.

It was in Grey.

CHAPTER 26

FOXTAIL LED LACHLAN upstairs. Meriel and Gareth went with them.

Grey remained in the shop. With another sigh, he found a broom and began sweeping the glass into a pile. I didn't go with the others. I just stood there, staring at the stain inside Grey.

It wasn't like the primeval magic in Lachlan. It wasn't alive. And it didn't have a color. It was black, an ugly, dead mass, and it spread throughout his stomach and into his chest.

I put the patch back on. I didn't want to see that thing anymore.

Grey stopped sweeping and turned to meet my gaze. "Somethin' wrong, boyo?"

It was hard to get the words out. "You're sick," I said.

He smirked. "Took you long enough to notice. The Old Man had me pegged six months ago."

That's what the Old Man had been trying to tell me in my head. Now I saw—really saw—the signs in Grey I'd missed. The weight loss. His resignation at the destruction of his shop. His allowing all of us to stay here, even encouraging it. He didn't want to be alone.

He was dying. And he knew it.

Why hadn't I?

You didn't want to know, the Old Man said. *You saw the signs, you knew what they meant. If Grey was a mark, you'd have recognized it right away. You just didn't want to know.*

Grief welled up from deep inside. Grey had been good to me. Before I'd met Lachlan and the others, I could count on one hand the number of people I could have said that about.

"How long?" I said, voice breaking.

"Don't know, exactly," Grey said. "Physick thinks another month or so."

"Is there nothing you can do? What about a healer?"

"How much did Daphna say it would take to fix your scars?"

"Fifty thousand crowns," I said.

"So how much do you think I'd need to save my life?"

"But . . . all those jobs you brokered for us. The goods you shifted. Your cut."

Grey shrugged. "Never been much of a saver, boyo." He rested the broom against a shelf. "But now that you know what's going on, I have something to show you." He rooted around in his things behind the counter and called me over. "Look at this."

He held out a ring. It was made of pure, smooth crystal that sparkled in the light of the oil lamps. The ring was brilliant craftsmanship, a design I'd never seen before. Instead of a single band, it was seven narrow bands intertwined, looping in and out among themselves in an impossibly complex pattern.

It was stunning. "Where did you get this?"

"The Old Man," Grey said. "He was supposed to pay me for a job I sent his way 'bout a year ago. Said he didn't have the crowns, so he gave me that ring instead. Claimed he stole it from a Weaver on a gaff you two ran in Kilmallock a few years back."

I frowned, trying to recall the job. We'd only ever pulled one gaff in Kilmallock, and it had nothing to do with a Weaver. We'd been hired to snaffle a small metal case from inside a duke's home. We'd posed as servants, the Old Man playing my father, and got hired.

For anyone else, it would have been a two-month con to find where the duke hid the case and get the keys to crack the safe. The Old Man had it in a week and a half. I still remembered the thing. It was made of some strange orange metal, with no apparent way to open it. I couldn't recall ever seeing this crystal ring.

Though I did remember now . . . there was one night there, a party. A Weaver was supposed to attend. The Old Man told me to stay away. No matter what, I was not to go anywhere near the ballroom. *Can't trust spellslingers*, he said, same as always. At the time, I was still following the Old Man's orders, so I'd kept clear of the ball, like he'd said.

He must have snatched the ring that night, at the party. Made me wonder just how often the Old Man had snaffled a little extra for himself.

"He told me," Grey said, "that ring's full o' powerful magic. That it's worth a lot more than what he was supposed to pay."

I was too curious not to look. When Grey began tucking his things back under the counter, I peeked at the ring with the Eye, just long enough to see the truth. There wasn't even a hint of a glow.

"It's not enchanted," I said.

"The Old Man promised it was. Swore it up and down. Said he'd make it ten times right if he was lying."

"Course he did, Grey. That's how the gaff works."

Grey laughed. "I know. That's the point. He was cheating me. I *knew* he was cheating me. *He* knew I knew he was cheating me—and he still did it anyway! He was even smiling as he handed it over. Couldn't help himself."

Grey laughed again. "That's why I kept the thing instead of selling it. It reminded me of the old swindler. Anyway, I want you to have it."

"Me?"

"Yeh, you. You think I got anyone else to give things? Besides, I'm pretty sure the Old Man would like that it ended up in yer hands."

I shook my head. "He didn't really care about me, Grey."

"Sure he did."

"Grey—"

The clockmaker cut me off. "I knew the old cheat for thirty years," he said. "Since I was just an apprentice, younger'n you are now. He worked with a lot o' swindlers over the years. Most he kept around a few weeks, just a single job, then gone. A few he kept a bit longer. Most I ever saw? Six months. That was it.

"He kept you around for *eight years*, Cal," Grey said. "No matter how much you vexed him, he stuck by you."

"Because I was useful, Grey. I was a good gaffer."

He snorted. "Not denyin' you got skill, boyo. But you think you're the best he ever snaffled with?" Grey sighed. "Look, I don't know what happened between you two. None o' my business.

But here's what I do know: When he left, he could've ditched you anywhere in the world. 'Stead he left you with me. He did that 'cause he knew I'd let you stay however long you needed. No matter how much of a pain in my backside you are. Know anywhere else you could do that?"

I shook my head dumbly.

"Yeh. That weren't no accident. The Old Man didn't *do* accidents. So don't say he didn't care. He cared more for you than anyone I saw in a lifetime."

I bowed my head. I couldn't believe that. I couldn't trust it. Because I *wanted* to believe.

"As for me," Grey said. "It's a funny thing, dyin'. Makes you think less of what you got and more of what you never had. I ain't made no mark on this world, Cal. No family, no name. This shop's all I got, and that'll go right back to the guild when I pass: Ain't no one going to think of me when I'm gone. 'Cept maybe you. So do ole Grey a favor for once, and take the Old Man's ring. And maybe when you see it, it'll remind you o' both of us."

I couldn't help it. I threw my arms around Grey and cried.

"Nah, boyo, come on," he said quietly. "Let's have none o' that." But he didn't push me away.

CHAPTER 27

W E S E T O U T on Lake Galway the next morning. I stood on the
deck of the ship Daphna had found for us and held the crystal
ring up to the rising sun.

I didn't know what it was about this ring that struck a chord
in me, but I'd loved the thing even before Grey had handed it
over. The crystal had sparkled beautifully in the lamplight of the
clockmaker's shop, but it really took the sunlight to do it justice.
As the seven bands intertwined, the crystal broke the sun's rays,
shining rainbow arcs onto the deck, colors shifting as the boat
bobbed along the waves.

I wore the ring on my right middle finger, the only one big
enough to fit the loop. Grey was right: Looking at it made me
think of him and the Old Man both. After a while, it became too
much, and I let my hand fall. Maybe one day those memories
would be sweet. Today they just filled me with grief.

I had work to do, anyway. Daphna's runner had come to Grey's
about an hour after Lachlan's . . . I didn't know what to call it. Outburst? The runner had told us to get whatever we needed ready.
Daphna had arranged our expedition. We'd be sailing to the
wreck of the *Silver Star* at dawn.

All five of us had pitched in to put the clockmaker's shop
back in some semblance of order. There wasn't much we could

do about the windows except board them up, but we'd swept away the glass and stood all the clocks upright. Not that he'd be selling them anymore.

I stayed up most of the night with Grey, the two of us swapping stories of the Old Man by the fire, me wishing all the while for the night to remain just a little longer. But time waits for no one.

"What will you do?" I asked when morning finally came, still trying not to cry.

"I'll enjoy the last o' life while I can," Grey said. "Go on, then, boyo. Shuna walk with you."

And that was our goodbye.

The ship Daphna had hired was called the *Bashful Turtle*. This was not exactly a name that inspired confidence. But Daphna, who'd been waiting for us at the docks, said the ship and her commander, Captain Trallam, were solid.

Trallam wasn't what I expected. I thought he'd be more a roguish type—the sort Daphna enjoyed spending time with, like the Old Man. Instead, the captain turned out to be something of a gentleman, a former navy officer with graying temples and a military bearing, though he'd left the emperor's service decades ago.

He welcomed us aboard politely, if not warmly. Though he tried to hide it, he was put off by the fact that we were all so young. He was even more disgruntled when he asked for the coordinates of the wreck and I answered by pointing across the lake and saying, "That way."

The *Bashful Turtle* was a brig, a hundred and ten feet long, with two square-rigged masts and fore-and-aft sails. Captain Trallam had the ship pull away from the docks as soon as we came on board, speaking his commands softly to the first mate. "Cast off, Mr. Leeds," he said, and Mr. Leeds, a rougher sort than his captain, bawled the orders to the crew.

The five of us stood up front—the "fore," as the sailors called it—as the brig lanced through the water, the sun rising above the mainsail, chasing us. Spray kicked up from the prow. Lachlan tried to catch it on his tongue, soaking himself in the process. Meriel joined him, carefree, and Foxtail twirled her dress behind them in the mist. Gareth looked content, but he stayed back, not wanting to get wet.

In spite of my sorrow over Grey—or maybe because of it—it was nice seeing them all having fun. Lachlan especially, who'd been terribly upset about his role in the destruction of Grey's shop. The excitement of the boat ride let him put it out of his mind, but it was still very much in mine. I kept peeking at him with the Eye to see the stain.

It hadn't grown any further than the size of my hands. But I didn't exactly consider that good news. As the events in Grey's shop had made clear, "growing" didn't mean "growing constantly." The stain had simply jumped from smaller to larger. Who knew when that might happen again?

My gloomy thoughts were broken by Meriel. She grabbed my hands and dragged me into the spray, laughing. I resisted for a bit, more on principle than anything else, then let myself get wet, too. We'd be going into the water soon enough.

Captain Trallam looked on in silent disapproval. As for Daphna, she alternated between watching us with an inscrutable gaze and flirting shamelessly with the younger men on the crew. She'd come fully armed for it, with heavy makeup, bright jewelry, and a breezy silk gown that covered less than one might have liked.

Meriel scrunched up her face at Daphna's flirting. "What is she, three times that man's age? So creepy."

This was not a fight I was interested in. Besides, I was supposed to be navigating. I pulled away from the others and snuck a look with the Eye to spot the Blade of Heaven.

Our direction was a little off, so I called up to the captain, "A little more to the right."

Trallam paused a moment. My guess was he was deciding whether to educate me on proper navigation—or maybe just regretting taking this job. "Five degrees starboard, Mr. Leeds."

"Five degrees starboard!" Lachlan shouted after him, soaked and giddy. From the look Mr. Leeds gave him, I wagered even odds Lachlan would get tossed overboard before we got there.

In the meantime, Daphna paused in her flirting to watch me. When we'd first come on board, it was Foxtail who had captured Daphna's eye. Foxtail was wearing her veil again, of course, but her hidden face and lack of response when Daphna greeted her made the woman curious about just who this girl was. So she'd watched her for a while. But with no way to see past that veil, Daphna soon turned her gaze to me.

I tried to keep my back to her when lifting the patch, moving my arm as if only rubbing a sore eye. But Daphna was no fool. She suspected I had some enchanted device hidden somewhere that was directing me to the shipwreck, and all my contortions were just a smokescreen to hide what it was. When she sidled up to me, I could tell that was what she was after, even though she asked about something else.

"So who's the little one?" she said.

"Foxtail?" I said. "She's our second-story girl."

"Unusual to wear a veil on the water."

"She's shy."

Daphna raised an eyebrow.

I grinned. "She doesn't like showing her face to strangers," I said, as if telling Daphna the real answer. "Had a bad time with the Stickmen once. If you hang around long enough, she'll let you see who she is."

I couldn't tell if Daphna bought that, because she lingered only a little longer before returning to flirting with the crew. In truth, her questions made me think again about what Gareth had said. I believed he'd got it right that Foxtail's mask hid her from magical detection, though why that mattered, I still had no idea. Either way, something else was troubling.

Foxtail was avoiding me.

For a while, I'd thought it was just coincidence. I'd been away from the shop a lot in Redfairne, first with Meriel, then with Gareth. I'd spent a lot of time talking to Grey, too. And Foxtail was a solitary sort of girl, anyway. She'd proved that back in Carlow.

But I'd also noticed that anytime I joined the group, she

avoided looking in my direction. I'd tested her further at Grey's, coming up to her while alone. The first time, she went to join the others. The second time, she slipped out the window with a wave of apology, going on the prowl, as if she'd meant to head out all along.

Of all my friends, Foxtail was the hardest to read, for the obvious reason that she didn't have any facial expressions to give her away. But I could read her body well enough. And every move she made said she wasn't comfortable around me anymore.

Best I could tell, this had started after we'd left Bragan's farm—right after I'd seen her with the Eye. She'd definitely realized I knew she didn't glow. And for some reason, that made her shy away from me.

I hadn't forced her to talk with me yet. But we'd have to have that discussion soon.

It hadn't been clear to me how we were going to be able to search underwater. As we approached the wreck of the *Silver Star*, Captain Trallam showed us how we'd get down to the bottom.

In the center of his boat was a crane. Attached to that crane, with a thick black cable, was what he called a diving bell. It was shaped exactly like a giant bell, ten feet high, eight feet wide at the base. It was made of steel, with two circular glass windows on opposite sides. Inside the bell, a narrow bench ringed the base with several handholds above it. Captain Trallam said we'd need to climb into the bell, sit on the bench, and hold on as we were lowered so we wouldn't accidentally fall into the water.

The diving bell was open at the bottom, like a real bell. "I don't understand," I said. "Where's the floor?"

"There is no floor," Trallam said. "The open bottom is how you'll get in and out."

"But . . . won't the bell fill up with water as soon as you lower it into the lake?"

"No." The captain did a decent job of concealing his sigh over the fact that we clearly didn't know what we were doing. "It's like putting a glass upside down underwater. When we lower the bell below the surface, the shape traps air inside. You'll still be able to breathe, even at significant depths."

"Won't we r-run out?" Gareth asked nervously.

"Not while you're inside. You see the cable at the top? It's hollow, and it's attached to an air pump on deck."

He nodded toward a large boxlike contraption next to the crane. It, too, was made of steel. Bolted on opposite sides were wheel cranks. Two of the *Bashful Turtle*'s crew were already testing the pump, turning the wheels. I could hear air rushing through an opening inside the bell, at the top. It didn't look like easy work.

"My crew will keep the air pumping," Trallam said. "Once you're inside, we'll let out the cable, and the bell will drop. This distance from the coast, the lake floor will be around three, four hundred feet down. There should be just enough cable to reach the bottom." He regarded us critically. "Though I don't know how you're going to swim around down there without a diving suit."

"That's my job, Captain," Daphna said.

She handed me a small pouch. Inside were a dozen smooth

gemstones, oval in shape, each one an inch long. Amethyst, by the looks of it, a deep, rich purple.

"Those are air stones," Daphna said. "To activate one, grip it tightly in your hand and say '*aeragh*.' It'll create a bubble of air around the stone large enough to surround you and let you breathe. Whatever you do, don't let go. The air is around the *stone*, not you. If you lose it, you'll drown."

Amazing. I turned one of the stones over in my fingers. I wanted to peek at it with the Eye, but I'd have to wait until we were alone.

"The bubble it creates," Daphna said, "will be strong enough to keep the water out, so you should be able to walk around more or less normally down there. But if all five of you are going down, you'll have to move fast. Each stone usually gives a couple hours' worth of air, but that's measured for one person only. Sharing them means the binding will burn up quicker. Also, don't knock them about. If a stone cracks, it'll release all its magic at once."

"What'll that do?" I said.

"Turn you into fish food."

"How l-long will each stone last, then?" Gareth asked.

"With all five of you breathing inside the same bubble? Twenty, twenty-five minutes each. Maybe."

There were six stones in the bag. Daphna said that was all she could get on such short notice. This gave us a little more than two hours to find the Dragon's Teeth.

I gave the stones to Gareth to carry. Lachlan begged Gareth to let him hold one, but Meriel hushed him. "Later."

In the meantime, Captain Trallam handed me a couple of light globes, each about the size of an orange. "You'll need those," he said. "It'll get darker the farther down you go."

He still thought we were mad to go ourselves. Daphna wasn't that keen on it, either. But that decision was already made. "Anything else we should know?" I asked.

"Watch out for sharks," Trallam said. "They prowl these waters, sometimes."

"*Sharks?*"

"What's a shark?" Meriel said.

I looked over at Gareth. His eyes were wide. "B-but sharks only l-live in the ocean."

Captain Trallam shrugged. "There's lots of sea life round here. Must swim up the river. Pocket of salt water or something."

I could tell that didn't make any sense to Gareth—especially since the sea was hundreds of miles downstream—but he didn't challenge the captain. Still, the whole thing made me think back to the woods near Bolcanathair. That leopard wasn't supposed to be there, either.

Trallam waved over a crewman standing near the diving bell. He was carrying a strange sort of weapon: a long, railed device with a trigger and handle. There was a narrow, barbed spear latched to the rail.

"Sharks usually leave divers alone," the captain said, "as long as you don't provoke them. But take the harpoon just in case. You only have one shot, so make it count."

"What's a shark?" Meriel said a little louder, ready to poke me.

"You ain't never heard of sharks?" Lachlan said curiously.

"It's a big . . . it's . . . a giant monster fish," Gareth said. "With rows of teeth."

"Oh, sure, Gareth," Meriel said. "A monster fish with teeth. Bet it eats people, too."

"It does," Lachlan insisted.

She rolled her eyes.

I handed the harpoon off to Meriel. It was heavy and clunky, and she looked a little dubious as she took it. "You guys aren't really serious about what a shark is, are you?" she said. "Cal?"

I didn't answer. I'd drifted away from the group so I could give a quick look through the Eye. The beam of light descending from the sky swelled until it blotted out most of the blue.

"Here, Captain," I said. "Weigh anchor."

We'd reached the Blade of Heaven.

CHAPTER 28

THE DIVING BELL was roomier than I'd imagined.

The contraption had been designed for two adults wearing bulky steel-domed diving suits, so we had plenty of space for all five of us around the bench. While we were spared the discomfort of the suits, Captain Trallam did make us put on thick gloves and weighted boots. Without them, he said, we'd shoot up to the surface if any of us left the air bubbles—a trip that no one would survive. The boots weren't made for smaller feet, so we had to stuff cloth inside to make them fit.

We were already sopping wet. The crane had first lowered the bell into the water, just touching the surface, so we'd had to swim under the lip to get inside. Lachlan shook out his hair, spraying us.

"Stop that," Meriel complained.

"Sorry, luv."

Lachlan was a little dismayed. He'd had to leave Galawan behind with Daphna, lest the little sparrow get waterlogged. Lachlan would have stayed on deck with him, but he obviously wasn't going to miss his chance to go diving. Even if he hadn't wanted to come, I'd have made him. With that stain capable of growing anytime, I wasn't keen to let him out of my sight. Not that I could do anything if it did.

The bell jerked, and everyone gave a little gasp as we began to go down. We shivered, half from tension, half from the air blowing from where the cable attached to the top, running a breeze over our wet clothes. We crowded around the porthole windows, peering into the blue as we descended. And then any thought of the chill vanished as we saw below the surface.

It was amazing. Like visiting another world. At first, sunlight glittered through the waves overhead, making the water sparkle. Curious canary-yellow fish swam around the diving bell, joined by larger shimmering orange ones, staying nose to window until they lost interest in their own reflection. There were other things, too. An eel—

"Artha's snuffling snout," Meriel said, wide-eyed.

I couldn't remember Meriel ever cursing like that. I craned my neck to see what she'd spotted. When I saw it, I was just as astounded. "Gareth. *Look.*"

It was an octopus—something else that wasn't supposed to live in fresh water. It didn't look very big, maybe a foot long. But I'd never seen one alive before.

It glided down with the diving bell, reaching out an exploratory tentacle to touch the steel. I'd thought octopuses would be dumb, clumsy, awkward things, but the creature moved with such grace, it was impossible to believe it was anything but intelligent. It groped its way along the bell, studying the device. I was disappointed when it finally moved out of view.

Farther down we went. Pressure swelled in our ears, just like when we'd gone up on the airship. Swallowing made them pop. Outside, the light dimmed as we sank deeper below the surface.

Colors became harder to see, until everything was just shades of hazy blue.

"Gareth," I said, and he broke out one of the light globes. It cast an eerie glow inside the bell.

It was then that I noticed Lachlan didn't look well. "You all right?" I said.

He tried to smile. "Don't feel so good, guv."

"I told you not to eat those clams," Meriel scolded him.

I wasn't so sure bad shellfish was the problem. No longer needing to hide the Eye, I looked him over. The stain inside was still the same size. But it was more agitated than I'd ever seen. It banged around him, as if trying to escape.

I got the strangest feeling watching it. *It doesn't like it down here,* I thought.

Curious, the Old Man said. *Why would that be?*

Water lapped at my boots. I looked down to see the water at the bottom of the bell had risen. Captain Trallam had warned us this would happen, from the higher pressure down below. I was suddenly very conscious of the breeze blowing from the tube overhead. I hoped the sailors working the pump didn't decide to take a break.

"Should we use an air stone?" Gareth said.

I stopped him from reaching into the pouch. "Not yet. We only have a couple hours' worth. Let's not waste any air we don't have to."

But the water continued to rise the lower we went. When it reached our chests, Meriel said, "Cal," and I agreed.

Gareth passed me the light globe and pulled one of the air stones from the bag. He gripped it tight.

"*Aeragh*," he whispered.

There was a rush of air, strong, almost like the blow of a gale. It pressed us against the side of the bell for a moment. Then the wind stilled.

Looking down, we could see the water had been forced out of the bottom of the diving bell. The water's surface was no longer wavy, either. Instead, it was smooth and curved, as if a giant glass bubble was resting on it.

"Shuna's blessed bum," Lachlan said in amazement.

It was pretty incredible. But something else drew my eye—or rather, the Eye—even more.

When Gareth had first taken the air stone from its pouch, it had been tucked away in his hand. Now I could see it glowing in his palm. Nestled against the red of his skin, the stone shone a bright violet. It was exactly the same color as Lachlan's stain: air magic. But what really caught my attention was the primeval itself. It wasn't so agitated anymore. It had relaxed.

Lachlan seemed better, too, like he no longer felt sick. If anything, he looked delighted. He stared at the air stone, and in his eyes was a glint of . . . not quite greed, but something like it. A craving.

"Let me hold it," he said.

That's it, I said to the Old Man. *The primeval magic inside him was linked to air magic. And it didn't like being surrounded by so much water.*

The wrong element, the Old Man said. *Interesting.*

"Interesting" wasn't the word I'd have used—especially because I really didn't like the way Lachlan was looking at the stone. He was a curious sort, sure. But that craving . . . I didn't think it was coming from him.

It was the *stain* that wanted him to hold the stone. To be nearer its own kind.

Just like with Lopsided.

Lachlan reached for the stone. Gareth moved to give it to him. They were both surprised I pushed his hand away. "Leave it alone."

"Aw, c'mon," Lachlan said. "Just for a sec. I'll give it back."

"I said no. No one handles those things except Gareth."

"Why?" Lachlan complained.

I gave Gareth a pointed look. I didn't think he'd seen the greed in Lachlan's eyes, but he understood my message well enough. *Under no circumstances does Lachlan touch that stone.* The last time the primeval had had its way, Grey's shop had exploded. I didn't know if that would happen with the air stones, but I sure wasn't willing to find out.

Thankfully, Meriel drew our attention away. "Cal."

She nodded toward the water below. We were down far enough that we could see the bottom of the lake approaching. Time to slow the bell.

The captain had told us what to do. There was a metal ball attached to a swing bar near the top of the bell. We were to slam it against the side, and the sound would then carry up through the cable to the top. One knock to slow, Trallam had said, two knocks to stop. Five to say *we're done, pull us up.*

What he didn't tell us was how loud the clapper would be. We winced at the gong, unable to cover our ears without letting go of the handholds.

Still, the bell slowed its descent. We watched the bottom approach. When it came time to stop, I let Lachlan bang the clapper twice. The bell jerked to a halt.

We all looked at each other for a moment. We were actually at the bottom of Lake Galway.

And none of us were prepared for what awaited.

CHAPTER 29

LACHLAN GASPED.

"It's so beautiful," he said.

It was—and nearly as impossible to believe. When the diving bell had come to a stop, we'd climbed out the bottom. Now we stood on the lake floor, staring at a world of wonder.

I didn't know what I'd expected to find. I suppose, from walking along the shoreline, I'd thought the bottom of Lake Galway would look the same: an endless expanse of mud.

But we stood instead in a place teeming with life. Covering the ground were great waving leaves; branching, spiky growths; and soft fields of what looked like mushrooms, all joined together in one giant living organism. Fish of rainbow colors swam through the mass.

I'd assumed the lake floor would be flat. Instead, the ground was uneven, like an underwater hill country. Crustaceans of all kinds skittered up and down the slopes. Some I recognized: a lobster, a shrimp, a crab. Others were a complete mystery, things with spiked insect legs and six claws, opaque white eyes dangling on the end of antenna-like stalks.

We stood right in the middle of it, on the peak of the highest hill. The air stone in Gareth's hand projected a bubble around us, a perfect sphere of enchantment holding back the water. It was almost like we'd been sealed in an empty ball of glass, then sunk, left to fall to the bottom of the lake.

But unlike some mythical glass ball, there was no barrier between the water that surrounded us and the air that kept us alive. Carefully, I approached the boundary of our bubble and stretched out my hand. It slipped into the cool lake water easily, leaving ripples on the surface, as if I'd just touched a pond.

Small jellies floated by, ignoring the fingers I'd plunged into their world. There were plenty of fish around, and they floated toward us, curious. One of them got too close. When it swam into our bubble, it fell to the ground, flopping among the leaves. I tossed the fish back. The ripples radiated outward from the splash, then stilled, smoothed to a perfect sphere once again by the stone's magic.

The others, just as amazed, couldn't resist trying the same thing, except for Gareth, who, holding the stone, couldn't reach the edge. The bubble the enchantment projected was about fifteen feet in diameter, centered on the stone, leaving just enough room for the five of us to walk about.

Inside our sphere of air, the lake floor remained wet, but it was easily walkable, like a beach just drained from high tide. It didn't smell like the beach, though. The scent was hard to put into words. Sort of fresh, like a frosted meadow, but with a faint hint of something oily.

The mushroom-like growths squished as we stepped on them, and then there was a new scent in the air, slightly sweet and powdery. The harder, spiky growths crunched and broke underneath our weighted boots. Lachlan took off one of his gloves to touch the spikes.

"Don't!" Gareth said.

Lachlan jerked his hand back. Gareth had practically shouted. I couldn't remember him raising his voice like that before.

"What is it?" I said.

"The g-growths," Gareth said, worried. "They look like coral."

Daphna had mentioned back at her villa that there was coral near Redfairne. "What's wrong with that?" Meriel said.

"It might be poisonous," he said, and Meriel made Lachlan put his glove back on. "But . . . I mean . . . it shouldn't be here." Gareth looked at me. "Coral doesn't grow in fresh water, either. None of these things do. This isn't r-right."

He wasn't the only one who thought so. As beautiful as the reef was in my own human sight, through the Eye, it was positively ablaze. Colors of every shade and hue carpeted the lake floor, glowing in a dazzling seascape. From the Eye itself, however, I felt something, and it wasn't awe.

The Eye was *confused.*

Whatever it had expected to find down here, this wasn't it. That was slightly worrying, because the Blade of Heaven couldn't be clearer. The beam of white light sliced down through the water, piercing the reef some fifty yards away from where we stood.

Foxtail tugged on my sleeve.

"What is it?" I said.

She waved her arms at the boundary of our air bubble. Then

she pointed at the stone Gareth was holding, set her hands as if she was measuring the length of something, then made the distance smaller. *The bubble is shrinking.*

She was right. Watching where the boundary of the bubble met the ground, we could see the sea life the air had previously uncovered slowly getting swallowed by the advancing water. A quick glance with the Eye at the air stone showed the light of enchantment dimming inside it. This one was almost out of juice.

I'd left my pocket watch up on the *Bashful Turtle*, so I didn't know exactly how long it had been since we'd activated that stone. But somewhere between twenty and twenty-five minutes, like Daphna had warned us, seemed about right. "Get another one."

Gareth took a second stone from the pouch tied to his belt and spoke the command word to release the enchantment. Again we felt that rush, and the heavy wind, and then our air bubble pushed the water away, keeping our sphere at a steady fifteen feet.

"What do I do with the old one?" Gareth asked me.

"Aw, it's dying," Lachlan said, looking at it sadly. "Give it here, let—"

I shoved him back as he reached for it. "What did I say about those stones?"

"Artha's rump," he said, sulking. "You don't have to yell at me."

"Then do as you're told." I turned to Gareth. "Let's try something."

I motioned for Gareth to throw the dying stone down the

nearest slope. When he did, its air bubble stayed with it, following the stone as it bounced into the valley. It was obvious now that its power was nearly gone, and not just because the Eye saw its glow fade. The bubble that surrounded the stone grew smaller, shrinking faster and faster, until it finally collapsed, no more air around it.

It was sobering to watch. Enough sightseeing. "That'll be us if we don't hurry. Let's get going."

We walked along the top of the hill, making our way toward the Blade of Heaven.

It was an odd and wondrous experience, like moving through a giant aquarium. Lachlan stopped sulking about the air stones almost immediately. Different colored fish kept falling into our bubble as we advanced. Happy to help, he tossed them back into the water. "Sorry, little guy. There yeh go."

We had to move cautiously. Though our boots were enough to protect us from the coral spikes, the mushrooms made the lake floor slippery. We nearly lost Lachlan down the hill, when he stepped close to the edge to rescue a fish and had to scramble for footing. Meriel's hand on his collar was the only thing that kept him from sliding into the valley.

"Would you watch where you're going?" she said, exasperated. "I swear to Shuna, I don't understand how you always find so much trouble."

"I don't," he protested. "Trouble finds *me*."

Gareth, keeping a good hold on the air stone, was fascinated by how it worked. There was a little pressure, he said, when he walked with it. Like the air was pushing the water out of the way. He discovered the easiest way to move was with the stone held to his chest, then he'd lean into it, using his whole body to push forward. I could tell he wanted to study the stones more, but we couldn't waste time on that.

We finally reached where the Blade of Heaven was stuck into the earth. Except when we got there, I saw nothing but coral. We kicked it away with our boots, working at it long enough that Gareth needed to bring out a new air stone. But all we revealed was more coral underneath.

"Where are the Dragon's Teeth?" Meriel said.

"I don't know." I saw nothing special. Worse, the Eye saw nothing, either. And I could feel its frustration growing.

Something was very wrong. The Eye expected the Dragon's Teeth to be here. If they weren't . . . where could they possibly be? And how would we find them?

"Maybe this is the wrong spot," Gareth said.

"It can't be," I said. "The Blade of Heaven is right here—"

But then I realized: It *wasn't* here. Not exactly.

At the top of our hill, the beacon that guided us had begun to narrow, like a sword reaching the end of its blade. It occurred to me: What if the *tip* of the Blade of Heaven was the true marker? If that was the case, then from the angles of the beam, it looked like the point of the blade would be about fifty feet down.

Under the coral.

"I think we have a problem," I began.

Then I discovered we'd missed the biggest problem of all.

CHAPTER 30

Something slammed into my back.

Whatever it was struck me like a sledgehammer. I flew forward, ramming into Gareth. I had a vague glimpse of the others as I bounced off them, too.

Then I was in the water.

The lake was icy cold down here. I heard someone's muffled scream as my ears filled with liquid. I spun about, until the drag slowed me to a stop. I was dazed, disoriented.

What hit me?

My vision was blurry; my real vision, anyway. With the Eye, I could see just fine. The colors of the coral reef blazed in front of me—

I'm floating facedown, I thought.

Something dragged at my feet, pulling. I kicked out, panicked, until I remembered: my weighted boots. My legs sank to the bottom.

But the panic remained, growing. *I'm in the water. I can't breathe.*

A cool voice entered my head. The Old Man. *Stop panicking like a mark and control yourself, boy.*

Yes. Calm. Look for the air.

Where was it?

The reef shone with light. The life everywhere was glowing,

and the sloping hills and ridges of the lake floor only made things more confusing. I couldn't find it. I couldn't *find* it.

Only the Old Man's chiding kept me from losing my mind. *You can't see air, boy. Look for the stone.*

Right. The stone. Enchanted, it would glow.

There. Brighter than anything else, shining purple. Red shapes flitted around it. My friends.

It was moving. I moved toward it. And then—

Air. Glorious, wonderful air.

I fell into the bubble, drawing a ragged gasp as mushrooms squished under my knees. My gloves crunched a spike of coral.

Foxtail hauled me back to my feet. "What hit me?" I said, still a little dazed.

Gareth couldn't answer; he was stammering too much.

"Shark, guv," Lachlan said, wide-eyed.

"I thought it was a joke," Meriel said, stunned. "How could it not be a joke? What possible reason could the Spirits have to make *giant monster fish!*"

Foxtail turned me around, probed at my back. My shirt was torn where the shark had rammed into me. I wondered why it hadn't just grabbed me and swum away. Maybe entering the air had thrown off its aim? It couldn't possibly have expected the bubble to be there.

Everyone whirled, looking for the shark. "Cap'n Trallam said they wasn't supposed to attack unless provoked," Lachlan said. "We didn't do nothing."

Gareth finally found his voice. "Nothing down here is r-right," he whispered. "Nothing."

I had to agree. I could still sense the confusion from the Eye.

Meriel gripped the harpoon tight, turning this way and that, searching for a target in the blue. "Where did it go? Can you see it?"

Everyone looked into the water.

"There!" I said.

The Eye spotted it first. Its glow—red so tinged with blue it was almost purple—silhouetted the shark against the reef. The beast was sleek and streamlined, with fins on its back and sides, bladed tail propelling it through the water at frightening speed. It turned its nose toward us and started another charge. "It's coming!"

Meriel looked around frantically. "Where? *Where?*"

"Right there!" I pointed, but it was useless; she didn't have my Eye-sight. "Give me—"

I tore the harpoon from her grasp. Carefully, I aimed it at the oncoming shark.

Its jaws began to open.

I pulled the trigger. The springs released, and the harpoon shot into the water, tiny bubbles trailing from the spearhead. The gun kicked back, thumping me hard below my collarbone.

The harpoon screamed toward the oncoming shark—

But it missed.

I didn't know if the shark had dodged or if it was my own bad aim. Either way, the harpoon passed two inches from its mouth, nicking the beast's left fin before vanishing into the murk.

"Look out!"

There was barely time to shout. The nose of the shark broke through the air bubble. More by instinct than anything else, I jerked the empty harpoon gun up, the back of it braced against my chest.

If I'd been lucky before, then Shuna was surely blessing me now, because the front of the gun rammed into the shark's mouth. A dozen razor-sharp teeth went flying.

And then I was flying, too. The butt of the gun slammed into my chest with so much pain, I was afraid I'd broken my ribs. I rammed backward into the others, knocking someone beneath me as I fell.

It wasn't Meriel. She'd danced away, dodging the rush with a pirouette. Throwing knives already in hand, she twisted, flinging both blades after the departing shark.

But her attacks were useless. The moment the knives plunged into the water, the drag slowed them. They only went in a couple feet before they sank, disappearing among the coral.

I pushed myself up, gloves squelching more mushrooms. The person I'd knocked down was Gareth; he himself was lying on Foxtail's legs. Meriel and I helped them to their feet.

"We don't have anything left to fight with," I said, wincing at the pain in my chest. "We have to get back to the diving bell— *Where's Lachlan?*"

The boy was gone.

CHAPTER 31

Desperate, I stared after the departing shark.

Had Lachlan been grabbed? The Eye followed the shark's glow through the water. I saw it . . . but no Lachlan.

Then where was he? I looked around frantically.

Oh no.

The last attack had knocked him down the coral-crusted slope. Panicked, he thrashed about, and that only made things worse. Instead of letting his weighted boots bring him to rest, his kicking pushed him farther into the valley.

"Stop moving!" I shouted, but it was useless. He couldn't hear me. In his panic, it wouldn't have made a difference.

Gareth grabbed my arm. "The air stones," he said.

Yes. We could throw him an air stone.

But I'd failed to understand what Gareth was telling me. "The pouch," he said. "It's *g-gone*."

I stared in horror at his belt, where the extra air stones had been tied. "What happened to it?"

"When the shark attacked . . . someone g-grabbed me . . . I think it was Lachlan. He p-pulled it away."

So he'd torn the pouch off with him. Did he still have it?

I didn't see it in Lachlan's hands. But I did spot something bouncing off the reef about ten feet away from him. I couldn't see it, exactly; the object kicked up floating clouds of dirt from the lake floor as it rolled. But it had to be the pouch.

Foxtail spotted it, too. She fumbled about in the folds of Meriel's dress, coming away with a pair of knives. Then she dove into the water after the pouch.

"Wait—" I began.

Too late; she was already gone. I cursed. The better play would have been to leap down after Lachlan, bringing our air bubble to where he was. Meriel, Gareth, and I could still do that; we'd have to let Foxtail recover the stones on her own. If we didn't reach Lachlan soon, he'd drown.

Hurriedly, I told the others the plan. Meriel and I grabbed Gareth's arms, holding on for dear life. Then, together, we jumped.

It was a strange sensation, falling through the water like that. I'd figured it would be just like jumping down a hill. Instead, our air bubble, pushing the water out of the way, slowed our descent. It was like Ayreth had suddenly lost half its gravity. We fell in slow motion.

I didn't have time to wonder at it. As we bounced down the slope, I kept the Eye on Lachlan. So I forgot about the shark.

Meriel hadn't. "It's coming back," she warned us.

She gripped one of her knives in her free hand, like a dagger. I'd picked up the empty harpoon gun, thinking maybe I'd be able to fend off the shark with it again. But it wasn't aiming at us. It was going toward—

"Foxtail!" I shouted.

I wouldn't have thought she'd hear me in the water. She was swimming parallel to us, still chasing the pouch with the air stones bumping down the slope. But—as I'd seen before—her hearing was much better than ours. She looked over and saw us floating down, pointing frantically at the oncoming shark.

She turned to face it. When she dove into the water, she'd tucked Meriel's knives into her belt. Now she pulled them out, gripping both like daggers, ready to stab.

But the shark wasn't going for her, either. It swam below her— and gobbled up the pouch bouncing down the reef.

I didn't understand what had happened. Did it think the pouch was food? With the way it was kicking up clouds, I could see how it would have looked alive.

Gareth watched it happen, too. For a moment, he looked puzzled. Then his eyes went wide.

"The magic," he said.

I didn't know what that meant, and I didn't have time to ask. We hit the bottom of the slope, crushing more of those strange mushrooms. But we'd finally caught up to Lachlan.

He fell into our bubble. Still panicking, he thrashed about, spitting water. Meriel fell on him, pinning him to the squishy mass below.

"We have you," she said. "Calm down, Lachlan. Calm down."

He hacked out one last glob of water, taking gasping breaths. "Artha's bulging bum. Thought I was done for."

Gareth grabbed my arm. "The air stones," he said. "Th-that's what the shark was after. That's why it attacked us. It was attracted to the m-magic. *All* this life is. *That's why these creatures are here.*"

I stared at him. The sharks, the octopus, the coral reef itself . . . kept alive by magic?

We'd known something was odd. Even the Eye hadn't been expecting to see this life. *Something* out of the ordinary must have brought it here. Magic made sense.

And with the air stones . . . we'd just brought more magic with us.

So the shark hadn't missed me after all. It had been aiming for something else the whole time: the stones hanging from the pouch on Gareth's belt.

Well, it had eaten them now. So . . . why was the shark turning toward us again?

Still have an air stone, don't you? the Old Man said.

Of course. And we couldn't throw this one away.

"We'll never make it back to the bell in time," I said. "We have to find somewhere to hide—"

My words broke off as the Eye spotted new shapes approaching in the distance.

I studied their outlines. And my heart sank with despair.

More sharks.

I counted the glows. One, two, three, four . . . five. Five more sharks coming our way.

I told the others, trying not to panic again. But . . . "I don't know what to do."

"One of us could l-lead them off," Gareth said.

"How?" I said.

"Blood. Sharks go into a frenzy when they s-smell blood."

Meriel sighed and brandished her knife, ready to cut her palm. "I'll do it."

"No, wait," I said. "There has to be some other way . . . Foxtail!"

With the pouch snatched away by the shark, Foxtail had turned and swam toward us. She'd almost made it to the air bubble. But she'd stopped when Gareth had spoken. Then she'd turned to face the oncoming sharks. She'd heard what he said.

Now she swam off. When she reached about ten yards distant, she let herself sink to the bottom and crouched there.

The first shark that had attacked us was much closer than the others. It had already begun another run.

"Foxtail!" I shouted. "Don't!"

She shifted, putting herself between us and the shark. She held on to both of her knives.

Closer now.

"Foxtail!"

I thought the shark was going to attack her. I thought she was going to sacrifice herself.

But the shark wasn't coming for her. It was aiming for the air stone.

And Foxtail *wasn't* sacrificing herself. Instead, as the shark swam over her head, she sprang from the lake floor—and plunged both knives into its belly.

The shark writhed. It twisted, dragging Foxtail behind it, blades stuck deep in its flesh. Its jaws snapped as it turned, trying to fight back against whatever terrible thing had injured it.

Blood flowed from its wounds. Two dark clouds, shining

blue-red in the Eye, billowed out behind it as it swam. The shark veered off, trying desperately to get away from its attacker.

Foxtail wouldn't let it. She twisted, wrapping her legs around its midsection. Keeping one dagger in its belly as a handhold, she plunged the other into the shark, over and over again.

More blood billowed as the shark swam away. Then we couldn't see her anymore. I glanced back at the other five sharks, but they'd changed direction, too, chasing the sweet scent of blood across the bottom of Lake Galway.

We watched, stunned, as they disappeared into the black. The Eye kept them in view well past my own human sight, their shapes shrinking until they were little more than dots.

And then I was blinded by light.

An enormous sphere of purple blazed in a flash, off in the distance. A second later, our air bubble was squashed almost flat. The pressure wave flung us back against the reef. The explosion roared in our ears. The blast ripped the coral, the mushrooms, and the waving leaves from the lake floor.

Then all was silent.

"The air stones," Gareth said, horrified. "The ones the shark swallowed. They cracked."

They'd released all their magic at once, as Daphna had warned us. I looked into the distance with the Eye. There were no more sharks. The blast had torn them to pieces.

But what about . . .

"Foxtail," Lachlan gasped.

CHAPTER 32

SHE COULDN'T HAVE survived that blast. Nothing could.

"No!" Distraught, Lachlan tried to dive in after her, as if there were anything left of her to find. Meriel held him back. "Let me go! *Foxtail!*"

Meriel clung to him. It was half restraint, half hug. "It's too late," she said, deathly pale.

Except . . . it wasn't. Gareth stared into the murk. "Look."

Swimming toward us, mask reflecting our light globes, was Foxtail.

Stunned, Meriel let Lachlan go. He jumped up and down, screaming with glee as Foxtail emerged from the water. She began wringing out her dress nonchalantly, as if she'd just come in from a walk in the rain. Lachlan slammed into her with a hug so hard they nearly toppled back into the lake. Gareth wiped a hand across his face, still pale, as Meriel and I wrapped them in our own joyous embrace.

I covered the Eye. Partly because I was getting a little dizzy, but mostly because I was pretty sure Foxtail didn't like being around it. "How did you survive that blast?" I said.

Foxtail wagged her finger from side to side. She made two fists, as if holding on to something, then released them. *I wasn't in the blast. I let go of the knives, and the sharks chased the blood.*

I hadn't seen any of that—and of course I hadn't, because the Eye couldn't see Foxtail at all. I laughed, delighted. But even as I did, I realized something else about Foxtail, too.

She'd been out of our air bubble for a couple minutes. Yet standing in front of us, her chest wasn't even heaving. Which meant her mask not only shielded her from the Eye's sight, it let her breathe, even underwater.

Foxtail looked at me, and though of course I couldn't see her expression, something in the way she moved said she could tell I'd just figured that out. She stood there, hesitant, almost cautious, as if waiting for me to say something bad.

I took her by the shoulders. "That," I said, "was the most heroically insane thing I ever saw."

She relaxed, as if relieved.

Then she patted my cheek.

As happy as we were about Foxtail—and the end of the sharks—the attack had devastated our expedition.

We didn't have any air stones left. We weren't in danger of drowning; Gareth had cracked a fresh stone right before the first assault, and it would take us only a few minutes to climb back up the slope and get to the safety of the diving bell. But we'd never find the Dragon's Teeth now.

During the attack, the only sense I'd got from the Eye was that it had simply been annoyed by the inconvenience. Now that the sharks were gone, its frustration had returned. "If I'm right," I said, dejected, "and the point of the Blade of Heaven marks where the Teeth are, then they're buried under that mound of coral and sand."

"So let's get digging," Meriel said.

"It won't make a difference. We don't have enough time."

"Why not?" Lachlan said.

I'd have figured the answer was obvious. "It would take hours to get through all that. Maybe days. We only have a few minutes left in the air stone." I cursed. "Everyone back to the bell."

"Hold yer socks," Lachlan said. "Let's just fix the stone."

"How are we supposed to—*no!*"

I tried to stop him, but this time, Lachlan was ready for it. He ducked under my outstretched hand and snatched the stone from Gareth.

"*Lachlan, don't!*"

I moved to grab it back, but he'd turned away from me. He stared at the stone for the briefest moment, eyes alight. Then he clenched it in his palm.

Suddenly, a fierce violet shone through his fingers. The same rushing came as when Gareth had first activated the stone, but much louder, near deafening. We clasped our hands over our ears, staggered by the pain.

Then came the wind.

It flung us backward, away from Lachlan. We were sent sprawling, tumbling across wet leaves and mashed mushrooms. My stomach rose in my throat at the memory of being knocked out of the air bubble. We were all going to drown this time, flung far into the water.

But there was no water to slide into. The bubble swelled, air driving the lake back. A howling wind whipped our clothes, making it hard to breathe. The force of the gale shredded the reef, ripped the rest of the coral away like an explosion. Fragments of leaves and broken spikes swirled around the dome, then splashed into the water.

Then, just as suddenly, the gale stopped. The air was still, smelling of the sweet powder of the mushrooms and the wet freshness of a thunderstorm. We covered our heads as the bits of vegetation above us sank and fell through our bubble like apocalyptic rain.

Lachlan stood alone in the center of it. The bubble the air stone had created, once fifteen feet wide, now measured a hundred. Through the Eye, the stone blazed as bright as the dragon staff once had.

And the Eye was pleased.

(yes yes yes)

I felt it inside as it gazed upon the air stone, a steady beat of satisfaction.

We stood. Our clothes were filthy with mud and mushrooms.

Lachlan grinned, a smile of innocent delight. "See, guv? Too easy."

Gareth stared at him. "H-how did you do that?"

"Dunno, really. Just thought, *Aw, that's a shame,* 'bout the stone dying and all. Then I got this idea 'bout breathing life back into it. Like with Lop."

"You exploded when you fixed Lop," Meriel said.

Lachlan looked surprised. "Huh. Hadn't really thought of

that. But I don't feel sick this time. Not like before. Maybe I'm all fixed, eh?"

No. It was exactly the opposite.

The idea to "save" the stone hadn't been his. It was the stain that had compelled him, the stain that sought out its own kind. The stain had powered it, just like Lop.

And also like the last time, the stain had grown.

It was twice the size as before, nearly big enough to fill Lachlan's whole chest. It shifted inside him, swirling around, bounding off the confinement of his soul. Its shape changed constantly, and for brief, flashing moments, instead of an amorphous blob, I could make out a strange patterned spiral within, almost like Weaver runes. And the way it moved ... the only way I could describe it was *happy*.

"Give the stone to Gareth," I said quietly.

"But why? It feels so good—"

I yanked it out of his hand. He stumbled back, like he was worried I was going to hit him. "Shuna's paws, guv. Was just trying to help."

Whatever Lachlan felt when he held the stone, all I detected was a warmth in my palm. Part of me was afraid that when I took it from him, the bubble would collapse on us, that the primeval magic was the only thing keeping it powered. But a bigger part of me was worried about what it would do to Lachlan if he kept holding it.

It wasn't just the stain's growth that concerned me anymore. It had clearly begun to affect Lachlan's mind, too. He didn't seem to realize what he'd done should have been impossible. Like it was normal for a ten-year-old thief with no Weaver training to enchant magical artifacts with nothing more than a wish.

The stone's blaze remained steady in the Eye. There was so much magic in there now. How long would this enchantment last? Days? Weeks? Years? And what would it do to Lachlan the longer he was around it?

I didn't want to find out. If I could have, I'd have taken us all back to the diving bell and fled for the surface. But Daphna had no more stones to give us. Which meant either we used this primeval-powered magic to find the Dragon's Teeth or we gave up forever. If we failed now, we failed for good.

Life isn't always a choice between good and bad, boy, the Old Man had once said. *Sometimes you have to choose between the lion's claw and the tiger's bite.*

Staying down here might make the stain grow further inside Lachlan. But if we left, he was doomed for sure. Lion's claw, tiger's bite. *Not much of a choice at all, Old Man.*

"Let's hurry," I said. "Find the Dragon's Teeth and get out of here. Though Artha only knows where they are."

Gareth blinked. "I know, too," he said, surprised.

"You do?" Meriel said. "Where?"

"There."

He pointed to the side of the slope. I followed his gaze. The reef here had been battered, all life stripped away. To the Eye, the hill was nothing but a blank, lightless slab. "Under the mud?"

"That's not mud," Gareth said. "It's *wood*."

He scrambled halfway up the slope, digging his fingers into the dirt, tearing chunks of it away. And there, under the dripping wet, were the dull brown grains of water-swollen oak.

"This," Gareth said, "is what's b-been attracting all the life. The sharks, the fish, the coral. We were looking for Veran's shipwreck. We couldn't see it b-because it's been overgrown."

He stared up at it, awed. "This . . . this whole ridge . . . it's the *Silver Star*."

CHAPTER 33

"Quickly," I said, but everyone was already on it. We climbed up through the mud, brushed it off, and pushed against the wood, looking for some way inside.

Lachlan was the one who got us through. Higher up on the slope, he stomped hard against the boat. Suddenly, the ground collapsed, a great hole opening underneath him. He fell, disappearing with a cry into the mound.

"Lachlan!" Meriel said.

We scrambled up to the hole. Gareth brought his light globe so we could see. Lachlan had fallen through rotted wood into what looked like the remnants of a ship's cabin. He looked up at us, squinting at the light and rubbing his backside.

"Found it, guv," he said.

It was like stepping through a portal into history.

We walked the cramped corridors of the *Silver Star* in awe and horror. This ship had sunk two thousand years ago, but shockingly, most of it was still intact. Gareth wasn't sure how it had survived.

"Maybe the reef preserved it underneath," he said, running his fingers over the wood as water dripped from the beams overhead. "Or it could be . . . I mean . . . something else."

He meant a binding, of course. The same enchantment that had drawn the life here, and kept it here, and created insane things like sharks that ate magic instead of people.

Whatever it was, it hadn't preserved everything. Though very little coral had penetrated the hull, most of the ship's interior was coated with a slimy green mold, stinking of mildew and decay. In some places, the slime had hardened, leaving a greenish-gray plaque that stuck like glue to the wood. And if the slime was all we'd had to contend with, it wouldn't have been that bad.

But also, everywhere, were the dead.

Skeletons littered the decks, still wrapped in tattered woolen tunics and the remnants of armor, steel scales overlapping, decayed to rust. Their weapons, lying nearby, had fallen apart alongside them, fragments of spear blades and short swords, leather grips rotting with mold. It was impossible to tell whether these men had died in battle or whether they'd been alive when the ship went down, and they'd drowned in the waters of Lake Galway. But it was a stark reminder that what had happened here was a terror, and we were walking through a tomb of ancient remains.

Yet there was something else about this place that was different. Something unnatural. It gave me an eerie feeling I couldn't shake, like the skeletons would come to life to wield their broken weapons once again. The *Silver Star* hadn't landed level on its bottom; the fact that everything was canted at an odd angle just made it worse.

Whatever I sensed that was troubling me didn't seem to bother Foxtail at all. She paused over one of the skeletons, then pried a blackened circle from the uniform. The scale armor beneath it crumbled into flakes of rust.

Foxtail removed her glove and scratched at the circle with her fingernail. Then she held it out for me to see. It was shiny underneath, pure silver.

Meriel grabbed it and tried to scratch off more of the tarnish. "What is this?"

Gareth marveled at it. "I think . . . I think it's the insignia. Of the Emperor's Guard."

"That worth something special?" Lachlan said.

"It's . . . yes. I mean . . . if it really is the insignia . . . it would be worth thousands of crowns. Maybe more."

Meriel's eyes bulged. She pocketed the brooch and yanked a second one from a nearby armor.

"Meriel," I warned.

"You promised I could fill my pockets," she protested.

"Yes, but we can't steal everything."

"What Daphna doesn't see," she said lightly, "Meriel gets away with."

In truth, despite our deal, Daphna was no doubt expecting us to hide away an item or two while we were down here. And there were plenty of dead guardsmen to loot. Lachlan took a crest for himself. So did Gareth, though I didn't think he cared about its value. He just wanted a piece of history.

Foxtail looked on with interest but took nothing. I did, but only to show Daphna. These insignia were proof that we'd found the *Silver Star*.

Yet there was much, much more than silver crests down here.

As we searched, we came upon a room with a long table. It had been secured to the floor, so it hadn't slid away when the ship had tilted. The wood was warped and split from being underwater, which was a real shame. It had once been a magnificent mottled walnut, different shades still showing through the water stains.

The chairs around it hadn't been nailed down, however. Two leaned forward with the ship's tilt, propped against the table. The other four had tumbled down and now lay against the wall. Crusty piles of that green mold coated the floor around them.

"This must have been the emperor's dining room," Gareth said.

"The emperor?" Lachlan said, impressed. "Really?"

"It was his ship, remember."

"Either way," Meriel said. "Dining room means dinnerware, and I have so many lonely pockets. I'd best find them some little silver friends—hey, what's this?"

There was a glint of metal among the crusted objects against the wall. She pried one away, then tore at the plaque, snapping off big green pieces of it.

"Looks like a plate," I said.

The metal was an odd pale yellow. "Is that gold?" Lachlan asked.

"Electrum," Gareth said, surprised.

"What's that?"

"An alloy. Of gold. And silver, I mean."

"Shuna's paws," Lachlan said. "Never heard of that before. I just learned something, I did."

Meriel snapped a few more pieces of crust from the plate. "Hey, there's a face on it."

Gareth gasped.

In the center was a visage of a boy in profile. The face was made of pearl, reflecting an iridescent sheen in Gareth's light globe. The boy's hair was wavy, cut short, and fashioned out of boulder opal, a rich brown flecked with blue and green. His eye was a single sapphire, perfectly round.

It was stunning. But its beauty wasn't what took Gareth's breath away.

"That's *him*," he said.

"Who?" Lachlan asked.

"Galdron III. The child emperor. That's his visage."

"Why is that a surprise?" Meriel said. "Like you said, this was his ship."

"Yes. But . . ." Gareth took the plate from her, staring in awe. "Every image of Galdron was lost in the First Civil War. He was so young that not many had been made yet. Just a couple of statues and a portrait. He hadn't even begun to mint coins. The only images of him we have are drawings made from the description of him in the h-histories. There's nothing like this anywhere else in the world."

"So," Meriel said slowly, "how much would this be worth?"

"There's no . . . it's . . . I wouldn't know how to set a value. It's priceless."

"And it's *Daphna's*," I reminded her. "Unless you have a pocket in that dress big enough to hold it."

"But . . . it's a dinner plate," Meriel said. "There's probably a whole set under that muck. Can't we keep just one?"

"This is not what we came for." I tilted my head toward Lachlan, who was happily snapping away more muck from the floor, trying to find another plate. "Remember?"

Meriel looked at him. "Oh . . . fine," she muttered. "I still think you're getting soft."

We kept searching the wreck. We found more artifacts: a platinum torc, a gilded proclamation of the *Silver Star* as Galdron's ship, and marble figurines of Fox and Bear. All this was great for Daphna. And terrible for us.

Because the Dragon's Teeth simply weren't here.

It wasn't just our own sight that missed it. I walked through the entire wreck with the Eye. For all the value we'd discovered, I didn't see any glow anywhere other than the mold and the few spikes of coral that had managed to infiltrate the ship.

"Nothing," I said, my own frustration echoing the Eye's. "How can there be nothing?"

"Maybe someone looted the ship already," Meriel said.

"Looters would have taken the valuables we found." It was clear no one else had set foot in here since the men at our feet had died. Besides . . . "What happened to the Blade of Heaven?"

Gareth looked up. "It's disappeared?"

"I can't see it anywhere." There was no chance I'd miss it. It was blazing bright, even underwater.

"Then maybe . . . I mean . . . there might be a hidden compartment somewhere."

Lachlan motioned toward the stern of the ship. "How 'bout over that way, guv?"

"Why that way?"

"Got air over there."

"There's air all around us, Lachlan," Meriel said.

"Nah, luv. This air's from the stone. That's different air that way, that is."

"Different?" Gareth said. "How?"

"Dunno." Lachlan looked confused. He smacked his lips, as if there was an odd taste in his mouth. "Something funny about it."

This had to be an effect of the primeval again. I checked the stain with the Eye, but it hadn't grown any further. It shifted around his soul, but smoothly, not agitated like before.

"Where exactly is this air?" I said.

"Dunno that, either. Just . . . over there." He motioned vaguely toward the stern of the ship again.

Puzzled, we made our way in that direction. At the end of the corridor, narrow steps led down into a cargo hold. The hold was mostly empty, just a few barrels of rotted food and soured wine, stinking of vinegar.

"We searched this room already," Meriel said.

I saw no Blade of Heaven here, either. "Lachlan, this air. Can you—"

"Cal," Gareth said.

He was staring at the back wall. The wood was covered with coral.

Not much coral had penetrated the ship, just a few spikes here and there. But this wall was absolutely thick with it. I remembered what Gareth had said earlier: Whatever strange thing was down here must have been what attracted all the life.

I looked the coral over. It glowed in the Eye, no different than the reef outside. Except its glow meant—

The Eye can't see past it, I thought.

There was a pile of baling hooks in the corner. Most of them had rusted away, but a few, trapped under hard green plaque, had been spared the ravages of the water. I snapped off the mold, then started hacking at the coral.

The others joined me; Meriel and Gareth with their own hooks, Foxtail and Lachlan with their weighted boots. Once again, Lachlan found what we were looking for. Kicking at the coral, his foot plunged through.

"Uh . . . a little help, eh?"

We pulled his leg free. Then Meriel and Foxtail smashed away the rest of the coral to reveal what was behind it.

We'd found a tunnel.

CHAPTER 34

THE TUNNEL WASN'T natural.

That was obvious from the shape of the walls. They were smooth, forming a near-perfect circle, angled downward into the earth. Gareth pointed something else out, too: At the tunnel's edge, the *Silver Star*'s hull had been driven into the dirt. Someone—or some*thing*—had blasted their way out of here.

Cautiously, we went down, the light globe illuminating our way. The passage began steep enough that we had to crouch as we descended, one hand on the dirt to keep us from slipping. Fortunately, there was none of that green slime. Despite the growth in the cargo hold, there was no coral here, either. Whatever had attracted life to this place, something had stopped it from growing into the tunnel.

Fifteen yards down, the tunnel changed. Earth gave way to rock, and the slope of the tunnel became less steep. Soon afterward, we came upon water. The passage descended into it, and no matter how hard we tried, our air stone simply couldn't shift the water away.

"That thing's still working, isn't it?" Meriel said nervously.

It had to be, otherwise we'd all have drowned. Gareth had a thought. "The stone doesn't . . . I mean . . . it doesn't turn water into air," he said. "It just pushes it out of the way. Maybe there's n-nowhere for this water to go."

Foxtail tapped her chest. *I'll check it out.*

Taking our second light globe, she waded into the water, dress swirling around her. When it reached her waist, she dove under. We watched the light globe move away until nothing reflected in the ripples. Then we waited.

It took less than a minute for her to return. Foxtail half emerged from the water, dress soaked and stuck to her body. She gestured at us until we understood.

There's air over there. It's just a short swim.

Meriel shrugged, then dove in. I went next.

Even with Foxtail's reassurance, there was something scary about diving underwater when you couldn't actually see where you were going to end up. Fortunately, she was right. The water was crystal clear, illuminated by the light globe she'd dropped at the bottom of the tunnel, and surprisingly warm. It was easy enough to reach the other air pocket, which wasn't even ten yards away. The passage curved upward, and I swam with it until I broke the surface.

Meriel gave me a hand up as the others followed. Gareth couldn't swim any better than Lachlan, so Foxtail brought each one over by simply grabbing on to them and kicking her legs. I'd never much liked swimming, myself—the only times I'd been underwater was fleeing through causeways and sewers with the Old Man, chased by irate Stickmen or murderous hired guards— but today, I was grateful the Old Man had taught me how.

Gareth clung to Foxtail for dear life as he emerged. She had to gently pull his fingers off her to go back for Lachlan. When the younger boy came through, he snorted water out of his nose, looked around, and cheerfully said, "Told you, guv."

There was indeed air here; Gareth had left our air stone on the other side. I smelled just the faintest bit of must, almost undetectable after the powdery scent of the mushrooms and the mold in the *Silver Star*. We wrung our clothes out and moved on.

The path curved upward until we finally entered a cavern. Unlike the tunnel, this cavern had formed naturally; its walls were craggy and unshaped.

And there we saw: we weren't the first to discover it.

CHAPTER 35

A SKELETON LAY against the far wall.

Its bones were wrapped in a tattered robe. Silver glinted in the light of our globe: a ring around one of the fingers. The other hand—what was left of it—rested on a book.

"That's him," Gareth said in awe. "Veran IX. The Childkiller."

The old High Weaver. We stared at the bones.

Why was he all the way down here? And if this was really Veran...

"Where're the swords?" Lachlan said. "Didn't he snaffle 'em?"

I couldn't see the Dragon's Teeth anywhere. Yet there was no question this was the place. Because when I looked with the Eye, I could see the Blade of Heaven. It pierced the roof of the cavern, glowing white. The tip of the Blade aimed straight at the book under Veran's bony hand.

And that wasn't the only thing I saw. Also under the Blade of Heaven was the ghostly figure of an animal. It was strange, and yet familiar; I had the surest sense I'd seen it somewhere before. Translucent, glowing a shade of soft gold, it lay curled, as if asleep, right where the book was. If it had been solid, the tome would have been inside it.

Surrounding the animal were sparkling ribbons of light, looping around and around, forever in motion. Strange glyphs spiraled around those ribbons, weaving a dance of beauty unmatched.

And suddenly, my right middle finger grew warm.

My ring.

My crystal ring. It was heating up.

I looked at my hand. In my Eye-vision, the ring still gave off no glow; there was no hint of an enchantment. But the ring grew warmer nonetheless, hot enough now to be uncomfortable against my skin.

Yet that wasn't the only thing I felt. As I turned the Eye back to that ghostly shape, uncontrollable rage welled inside me. How could this wretched creature be here? Where had it taken the Dragon's Teeth? How could it interfere with my plans?

Fury drove all other thoughts from my mind. I stormed toward the figure, raging. I would tear it to pieces. I would gut it with my own two hands. I would feel what tiny shred remained of its life gush over my fingers, warm and wet. I would drink its blood—

Something touched me. A tiny speck of a creature grabbed my arm.

Who? Who dared to try and stop me? I roared and swatted them away.

Then I was falling. Some monster bound me in ropes of iron, and I couldn't break free. let me go, I screamed at them. let me go let me go I'll kill every last one of you

I hit the ground hard. My chin smacked against the stone, jarring my mind. My thoughts were a jumble of hatred and rage

(I'll kill you I'll kill you all)

until a hand pulled the patch down to cover the Eye. Then my rage faded, boiling away like steam.

I was lying facedown on the floor of the cavern. Confused, jaw aching, I was bound by strong hands, holding me still.

I smelled the faintest hint of jasmine. Meriel had me.

I groaned. "You can let go now."

She released me. I rolled over, pressing my hand to my chin. It was bleeding where I'd smacked it against the ground.

Meriel crouched next to me, wary. Foxtail stood behind her. I'd made it halfway across the cavern before they'd hauled me down. Lachlan was on the ground, too. He rubbed his cheek as Gareth helped him up.

"You want to tell us what that was about?" Meriel said, and not kindly.

Foxtail put a calming hand on her arm. I lay there, trying to stop shaking. The last hint of the rage I'd felt swirled deep in my mind, then vanished with that same stifled frustration as always.

"The Eye." I propped myself up, still trembling. "It was the Eye. I've never felt such ... *hatred*."

It was the only word for it, and even that didn't match the depth of its fury, the visceral rage that had swelled from wherever the artifact lived in my mind. I still hadn't heard the thing's voice, exactly. It was more a tidal wave of feeling that had overwhelmed me.

The girls helped me up. Lachlan was checking to see he still had all his teeth. It was then that I realized it wasn't just my chin that hurt. My knuckles hurt, too. I had a vague memory of striking out at something.

"Did I do that?" I said.

Lachlan nodded. "A right proper hit, guv. Smack in the jaw, it was."

He didn't seem too upset about it. But I was. "I'm so sorry. I didn't mean . . ."

Lachlan waved off my apology. "Aw, don't worry none. Wasn't you inside, eh?"

It wasn't, not really. Foxtail, it seemed, had recognized what was happening and covered the Eye with my patch. But I still felt terrible about it.

Gareth was looking at me quizzically, a question on his lips. *What did the Eye see?*

I told them as much as I could, feeling foolish. "The Blade of Heaven is here. It's pointing at that book under Veran's hand."

Gareth glanced over at it. It was taking everything in him, I could tell, not to rush over and open it, to unlock its secrets.

"There's something else here, too," I continued, and I shifted my ring on my finger. The crystal remained uncomfortably hot. "I don't know how to describe it. It's like it's there . . . but *not* there. Like a ghost. That's what set off the Eye. When it saw that . . . creature. The Eye hates it. With a brutal, burning hatred. That's when I lost control."

"What did this creature look like?" Meriel said warily. She'd had more than her fill of undersea monsters today.

"Well . . . you're going to think this is crazy," I said. "But it looked like a sheep."

"A *sheep?*"

I spread my hands. "I know how that sounds. But it was a

sheep, I swear. It had ribbons of light all around it. The thing is . . . I'm sure I've seen that sheep before."

Meriel looked at me like I'd lost my mind. "You know sheep now?"

"Do you remember that painting in Mr. Solomon's gallery?" I said. "The scene of Fox and Bear by the pond? There were two other animals with them. One was a crow. The other was—"

Gareth stiffened. "A sheep," he said.

"Right. It was curled up, sleeping by the trees behind Fox and Bear. The thing is, when I saw that painting—just like when the Eye saw the figure here in the cavern—I had the strangest feeling about it. That sheep wasn't asleep. It was—"

"Dead," Gareth whispered.

I shivered. None of the others seemed to know what we were talking about. But the fact that Gareth had had the same thought when he saw that painting gave me a chill, and I wasn't sure why.

"So," Meriel said slowly, "that book is being guarded by an invisible dead sheep?"

"Like I said, I know how it sounds. But it's true."

"Shuna's snout," Lachlan said. "What're we supposed to do, then? Just leave it there?"

"We can't," I said. "I don't know why the Blade of Heaven is pointing to the book instead of the Dragon's Teeth. But that book is why we were brought here."

"Sure, guv, but if it's going to make you lose yer marbles again . . ."

I'd have to keep the patch on. I'd rather use the Eye to be able to spot any danger, but after what had happened, I couldn't take the risk. The Eye's hatred had been all-consuming. I never wanted to feel that way again.

And yet despite the Eye's feelings, I didn't get the sense the sheep would be dangerous. For that brief moment, when I'd seen the creature with my own mind, before the Eye had taken over, I hadn't been scared at all. If anything, I'd felt a sense of . . . peace.

I moved to take the book. Meriel stopped me, the back of her hand against my chest. "Maybe I should do this one," she said.

Cautious, she stepped forward. She looked back at us, as if to reassure herself we were still there, then stood over the book, hesitating.

She waited.

Nothing happened.

Finally, she said, "Oh, this is ridiculous," and she reached down to take the book. She touched it.

And the air in the cavern changed.

Something seemed to grow in the cave. A *presence* swelled to fill the whole space.

But this one didn't make me afraid. The presence washed over me

and suddenly I was wrapped in a soft, welcoming heat, the warmth of a crackling hearth. I smelled freshly baked bread, the sweet scent of cinnamon and honey. And though I'd never really known one, a word thrummed through my soul.

Home

it said.

The presence flitted among us. The crystal ring burned my finger as ghostly tendrils brushed against my skin, then moved on. I got the strangest sensation that the presence was touching our hearts, weighing them, measuring what was inside.

Then it hovered over me, over us all. And a voice spoke in my head, motherly, gentle, and kind.

Your path will be painful, child, it said. *I wish I could walk it with you. But my time is done. Take my blessing, and know that you are loved.*

Then it was gone.

CHAPTER 36

I CLUNG TO that feeling as long as I could.

I shut my eyes, trying to imprint every detail in my memory. I stood there, desperate to hold on to it, until the warmth inside finally faded.

The burn of my crystal ring faded as it went. I looked at my hand and saw the skin underneath the ring was red, flushed with the heat it had given off.

When I looked up at the others, I knew they'd felt the same presence, heard her words. Meriel stood trembling, eyes wide and red, vulnerable, like a little girl. Foxtail was on her knees, head bowed, palms pressed against her chest. Gareth's face was in his hands. Lachlan wept openly, tears streaming down his cheeks.

"What was that?" he sniffled. "Was it... Shuna?"

"No," I said, and I looked over at Gareth, remembering his question to Professor Whelan. "But I think it was something like her."

None of us wanted to move, as if doing so would break the connection to what we'd felt. But we couldn't stay there forever. Eventually, Meriel kneeled beside the book, reaching out hesitantly this time. When she touched the leather, she let her hand linger, hoping the presence would return.

But it really was gone for good. Meriel sighed, then slid the book from under Veran's bones. She opened it.

And frowned.

"What's the matter?" I said.

"It's gibberish."

We crowded around to see as she flicked through the book. Each page had an entry on it, written in a strange scrawl, some alien language, the words totally unfamiliar. At the top left of every page was a sequence of numbers. Dates, I guessed, which would make this book some kind of record.

"It's not gibberish," Gareth said, excited. He took the book from Meriel. "This is the Old Tongue."

Right. Veran had lived two thousand years ago. Of course he didn't speak our language.

"Can you read it?" Lachlan said, peering at the strange scrawl.

Gareth nodded, running his fingers over the pages with reverence. He translated the beginning of a small paragraph written just inside the front cover.

> To you who has found this:
>
> This is my journal. I am Veran IX, High Weaver, and I murdered my emperor, the child, Galdron III.

I'd guessed the book was a record of sorts. It was still stunning to hear the words.

"Veran stole the Dragon's Teeth," Meriel said, confused. "Why would he keep a journal of what he'd done?"

"He answers your question," Gareth said, and that made her eyes widen. He read on.

I can only imagine what you have heard about me. I knew the actions I took would cast me as a monster. Perhaps I actually am that monster.

I leave this record for you to decide. In it you will find the truth of what happened. I accept whatever judgment you make, but I hope you will find it in your heart to forgive me.

Gareth turned the pages slowly, reading.

"Well?" Meriel said impatiently. "What does it say?"

"He's just . . . I mean . . . it's mostly about him becoming High Weaver. There's nothing about . . ."

Gareth stopped. He blinked a couple times, then translated the passage.

Of all the duties of the High Weaver, tutoring the emperor is the one I dread the most. What do I know of children? Perhaps I could pass it off to an apprentice. Call it training . . .

No, that would be an insult to His Imperial Majesty. I will do my best, Artha spare me.

Gareth turned a few pages, then stopped.

I have never been so wrong about anyone. Before I met young Galdron, I expected him to be a copy of his father: foolish, lazy, and cruel. Instead, I found him to be a gentle boy with a sweet disposition, and remarkably intelligent.

Yet there is steel in him, too. With the aid of the loyal

General Heath, our young emperor has managed to stall the budding rebellion of the various factions that had jockeyed for power under his father. It is almost impossible to believe this boy is Ciaran IV's son. Perhaps our lessons will not be a waste of time after all.

Gareth continued turning pages, skimming the entries. "There's a lot about Galdron's tutoring..." He trailed off, frowning.

"What is it?" I said.

He read a new passage.

I never would have imagined it, but my lessons with Galdron have become the highlight of my week. This child is a genius, his intellect keener than even my closest colleagues. Though only nine years old, Galdron has an intuitive grasp of nearly every subject I introduce. It is a shame our emperors are forbidden from studying enchantments. He might well have turned out to be the greatest Weaver in our order's history.

As it stands, I have little doubt that, in the future, he will make his mark as our greatest emperor. Yet he still retains such childlike innocence. His favorite subject remains Fox and Bear, and he pleads with me every lesson for a story. I am slightly embarrassed to admit that I always read him one, and as he leans into me, listening, I find myself wishing he was my son.

Lachlan frowned. "I know I ain't the cleverest," he said, "but that old storyteller said this Veran bloke was scheming for the throne, weren't he? This don't sound like a man who hates the emperor none."

It didn't, not in the slightest. So what happened?

Gareth turned more pages, then read a new passage.

> Something is wrong with Galdron. He has always looked forward to our lessons, but recently, he has been tired, sluggish. I have asked him what is wrong. He tells me it is nothing. I do not press him further, but I am worried. I will ask the physicks to examine him.

The next page:

> Galdron finally broke down and told me what has been troubling him. He has been having nightmares. I asked him what he dreams about, but he says he cannot remember. Only that he wakes up every night in nameless terror. The poor child is now frightened to go to sleep.
>
> Are these merely nightmares or something worse? Two months ago, I taught Galdron the nature of Shadow, and how it may be used to communicate with greater beings like the Spirits. I told him little more than this, surely not enough to allow him to explore that realm and unlock its secrets.
>
> But now I wonder. The boy is almost too clever. Did he begin to research Shadow on his own? He says no, but he seems ashamed of himself, so I am not sure I believe him.

Shadow, I thought. Bragan had mentioned it back on his farm. In fact, he'd said almost the same thing about Shadow and dreams.

Gareth continued reading.

> My business kept me late, so I spent the night in the palace. I awoke at two with a terrible feeling of dread I could not shake. I rose and paced the halls, hoping to tire myself enough to return to sleep.
>
> It was not long before I came upon the throne room. No one should have been in there at this hour, but I spotted light from a torch. Investigating, I found Galdron standing by the throne.
>
> He was in his nightclothes. He stood with his back to me, facing the rear wall. At first I thought he was looking at the Great Sun Seal, but when I approached, I saw his gaze was aimed beside it, upon a space entirely blank.
>
> He remained there, unmoving, long enough that I began to feel frightened. I called to him. He turned and looked surprised to see me. When I asked him what he was doing, he had no answer.
>
> I took him back to his room and saw him safely tucked into bed. Then I admonished his guards. There are still rumblings of rebellion. How could they have let the emperor wander the halls alone? They swore to Artha and Shuna both that His Imperial Majesty had never walked by them.
>
> I have heard talk of a secret passage the first emperor, Aeric, had built to allow him to leave his quarters without

anyone knowing. Perhaps that is how Galdron got out. In truth, that bothers me less than his strange behavior.

What was he looking at?

The next entry:

I remained at the palace for one more night, without telling Galdron I was staying. I did not try to sleep this time. Instead, I waited in the throne room, hiding behind one of the pillars.

Much of the night passed uneventfully, enough that I began to think I was being foolish. But then around two o'clock, as the night before, Galdron came in alone, torch in hand.

He walked to the same place he had the night previous. Once again, he stared up at the blank wall. But this time, he began to speak.

"Yes," he said. Then, "Yes . . . I am . . . I will."

Fear gripped me. He wasn't just speaking. He was listening to someone.

I didn't understand what was happening. But I couldn't let it continue. I stepped from the shadows and called his name. "Galdron!"

He turned. This time, he didn't seem surprised at my appearance. "Hello, Master."

"Who are you talking to?" I said.

He smiled. "Artha."

Surely he was dreaming. Sleepwalking.

"Now that she and Shuna are enemies," he continued, "the Bear needs a friend."

I played along, trying to understand. "What does she need a friend for?"

"She wants me to take up the Dragon's Teeth."

My veins turned to ice. But before I could ask him anything more, he walked away.

Gareth turned the page.

I spent the rest of that night and all day researching what I could. I began to wonder if Galdron really had spoken to Artha. There is an idol made of gold in the palace treasure room, deep underground. Legends claim that the idol has a direct connection to Artha—that it can, given the right conditions, actually summon the Bear.

I set my apprentices immediately to finding what they could about that idol, but none of them could discover what the means of using it was. All we learned for certain was that the idol had been placed there by Aeric, brought back from one of his conquests, and since then had never moved—in fact, it apparently couldn't be moved anymore. Beyond that, all our records said was that the statue remained impervious to all testing.

Could Galdron have stumbled upon a way to use it? Perhaps previous Weavers had failed because it only responded to blood of Aeric's line. Either way, what worried me more was the idea that His Imperial Majesty would take up the Dragon's Teeth.

While my apprentices searched for information on the idol, I learned more of those cursed blades. No one has used them—in fact, no one has even touched them—since Aeric laid them in the treasure room a thousand years ago.

But from what I read, they are unquestionably artifacts of ancient power. One blade, which Aeric called Camuloth, appears to be a siphon, capable of draining any magical energy from any source. The other blade, Belenoth, is a transmuter, capable of reshaping that energy into any form the wielder wishes.

Yet the fact that Aeric locked the blades away, decreeing that no one, not even another emperor, should ever touch them on pain of death, makes me believe there is something far more sinister about them. In fact, they remind me of that other Dragon artifact, the Eye, which remains bound in the cavern below the Enclave. As High Weaver, only I have the right to enter the Eye's cave. I did it once, but I felt such malevolence from the Eye that I swore I would never look upon it again.

So what do I know for certain? Only this: Galdron is not dreaming. Someone, or something, whether Artha or something pretending to be the Bear, is speaking to him. And it wants Galdron to take up those blades. This must be prevented, no matter the cost.

The next entry:

I found Galdron in the treasure room.

He was standing before the sealed chest which confines

Aeric's swords, speaking to some unseen figure. This time I did not wait to challenge him.

My voice did not wake him as before. Instead, he looked at me coldly, like I was an enemy. I asked what he was going to do.

"I will wage a war of destruction," he said, "so all who oppose us are annihilated. Forever."

"You are the emperor," I said. "You already rule this world. None oppose you."

He smiled. And then I knew not to whom I was speaking, because behind that smile was not the boy Galdron. There was something else.

"You are nothing," it said. And Galdron left the room.

I do not know what to do. I cannot tell anyone what is happening. Any sign of His Imperial Majesty being unfit will tip the empire into civil war. Even loyal subjects like General Heath cannot be told. If Galdron violates the law by touching Aeric's swords, Heath will have to do his duty. Galdron will be executed.

Artha, if it is really you behind this, I beg you, release this boy from your will. Or you will tear Ayreth apart.

Gareth reached the final entry in the journal. The words here were damaged by tears that had splashed onto the page. Veran IX, High Weaver, had been crying.

I killed him.

I didn't mean to do it. I spent all day trying to find some binding that would release Galdron from whatever being had a hold on him. My only hope was to appeal to the child within and get him to listen to me. I was certain that if I could do that, I could reach him.

I miscalculated badly. When I went down to the treasure room to wait for Galdron, he was already there. He'd broken the seals on the chest and taken up Aeric's blades. By that action, Galdron's death sentence had been signed.

Yet I would have told no one if I could have stopped him. I begged him to put the swords down, to remember me. To remember himself.

Instead, he advanced on me. I released a binding of air to push him away from me, just as a defense. But he was so small. He stumbled—he hit his head—

By Artha, what have I done?

There was a break in the page here, the ink smeared. When Veran had composed himself again, he continued.

My sentence is death now, too. It makes no difference that Galdron took up the Dragon's Teeth. I have killed my emperor. For that, I deserve to die.

I decided to do one last thing for the child. I would not let his name be stained by his actions. Instead, I would take the blame for stealing the blades. Let everyone believe that I was the one who broke the seal, then killed Galdron when he begged me to stop.

As I made that decision, my path became clear. I could not let Aeric's swords fall into the wrong hands. Something wanted them back in the world. Whether that was Artha or something evil, I do not know. Regardless, I intend to spoil its plans.

I did not bother to leave a note of confession with the body. My fleeing with the blades will tell the story well enough. I hurried down to the docks, carrying the swords in their scabbards. When I was certain others on the wharf could hear me, I told the captain of the Silver Star that His Imperial Majesty had commanded him to carry me across the lake to Redfairne.

The captain did not question my orders. He simply set sail. I suspect it did not take much longer for the alarm to be raised, and my path tracked. No doubt there were ships sent after us before we'd even reached halfway across Lake Galway.

It is imperative that they do not find me. More important, whatever happens, they must not find the Dragon's Teeth. So I never let the Silver Star reach its destination.

A few miles from Redfairne, I forced all the sailors belowdecks. Then I went down to the cargo hold and blew a hole in the bottom.

The ship sank instantly. My magic saved me, held me safe within a bubble of air. It could not save the others. Add their deaths to my ledger. I, and I alone, am to blame.

When the Silver Star finally hit bottom, I was able to sense something odd below: a cavern, a pocket of air trapped within. With the last of my enchantments, I bored a tunnel through the lake floor until I discovered that cavern. I wonder what created it. A Spirit, perhaps, who wished me to finish my story.

So here I die. Let the powers above scour the world for Aeric's blades, the tools that may bring about the world's destruction. They will follow my trail to Redfairne and beyond, searching.

They will never find them. For the Dragon's Teeth, and the evil behind them, shall die with me in this cavern.

CHAPTER 37

MERIEL STIRRED, AS if waking from a dream. "That's it?"

Gareth flicked through the last few pages. They were all blank. "That's the final entry."

Lachlan looked around, confused. "Then where're the blades?"

Good question. Because there was nothing else here. We looked everywhere, in every nook and cranny in the rock, but there was nothing to be found.

"Could Veran have left them in the *Silver Star*?" Meriel said.

"That's not what he wrote in his journal," I said. "Anyway, we searched that whole ship. The Dragon's Teeth weren't there."

"Is it possible someone beat us to them? Already took the swords?"

If they did, then we were lost. We'd have no way of tracking whoever took them—which could have happened anytime over the last two thousand years.

I had to hope Veran had hidden the blades instead. But our search had already turned up nothing. Unless . . .

"What if he used an enchantment to hide them?" I said.

Gareth considered it. "He might have. The cavern . . . I mean . . . maybe the rocks are some sort of illusion."

I was scared to use the Eye again down here. Still, what else were we to do? "I'm going to take a look."

Meriel and Foxtail stepped close, watching.

"Please don't hit me unless I go crazy," I said.

"How will we be able to tell the difference?" Meriel said inno-cently.

I inched the patch up, just enough to peek under it. Then I looked around the cavern.

I saw nothing—at least, nothing new. The Blade of Heaven was still there, pointing to Veran's journal in Gareth's hands. But other than our own glows, there was no light anywhere that might reveal a hidden passage, or any sort of enchantment still working. Even the ring on Veran's skeleton had lost whatever magical energy it had once contained.

You're missing something, boy, the Old Man said.

What else is new? I sighed. *I don't know where to look.*

You don't need to look. You've already seen it.

Seen what? There's nothing here but the Blade of Heaven.

The girl's right, the Old Man said. *You're getting soft.*

I frowned. *What's that supposed to mean?*

The Old Man didn't answer.

Seriously, though, why would he say I was getting soft? That was Meriel's line for me every time I didn't act like the thief he'd trained me to be. What did that have to do with anything now?

Unless the Old Man meant . . . I *should* be acting like a thief?

I mulled that over, but it didn't make sense. What was there to snaffle down here? We'd come to loot the Dragon's Teeth, but they were gone.

And then I had a vision of the Old Man. He was puffing on

his pipe, looking at me with that sardonic expression of his, one eyebrow raised.

Isn't that the point? he said.

That the Teeth aren't here? I said, confused.

But as I thought about it, a new question entered my mind.

Why *weren't* the Teeth here? Veran had taken them with him. He'd said so, right in his journal. In fact, he'd made a whole show of it, making sure everyone at the dock saw him carrying a pair of swords before getting on the—

Oh.

Oh.

The Old Man winked.

I turned to the others. "It's a *gaff.*"

"What is?" Meriel said.

"Veran. His story about the Dragon's Teeth. It's a gaff. He's playing us. Just like he played everyone else two thousand years ago."

"Shuna's paws," Lachlan said. "You mean everything in that whole book's a lie?"

"Not all of it," I said. "The part about Galdron hearing voices, losing his mind, taking the swords? That I believe. That Veran killed Galdron to stop him waging a war of destruction across Ayreth, and that he was heartbroken about it? I believe that, too. No, it's his story about the *Teeth* that's false."

I paced around the cave. "Look what Veran does after Galdron's death," I said. "The seal on the chest is already broken, so he can't just put the Dragon's Teeth back. What's more, he doesn't *want* to. Regardless of who that voice Galdron heard was"—and at this point, I think I had a pretty good idea of who, or rather, *what* was speaking to the boy—"Veran doesn't want the swords to fall into anyone else's hands."

"So what does he do?" I said. "He goes down to the docks *and makes sure everyone sees him carrying two swords.* Then he commands the captain of the *Silver Star*—again, in front of everyone—to take him to Redfairne. When he scuttles the ship, he eliminates the only witnesses who might know where the Dragon's Teeth have gone. If anyone chases Veran to Redfairne, they'll never pick up his trail—not there, not anywhere—because there's no trail to pick up. People will search, but they'll never find him. The Dragon's Teeth will stay lost forever.

"And that's the whole point," I said. "Veran *wanted* everyone to think he had the swords, so when he disappeared, everyone would assume the swords were lost, too. *But he never took the Dragon's Teeth. He only made it look like he did.*

"That's the gaff," I said. "The swords everyone saw him carrying were fakes. He hid Aeric's real blades somewhere else."

I looked down at what remained of Veran. *You sly old fox.*

"How do you know this for sure?" Meriel said.

"Because if he'd had the Dragon's Teeth with him, then they'd be here, next to his bones. Or somewhere on the ship. A gaff is the only answer that makes sense."

"Then where are they?"

"No idea. But the answer is somewhere in that book." I motioned toward Veran's journal.

"How do you know?" Gareth said.

"Because the Blade of Heaven is still pointing to it."

"Couldn't that be part of Veran's gaff?" Meriel said.

"No," I said, *"because Veran didn't create the Blade of Heaven.* He didn't want the Dragon's Teeth to be found, remember? Why would he create a beacon to where he hid himself? He wouldn't. It's not his enchantment."

"Whose is it?" Gareth asked, wide-eyed.

"I think it was made by the . . . being . . . that was waiting here for us when we arrived." For whatever reason, it wanted us to find the swords. And I didn't think we wanted to let it down.

Foxtail spread her hands. *So what do we do?*

"Run through the journal again, Gareth," I said. "This time, I'll look with the Eye."

We all huddled around Gareth as he began to turn the pages. Since I couldn't actually read the thing, I just watched for anything that stood out with the light of enchantment: a page, a paragraph, a sentence, a word. Something.

But as he flipped through the book, I saw nothing at all. The closer he got to the end, the more flustered I became. Had I got it wrong?

Finally, Gareth reached the last entry.

Nothing.

"It has to be here," I said, heart sinking. "What about the last few pages?"

"They're blank," Gareth said, turning them over. He got to the final page, then began to close the cover.

I slammed my hand down to stop him.

A glow.

There was a glow on the very last page. It was the same bright white as the Blade of Heaven. And as I stared at it, I began to see this glow wasn't shapeless. There were letters.

Words.

I couldn't understand them. I told the others. "What do they say?" Gareth asked.

"I'll have to spell it," I said. I read them off, one by one, until I'd got them all.

ceyrdis thusann?

Gareth looked pensive.

"What's it mean?" Lachlan asked him.

" 'What are you?' " he said.

"Don't you mean '*who* are you?' " Meriel said.

Gareth shook his head. "It says 'what.' "

"That doesn't make any sense."

Except it must have. Because as Gareth translated, the words responded. I watched through the Eye as the letters shifted, changing so I could understand.

what are you?

And as I stared at that glowing script, I suddenly remembered what the Eye had called me, back in the cave where I'd found it. I'd asked it a question. *Why do you keep calling me that?*

And the Eye had answered: it is what you are.

"A foxchild," I said, surprised. "I'm a foxchild."

Suddenly, the words flared. They burned a brighter white, then vanished.

And new words appeared, one by one, on the page. They didn't glow, and they weren't enchanted. They just appeared, written in the same decaying ink as the rest of the journal, as if being written before our eyes.

Gareth nearly dropped the book in surprise. He stared alongside us as Veran's handwriting filled the page.

And then it was done. I couldn't read these words; they were in the Old Tongue, the same as the rest of the journal. Veran had scratched them down, then something—the same presence, I thought, that had created the Blade of Heaven—hid them with its own magic. Until someone arrived with the Eye to reveal it.

Gareth waited until he was certain there were no more words to come. Then he read us Veran's final secret.

I had a dream.

I have been dying here, dying of starvation, for so long. At first, I thought I was hallucinating. But when I woke, I felt better than I had in a long, long time. The dream was real. And in it, I visited Shadow.

There I stood on the edge of a cliff. I wanted to jump, to end it all. A voice stopped me.

I turned to see who it was. It was an animal. A sheep.

"Tell your secret," she said.

"Everything I've done," I said, "has been to hide the truth. I can't let it get out."

"And yet there will be a time," the sheep said, "when the truth must be revealed. Or something worse than what you fear shall come to pass."

I had no plans to change my mind. But this being looked upon me with such love, such warmth, that I knew her words to be true. So I trusted her. And now, whoever you are, I am trusting you.

My escape with Aeric's swords was but a ruse. I never removed the blades. Instead, I placed the Dragon's Teeth in a secret chamber, hidden behind the immovable idol of Artha. Then I bound that chamber with the strongest, most deceptive enchantment I know. This magic hides itself from all scrying, so no one will ever stumble upon it by accident.

The binding can only be released by a keyword. In my despair, I chose it to honor Galdron, whom I murdered. My emperor, the boy who I wished was my son.

The keyword is: beloved. Understand, you who read this, the power those swords can wield. If you take them up, I pray you wield them well.

These are the last words of Veran IX, High Weaver.

Meriel looked at me, amazed. "You were right."

"One of these days," I said, annoyed, "one of you will remember: gaffs are my job."

"Shuna's snout. Crackers and jam, this is," Lachlan said, excited. "All we got to do now is steal them swords. Always wanted to break into the emperor's palace."

"They're not in the emperor's palace," Gareth said suddenly.

"But that's what this Weaver guy said. Weren't it?"

I thought so, too. But Gareth pointed out, "Veran IX died two thousand years ago."

"We know," Meriel said. "So?"

"The palace isn't . . . I mean . . . the palace isn't the p-palace anymore. Half of it was burned during the First Civil War. When the war ended, and the new emperor took the throne, they built a new palace on Bearslook Hill, opposite Bolcanathair."

"What happened to the old palace?" Lachlan said.

"It was rebuilt," Gareth said. "I mean . . . the part that burned down was. The new occupants built it in a different style, one that would serve them. They're still there today."

I didn't like where this was going. "And these new occupants . . . ?"

"Are the Weavers." Gareth looked at me in surprise. "The old palace became their new guild hall. The Dragon's Teeth are in the basement of the Enchanters' Enclave."

CHAPTER 38

DAPHNA COULDN'T BELIEVE it.

With nothing remaining for us in the cavern, we'd left Veran's bones to rest in peace and exited the wreck of the *Silver Star*. The walk back to the diving bell was eerily quiet. All the fish had disappeared, leaving only the coral reef underneath. The magic that had attracted the life to that cave was well and truly gone.

The air stone Lachlan had enchanted, however, showed no signs of dimming. Once we were safe in the diving bell, Foxtail took the stone and dropped it far from the wreck, so no one would find it, before the bell carried us up to the surface. The primeval had infused the stone so strongly, it would have prompted some uncomfortable questions if we brought it back.

Now Daphna stood with us on the deck of the *Bashful Turtle*, staring with naked greed at the visage of Galdron III. She gripped the electrum plate tight, as if she was afraid the rocking of the boat would make her stumble and lose the thing over the side.

"My dearest, dearest Cal," she said, laughing breathlessly. "I thought you were mad." She cupped my cheek affectionately. "I still rather do. Are there more of these down there?"

"I'm sure of it," I said. I told her about the dining cabin we'd stumbled upon and the crusty green muck. "Lots of other things, too. And it's all yours."

"How did you survive?"

"What do you mean?"

"We saw the explosion," she said. "There was a flash of light from below, then a giant bubble burst the water at the surface. Captain Trallam was sure you were all dead."

"Oh, that," I said casually. "That was us feeding air stones to a shark."

"A shark!" She laughed with delight. "Sweet Cal. See how good a team we make? I trust you'll bring all your jobs to me from now on."

"I'm glad you said that. Because this one's not quite finished."

She glanced at the others, who were wringing out their clothes farther aft. "Yes, I didn't notice any swords when you returned. No luck?"

"Some luck," I said. Along with the few silver insignia of the Emperor's Guard we'd snaffled, I'd thought it wise to hide Veran's journal before we returned to the surface. Since the final page revealed the location of the Dragon's Teeth—and how to get them—I was sure if Daphna discovered it, she'd try to cheat me and go for the swords herself. So we'd bound the journal firmly to keep it watertight, then strapped it to the inside of Foxtail's leg, under her dress.

"We didn't find the swords," I said, "but we did find where they're hidden." Let Daphna guess how we'd discovered that. "We'll need your help getting inside."

"Anything. Where do we go?"

"Carlow. The Weaver Enclave."

Daphna blinked. Then she laughed. "That's funny. The Weaver..." She trailed off. "You can't be serious."

I shrugged. "I go where the loot is."

"You *are* mad. Even the Old Man knew better than to provoke the Weavers."

"Yeah, well, he's not here. I understand it won't be easy getting in—"

"Oh, you have it wrong, Cal. It'll be the easiest thing in the world getting you in. The problem will be getting you *out*. Do you have any idea what they'll do to you when they catch you?"

I remembered the horrors I'd seen and heard in Darragh's laboratory. Groaning voices, helpless creatures—or maybe they'd once been people—twisted by magic into monsters, living nightmares. I had to force myself to sound unconcerned. "I've seen Weaver experiments before."

That made Daphna pause. "Where would you have seen those?"

Oops. I shouldn't have said that. Daphna wasn't wrong about the Old Man. He'd kept us far, far away from the Weavers.

I did my best to cover my mistake. "The Old Man broke the rules when it suited him," I said, which was true. Just not about this. "I've been in a Weaver's home before."

"The Enclave isn't a *home*. It's a compound full of enchanters who will gladly turn your entrails into jingle strings. Where exactly are the Dragon's Teeth being kept, anyway? And why don't the Weavers already know about them?"

This was the tricky part. Still worried about Daphna cheating us, I didn't want to say more than I had to about where the swords were hidden. Frankly, I didn't want to say *anything*. But if we were going to pull this job, we needed to know as much as we could about the Enclave. And no one but Daphna would tell us.

I had to take the risk. "The Weavers don't know about it," I said, "because they were hidden a long time ago by one of their own. We have to get into the old palace treasure room."

I'd never seen Daphna dumbfounded before. "The ... the treasure ... this *is* a joke. You're having me on."

I didn't answer that.

"You foolish boy," she said. "The old treasure room is where the Weavers keep their most dangerous artifacts."

I shrugged again, trying to project an air of confidence. "Like I said, I go where the loot is."

"Cal. There are wards, glyphs, alarms."

"Then you'll have to find me whatever tools we'll need to break them."

She stared at me. I watched her carefully, looking for any sign I could exploit.

The biggest sign you'll see, the Old Man had once taught me, *is sometimes no sign at all.*

I knew just what he'd meant. What I was proposing was insane. So why wasn't Daphna refusing outright?

She owed me nothing. The haul from the *Silver Star* would make anyone not only famous, but fabulously wealthy—and she was already wealthy enough. She could easily say no.

She hadn't. Which meant she was actually considering helping me. And the only reason to do that would be . . .

"You must want something," I said smoothly. "Something the Weavers have. Something you can't wheedle from them, can't buy at any price. Help us crack the Enclave treasure room, and we'll steal it for you."

She studied me, still silent.

"Look what we found already," I said, pointing to the electrum plate. "No one's seen anything like it in two thousand years. It doesn't exist anywhere else in the empire."

She stared at Galdron's visage, her mind working.

"And remember who taught me," I said. "There was nothing the Old Man couldn't snaffle. I can do this. *We* can do this."

She hesitated. "If you get caught . . ." she said quietly.

"They'll never know you were behind it. We don't turn nose. Not one of us."

She laughed without humor. "You may not have a choice."

The tone of her voice was saying *no*. But the glint of desire was blazing again in her eyes. There *was* something she wanted in the Enclave. Something she'd never get otherwise. And the Old Man really had taught me well.

Need, greed, and speed. I already knew her answer.

She was in.

CHAPTER 39

IF THERE WAS one thing we all agreed on, it was that we weren't going to be staying in Carlow.

Instead, the *Bashful Turtle* dropped us off at Quarry's Point, a village on the coast of Lake Galway, eight miles south of the city. The town was too small to have a proper dock that could accommodate a brig the *Turtle*'s size, so we had to disembark by rowboat. Captain Trallam was glad to see the last of us, I think, though he remained unfailingly polite to the end.

Since Quarry's Point was a waystop on the road to Carlow, there were several inns available. We chose the most remote, the Blue Boar, at the edge of the village proper, by the woods. The villagers were friendly people, used to travelers passing through on their way to the imperial city, so I engaged a few in conversation down in the tavern.

They told me things had cooled in Carlow since we'd fled. Lava no longer flowed from the side of Bolcanathair, and the volcano had stopped smoking. The air still felt thick with it, and it had turned the morning sky a brilliant orange, like after Bolcanoig's eruption a month ago in the east, but the ash that had fallen had largely been swept away by either street cleaners or the wind. The general feeling was that the volcano was no longer going to blow.

As for the Stickmen, now that fewer people were trying to flee the city, the lockdown had been eased. They were still inspecting travelers exiting the gates, and patrols were heavier than usual, but we shouldn't have any trouble getting in.

That was good to hear. Still, there was no point in pressing our luck. Since Daphna would handle all the legwork for this job, the five of us decided to remain in Quarry's Point while she visited her contacts in Carlow.

"This might take a while," she warned me, speaking privately in my room. "I can't risk alarming anyone. I'll have to dance around what you really want to do."

I supposed it was the best we could hope for. Still, after Daphna was gone, Meriel stood in my doorway, hands on her hips.

I sighed. "Did you want something, Meriel? Or are you posing for a statue?"

"I don't trust her," Meriel said.

"I don't either."

"We're walking into the heart of our enemies, and she's the one making the delivery. What if she turns nose on us to the Weavers?"

"Same as any other job. We run."

"You think they'll give us that chance?" she said.

I didn't. But I said, "What else can we do? Daphna's our only way into the Enclave."

"I bet we could find a way inside ourselves."

"Probably," I said, "but how long do you think that would take?"

She understood what I meant. We were running out of time.

Lachlan was sick again. And this time, it was much, much worse.

He'd seemed fine when we returned to the *Bashful Turtle*. He talked animatedly to any of the crew who would listen about the shark attack while I showed Daphna the loot. Then, about an hour later, as he told the shark story for the third time, he'd suddenly doubled over and vomited.

The crew had laughed at him. Another land-legs falling seasick; they'd seen it often enough. But a quick peek with the Eye showed the stain writhing around inside him, more agitated than I'd ever seen it before.

The girls quickly took him to the ship's rail and laid him on the deck, splashing water on his face to cool him down. He threw up a few more times, then fell into a fitful sort of drowsing. Our fear then, beyond what was happening to Lachlan, was that he might have another outburst, like in Grey's shop. If the primeval magic blew a hole in the hull, it would sink the ship. It had made for a pants-wetting overnight trip across the lake.

Fortunately, we'd been spared any more problems. As the sun broke on the horizon, we'd arrived at Quarry's Point, got Lachlan into the rowboat, then bundled him away once we'd rented rooms at the Blue Boar.

I'd hoped he'd get better quickly, that the stain's thrashings were just a reaction to all that water. But even on land, he lay in his bed, shivering when awake, tossing and turning when asleep, sweating the whole time. Foxtail kept making him drink to stave off dehydration. Beyond that, there was nothing we could do.

It took him two days to get well again—mostly. This morning, Lachlan had finally risen from his bed hungry. He stuffed his face with sausage, eggs, and alshic, a fermented fish popular in coastal towns. But another look with the Eye showed how much trouble we were really in.

The primeval violet now filled more than half his body. And it was beginning to take him over.

Even after his apparent recovery, every once in a while, Lachlan would blank out, staring at nothing anyone else could see. At those times, the stain swirled inside him with a sense of excitement, like a fighter who knows the battle is tipping in his favor.

He was tired a lot, too. Normally, Lachlan would be bored and looking to explore the village, the beach, the surrounding woods. Instead, he just seemed listless. He could barely even rouse himself to play with Galawan.

So, no, I didn't trust Daphna. But like the Old Man said, lion's claw or tiger's bite? Sometimes the world doesn't give you the choice.

◠◡

We stayed another two nights in Quarry's Point, waiting for Daphna to return. Meriel was on edge the whole time, expecting the woman to rooker us and ride in with a circle of Weavers.

Foxtail didn't trust her either. The girl checked in with us in the early morning and evening to see that everything was all right, but otherwise, she refused to stay at the Blue Boar. Every sunrise, she showed up smelling faintly of pine, which had me believing she was camping out in the woods. Smart, because if Daphna did betray us, at least she'd never find Foxtail.

Gareth buried his nose in Veran's journal, studying it with interest. And Lachlan finally returned to his normal self, at least on the outside. The stain inside him hadn't changed.

"Dunno what was wrong, guv," he said cheerfully. "Must have picked up a bug somewhere."

More than he realized. Though he still hadn't questioned any of his strange abilities. I told him not to worry. After all, I said, he'd almost drowned in Lake Galway. There were bound to be some aftereffects.

I knew, however, that the primeval's calm was only temporary. So when Daphna finally returned, I was relieved.

To Meriel's surprise, Daphna hadn't turned nose. Instead, she'd done even better than I'd hoped. She brought us a detailed floor plan of the Enclave, along with a satchel of enchanted items we'd need to pull off the heist. She explained what each of the items was for and what we'd have to do with them. That was the good part.

The bad? She told us we had a new partner.

"Who?" I said, alarmed.

"A Weaver," she said. "He prefers to remain anonymous."

Meriel was furious. "You had no right to bring anyone in on the job."

Daphna regarded Meriel coolly. "He's the one who provided the bindings, darling, so it was bring him in or do it on your own."

"Then we'll do it on our own!" Meriel said, but that was just her temper talking. She already knew we didn't have that option.

"So what's the new deal?" I asked. "What does he want in exchange?"

"You'll have to steal *two* extra items from the treasure room now," Daphna said. "The first is an elixir. It's in a ruby-red bottle, wrapped in a cradle of gold foil. It'll feel warm to the touch and throb when you hold it, like a heartbeat. That's my cut. Bring that for me, and we're square."

"Fine. But what does *he* want?"

"A statue of a deer. It's one foot tall and made of skystone. It should look charcoal gray, almost black, and it'll feel heavier than it looks."

"A statue? That's it?" Meriel said skeptically.

Daphna's contact could have asked us for just about anything in that treasure room. Which meant it wasn't an ordinary statue. "What does it do?" I said.

Daphna shrugged. "I didn't ask. It's what he wanted, and he wouldn't agree to anything less. The tools for the deer, take it or leave it."

"And if we leave it?" Meriel said.

"Then you'll have a very angry Weaver on your tail."

"How will he know our names?"

Daphna smiled. "I'll give them to him, of course."

Meriel spat. "So you *will* turn nose."

"You'll be the one busting the deal, sweetie. Consider it insurance against you trying to run off without paying. When this is over, he'll either get his statue or he'll come looking for a hide to strip. I don't intend that hide to be mine." She turned to me. "Understood?"

I nodded. "When's the best time to hit the place?"

"Late," Daphna said. "The Enclave never closes, so there'll always be Weavers around no matter when you go. But the fewest will be in the small hours after midnight."

"Then we'll go tomorrow night," I said. That would give us time to get ready.

Besides, as I went over the plan, I realized we'd need an item or two of our own.

To get our tools, Lachlan needed to meet his contacts in Carlow.

I didn't like the idea of sending him into the city. It wasn't the Stickmen I was worried about. As a former runner for the Carlow Breakers, Lachlan knew the place like the back of his hand. He had plenty of ways to get around unseen, and anyway, he wasn't carrying anything that would get him into trouble. The High Weaver was only searching for the stolen Eye.

My concern was more about the primeval magic inside him. While it was true he felt better now, I didn't really want him out of eyesight—or more to the point, out of Eye-sight. It was the only way I could keep watch over the stain.

In the end, I had to let him go without me. Bringing the Eye back to Carlow before we needed to was simply too much of a risk. And Gareth pointed out something interesting: The stain only grew when it was able to use Lachlan to enchant something. Gareth suggested as long as we kept Lachlan from powering sources of air magic, we might be able to keep the primeval in check—or at least slow its growth.

Since the tools we needed Lachlan to get for this heist weren't enchanted, that wouldn't be a problem. So we sent him off with a shopping list. Meriel went with him, partly for added protection, but mostly to keep an eye on him and ensure he didn't fall ill again.

Gareth was content to spend his time with Veran's journal. I had no idea how anyone could study the same book for five days straight, but there he sat, hunched over the little writing desk in his room, happy as a clam.

As for me, I was getting restless. I didn't know what awaited us at the Enclave, I didn't know what would happen with Lachlan, and most of all, I had no idea what we were supposed to do if we ever did get our hands on the Dragon's Teeth. But seeing Lachlan recovered, at least temporarily, and remembering my goodbye with Grey, made me think of all the things that mattered to me—and how easily they could be taken away. So when Meriel and Lachlan returned with the tools we needed, I said, "Let's do something fun tonight. Let's have a fire."

"You want to burn down our inn?" Meriel said.

Everyone's a comedian. "I was thinking out back. A campfire."

"Ooh! Yeah, guv!" Lachlan said. "We can play games. And tell stories!"

And so it was on. The Blue Boar had a firepit out back, so I arranged for a pig from the local butcher to roast on the spit. I'd also picked up a few other things that day with a wad of crowns

I'd borrowed from Daphna before she'd returned to Carlow.

Being in Quarry's Point had certain advantages, such as every trader from the south passing through here. So I scoped out their carts as they traveled the Emperor's Highway and stopped the ones where I found something I liked. Gifts for my friends.

I handed them out while Meriel carved the pig. Gareth got his presents first: a fine deck of cards with a map of Ayreth on the back, and a small book.

"It's a pocket dictionary of the Old Tongue," I said.

Gareth blinked, staring down at the gifts in his hands. He ran his fingers over the leather of the book's cover, then looked up at me.

"I figured it might come in handy," I said.

He wasn't used to kindness. He almost didn't know what to do with it. "Thank you," he said seriously.

"Do us a trick, then," Lachlan said.

"Hold on," I said. "I have something for you, too."

"For *me*?"

I gave him a book as well: an edition of Fox and Bear stories, full of illustrations, since he couldn't read. The cover plate showed Shuna and Artha when they were still friends, standing atop a mountain, gazing over Ayreth below and grinning.

Lachlan was so happy. He jumped up and down and hugged me. "My very own book," he said joyfully as he leafed through the skillful drawings inside. "Will you read it to me, Gar?"

They sat by the log, Lachlan prodding Gareth to start the first story, too excited to even wait to see what the others got. For Foxtail, I'd picked up a new veil. Hers had been banged about and waterlogged—she'd had to keep it on until she slipped under the diving bell in Lake Galway, which had caused more than a few raised eyebrows on the boat—so I'd found the finest veil I could, with pretty little lace flowers in the mesh.

Foxtail seemed as delighted with her gift as Lachlan had been. She cast her old hat aside and donned the new one, twirling girlishly. She pressed her hands to her heart and held them out to me. *Thank you.*

"Got you this, too," I said, and I tossed her a little jar. "It's mirror polish."

She stared at it for a moment, then began to laugh silently, shoulders shaking. I was glad she liked the joke, especially considering how distant she'd been with me lately. Even funnier, she actually tried the stuff, putting it on her mask like it was skin cream.

She took her veil and went to twirl in front of the others, showing off. That left me with Meriel, who'd paused in carving the pork and was eyeing me warily. I pulled out a little box. "This is for you."

She regarded me for a moment, then opened the box slowly, as if a spring-loaded mouse would leap out at her. But there was no mouse inside. She gasped as she saw what lay within.

It was a thin gold necklace. At the end was a tiny pendant of malachite, with alternating bands of light and dark green, in the shape of a dragon.

She looked up at me, not quite believing it wasn't a joke. "What's the catch?"

"There's a clasp on the back," I said.

"That's not what I meant."

"I know."

She looked back down at the necklace. She picked it up, let it dangle from her fingers. Then she held it out to me and pushed her hair away. "Put it on me."

"Turn around."

She turned. I stepped close, close enough to smell her jasmine perfume. I clasped the chain on her, then stepped back.

She looked down at the little dragon. The green and gold really set off her skin. She glanced up at me, flustered, not sure what to say.

Lachlan spared her. "Wow, that's pretty!" he said. "And it's a dragon, too! Let me see." She leaned in so he could have a look.

"And if that's not enough," I said, tossing them a sack, "here's some candy."

Meriel caught it. Lachlan could barely believe the mass of sweets inside. "Guv! Where'd you get this?"

"Bought it from a sugar-peddler on the way through. It's good stuff." I should know; I'd already gobbled down a decent amount of it this afternoon.

"I feel bad," Lachlan said. "We didn't give you nothing."

"Sure you did." I tapped my eyepatch. "None of you had to come with me to get this back. None of you needed to risk your lives. There was no payoff for you. You did it anyway. It's a debt I can't really repay."

"Aww," Lachlan said, getting all teary. He came around the fire and hugged me. "Ain't no debt at all, guv."

We spent the evening around that fire. And there was no talk of the Eye, or the Enclave, or the job. Instead, we did just as Lachlan wished. Gareth read from Fox and Bear, absently shuffling cards from his new deck one-handed. He performed a bunch of tricks for us afterward, ramping them up with such skill and complexity that by the end, if he'd have said he was using real magic to make those cards do what he wanted, I'd have believed him.

Meriel entertained us with some knife throwing, knocking off pinecone after pinecone with perfect accuracy. Foxtail showed off, too, scampering up the tallest tree, frilly dress, flowered veil, and all, until she stood at the end of the highest branch, perched like a bird. It made Gareth—never one for heights—so nervous, he had to peek through his fingers.

Then we played games for the rest of the night: cards and contests. The favorite turned out to be the knife toss. We made a target on a nearby tree, then took turns throwing at it—Meriel judging instead of playing, of course—closest to the center won. The biggest shock came when Gareth managed, in a complete fluke, to nail the bullseye, just edging out Foxtail's previous throw. Everyone cheered as he stared with stunned pride at his happy accident.

By the end, we were all just lounging about the fire, stuffed with roast pig, sticky sweets, and fun. As the moons rose higher, we grew tired. Foxtail gave a quick wave—and one last twirl—before disappearing into the woods. Lachlan was already snoozing.

Meriel nudged him. "Come on, sleepyhead. Up to bed."

He woke with a start. "No. Another story. Please?"

"Some other time. We'll be up late tomorrow, remember?"

Her mention of the job brought seriousness back to our hearts. Gareth stood and, cradling his new deck and dictionary, nodded to me as he left. Meriel hauled Lachlan to his feet and prodded him toward the inn. Halfway there, she paused. She turned back to me, holding her dragon pendant between her fingers.

"I should have thanked you for this," she said.

"Looks good on you," I said.

That left her flustered again. I gave her a three-fingered salute.

"See you tomorrow," I said.

After a moment, she said, "Shuna watch over you."

Then she went inside.

∩∪

I probably should have gone in, too. But like Lachlan, I didn't want the night to end. I just lay there awhile, hands behind my head, staring up at the sky. With the smoke from the volcano finally dissipating, it was the first time in a week I saw our twin moons.

No longer full, they weren't nearly as bright as they'd been the night of the syzygy, and a faint haze of smoke-cloud still washed out their light. Nonetheless, lazing there made me think of times long past, when I'd lain beside a different fire, the Old Man smoking his pipe, the two of us on our way to pull some job or another.

I held my right hand up to Cairdwyn, watching her moonlight glitter through my crystal ring. *Turns out this thing's enchanted after all*, I said to the Old Man. *Did you really know that when you traded the ring to Grey? Or were you snaffled by your own jolly gaff?*

How dare you, boy, he said in mock outrage. *I've never been snaffled in my life.*

Then what is this ring actually for? I asked. *All it seems to do is heat up.*

Ah, he said sagely. *It must be for making grilled cheese.*

Even though he wasn't really here, I still found myself smothering my laughter, as I always had when we were together and he'd made a joke. I couldn't let him get one up on me, after all.

Seriously, though, I said. *I can't figure out what the ring's good for. It doesn't glow in the Eye, even when it gets warm. And it only did it once, under Lake Galway.*

What do you care what it's for? he said. *I thought we had this discussion already.*

I know, I know, I said. *Fiddling with nature is for fools.*

Exactly. You shouldn't even be wearing that thing.

"But I *like* it," I said quietly, holding it up to Mithil now. "That's why you didn't let me see it when you snaffled it, isn't it? You knew I'd want to wear it—"

One of the bushes moved.

On the other side of the fire. I saw it move; I was sure of it. There was no sound of rustling leaves, but branches had swayed, like something was pushing them aside—

I sat up.

I'd suddenly remembered that leopard we'd seen outside Bolcanathair. Unless someone had caught the beast, it would still be prowling around Carlow. Slowly, I pushed myself to my feet, placing one of the logs between me and the woods, peering into the trees with the Eye.

It was strange. I could see the glowing green leaves well enough, but not what was pushing them. It was almost as if . . .

Ah. I blew out my breath in relief. "Hello, Foxtail."

The branches stopped moving.

I sighed and put my patch back on. "Come on. I know you're there."

Foxtail stepped from the bushes, looking a little sheepish. She wasn't wearing a veil, and she'd been sneaking about silently, which meant that she not only hadn't expected me to notice her, she hadn't *wanted* me to notice her.

I sat on the log. "Come sit with me," I said. "Enjoy the fire some more."

She waved at the moons, then at the inn, then at the woods. *It's late. We should probably get some sleep.* She began heading back into the trees.

This was ridiculous. "Are you going to keep avoiding me forever?"

She stopped. Then she spread her hands. *Who says I'm avoiding you?*

"I swear," I said, "the next time one of you forgets what my job is . . ."

That made her look sheepish again.

"Will you please come talk to me?" I said.

She hesitated, but she joined me. She took a spot on the log, though not too close.

"I know what's bothering you." I tapped my eyepatch. "The Eye can see magic, and life."

She nodded. *I know.*

"But it can't see you."

She hesitated. Then she nodded again. *I know that, too.*

"I didn't understand what that meant at first," I said. "So I asked Gareth. He thought it was because of your mask. In fact, he thinks that's what the purpose of your mask *is*. To hide you from being detected by magic. Hide you from the Eye. It does other things, I'm sure, but he's right, isn't he?"

Foxtail didn't move.

"For days now, I've been trying to think why you'd want to hide like that. Then I remembered that—"

I stopped myself from saying *Shuna*. The Fox had warned me I couldn't tell anyone that we'd met. I didn't think that quite applied to Foxtail. She was, after all, responsible for sending me on my first . . . trip?—I didn't know what to call it—to meet Shuna. I still decided not to take any chances.

"I remembered," I said instead, "that our, uh, mutual furry friend warned me not to tell the Eye that I'd spoken to her. And then down below Lake Galway, when I saw . . . *what* I saw . . . I began to wonder.

"I once asked our friend if you were some sort of magical being. She said no. I've been starting to think maybe she was lying. Is it possible you don't want to be seen by the Eye because . . . you're really a Spirit?"

Foxtail seemed shocked by the idea. Then she threw her head back, shoulders shaking, laughing silently. *No.*

"But you're not an ordinary girl."

She held her hand out to me. *Don't I feel like an ordinary girl?*

"I've held your hand before," I said. "I know you don't feel different. But you *are* different, aren't you? In some way, some way that's important, you're not like the rest of us."

Foxtail let her hand fall.

"That's it, isn't it?" I said. "That's why you've been avoiding me. Because you realized the more I thought about it, the closer to the truth I'd get. And you don't want me to figure it out."

She looked into the fire.

"I understand that might not be the only reason. Maybe, like you-know-who, you have rules that forbid you from telling us what's behind that mask. Still, whatever the truth is, I want you to know: I don't really care. You saved my life. Twice, actually. No matter what your secret is, you'll always be my friend."

She stared into the fire a moment more. Then she stood and came over to me.

I expected her to pat my cheek like she always did. A charming dismissal. Instead, she gave me a hug, soft and tender.

I hugged her back, until she let go. "So will you stop avoiding me?"

Now she patted my cheek. But she nodded, and I was sure, under the mask, she was grinning.

I grinned back. "Good. Then sit with me. I'm having trouble working something out, and I'd like to throw a few ideas at . . ."

I trailed off as she cocked her head. *Wait.*

"What's the matter?"

She waved me off. *Shush.*

She listened some more. Then she turned back to me and held out both her hands.

Puzzled, I took them. She pulled me from the log. Then she turned me around so I faced the forest. She pointed.

"What's out there—"

She gave me a soft slap on the backside.

"Hey!" I said. "What was that for?"

The grin returned. She nodded meaningfully toward the woods, moving two fingers like legs. *Go.*

"What in Shuna's name are you on about?" Then I realized I'd stumbled into the answer. "Ah."

There were a pair of lanterns hanging from the wall of the inn. I took one and, with a nod to Foxtail, headed into the woods.

I wasn't sure which direction I was supposed to go, so I just walked among the trees, away from the village. The path probably didn't matter, anyway. Because a hundred yards from Quarry's Point, I came to a clearing.

And there, in the middle of it all, waited a fox.

CHAPTER 40

She sat in the open, facing Bolcanathair, so her body was in profile. She was gazing up at the moons, at the haze they made in the clouds. She had deep-red fur and a soft white underbelly, and I had to admit that she was undoubtedly the best-looking fox in all of Ayreth.

"Why, look who's dropped by," Shuna said, ears out in a foxish smile. "Hello, Cal."

"Tell the truth," I said. "Did you strike that pose on purpose, staring up at the moons, so you'd look majestic?"

She made a face. "Too much?"

"Well, like the Old Man used to say, a little goes a long way. What are you doing here?"

"Every time I meet you, I'm amazed at how rude you are. Can't a patron Spirit stop by to see her favorite gaffer once in a while?"

"She could," I said, "but I'm guessing tonight you have some other scheme in mind."

"Nothing so calculating. I heard about your upcoming job and wanted to wish you luck."

Her answer made me think of the time I rode down to Marsden with the Old Man, annoying him with my questions about the Spirits. "Does that actually do anything?" I said.

"Does what do anything?"

"Wishing me luck. You know, we drop septs into Fox shrines before a job, make the sign of the Fox, and so on. But does that *actually* bring us luck? After all, aren't you forbidden from helping us? Because of the Pact?"

"Well, well," Shuna said. "Someone's been reading the old stories."

"So it's true?" I could barely believe it. "You really made a pact with Artha not to interfere with humans?"

"I didn't say that."

"So . . . you didn't make a pact?"

"I didn't say that, either. You know I can't answer those kinds of questions."

"Because of your rules," I said. "But *that's* where the rules come from, isn't it? From the Pact."

"I didn't—"

"Say that." I sighed. "Yes, I know. I wonder if Artha would tell me the truth?"

Shuna was amused by that. "And just how do you think you'd find her?"

"Apparently, there's an idol in the Enclave treasure room that can summon her."

"*That's* where that is!" Shuna said, delighted. "I'd completely forgotten where it went."

I blinked, stunned. "Wait . . . you mean the idol actually *works*? I could really summon the *Bear*?"

She looked at me warily. "You're not truly thinking of doing that, are you?"

"I wouldn't even know how."

"Good. Because while you're charming and all, I don't think my sister would like you very much."

Something occurred to me. "Hey, if there's an idol of Artha, is there one that summons you, too?"

"Sure. It's in Sligach. At least I think it is. The last time I saw it was what, thirteen, fourteen hundred years ago? I might be remembering wrong."

"Did someone use it?" I said, curious.

She nodded. "A Weaver. What was his name again? Gralt? Geralt? Something like that."

"What did he want?"

"He asked me to help him become High Weaver. Promised if I did, he'd switch the Weavers' patronage from Artha to me."

"Did you do it?"

Shuna laughed. "Of course not. Why would I care about that? I told him to get lost. I also told him if he summoned me again, I'd bite his nose off."

That sounded more like the Fox I knew. Though . . . "You couldn't actually have bitten his nose off, could you? Because that would break the rules."

"Yes, but *he* didn't know that."

"Then how come you were allowed to bite me?" I complained. "When I wouldn't get out of that bed?"

"Oh, come on. It was just a nip on the backside. It's not like I actually injured you."

My heart skipped a beat. Did she just let something slip?

"So that's the boundary of the rules?" I said. "Getting hurt?"

She began to answer. Then she caught herself and grinned. "You really are my favorite gaffer, Cal."

Even though I was still a little miffed with her, I had to smother a smile. "All right, then, just tell me this: Does the Pact *prevent* you from helping or hurting us? Or does it just mean you can, but if you do, your sister gets to punish you?"

"What's the difference?"

"Huge," I said. "One means you can't do it. The other means you could, but you won't."

"Suppose I could," Shuna said. "Would you give your biggest enemy the chance to punish you?"

Considering my biggest enemy was either Artha, High Weaver Darragh VII, or the Eye, I'd have to say no. "I guess not."

"There you are, then."

"But what punishment could a Spirit face?"

"All in all, I'd rather not find out." Shuna swished her tail. "Anything else you want to know?"

"Yeah. How many Spirits are there?"

That made her pause. "What a strange question. Why in the world do you ask?"

"Because I think I met another one."

"Another *Spirit*? I doubt it. What makes you think so?"

"This does," I said.

And I held up my hand with the crystal ring on it.

I'd never seen the Fox startled before. She stared at the ring on my finger. "Where did you get that?"

"Grey gave it to me."

"Grey?"

And here I thought she knew everything. "The clockmaker I was living with in Redfairne. He got it from the Old Man, who stole it from some Weaver."

"What Weaver? What was his name?"

"I don't know."

"Cal," she said, and there was no humor in her voice anymore. "This is important. What was the Weaver's name?"

I was a little rattled by her intensity. "I don't know. Honest. The Old Man swiped it while we were on a job in Kilmallock. I never met the Weaver he took it from. I didn't even know he'd snaffled it until Grey told me. Why? What's the deal with this ring?"

She put on a casual air again. "It's just ... been a long time since I've seen a design like that."

"So?"

"So you'd better be careful with it. It contains a tremendous amount of power."

"How, exactly? No, let me guess: You can't tell me."

"I wouldn't even if I could," she said. "You really shouldn't have that thing."

"It has something to do with Spirits, though, doesn't it? It detects when you're around."

Shuna hesitated. "What makes you say that?"

"Because it started heating up before I even got close to this clearing. And right now, with you next to me, it's so hot I can barely stand it."

My skin was burning. It was all I could do not to take the thing off.

"If this ring can detect you," I said slowly, "I wonder what would happen if I touched you with it?"

I held my hand out. Shuna scampered away, alarmed. Then, when I took another step closer, her mood turned playful. She went down on her front legs, then darted off as I came close. We did that a couple more times before I realized that somehow, I'd ended up playing catch-me-if-you-can with a Spirit.

I gave one final leap at her, trying to catch her off guard. I landed face-first in the grass. She'd already sprung away.

"I'm a fox, Cal," she said, laughing, as I removed grass from between my teeth. "You'll never catch me unless I want you to."

"It's hardly a fair contest," I said. "There's about twenty pounds of pork in my stomach."

"Excuses, excuses."

I brushed myself off as she sat next to me. "But seriously," I said. "If I did touch you with the ring, what would happen?"

"Something very interesting," she said. "So I'm going to ask you not to do it."

I regarded her for a while, trying to figure out what she was getting at. I got the feeling she was trying to tell me something without actually telling me something. Something that bumped up against her rules.

"All right," I said. With her sitting so close, the ring was too hot to wear, regardless. I took it off and put it in my pocket, where it burned against my hip. "Anyway, that's why I asked you about Spirits. Because the only other time this ring heated up was when I saw what I'm pretty sure was another Spirit."

"And where was this?"

"Under Lake Galway."

"*Under* it?" Shuna looked amused. "I don't think so."

But I did. "It wasn't an ordinary Spirit, like you. It was more like . . . I don't know. The remnant of one. The last breath of its ghost, remaining behind to guard the path to the Dragon's Teeth. Because while it looked asleep, I'm pretty sure that Spirit was dead."

The Fox went very quiet then, all playfulness gone.

"What's wrong?" I said.

"What did this Spirit look like?" she said slowly.

"A sheep."

Suddenly, Shuna looked stricken. Her tail went down, and her ears went back against her head. She stood and walked a few paces away, her back to me.

"This . . . sheep," Shuna said, voice thick. "Did she do anything?"

"Yes," I said. "Before she left, she spoke in our minds."

"Do you remember what she said?"

Every word. Even thinking about it brought the warmth back to my heart. "'Your path will be painful, child. I wish I could walk it with you. But my time is done. Take my blessing, and know that you are loved.'"

Shuna curled up on the grass, head on her paws, tail hugging her body.

I didn't know what to do. The Old Man had never taught me anything about foxes, but it wasn't hard to read Shuna's grief.

"I'm sorry," I said.

Not long ago, Shuna had comforted me when I was in despair. Now I knelt in the grass next to her and placed my hand on her back, stroking her fur. She didn't say anything.

"Thanks ... thanks for coming to wish me luck," I said, because I didn't know what else to tell her. "I really do appreciate it. Even if I pretend otherwise."

She nodded.

I stayed there for a while, just resting my hand on her fur. Then I stood.

"I'm sorry," I said again.

I left, going back the way I came. I turned around once more to look, just as I entered the trees. Shuna remained curled up in the grass.

I let her be.

CHAPTER 41

It was strange being back in Carlow.

It had barely been a week since the five of us had fled the city. Running away with Stickmen on my heels was hardly new to me; I'd spent plenty of years with the Old Man bolting from place to place, one step ahead of the skullcrackers.

But I'd never been back anywhere so hot so quickly. Come to think of it, I'd never turned any city so hot before, ever. Stickmen, Weavers, *and* Pistoleers gunning for my head? I couldn't decide if the Old Man would be embarrassed or proud.

Whatever the case, we rode back to town in style. Lachlan had arranged for a carriage to pick up the five of us from the Blue Boar and carry us into Carlow. A nice one, too, with a golden fringe around the canopy and comfy velvet seats.

"Artha's paws," Lachlan said, bouncing up and down on the cushions. "I could get used to this."

Would be nice. For now, this was just part of our disguise. I had no reason to believe it wouldn't hold—at least until we reached the Enclave—and we'd all dropped a sept in the Fox shrine, as usual. Still. Shuna's kind wishes or not, I wouldn't feel good about this job till it was done.

We actually did get stopped by Stickmen, not long after we'd entered the city's southern gate. It was just after midnight. One man stepped in front of our carriage with an upraised lantern while his partner waited by the side, hand on his truncheon. The driver reined the horses to a halt.

"Spot search," the Stickman told the driver.

"Everyone play it cool," I muttered. "Remember: the key to being somewhere you shouldn't is acting like you belong there."

The Stickman who'd stepped in front took hold of the horses' bridles. His partner came round the side and peered into the open window.

I didn't know what the Stickmen's purpose was, whether they were looking for the Eye or just planning to shake down wealthy travelers into their city. I never got to find out. The Stickman stopped as soon as he saw our disguises.

We weren't dressed in anything outlandish. We'd all just put on respectable, decently tailored clothes, Foxtail in her veil as usual. No, what made the Stickman freeze were the necklaces we were wearing.

They were copper seven-pointed star pendants. The mark of apprentice Weavers.

"Problem?" Lachlan said, sounding snooty.

Whatever words the Stickman had for us died on his lips. Instead, he tipped his hat to Lachlan and said, "Sorry 'bout that, sir." He stepped back and waved to the driver. "Move along."

Our carriage pulled away. "Did you hear that?" Lachlan

laughed. "He called me 'sir'! Shuna's sniffing snout. I *could* get used to this, I could."

Back in Quarry's Point, Meriel had looked a little disappointed that she'd had to hide her new pendant and don the seven-pointed star instead. Now we were all glad to be wearing them. It was amazing how one bit of copper changed everything.

What we were doing—pretending to be Weaver apprentices— was a crime, of course. It was forbidden to claim membership in any guild you weren't actually a part of. Even worse to be a Weaver, because if you were caught, the Stickmen would hand you over to the Weavers for punishment.

But since we were about to commit a much worse crime tonight . . . Well, as they say: in for a sept, in for a crown.

Lachlan enjoyed the whole ride through the city. And it was good to see him still doing so well. As much as we needed these Weaver pendants, I'd been worried about having him wear one.

Our disguises might have been fakes, but the necklaces weren't. These pendants were the genuine article, provided by Daphna's secret ally. She said we'd need them to get into the Enclave. After Daphna delivered them, I'd looked them over with the Eye, just to see what we were dealing with. Each one glowed a faint, soft white.

It was no surprise they were enchanted. What concerned me was whether the stain would react to that enchantment. If I'd had the choice, I wouldn't have given Lachlan a pendant at all. But since he either had to wear one or we'd have to leave him behind, I tested it first. Before handing him his pendant, I'd hidden it in my palm and brought it close behind his back, watching the stain through the Eye. When it didn't seem to react, I handed the necklace over.

I watched as he put it on. This time, the stain drew close to where the pendant touched him, as if curious. But it didn't appear to respond beyond that. It looked like Gareth's theory was correct: the stain really only reacted to magic of its same type.

There was something else that worried me, though, and it wasn't the primeval. It was the Eye. When it saw the stain swirl toward the Weaver pendant, I felt a sense of anticipation

(soon)

coming from somewhere inside. I didn't know what it meant. It left me restless.

My worrying had always annoyed the Old Man. *Stop inventing trouble*, he said in my head. *You can't do anything about it, anyway. Deal with whatever comes when it comes.*

His advice may not have been gentle, but it was good. The more I thought about it, the more his words settled me. *You're right*, I said in a rare moment of feeling grateful to him. *Thank you.*

Don't thank me, he said. *You're doing exactly what I told you not to do: poke the Weavers. I think you're a fool.*

For some reason, his insult made me feel better. *Good to know some things never change, Old Man.*

He winked.

∩∪

We stuck our heads out of the carriage to see the Enclave.

The Enchanters' Guild hall was like no place I'd ever been before. Huge walls surrounded it, made of something smooth and shiny black, like giant, unmarked sheets of obsidian.

"They sing," Lachlan said.

"What?" Meriel said.

"Them walls. They sing when the wind blows. Can hear 'em as far as the Rat Quarter in a storm."

"What do they sound like?" Gareth asked, curious.

"Flutes," Lachlan said. "Sometimes it's pretty. Sometimes it makes yer head hurt."

Gareth stared up at them. "What are they made of?"

"Dunno. Been here hundreds of years, though, and they ain't got a scratch on 'em."

Beyond the walls, the Enclave was laid out like the symbol of the Weavers, a seven-pointed star: seven wings joined by a central hub. Each wing was marked at the end by a spire, each made of a different material, though nothing so odd as the walls. Just different colored stone and brick, with one spire made entirely of glass. I had no idea how the thing didn't shatter.

I was sure there were other wonders, but we arrived in the black of night, so we didn't get to see the full majesty of the place, just what was lit by light globes. Regardless, we weren't here to go sightseeing.

The driver pulled up at the entrance. The Enclave's main gate was two giant doors, forty feet high and ten feet wide, fashioned from the same black material as the walls. Here, however, the obsidian was marked. Each door was carved with lines and curves that looked a lot like Weaver runes. I wasn't sure if they actually held any enchantment, and I wasn't going to uncover the Eye to test it. I had the strangest feeling we were being watched.

This was the first of the three hurdles Daphna had said we'd need to pass to enter the treasure room. Number one: get inside the complex.

Fortunately, this would be the simplest. *How will we get past the guards at the gate?* I'd asked her yesterday.

Easy, Daphna said. *There aren't any.*

I'd thought she was joking. She wasn't.

It will serve you well, she said, *if you imagine the Weavers being exactly like their patron Spirit, the Bear. Like Artha, they are intelligent and curious. Also like Artha, they are hot-tempered, arrogant, and entirely assured of their own superiority. They place no guards at the gate because they don't believe they need any. They use magic to guard their complex, not people. Magic—and the complete certainty that no one would ever dare cross them.*

When she'd told me that, it occurred to me just how true it was. We'd seen it both times we'd stolen the Eye. Originally, the High Weaver's palace had been protected only by magic; he hadn't brought in human guards until most of his wards had been broken. Mr. Solomon, too, fit Artha's mold: he'd been hot-tempered, arrogant, and entirely assured of his own superiority. That arrogance was what we'd used to beat him.

When I told Daphna that sense of superiority seemed like a big weakness, she almost looked offended. She was, after all, a descendant of powerful Weavers herself.

It's worked for them for centuries, Daphna said. *No thief has ever broken into the Enclave. Not because it's impossible. More because no one's ever been so foolish.*

The Old Man laughed. *Told you*, he said.

But we knew how the ward on this door worked. It only allowed those inside who belonged there: Weavers. And tonight, with our pendants, Weavers—Weaver apprentices, to be specific—was what we would be. The seven-pointed stars they wore weren't just for show; the Weavers also used them as keys.

Normally, an apprentice Weaver got his pendant when he joined the guild. It was a big deal, from what Daphna told us. Only the most promising students, or descendants of Weavers themselves, were even allowed to undergo the four-month trials before selection. Those who passed the trials were then brought before the Admitting Council. The council had nine members, all Master Weavers, and the pledge had to get at least seven of them to agree to their admittance.

If they were accepted, there was a huge ceremony and celebration, as the young boy or girl embarked on a path to enlightenment—and a guaranteed future of status, power, and wealth. We got none of that, unfortunately. Just the pendants, provided by Daphna's inside man.

Everyone was feeling their nerves now. Standing at the entrance to the Enclave, there was something inhuman about these rune-carved doors. They promised an alien world behind them, something no mortal should tamper with. And I was doubly nervous, for a different reason. If Daphna—or her secret Weaver ally—was going to betray us, this was the most likely place to do it. The streets, thick as they were with Stickman patrols, were nothing compared to what waited beyond these gates. Inside was Weaver ground. If they let us in to trap us, we were never getting out.

I did as the Old Man had taught me and forced myself to not hesitate. I stepped up with the pure pretended confidence that this was where I belonged.

The moment I came close, the door shimmered, as if the black was made of liquid. A new symbol appeared among the swirls: an impression of a seven-pointed star, exactly the size of my pendant.

Here goes nothing, I thought. Chain still around my neck, I pressed my pendant into the door.

And then suddenly a new door opened. The obsidian-like portal shimmered again, and a smaller portal swung open inside it, no larger than an ordinary door to a house. I took a deep breath and went inside.

When the door sealed behind me, I really thought it *was* a trap. But no one was waiting, and nothing sprang out to nab me. It appeared that our apprentice pendants only let one of us in at a time. The others stepped through one by one, using their own charms to get through the gate.

And we were in. It was bizarre to think how easy that was, even though I'd been told—and taught—to expect it. *Nothing makes a job simpler than an inside man*, the Old Man had always said, and that was certainly true.

Now we were on a wide stone path that led to the main entrance of the Enclave's seven-armed complex. To the right and left was a well-manicured lawn, with patches that looked like outdoor training grounds. In the distance, we could see a group of apprentices practicing in the wee hours of the morning. Three of them watched as a fourth stretched out a rod and threw sparks toward a training dummy.

Lachlan stared, eyes wide. "Shuna's snout. Best hope that don't happen to us, eh?" he said, and he made the sign of the Fox.

I covered his hand. "Weavers belong to Artha, remember?" I muttered.

"That's true, innit?" He thought about it. "Never asked Artha for nothing before. Is there a sign for the Bear?"

"If there is," Meriel said quietly, "I don't think we want to make it."

CHAPTER 42

THE ENCLAVE WAS a place of wonders.

According to the map Daphna had sketched for us, the entrance to the main complex was called the Hall of the Elements. It was easy to see how the space had got its name.

The hall was shaped as a perfect cube, Daphna had told us, precisely three hundred and forty-three feet a side—seven times seven times seven, Gareth noted. It was fashioned entirely out of marble, every inch of which was carved. This extraordinary sculptured mural wrapped the entire room, with different scenes telling the history of the Weavers.

Their story began above the door we'd entered, an enormous statue of Artha handing what looked like a globe to an old man with a beard—though I had the sudden sense that the orb was no globe, but the Eye. The scenes continued clockwise around the hall. There was the founding of the first Weaver Enclave in the woods that would become Carlow, there was the battle against Aeric, there was the Weavers blessing the newly crowned emperor, and so on. The door on the opposite end of the cube led to the central hub, where another statue of the Bear rose above the exit. Here she stood regally, gazing benevolently at all who passed beneath her paws.

Illumination was provided by forty-nine light globes, each one seven feet in diameter—the Weavers sure did love their sevens. The globes floated in the air, turning in lazy circles near the ceiling, which was painted with lines, angles, and curves, as if covered with runes. The ever-changing play of light and shadow made the carvings in the mural look as if they were alive, moving. It was like watching history play out before our eyes.

There were more wonders, too. Around the room, vases, alternating large and small, stood on pedestals. The plants and flowers they kept bloomed brilliant colors, but they were varieties like nothing I'd ever seen in nature. There were massive bulbs, octagonal leaves, and even something that looked like a snapdragon that stretched toward you, mouth open, as if to take a bite when you passed by.

Yet what was truly stunning was the dais in the center. Atop it was a square fountain, though it contained no ordinary spout of water. Here was what gave the Hall of the Elements its name, for living side by side in the fountain were the four elements that made up the world.

In one corner was a roaring pillar of fire. Near the ceiling, the fire burst, creating bright flashes, popping like muffled fireworks.

The next corner was a mass of earth and stone, intertwined with creeping vines. The whole column slithered, shifting constantly, shaping itself into a bear, then a pillar, then a man, and back again, the cycle continuing forever.

The corner opposite the fire was water. At the top, it was a pillar of ice. Halfway down, it began to melt, until it became a flowing crystal stream pooling at the bottom.

And in the final corner of the fountain was a twisting column of air, its currents made visible by what appeared to be a thousand tiny dandelion seeds. Except these seeds sparkled with rainbow colors, so the air looked as if it were adorned with precious jewels.

"Artha's bulging bum," Lachlan said, staring in awe. All of us stared with him, Gareth most of all, the boy unable to decide whether to gawk at the history unfolding in marble or the magic in the central fountain.

So much for looking like we belonged. Though Daphna had mentioned this wouldn't be such a problem. *It's not a big deal if you stop for a while. A lot of Weavers go to the Hall of the Elements to admire its beauty. Particularly the apprentices, who aren't yet used to seeing that kind of thing.*

Standing in the middle of it, I understood. Like the entrance to Daphna's home, like the black gates that guarded the Enclave, this hall was designed to impress—and intimidate.

And to make a promise as well, the Old Man said. *Look at my power. Soon to be yours, apprentice.*

That was clear now. Even for me, there was something intoxicating about it. I had to pull myself away. We had a job to do.

Though the hour was late, there were a surprising number of Weavers coming and going. Daphna had warned us that the Enclave was never really empty. Experiments often ran for months, she said, and many required careful monitoring. What's more, it was exam time for apprentices. In addition to their usual duties, aspiring Weavers were required to take a core set of classes at the academy, so they could learn the basics of their art without eating up their masters' time with trivial questions.

All this worked in our favor. Unless someone caused trouble, the Weavers would barely even notice apprentices wandering around, and new faces in the Enclave weren't unusual, so no one paid any attention to us.

Though that seemed about to change. The Hall of the Elements was merely the entrance to the broader complex. Our goal was the old palace treasure room. To get there, we first needed to reach the central hub. Daphna had insisted that all the wards we'd need to deal with would be magical, that the Weavers didn't use human guards.

Yet now someone stood in our way.

The path to the central hub was through a corridor. Inside it, an older girl of about sixteen leaned against the wall, looking bored. Her copper pendant marked her as an apprentice.

She glanced up at everyone who passed. If they were Weavers, she simply looked away, bored again. Apprentices, however, she stopped to ask a question. It looked like she'd been stuck there to keep watch for something.

That made me pause. What was she asking about? Had Daphna's poking around made someone suspicious?

The Old Man had taught me how to deal with this kind of thing well enough. I could probably fake my way through it. Unless, of course, the girl asked questions about enchanting that only a real apprentice would know. And if she demanded to see under Foxtail's veil . . . I couldn't take that chance.

All right, new plan. If talking our way past the apprentice was too risky, then we needed to distract her instead. I looked about the room for something useful.

My eyes fell immediately on the nearby vases. If one of those fell over, it would make a big noise. The only problem was getting caught next to it. Blocked well enough by the doorway, one of us could tip it over unseen. But if the apprentice came out and noticed someone hurrying away, the game was up.

I told the others what I was thinking.

"I could break one," Meriel said quietly.

She turned her hand over. One of her throwing knives was already hidden in her palm.

I considered it, then shook my head. When the apprentice investigated, she'd find the blade among the dirt. She'd be certain to call some sort of alarm.

"What about . . ." Meriel made a choking motion with her hands.

That was how we'd got past the apprentice who'd surprised us in the High Weaver's palace. Yet again, that was a risk we couldn't take. There were too many people around. And where would we hide her unconscious body?

No, we needed something where no one got hurt. I stared up at the fountain of elements. Maybe there was some way we could sabotage it?

That's a huge chunk of ice, I thought. *If we could crack it somehow, it would shatter all over the—*

No. Wait. *Ice,* I thought, and I suddenly remembered a gaff the Old Man and I had played a few years ago. A distraction.

"Meriel," I said under my breath, "can you chip a piece of ice off the fountain?"

Though somewhat confused, she did as I asked. We sat against the fountain's edge, pretending to enjoy the room. Then she swiped out with her blade and hacked off the tip of the giant icicle. It dropped into the pool with a splash.

I fished it out. Then I stuffed it in my mouth.

"What're you doing, guv?" Lachlan said curiously.

I motioned for them to wait on one side of the hall, near the corridor. Ice freezing my tongue, I went to the other side, to the vase nearest the doorway.

The plant inside was one of those snapdragons. The flowery mouths reached for me. In possibly the creepiest experience I'd had yet, they began tugging at my hair.

I steeled myself to ignore them and gave a quick glance around to make sure no one was watching. Then I moved the vase to the edge of the pedestal, balancing one side of it on the piece of ice I'd hidden in my mouth.

Tongue numb, I moved to the other side of the door and glanced down the corridor. The apprentice inside still looked bored.

And so we waited. It didn't take long. The ice, warmed by my heat, was already melting and slippery. The bottom of the vase pressed on it, and within a minute, began to shift.

Now.

I stepped into the corridor.

The ice gave way, shooting out from under the ceramic. The

vase rocked and, unsupported at one edge, toppled from its pedestal.

CRASH

I jumped, pretending to be startled. The apprentice jerked her head up, equally surprised.

"What happened?" she said.

I stared off to the side, a puzzled expression on my face. "The vase. It just . . ."

I deliberately didn't finish my sentence. *If you can offer up a mystery*, the Old Man had once taught me, *your mark will want to investigate it for herself.*

Frowning, the apprentice left the corridor and stepped past me into the Hall of the Elements. She stared, genuinely puzzled, at the mess, which had attracted a crowd. Shattered ceramic lay strewn across the floor, mixed with dirt. The snapdragons mouthed the air angrily, their roots moving like horrid, wriggling toes.

"It just fell over," a man with a silver pendant said, sounding confused.

The apprentice didn't even consider blaming me for it—after all, I'd been in the corridor when the vase broke. When she moved to inspect it, I ushered my friends ahead of me into the passage.

"Strange," I said. Then I took off, too.

And we were through.

CHAPTER 43

We went as quickly as we dared.

It wasn't wise to run. We might make some Weaver wonder why a gaggle of apprentices was sprinting through the halls. Still, it wouldn't pay to dawdle.

The girl who'd been standing guard wasn't likely to raise an alarm. By the time she'd sifted through the shards and dirt, looking for why the vase had toppled, the ice would have melted. I doubted she'd put two and two together even if she found it. Odds were, she wouldn't think of me again.

Nonetheless, the more we lingered, the greater the chance something bad could happen. And I wasn't even sure our next move would work. Because now it was time to get past the second hurdle.

Getting underground.

That's where the treasure room is, Daphna had told us. *Deep below the seventh spoke of the Enclave.*

This would be the trickiest part of the job, so we'd spent a lot of time preparing for it, huddled around the map in our rooms in Quarry's Point. Daphna had shown us exactly where we'd need to go. The seventh spoke was the wing farthest from the entrance, in the upper-right arm of the star-shaped complex.

This was the emperor's old palace, Daphna had said, *before the First Civil War. Now it's mostly staterooms and lodging for Weavers visiting from outside Carlow.*

Meriel had studied the floor plan. *Where's the way down? I don't see the stairs.*

There aren't any, Daphna had said. *Not anymore. As a security measure, the old palace stairs were demolished and replaced with a lift. It's a levitating platform, operated by touching a crystal. But to activate the crystal, you need a pendant as a key.*

Ain't that what you brought us? Lachlan had asked, holding up his copper pendant.

Daphna shook her head. *Those aren't good enough. It's not just the treasure room below. The seventh spoke is where the most important laboratories are, used for the most delicate experiments. They're restricted to Grandmaster Weavers and anyone working with them. Apprentices can go down, but only if a Grandmaster's pendant activates the lift.*

We'd asked her what a Grandmaster was. She told us that was the rank just below the Circle of Seven, the Weavers' governing body, of which the High Weaver was the leader. Grandmasters had pendants made of gold.

We'd all looked at our poor copper stars. *Could we steal one?* I asked.

She'd looked at me like I was mad. *You're not going to lift a pendant off a Grandmaster.*

So how do we get down?

You'll need to channel the Old Man, Daphna said, *and convince one of them to take you.*

I'd spent some time talking with Daphna afterward. Being her father's daughter meant that she was one of the few non-Weavers who'd actually been inside the Enclave—and one of only a handful who'd stayed at the seventh spoke. So she could tell me what it was really like inside.

Besides the various staterooms, she'd said, the main Weaver library was there, with adjoining study rooms. What I really needed to know was if there was any connection other than the lift between the ground and the underground. If the basement was sealed, for example, why didn't they run out of air down there?

I was worried that they'd just use magic. Fortunately, Daphna said there were vents to allow air to circulate. *Too small to squeeze through, if that's what you're thinking,* she'd said. *Not even that veiled girl would fit. There are wards on the ducts, anyway. In case any of the experiments below try to climb out.* She'd wiggled her fingers. *Zap.*

Not a problem. My plan didn't have anything to do with going down the vents. It was all about what was coming up.

In a way, the Enclave's central hub was even more impressive than the Hall of the Elements. It was a massive circular garden enclosed by a giant dome. The twin moons and stars shone so clearly through the glass, we could only tell the dome was there by the floating light globes reflecting off its curves.

A stone path led from the hall, branched off among the flowers, then rejoined to wrap around another circular fountain-like structure in the center. Farther paths branched away from that, each made of a different-colored stone, leading to the seven different wings of the Enclave.

The garden was meant for harvesting ingredients the Weavers needed for their bindings. Two apprentices and one Weaver—a Master rank, his pendant silver, with a crystal in the middle—were clipping buds next to the entrance with delicate pruning shears. They ignored us, as everyone else had so far.

The garden was beautiful, the dome spectacular. But what really made us gasp was the sphere turning in the center. Made entirely of light, it was a giant globe, showing all of Ayreth on its surface. Spots glowed on it. Some I recognized as cities. I had no idea what the rest of the marks were.

I stared in awe for a moment, until the Old Man said, *Focus, boy.* I tore myself away from the globe and pulled Gareth along with me, who would have happily gazed at the thing all night.

Daphna told us the path to the seventh spoke was made of white stone. We took it and entered what used to be the old palace, built by Aeric three thousand years ago.

It didn't look like the Weavers had changed much of Aeric's original design. As a result, the seventh wing seemed less magic-infused and more homey—well, more palace-y, I guess—than the rest of the Enclave. The walls were all warm dark wood, sculpted paneling, and soft carpet. I could almost imagine the old figures walking these halls: Aeric the conqueror; Galdron the child emperor; Veran, his killer—and savior of the world. An unbroken line through history to the start of it all.

Well, we'd made it, so now for the second part of our plan. Daphna had advised us that, at this hour, our best chance of finding anyone still awake was in the library. We headed straight there.

The library turned out to be a grand room, seven stories tall, longer than it was wide, with a study area on one end and stacks of books filling the rest. Stairs on either side led to the upper levels, where more tomes awaited.

I was almost shocked to see how many people were up. Most of the study tables were full. They were all apprentices, young faces buried in books, scratching notes, or arguing with each other. A librarian, his own pendant silver, dozed behind a counter, stirring only to glare the apprentices into silence when they got a little too loud and woke him.

"What's all this, then?" Lachlan whispered.

"Cramming for exams," Gareth guessed.

Poor Gareth. He sounded so wistful. All this knowledge, all these books, and all of it out of his reach. But there was no time to feel sorry for ourselves. "Check around," I whispered to him. "See if you can spot anyone wearing a gold pendant."

Gareth nodded and began wandering through the stacks. I sent Lachlan and Foxtail off next, searching for vents that might lead to the laboratories downstairs. Meriel and I took a seat in the study area, waiting.

Since I wanted to make it look like we were working, I pulled an oversized tome off the nearest shelf and carried it awkwardly to our desk. I flipped it open to find I'd chosen a historical roll of Weavers, an endless record of names and dates. How dull.

It occurred to me, a little too late, that we probably shouldn't have sat down at all. Some of the apprentices at the other tables were looking at us curiously and whispering among themselves. *Do you know those two? Who's their master?*

I was sure we'd be all right if someone questioned us. We'd come armed with a cover story: we were from Garman, here with our master, Quinn. It wasn't a tale that would stand up to scrutiny—for one thing, there was no Master Quinn—but it would hold us over for the night.

What I hadn't counted on was Meriel. She was, in a word, stunning, and several of the boys nearby couldn't take their eyes off her. One of the bolder ones, after a bout of goading among his friends, approached our desk with an easy smile.

"Get rid of him," I muttered under my breath.

The boy leaned on the table, awfully close to Meriel. "Have I seen you here before?"

Meriel smiled back pleasantly. "I don't think so."

"That's an interesting accent you've got. Just came to town?"

"Yes, we're from Garman."

"Really? That far? Seen much of the Enclave yet?"

"Nope."

"Well, then, why don't you come with me, and I'll give you a tour?"

"I have a better idea," she said, still smiling. "Why don't you go get stuffed?"

He flushed a deep red. "I . . . er . . ."

"Bye," Meriel said.

The boy walked stiffly back to his table, where his friends sat laughing at him.

The librarian woke. "*Shhh!*" he hissed, and they stifled their snickers.

"Smooth," I whispered.

Meriel looked confused. "You said get rid of him."

I couldn't really argue with that.

∩◡

Gareth didn't take long to return. To our relief, he'd been success-ful. "There's a Weaver...I mean...a woman. A Grandmaster. On the second floor. She has a gold pendant."

Lachlan and Foxtail came back successful, too. "Vents are between the shelves, guv. Two over here, and two on that side."

That placed one vent directly underneath the Grandmaster. Perfect. Time to play out our gaff.

We left the library and returned to the hall. There, Lachlan slipped Foxtail what he'd picked up from his contacts when he'd gone to Carlow with Meriel: two tiny vials containing different thieves' tools.

One was what we called a "puff." The liquid inside was a vola-tile, meaning it would fizzle into smoke as soon as it came into contact with air—in essence, a smoke bomb.

The other we called "dead juice." It contained a thin yellow liquid that I'd heard one thief describe poetically as "a thousand corpses rotting slowly in the summer sun." In other words: a stink bomb.

Foxtail, the stealthiest of us, executed our plan. She took the vials back into the library, cracked them, and dripped both liq-uids down the vent below the Grandmaster. Then we waited, hiding around a corner. It didn't take long.

"What in Artha's name?" came a cry—

And then the apprentices were piling from the library, cover-ing their mouths and retching.

The librarian followed them out, coughing, a faint mist of smoke swirling through the double doors. "What did you lot do?" he called after them. "Come back here!"

The apprentices began to scatter. They knew perfectly well how guilds worked: trouble rolled downhill. An apprentice would catch the blame, even if blameless. "It wasn't us!" one boy protested.

"A likely story!" the librarian said in outrage.

He was interrupted by the arrival of the Grandmaster. She stormed from the library, her bun of gray hair bouncing on her head as she strode, gold pendant around her neck. She covered her mouth with her sleeve, eyes blazing.

Her voice carried thunderously through the hall. "*Who is responsible for this?*"

The apprentices who'd already turned corners fled. Those few still in sight froze, as if moving would mark them as the culprit.

Now it was my turn. I'd have preferred no audience of apprentices, but it couldn't be helped. I assumed they'd stay out of it, anyway. They wouldn't want to catch the Grandmaster's wrath.

I staggered out from behind the corner, coming from the direction of the lift to the laboratory downstairs. Hand covering my face, I hacked and retched.

What started as an act quickly turned real as I caught a whiff of the dead juice. "A thousand corpses rotting slowly in the summer sun" didn't really do it justice. I went straight for the Grandmaster, trying my best not to throw up.

"Grandmaster," I said, coughing. "An experiment . . . down in the lab . . ."

I trailed off. For this gaff to work, I was relying on two things.

First: Everyone's initial reaction to a problem is always in terms of what's familiar to them. A Grandmaster Weaver would have spent her entire life studying, crafting, and using bindings. So if I offered her a magical answer to a question—*What is that smell?*—she'd almost certainly accept it as the truth. She wouldn't even think of something so mundane as thieves' tools.

And the second: In jockeying for status, guildmates frequently made enemies. And the more powerful the guild member, the more enemies they'd have made among their own. I was relying on this woman to despise someone else who mattered.

I staggered right up to her. The remaining apprentices, seeing a figure to blame, hurried away as the woman cast a baleful eye on me.

"This is *your* fault?" she boomed.

"Not mine." I retched. "It's Grandmaster"—*cough*—"Grandmaster..." I fell into a hacking fit, pointing frantically downward.

Leaving her hanging on the name but pointing to the labs downstairs gave her the time to fill in the answer with her most likely candidate. "Is it Grady? I saw him going down there. It is, isn't it?"

I had no idea who Grady was. But he'd fit the bill just fine. I coughed violently and nodded.

"Oh, we'll see about *this*," she said, and she stalked down the hall toward the lift. As soon as she'd turned, Foxtail slipped from the library and joined me. We followed the Grandmaster, doing our best to seem like cowed apprentices.

Meriel, Gareth, and Lachlan were already waiting at the entrance to the lift. This one was different from the one in the High Weaver's home. Though the platform was made from the same obsidian—it looked a near-perfect match to the Enclave's walls outside—this lift was three times the size, with no door separating the hall from the shaft down.

The woman strode onto the platform. The five of us joined her. This was the final test.

Would she object?

To my relief, like all of the other Weavers here, she treated apprentices no different than potted plants: they were just part of the landscape. So she didn't care about us at all. Instead, she went straight for the pedestal on the far side of the shaft. It was a simple column of the same obsidian, with red and blue crystals embedded in its face. Above them was an impression of the seven-pointed star.

She pressed her gold pendant into it. Under our feet, the platform began to hum.

"Hold the lift, please," a voice called from the hall.

I nearly jumped. That voice.

That *voice*.

I turned just as the boy who'd called came into view. He was a plain sort of fellow, about sixteen, with wide-spaced eyes and a sharp nose. He made to step onto the platform. Then he saw me.

And his jaw dropped.

CHAPTER 44

PADRAIG WILLS—APPRENTICE to the High Weaver, gambler, and the boy we'd gaffed to swipe the keystone that let us steal the Eye—turned white as he stared at me in horror.

Slowly, his gaze fell on the others. Meriel, the sweetie pie who'd led him to the slaughter. Gareth, who'd cheated him at cards. And Lachlan, who'd pushed Padraig's bet up so high he'd ended up losing it all. Foxtail had her new veil on, so he couldn't see her mask, but I could tell he recognized her from the hotel.

Padraig looked back at me. I smiled pleasantly.

"Are you coming or not?" the Grandmaster snapped at him.

Still facing Padraig, ever so slightly, I shook my head.

"I . . . I'll take the next one," Padraig said.

The Weaver touched the red crystal.

Padraig stared at us all the way down.

The others looked ready to bolt.

Padraig had seen them. They didn't know what to do. I carried myself casually, as if nothing had happened, hoping they'd follow my lead.

The Grandmaster, fuming, finally seemed to take notice of us. "Why are you wearing that veil indoors?" she snapped at Foxtail. "You look ridiculous. Take it off."

"Apologies," I said. "Darla here was injured in one of our master's experiments. Her face is . . . it will take some time to heal."

Foxtail buried her head in Meriel's shoulder, as if upset. Lachlan, getting into the swing of things, patted her back in sympathy.

"Yes. Well. Keep it on, then," the Grandmaster said, somewhat disarmed. "And tell your master I said to be more careful."

The lift continued downward, the stone showing its age as we sank. I estimated we went down sixty, seventy feet, a shorter ride than at the High Weaver's house.

The platform slowed to a halt when we reached the bottom. The hum subsided as the Grandmaster stomped off leftward down the corridor.

The old underground had never been built to impress visitors. Gone were the wide, finely paneled walls and smooth red carpets. This place was all limestone—floor, walls, and ceiling. A path had been worn beneath our feet, millennia of footsteps grinding the stone away. Light globes attached to the walls illuminated the passage, the only real upgrade from the torches that would have been used in the days of the old emperors. Otherwise, the place looked like a dungeon—which was exactly what it had once been. I tried not to think too hard about that. Or what terrible experiments the Weavers would use to torture us if we got caught.

And we were so close now.

We followed the Weaver toward the laboratories, straggling a little. According to the map Daphna had sketched, this was the opposite direction to the treasure room. Still, I didn't think we should make a run for it until the woman was distracted.

It didn't take long. We passed a series of labs, some occupied, some not, until we reached a closed door. The Grandmaster banged it open.

Inside, a portly man with a neatly trimmed mustache, wearing his own gold pendant, was startled by the intrusion. He jumped, knocking over a tower of stones he and his two apprentices had been carefully balancing. A glowing ball of green light flashed, then winked out with a *bang!*

"What the Fox!" the man cursed.

"Grady, you buffoon!" The woman stormed inside. "You've polluted the entire Enclave *again*!"

"Ramsden, you hag!" Grady shouted back. "You've ruined *three weeks* of work!"

I wished the Old Man were here. There was nothing he liked better than creating a distraction by starting a fight. I could almost see him rubbing his hands with glee.

At any rate, this was our cue to leave. We hurried down the corridor, back the way we came, stopped only by another of the steel doors opening. A third gold-pendant Weaver stuck his head out.

"What is all that commotion?" he said.

"Grandmasters Ramsden and Grady," I answered.

"Oh, for Artha's sake," the man said, and he clanged his door shut, rolling his eyes.

We kept going until we'd passed the lift and turned down a new corridor. The paths branched off in different directions, turning the underground into something of a maze. Foxtail, who'd memorized the map Daphna gave us, led the way.

But the others hadn't forgotten who we'd run into upstairs. Gareth grabbed my arm, worried. "Padraig," he said. "He s-saw us."

"We have to go back and stop him," Meriel agreed. "He'll turn nose."

"No, he won't," I said.

"How do you know—er . . ." She changed what she was going to say as I glared at her. "Why wouldn't he tell?"

"To start," I said, "he'd have to explain how he knew we weren't real apprentices. Even worse, if he turns nose, and we get rookered, he has to be worried: What if *we* turn nose on *him*? The fact that he's still alive means the High Weaver never found out Padraig was responsible for the Eye being stolen. I promise you, this very second, that boy's up there wetting himself, praying to Artha we don't get caught. He won't say a word. Not now, not ever."

Meriel remained skeptical. But there really wasn't anything we could do about Padraig, regardless. We couldn't get back topside now even if we wanted to. We'd need a Grandmaster to activate the lift again.

Fortunately, we had a better way planned for escape.

The treasure room was at the end of the twisting maze. There was only one door here: a ten-foot-wide square of metal, though what kind, I wasn't certain. It looked a bit like brass, but I didn't think it was. It was too dull, without that brassy shine.

The door had no handle, and no apparent hinges. It simply sat there, an immovable slab under a single dimly glowing light globe. Daphna had told us it didn't need any handles or hinges because it couldn't be opened by human hands.

It's held fast by a binding, she'd said. *Several bindings, actually.*

What do they do? Gareth said.

Kill you the moment you touch it. Then call the Weavers to come collect what's left of your body.

So how do we get inside? I'd asked.

With a different binding, she'd said, and she'd removed a disk from a lead box. The disk was seven inches wide. It looked to be made of red clay, but when I picked it up, it was much heavier than clay should have been. There were two runes carved into it, one on each side. Both symbols were more complex than just about any I'd seen yet.

When I peered at it later with the Eye, I saw the disk had a strange sort of shine. It blazed an intense white around the edge, nearly as bright as the dragon staff. Yet in the center, it was pure black. The light seemed to flow inward, disappearing, as if falling into an impossibly deep hole, though the brightness of the edge never faded. From the Eye itself, I got a distinct sense of interest, even approval, when it saw the thing.

What does this do? I'd asked Daphna.

It traps magic, she said.

What kind of magic?

Every kind.

I'd looked up at her, surprised. Was this the same sort of enchantment that shielded Foxtail? Or the magic that kept the Eye hidden under my eyepatch? *I didn't know a binding could do that,* I said.

It's one of the hardest enchantments to make, Daphna had said. *Magic doesn't want to be contained. That's why no binding, no matter how small, is easy for a Weaver to create. Forcing the energy into the runes drains their vitality. It's what makes them so tired.*

Interesting. I'd seen that happen with Mr. Solomon, and with Bragan, too, when he'd brought back Lachlan. I'd even felt the struggle myself, when I used the Eye to force the primeval magic back underground.

What you have there is incredibly dangerous, Daphna had said, nodding at the disk in my hands. *Not just to you, but to our ally. There are only a few Weavers in the guild who can bind an item of that power. If you get caught with it, the High Weaver will know who gave it to me.*

The disk, she'd said, for all its ability, still couldn't trap magic for very long. It would only stay intact for ten minutes or so, fifteen at the absolute most. Then it would disintegrate, leaving no evidence behind, and the magic it bound would be released. Since the seal on the treasure room door would be broken, that's when the alarm would sound.

So you'd better be out of there by then, Daphna had said. *Unless you want to fight off the entire Enclave.*

That left the question of *how* we'd get out. Fortunately, our Weaver ally gave Daphna that answer, too.

But we needed to get into the treasure room first. I stopped everyone around twenty yards from the door.

"I don't think we should get any closer," I said. "Foxtail?"

I'd given her the disk to hide under her skirt. She pulled it out and offered it to me. I nodded to Meriel instead.

"Have fun," I said.

Meriel made a face. "I throw knives, not weights." But she took it and prepared herself.

For obvious reasons, I'd kept the Eye covered since we'd entered the Enclave. But since it was only us down here, and I needed to be sure the disk did its job, I finally lifted the patch.

And the corridor came alive with light.

Weaver runes glowed on every single stone near the end of the hall, the symbols getting more dense as they approached the door. The metal itself pulsed with its own blazing shine, dark blue, every inch of it scrawled over with runes of its own.

Deep inside, that terrible excitement returned. The Eye knew exactly where we were. And it knew what was behind that door.

I glanced at the disk in Meriel's hands and hoped its magic would work. Most of all, I hoped our ally hadn't double-crossed us.

"Throw it," I said.

Meriel gauged the distance, gripping the disk tightly. Then she whirled around once to gain momentum and hurled the disk down the hall.

It spun as it flew, angled upward. As it passed through the web of Weaver runes around it, the symbols dimmed. Then it reached the door at the end.

The disk stopped just short of the portal, hovering in mid-air for one second. It flipped, once, twice, through no force I understood. Then it slammed into the brass-colored metal like a magnet. It stayed there, stuck slightly off center.

And the runes started to bleed away.

It was like gutters draining into a hole. All the light in the runes flowed in sparkling rivulets toward the disk. Except when they reached it, the light didn't disappear. It pooled in the clay, getting brighter and brighter, until the whole disk shone like the sun.

And as the light flowed, the runes faded. They became no more than black scratches, barely visible on the stone and the metal, until there was nothing at all but the disk, blazing white.

Then the giant door shifted. We heard a

chunk

chunk

chunk.

It opened.

And we stared at an absolute hoard of treasure.

CHAPTER 45

It wasn't what I'd expected.

The words "treasure room" conjure up dreams of wealth. Hills of gold, mountains of silver, rivers of jewels. There was none of that here.

What lay inside looked more like a warehouse. Long, oversized shelves rose high in the vault, rows and rows of them, small placards numbering the aisles. As we stepped inside, I saw the room was even larger than I'd imagined. The space wrapped around the hallway in the shape of an elongated U, countless more shelves laden with artifacts.

Some of the treasures *were* treasures, fashioned out of precious materials. I saw a golden mask, an ivory knife, a jeweled snuff box, and the like. Otherwise, most of the items appeared plain: a cracked mirror; a stopped clock; a wooden horse, fashioned crudely, as if by the hands of a small child. Yet what made this truly breathtaking wasn't their appearance, or even the sheer number of them.

It was the magic.

When the vault door opened, I still had the Eye out, scanning for traps that might otherwise be invisible. I spotted no more wards. Instead, what I saw was colors. Everywhere. Every item glowed, each with their own shade. Their light wasn't the soft glow of life but the hard, concentrated blaze of master enchantments. Inside the vault was a shattered, burning rainbow, so bright it left me stunned. The raw, collected might of the greatest Weavers in history, who'd bound these items over millennia.

I thought the Eye might react to these artifacts with interest, the way it had previously when looking at master bindings. Instead, all I got from it was

(go go go)

impatience.

Well, I suppose it was right. There was no time for gawking. I glanced at the disk attached to the vault door. The energy inside was pulsing, seeking an escape.

"Let's finish this," I said, and we began our search. Each of us had been given a different task. Foxtail would hunt for the statue of the deer, the prize our inside man among the Weavers had demanded. Meriel would look for Daphna's payment, the red elixir. Lachlan had an equally important task: to find the artifact that would give us our way out.

When Daphna had told us about the lift down to the lower level and the need for a gold pendant to activate it, I'd balked. *I can probably play a gaff that will get us down there*, I'd said. *But how are we supposed to get back up carrying all those artifacts? And in fifteen minutes, no less?*

You won't need to, she'd told me. *My contact has a better way to escape. There's a board in the treasure room made of ivory. It looks like a gameboard, with little sandstone statues for pieces. If you put the pieces* on the board in the right pattern, it can open a portal that lets you travel instantly from one place to another.

Gareth was awed. *Teleportation? H-how?*

Daphna shrugged. *That's far beyond anything I understand. Regardless, our friend gave me the pattern for Quarry's Point. Once you have all the artifacts, place the pieces on the board like this*—she handed me the instructions—*and it will open a portal for you. But hurry through: The path only lasts for a few seconds. If you don't enter it in time, you'll be stuck down there.*

That made me wary enough to remind Lachlan of its dangers. "Don't play around with it," I told him. "Just find where it is."

"Righto, guv. You can count on me," he said, and he began wandering among the shelves. Every so often, he'd stop to stare at something, marveling at it.

"Lachlan, please. We need you."

"Sorry, guv." He shook his head, as if trying to rattle some sense into it. "The colors are just so pretty."

I couldn't blame him for dallying. We'd already seen the stain was drawn to bindings of the same violet. And sure enough, those were the artifacts Lachlan stopped to stare at. Even now, I could see the primeval swirling inside him, dancing about like a child in a candy shop, not sure which jar to open first.

"I could . . . I mean . . . I'll go with him," Gareth said.

"No. I need you to help me find the Dragon's Teeth."

I let Gareth lead the way, heading deeper. Unlike Lachlan, I could see *all* the colors in the vault, and they weren't just distracting. They were so bright, it made it hard to tell what I was looking at. What's more, I didn't like the feeling inside. As I moved farther in, the Eye's impatience had shifted. Now it was burning with anticipation

(closer closer closer)

ready for what was coming.

Gareth and I moved to the rear of the vault. I could hear the others searching, the *clink* of items being shifted as they looked for their prizes. Some of the artifacts on the shelves, I noted, had papers tucked underneath, or rolled-up scrolls of parchment leaning against them. Notes, I guessed, on how to use the things. *Or warnings not to*, I could hear the Old Man say.

We continued our hunt. What Gareth and I were looking for wasn't the Dragon's Teeth, at least not exactly. We were looking for the item Veran had written about in his journal: the golden idol of Artha.

Neither of us could spot it. My stomach started to flutter; time was ticking away. I didn't dare look at my pocket watch.

Where was that stupid statue? "It's in here somewhere," I said. "I *know* it is."

"How?" Gareth said.

"Because my ring is getting warm."

I held up my hand. As usual, there was no glow in the crystal. But the ring was definitely heating up.

Then it struck me: *This* would be our guide. Gareth and I wandered the room again, me concentrating on the ring. Whenever it cooled, I backtracked. If it warmed, I kept going.

We reached one corner of the vault, shelves lining the walls. Now the ring was burning hot.

And yet no idol.

"It should be right here," I said, puzzled. It wasn't until I pulled out the Eye again that I understood.

The shelf in front of me was filled with shining treasures, like the others. But it was what was *behind* the shelf that was special.

The wall was glowing.

Through my real eye, the stones of the wall looked unremarkable. But through the Eye, the whole section behind the shelf glowed a single, dull purple. I reached past the artifacts—

And my hand disappeared into the wall.

Gareth gasped. "An illusion."

Quickly, we dumped the artifacts on the floor. Then we grabbed the shelf and pushed it aside. The screech of metal against stone made me cringe. I prayed to Shuna we were too far away for any of the Weavers to hear it.

The wall unblocked, we stood in front of the illusion. Both of us stuck our hands through this time. Gareth marveled at how his arm just disappeared. It looked so real, yet we could feel nothing.

Lachlan came running to meet us. "Found it, guv! Told you you could count on me—*oh!*"

He skidded to a stop, staring in delight at our arms sunken into the wall. I realized too late: of course he'd want to reach through, too.

And when he did, the illusion burst.

I saw everything that happened through the Eye. As Lachlan stretched his hand out, the stain leapt to the end of his finger. The violet of the illusory wall evaporated, curling into wisps. Some vanished into the air, but some of that essence lingered, swirling around Lachlan's hand.

Then the stain devoured it.

The wisps were sucked into his fingers, and the primeval thrashed against the edges of his soul. It swelled, growing as it consumed the enchantment that had bound the illusion. New patterns flashed inside him, lines and whorls and spirals sparking with violet life.

I stared in horror. Over three-quarters of him was no longer Lachlan red. But his face was lit up with joy. He let out a breath of satisfaction—*ahhh*—and suddenly Gareth and I were blown by a wind that made our clothes flutter.

I'd have known it wasn't natural even if I hadn't been able to see the truth. Lachlan's breath glowed with primeval violet, the wind his magic. And all the while, I felt

(yes yes yes)

from the Eye.

Lachlan didn't even realize what he'd done. He puffed himself up and said, "What was *that*?"

I was almost afraid to touch him. But I did, my hand on his shoulder, peering into his face. "Are you all right?"

"You joking?" he said. "I feel *amazing*."

I didn't know what to do. "I . . . all right. Sit down."

"Why?"

"I can't . . . just . . . will you trust me?"

He was surprised at that. "Course I will, guv." He sat among the artifacts we'd removed from the shelf and stared up at me with innocent eyes.

We had to end this. I turned back to where the illusion had stood and saw the alcove that had been hidden behind it. In the middle was a pedestal. And on that pedestal stood a statue of a bear.

No, not *a* bear. *The* Bear. This was the idol of Artha. My crystal ring burned.

The idol was beautiful: pure gold, a perfect rendering of the Bear in exquisite detail, not a single flaw anywhere on its form. It was smaller than I'd thought it would be, only eight inches tall at the shoulder. It seemed strange that something so little should be able to summon a Spirit.

From the crusted coat of dust on the pedestal, no one had been back here in centuries, maybe millennia, whenever the illusion had been created. Strangely, there wasn't a speck on the idol itself.

"Hey," Lachlan said. "That's Artha."

He began to get up. Gareth blocked his path even before I could.

"Lachlan," I said, "whatever you do, *don't* play with the idol."

He seemed startled by how serious I was. "Righto, guv. No worries."

What he needed was a distraction. "You said you found the artifact that will get us out of here?"

"Sure as Shuna's a fox."

"Bring it here."

"Will do," he said, and he ran off into the shelves. Free from the need to watch over him—at least for the moment—I examined the idol with the Eye.

Gareth whispered, as if the statue might come alive if he spoke too loudly. "Can you s-see anything?"

"Too much," I said. The idol blazed in gold, brighter than any artifact I'd spotted yet. I wasn't sure which was more disconcerting: the shine from the Bear, or the ring burning my finger.

Either way, this wasn't what we'd come for. We needed to get the Dragon's Teeth, then get out of here. Veran had claimed he'd buried them in the wall behind the idol. Except I couldn't see any magic there at all.

"Veran said he hid the swords from scrying," Gareth pointed out. "To do that . . . I mean . . . it would have to be undetectable."

"Like Foxtail and her mask," I said.

He nodded.

Then we'd have to trust that Veran had told the truth. His final entry had given us the keyword to unseal the hidden chamber, so I inched around the pedestal to stand in front of the wall.

I took a deep breath. Then I spoke.

"Beloved," I said.

Nothing happened.

I tried again, raising my voice. "Beloved."

Still nothing.

"Um . . . Gareth?"

Gareth had turned pale as the keyword failed to reveal anything. He'd already pulled Veran's journal from his satchel and was reading the entry again. "I was sure . . . I mean . . . that's what . . ."

Now I *did* glance at my pocket watch. It said we'd been in the vault for eight and a half minutes so far. And time was ticking away. If we didn't get out of here soon, the alarm would sound. And then . . .

Be patient with Gareth, the Old Man warned.

Patience was the exact opposite of what I was feeling. But as usual, the Old Man was right; pushing Gareth would only make him shut down.

So patience was what he got. Leaving him to his reading, I turned instead toward Lachlan, who hurried to join us, arms full.

He was carrying an ivory board with a pouch of sandstone pieces, exactly what Daphna had told us to find. Carved into the board was a grid of squares, seven by seven, with the Weaver star etched in one corner. Lachlan placed the board on the floor and dumped the pieces onto the stone beside it.

"What now, guv?" he said.

I looked the pieces over. They were simple, flat-based cones, each with a different animal carved at the top. "Now we wait," I said. "Remember, we can't put them on until we're ready to go."

Lachlan sat cross-legged, elbows on his knees, chin resting on his hands as he stared at the board. Not entirely trusting of his boundless curiosity, I pocketed one of the pieces—a wolf—so even if he got tempted to start playing with them, he wouldn't be able to complete the sequence and open our escape portal too early.

I glanced over at Gareth. He was rereading the final page in the journal, looking from the scrawl to the dictionary I'd given him, comparing the meanings of the words, muttering to himself. "It's right. It *has* to be right."

My nerves couldn't take much more of this. I looked back down at Lachlan, just to make sure he hadn't found some new way to cause trouble.

He hadn't. He was, however, frowning at the board.

"What's wrong?" I said.

"Something's missing," he said.

"I took one of the pieces," I confessed.

"Huh? No, that ain't it. Something's not right."

"What?"

"Dunno. It's just not."

Lachlan sprang to his feet and hurried off again, back in the direction in which he'd found the board.

This was really getting out of hand. My pocket watch now said ten minutes were up. I listened, half cringing, for the cracking of the disk on the vault door. I couldn't hear anything.

Keeping my voice as casual as I could, I said to Gareth, "What do you think?"

He'd gone absolutely white. But I could tell that he wasn't just scared. He was embarrassed, even furious with himself, for failing. "It says 'beloved,' Cal. I'm s-sure of it. It's 'beloved.'"

"All right," I said. "I believe you. So if the translation is right, then something else must be wrong. What could that be?"

Gareth frowned, thinking. "Maybe . . . we're not in the right place?"

"Veran's journal said it was behind the idol of Artha," I pointed out. "And that the idol couldn't be moved."

"Unless . . ." Gareth trailed off, staring at the Bear. Then he looked at me. He didn't have to say what he was thinking.

What if, in the last two thousand years, someone had *found* a way to move it?

If that was true, it was over for us. We'd never find its original position before we ran out of time.

There was only one way to be sure it was fixed in place. Gareth realized that, too. Hesitant, scared, he reached out with one finger, prepared to touch the idol.

Veran's journal said no one had ever figured out how to use the thing. It seemed ridiculous that just touching it would make it work. I still held my breath. I even sent a plea to Shuna. *Please don't let this summon the Bear. Please please please please please—*

Gareth touched it.

Nothing happened.

Both of us sighed in relief. Certain it was safe now, Gareth pushed on the idol. When it didn't move, he grabbed it and tried to yank it off, one foot against the pedestal for leverage. It wouldn't budge.

That was it, then. Gareth may not have been the strongest, but even he should have had no trouble moving an eight-inch figurine. This was clearly the right spot.

"Then the Dragon's Teeth have to be here," I said.

Gareth nodded, troubled.

"So," I said, "if the translation isn't wrong, and the location isn't wrong, what's our mistake?"

Gareth turned to the last page of Veran's journal again. I could see the frustration in his face. He almost looked like he was about to cry.

Maybe the Eye can help, I thought.

The Old Man spoke. *Forget the Eye. That's not it.*

Then how do we find the answer? I said.

Gareth already knows the answer. He just can't see it yet.

So what do I do?

Tell him it's staring him in the face.

How will that help? I protested.

Must you always be so contrary? Just do as I say, boy.

It seemed ridiculous, listening to a voice in my head who wasn't even there. On the other hand, the Old Man was never really wrong. So I said, "Gareth. The answer is staring you in the face."

He looked up at me, puzzled. He opened his mouth as if about to ask me what that meant.

Then he stopped.

He blinked.

And he looked back down at the journal.

"That's it," he whispered. "That's *it.*"

CHAPTER 46

I COULDN'T BELIEVE that worked.

"What's it?" I said.

"The translation's wrong," Gareth said.

"The keyword isn't 'beloved'?"

"No. Yes. I mean . . . the *t-translation* is wrong."

"Gareth, you're not making any sense."

"Look." He showed me the last page in Veran's journal. "What do you see?"

"Gibberish."

"It's the Old Tongue."

"You told us that. So what?"

"Veran wrote this in the Old Tongue," Gareth said, "because he *spoke* the Old Tongue. Which means, when he created his hiding place, he didn't *say* 'beloved.' That's *our* word. *We're not using the right language.*"

My heart skipped a beat. "So . . . what's 'beloved' in the Old Tongue?"

"*Muirneach*," Gareth said.

And the wall behind the idol began to crumble.

Gareth stumbled backward as tiny cracks appeared in the stone, branching out like a spider's web. Slivers of rock fell away, then chunks, as the upper section of the wall collapsed. The broken pieces crumbled further as they hit the ground, until what was left of the seal was nothing but dust.

I grabbed Gareth's shoulders, shaking him. "I knew you could do it. I *knew* it."

Gareth looked pleased. Ignoring the burning ring on my finger, I stepped around the idol and peered into the hollow.

We'd found our prize.

Two swords lay within. In shape, they looked identical. Each had a jeweled pommel, one glittering white, the other black as night. The cross guards looked to be made of some kind of smooth stone, curved upward, away from the grips. The grips themselves were ridged leather, fine quality, but worn. These swords weren't showpieces. They'd been used.

As for the blades, I had no idea what they were made of. Fergal, the old storyteller, had said it was no metal known to man. He was half right, because as far as I could tell, the blades weren't metal at all. They were milky white, nearly opaque, with a slight translucency that allowed light to just barely penetrate the surface. They looked almost like enamel

(like teeth, just like teeth)

but an enamel I'd never seen before.

The swords were double edged. Two inches wide at the cross guard, the blades broadened to three inches wide at their centers, then narrowed gradually to a needle-sharp point at the end. They were shorter than I thought they'd be, the blades themselves less than two feet long.

As the Eye gazed upon the Teeth, its emotions swelled within me, stronger than any before, except when I'd lost control in the underground cavern. Standing in that alcove, my mind roiled with greed, with covetousness, with

(yes yes take them yes take them TAKE THEM)

unbridled, naked desire. It wanted these blades more than I'd ever wanted anything in my life.

And I couldn't help but wonder: What strange magic did they hide? The Eye had grabbed hold of me when I'd taken it up. Now it refused to let go. Would the Teeth do something terrible as well?

I supposed, at this point, it didn't really matter. Like back under the High Weaver's home, I'd made my choice long ago. I took a deep breath, reached out, and grabbed both swords by the hilt.

I felt nothing strange at all. The Eye did exult when I took them

(yes yes YES)

but they created no effect I could see.

I held them, marveling at their beauty, their craftsmanship. Their balance was absolutely flawless; they felt nearly weightless in my hands.

Gareth gazed at them in awe. "Camuloth," he said, his eyes falling on the black pommel of the sword in my right hand. "And Belenoth," he said, looking at the one with the white gem in my left.

Camuloth, the soulstealer. Belenoth, the healer. We had them.

And now it was more than time to go.

Meriel had already joined us. She stopped and stared at the swords in my hands, even as she held what she'd been looking for: a ruby-red vial the size of a small glass, the bowl wrapped with an ornate gold-foil cradle. Foxtail came now, too, lugging a mottled gray stone statue of a deer which looked heavier than its size would suggest. Only Lachlan was missing, and he was on his way, jogging back to us, still troubled.

His expression changed to delight when he saw the Dragon's Teeth. "Shuna's blessed backside," he said. "That's really them, innit?"

Seeing him reminded me of the whole point of our coming here. The Eye wanted the Teeth for its own purpose. All I really cared about was healing Lachlan of the stain inside.

Except I had no idea how to do that.

Looking through the Eye, the swords barely glowed, just the faintest hint of enchantment. That struck me as awfully odd. Given their apparent value, their supposed power, I'd expected them to glow brighter than anything I'd seen yet. It made me think, for one terrible moment, that I'd been rookered, that these swords were fake.

But the Eye's reaction when I'd picked them up couldn't have offered better proof. What I held were the genuine Dragon's Teeth. Now, however, I was getting something else from the Eye. A new sense of

(finish. finish.)

anticipation.

Something about these swords was incomplete. I could feel

the Eye urging me on, but it had no way of telling me to do exactly what. The feeling was distracting, so I put the patch back on. The Eye burned, outraged, harsher than I'd felt from it before. Then, like usual, it faded to nothing in my head.

"This is great and all," Meriel said, "but shouldn't we be getting out of here about now?"

Indeed we should. My pocket watch said it had been thirteen minutes since we'd broken the seal on the vault. I was shocked we hadn't already set off the alarm. "Gareth?"

He pulled out the paper with Daphna's instructions and crouched next to the board. I handed him the wolf piece I'd pocketed as Lachlan kneeled next to him.

"Oh, let me do it," Lachlan said. "Please, guv?"

"All right," I said. "But hurry up."

Foxtail held on to the deer statue she'd pilfered. Meriel crouched to watch, setting the red vial down beside the board as Gareth read the instructions out loud. "With the seven-pointed star in the lower left c-corner . . ." He adjusted the board. "Rabbit: first column, second row."

Lachlan placed the sandstone piece with the rabbit exactly where Gareth pointed.

"Fox," Gareth read. "Second column, sixth row."

Lachlan found the piece with the fox and put it in the correct spot. They continued, placing the other animal pieces—wolf, leopard, sheep, deer, and bear—as Daphna had listed. As Lachlan placed the last one, we sat back expectantly.

"Now what?" Meriel said.

"That's it," Gareth said. "I mean . . . that's what Daphna said to do. The last piece . . . I mean . . . placing the last piece is supposed to open the portal."

"So why isn't it working?"

"Told you, guv," Lachlan said. "Something's missing."

Then, suddenly, a new voice spoke. A man.

"It needs to be attuned," he said.

And everyone scattered.

CHAPTER 47

I STOOD, FROZEN, while the others dove for cover, disappearing behind the shelves.

That voice. I knew it. I'd heard it once before.

I couldn't see the man. We were in the corner near the alcove with the statue of Artha, so he was obscured by all the Weavers' treasures. His voice echoed from the entrance to the vault.

Soon enough, however, I heard his footsteps. Leather heels clopped on stone as he walked along the stacks. Then he came into view, standing at the far end of the aisle.

He was tall and broad, with closely cropped hair and a neatly trimmed beard peppered with gray. His eyes burned with focused intensity; his gaze radiated power. And around his neck hung a seven-pointed star, the frame gold, each arm filled with a different colored gem.

Darragh VII, High Weaver, gazed at me from across the vault. He was carrying an orb the size of an orange, which glowed the same color.

Inside, I was kicking myself for being a fool. I'd assumed when the disk failed that the alarm on the door would make a sound. I hadn't realized the warning would be silent. Still, I stayed where I was. Running wouldn't do any good.

I heard the Old Man in my head again, one of his endless lessons. *It's always best not to get cornered,* he'd told me long ago. *But if you have to stand and face your pursuers, you have two choices. Cower in fear, if you think it will help. Or stand bold and keep them guessing. Make them wonder: Why is he so confident? What does this gaffer know that I don't?*

I didn't think cowering would offer anything useful. So. Boldness it would be.

"Sorry," I said, "I didn't quite catch that."

Darragh was surprised at my response. I think he'd expected cowering. Nonetheless, he said, "The plexion." He nodded toward the ivory board at my feet. "Your young friend said something was missing. He is correct. The board needs to be attuned before it will work."

"I don't know what that means."

"You first have to take it to the location you want to go. Then, when you place the pieces on the board, you—well, never mind. You don't have the training to understand. Simply put, you need to take the device where you want to end up before it will transport you there."

"Sort of defeats the purpose, doesn't it?"

"Yes. It's an impressive enchantment. Unfortunately, not a particularly practical one." He looked around the room. "Much like most of what's in here."

The High Weaver seemed content to talk, at least for now. This fit in nicely with another of the Old Man's rules. *Keeping your enemy running his mouth can only work in your favor.* Though I didn't know what possible favor this could bring. How had Darragh caught us, anyway? Even if the alarm went off on the door, it still would have taken him time to get here. More time than he had to find us.

That meant he'd come down to the treasure room not long after we had. Had Padraig betrayed us upstairs? Was it possible that he gave us up?

Padraig wouldn't have told him, I thought. *I'd have bet my life on it.*

You did bet your life on it, the Old Man pointed out.

It couldn't have been him, I insisted. *It doesn't make sense.*

Of course it doesn't. The right answer should be obvious. Especially considering Darragh already knows about that board at your feet.

Oh. Of course.

My heart sank when I realized the truth. It sank deeper when our betrayer came into view.

"Daphna," I said.

She stood behind the High Weaver, wiping dust from her sleeve. "Sorry, darling."

I'd known this could happen. It still hurt that she did it. She'd watched me grow up. She'd been nice to me. Somewhere inside, I'd really thought she cared. I thought it would matter.

"Why?" was all I could say.

She had enough decency to look guilty. "I needed the elixir," she said. "You might have been able to steal it for me. But Darragh could give it to me for certain. As long as I delivered him something in return."

"I *did* steal it." I pointed to the vial Meriel had left beside the board. "You would have got what you wanted, with no one the wiser. I was taught by the Old Man. You should have trusted me."

She shook her head at that. "You *were* taught by the Old Man, so I'm surprised *you* didn't know better. Why would I take a chance with you, risk angering the Weavers, risk you getting caught and telling them I'd helped you, when I could simply go to Darragh and have him offer me a sure thing? Oh, Cal. The 'friends' you think you've made . . . you forgot how things really are. Other people are a weakness. Always."

I shook my head. "So what is this elixir, anyway?" I said bitterly. "What matters so much that you'd betray me?"

"The only thing that matters at all," she said. "A second life."

For all that I'd gotten wrong about her, I still knew Daphna well enough to understand what she meant. "A potion of youth," I said. The one thing she missed the most, the one thing she never could accept. Growing old.

"It's—"

"Be quiet, Daphna." The High Weaver waved at her dismissively. "Can't you see he's keeping you talking to distract me?"

Daphna fell silent. What interested me, though, was what Darragh had said. I *hadn't* been trying to distract him. I'd been genuinely wounded by Daphna's betrayal—and yes, I was trying to find out what was in that vial, to see if it could help me gaff my way out of this. But that was all. Why would Darragh think I was trying to distract him?

He answered by calling out, "Everyone stop moving."

He waited a moment. When there was no response, he spoke

again. "I said *stop moving*. I am speaking to you, girl. The one with the knives." He held up the glowing orange orb and looked to his left. "Yes, I can see you. You are three aisles away, creeping in the shadows. Trying to 'get the drop' on me, as you thieves say. Yes. I see you *all*."

Well, that explained the purpose of the orb. It let him know exactly where we were and what we were doing. Which made it impossible to spring an ambush.

"Everyone," he commanded. "Return to your friend."

I couldn't hear anyone moving.

"If I have to repeat myself," Darragh said, "I will simply start killing you one by one."

"You're going to kill us anyway," I said.

"I am," he said. "You do, however, have a choice. Will the time that remains for you be peaceful? Or will it be painful?"

Gareth was the first to surrender. He hadn't gone far, just cowered behind the nearest shelf. I could hear someone else, too, far away to be Meriel, walking toward us, but whether that was Lachlan or Foxtail, I didn't know. They were obscured behind the artifacts.

Fuming, Meriel joined us next. She hadn't quite given up— from the way she was holding her hands, she had knives hidden in her palms—but any attack, I was sure, would be futile. Darragh had brought that orb of his to prevent surprises. He wasn't leaving anything to chance.

The Old Man raised an eyebrow. *Isn't he?*

What do you mean? I said.

With Meriel back in view, the High Weaver returned his gaze

to me. Or rather, to the Dragon's Teeth I was holding. "I must give you credit—Callan is your name?"

I nodded.

"You discovered the swords," Darragh said. "Impressive. Ingenuity, sadly, is sorely lacking in our guild at the moment."

It struck me as funny that Mr. Solomon had said the same thing. "Well," I said, "if you'll spare us, we'd be happy to join."

"Ingenuity, I like. Wit, I find tedious."

"Sorry."

"But you should be commended," he said. "What do you think? Are those the real Dragon's Teeth?"

"Honestly?" I said. "We've seen so many fakes, I don't know."

That was a lie, of course. A double lie, really. Not only had we never found fakes, the Eye knew well enough that these were the genuine blades. Still, why make it easy for him? We weren't dead yet. Maybe one or two of us could still gaff our way out of this.

"Let's make sure," Darragh said.

Still holding the orange orb, the High Weaver drew a rod from beneath his jacket. Daphna waited behind him, trying to look unconcerned. Though for all her talk of practicality, she wouldn't meet my eyes anymore.

Lachlan finally made it to where we were standing. He'd been shuffling his feet, moping at being caught. He joined us just as Darragh pointed the rod at me. I flinched.

"It won't harm you," Darragh said.

"What does it do?" I said.

"It will confirm whether everything I've been told is true."

I wasn't sure what that meant. Was it a lie detector? Or did he mean he was testing the swords I held? Either way, he moved the rod, studying it. He seemed to be concentrating on its vibrations; I could hear it humming in his hand.

What was that you said before? I asked the Old Man.

You claimed the High Weaver wasn't leaving anything to chance, the Old Man said. *But he is.*

How? I said.

Well, boy, what happened the last time you saw him?

The last time was in the underground laboratory beneath his home. I'd used the High Weaver's experiments—and the Eye's knowledge—to escape.

Yes, the Old Man said. *So what's different now?*

What was different was the Eye couldn't talk anymore. It couldn't help me find a way out. I'd barely even made it that time, after Darragh's apprentices had fired—

Wait.

I whispered to Meriel, keeping my lips as still as I could. "Did you see anyone else with Darragh? Besides Daphna, I mean."

"No," she whispered back, still glaring murderously at the two of them. "They're alone."

I frowned. When the High Weaver had last been after me, he'd chased me down with an entire troop of aides. Armed guards, armed apprentices; he'd brought as many men as he could grab along the way.

And that was all spur of the moment. Tonight, he'd *known* we were coming. Daphna had told him, and he'd used her to lure us down here. Yet he'd only shown up with her, and in a fight, Daphna would be useless.

So why had he come alone? Did he not think we'd be much of a threat?

Come on, boy, the Old Man said. *You stole the Eye out from under his nose. You've caused the High Weaver more trouble than anyone else in his life. Why would he think you weren't a threat?*

I tried to think it through. *If he's not confident we can't snaffle him again,* I said slowly, *the only reason to come alone ... is because he doesn't want any of the other Weavers to know what's happening.*

Why wouldn't he?

"Those *are* the true blades," Darragh said. "Remarkable."

As he spoke, I listened carefully to his tone. And I heard the greed in his words.

"He wants the swords," I said under my breath. "He wants the Dragon's Teeth for himself."

"Hand them to me," Meriel muttered. "I'll give them to him—right in his guts."

But now Gareth looked at me, confused. "He c-can't keep the T-Teeth," he whispered, his stammer worse than ever. "It's i-illegal."

Right. That three-thousand-year-old law of Aeric's was still on the books. No one was allowed to touch these swords, not even the emperor. Even holding them was a death sentence.

So what was Darragh doing?

He turned to Daphna and glared at her. "Those are the real Teeth," he said. "But the child doesn't have the Eye."

And then I understood.

Whatever it was the Eye wanted with the Teeth ... Darragh wanted the same.

CHAPTER 48

THIS WAS NOT good.

"You told me," Darragh said to Daphna, voice cold, "that these were the thieves who'd stolen the Eye."

"They are," she said nervously. "I'm sure of it."

So *that* was the reason she'd sought out Darragh to betray me. In the darkness of his underground laboratory, the High Weaver hadn't seen me well enough to identify who I was. But Daphna's Weaver friends must have told her the Eye had been stolen. Then I'd given her enough clues to put the pieces together. I let slip I'd done a job in Carlow; I told her we'd escaped the lockdown; I revealed I'd seen Weaver experiments. Even that I'd lost my own eye.

What a prize we would be to the one man who wanted us more than anything. To the man Daphna had known since she was a child. Of course she'd give us up; Darragh would grant her anything she wanted in return. It really was her smartest play.

"If he has the Eye," Darragh said to her, temper still smoldering, "then why can I not detect it?"

"His eyepatch," she said, shrinking under his anger. "I think there's something special about it."

Darragh turned to look at me speculatively.

"He kept lifting it on the boat," Daphna said. "Something's hidden underneath."

I cursed myself. I'd let her see so much. Stupid, stupid, stupid.

"Lift your eyepatch," Darragh commanded.

"You don't want me to do that," I warned him.

The High Weaver tucked the rod he was holding back in his robe. He brought out a different rod, smooth, blue-white, almost like marble.

I'd seen that kind of rod before. It froze things. If it froze them enough, they'd die.

He pointed it at Lachlan.

"Wait!" I cried as Meriel shoved Lachlan behind her. "Wait."

Darragh waited, rod held outward.

I gave in. There wasn't any point in resisting. There would be no charming Darragh, and no confusing him, either. I didn't have any gaff to stop him. If I tried, he'd just kill my friends one by one.

So I lifted the eyepatch as he'd ordered and revealed the Eye.

I saw the glow of magic again, the enchantments that shone on the shelves. I saw, too, the red lifeglow of Darragh and Daphna. Daphna had a hint of green in hers. Darragh had the strongest tint of icy blue I'd seen in anyone. The rod he held shone bright azure, as did his jewelry, the rings and bracelets blazing with cold light. His High Weaver's pendant was the only thing he had that wasn't blue. It glittered with iridescence, different colors flashing with dizzying speed.

He was missing one thing, though, which surprised me. The other two powerful enchanters I'd seen—Bragan and Mr.

Solomon—had both been covered with invisible runes tattooed all over their skin. Darragh didn't have any tattoos I could see.

Even more interesting was the reaction of the Eye. When it saw the High Weaver, I felt a swell of amused contempt. Darragh had been High Weaver for eighteen years, which meant he'd been the Eye's captor for nearly two decades. I wondered how many times he'd tried to remove the artifact from its cave, only to be stymied.

Darragh tried not to look surprised that I'd kept the Eye hidden in plain sight, but I could see the slight waver in his confidence that I'd somehow foiled his detection magic. He collected himself quickly, lowering the rod.

"Place the Eye on the floor," he said.

"I can't."

He lifted the rod again.

"I *can't*," I said desperately. "It won't let me."

Darragh frowned. "What do you mean?"

"It's grabbed on to me. It won't let me go."

The High Weaver studied me, considering.

"Listen," I said. "I promise I'm not trying to make you angry, but I'm telling you: You *really* don't want the Eye. It doesn't like you."

"Excuse me?" he said dangerously.

I spread my hands in apology. "It just doesn't like you. You tried to take it from the pedestal in the cave. It won't serve you. If you try to use it now, it's going to hurt you."

For the first time, the High Weaver looked rattled. "How would you—" He broke off as he realized the only possible answer to that question. "The Eye is *sentient*?"

"Yes," I said. "It's alive. And frankly, it's not very nice."

Inside, I felt a swell of mirth. The Eye was *laughing*. It really seemed to enjoy me talking back to Darragh. I guess it liked seeing the High Weaver squirm. Which was fine enough for it, I suppose, but that didn't help me any. All I was doing was treading water, trying to buy time before Darragh killed us.

It struck me then that it was possible, if I confused him enough about the Eye, he'd spare me—at least until he'd extracted every bit of information he could. But I could already see by the way his gaze flicked dismissively to my companions—from me to Meriel, to Lachlan, to Gareth, then back—he considered them worthless. He was about thirty seconds from killing every one of them—

Wait.

Every one?

Where was Foxtail?

Finally, you noticed, the Old Man said.

I stood there, as puzzled now as the High Weaver. Foxtail hadn't come back when Darragh had ordered my friends to return. She was still hiding among the artifacts. How . . . ?

My heart began to thump.

Her mask.

Darragh knew where we were because of that orb. It let him see our life energy, even when out of sight. *But Foxtail was hidden from magic by her mask.*

Yes, the Old Man said. *Now, what will she do with that knowledge? Hide until it's safe to come out?*

No, I thought. *She'll—*

"Get ready," I mumbled to Meriel.

"What?" she whispered back.

"Foxtail's missing," I said.

No longer focused on his own devices, the High Weaver heard us muttering this time. "What are you two saying?"

I gave him my best look of innocence. "Nothing."

"Be careful, Darragh," Daphna said. "Cal's mentor was a genius. The boy's trickier than you think."

Darragh regarded us with contempt. "None of them could possibly harm me. Nonetheless, you have a point. I have no use for the others anymore."

He began to raise the blue-white rod.

Just then, Daphna realized she'd been missing someone, too. "Wait—where's the veiled girl?"

"What veiled girl?" Darragh said.

That's when Foxtail showed him.

CHAPTER 49

HE NEVER SAW it coming.

Darragh VII, High Weaver, was the most accomplished enchanter of our time. His knowledge, his talent, his sheer power had lifted him to the highest level any in his guild could attain. He'd lived a life of magic, through magic. So he trusted magic, relied on it.

And that was his mistake.

He'd trapped us here, knowing that glowing orange orb in his hand would warn him if anyone tried to sneak up on him. It was how he'd caught Meriel.

But he'd never accounted for a girl like Foxtail. After a lifetime of success, he'd never imagined his magic could fail him. So when Foxtail sprang *her* trap, he didn't see it coming. Literally.

From her hiding place on Darragh's left, Foxtail hurled the stone deer statue straight toward him. End over end, it tumbled through the air.

Then it smacked him right in the temple.

The deer bounced off the side of his skull with a hollow-sounding *thunk*. His head snapped to the side, and he staggered, eyes going glassy.

"*Now, Meriel!*" I shouted.

She was already moving. Meriel flung both knives she'd palmed straight at the High Weaver.

If he hadn't been dazed, he could have defended himself. But off balance, his mind reeling, he brought up no magical protection. Both blades punched home, right in the center of his chest.

Daphna squealed in alarm as her childhood friend crumpled. Darragh's eyes went wide with horror. The orange orb slipped from his hand, shattering with a blinding blast as it hit the stone below. The freezing rod he held fell, too, bouncing on the floor once, blown sideways as the orb exploded. I heard it rattling as it rolled away, lost under the shelves.

Quick as lightning, Meriel pulled two more knives from hidden pockets and sent them flying toward the dying High Weaver. But the blades she'd hit him with earlier had triggered some magical defense. As Darragh fell, a ring on his left hand flared, and ice crystals began to form in front of him. Tiny like snowflakes, they grew with alarming speed until a wall of clear, pure ice surrounded him.

Her knives struck the frozen wall and bounced off, chipping ice shavings into the air. Daphna squealed again and fled deeper into the vault as Meriel drew two more blades. One she threw at the High Weaver, the other at the fleeing Daphna. Neither hit their mark: the crystal wall was impervious to her attack, and the knife flung after Daphna clattered harmlessly as she ducked behind the shelves.

I stared through the ice at the collapsed High Weaver. He stared back, unfocused, grasping clumsily at the blades sticking out of his body. I couldn't believe Meriel had killed him.

Except... she hadn't.

As Darragh's life began to fade in the Eye, a second ring flared, releasing its binding. Gareth huddled close to me, staring in horrified wonder as the blood that ran from Darragh's wounds crystallized into crimson-colored ice. Meriel's knives, protruding from his flesh, began to change, too. I heard crackling, like a frozen pond breaking under bootheels, and the daggers turned to ice along with the blood.

Then they shattered. The blades burst into frozen shards that glittered in the light as they fell. Left behind in the wounds instead were giant chunks of ice; sharp, ugly crystals that began to drip.

And as that ice melted, it formed new flesh. The High Weaver howled, the healing crystals as agonizing as the knives' cuts.

But he did heal. And soon his skin was unmarked, as if he'd never been injured.

The rings that had flared cracked, their enchantment spent. Slowly, the High Weaver brought himself back to his feet.

And unbridled fury blazed in his eyes.

"Oh . . . no," Meriel said, and she dove for cover behind the shelf. Lachlan and I did the same. Foxtail hid, too, presumably, wherever she was.

But Gareth was too slow.

Raging, Darragh clenched both hands. Then, howling a word I didn't understand, he punched his fists outward.

The crystal wall shattered at his command, sending frozen

boulders smashing into everything around him. One cracked Gareth in the back of his head, just as he dove to join us. He collapsed, sprawling in a heap on the floor.

"Gar!" Lachlan cried, dismayed.

Gareth was bleeding. We dragged him to cover, even as the bursting shards brought a hailstorm down upon us. Lachlan pressed his palm against the back of Gareth's skull, trying to stop the flow of blood as we were pelted with ice.

But the High Weaver was only getting started. He spoke another word, and suddenly the air was bitter, bitter cold. Winter had come to claim us.

"I will kill you all," Darragh whispered.

What could we do against such magic? I stared with the Eye at the Dragon's Teeth in my hand. The glow in them was so weak.

Tell me how to activate these, I said.

I felt that swell of anticipation again. The Eye wanted me to use them

(do it. do it. do it.)

but, silenced, it couldn't tell me the words. Frustration filled my mind, and not just my own. The Eye was getting angry.

Foxtail finally came into view. She was crawling over the tops of the shelves, trying to find some new surprise ground to attack the High Weaver. But Darragh spotted her and spoke again. Another one of his rings sparked and flashed a brilliant blue.

Then Foxtail was encased in ice.

"Foxtail! No! No!" Lachlan cried.

She froze there, on top of the shelf, teetering. The warning of the mad old thief Seamus I'd met in Clarewell Sanatorium burned in my mind. *Checker was frozen. Shattered like ice. Starling, too. Crack and crumble, she did.* If Foxtail fell . . .

Darragh roared. *"I will kill you all!"*

I gripped the swords in my hands. *Tell me what to do!* I screamed at the Eye. *Give me something!*

It gave me nothing but swelling frustration.

Meriel tried to sneak around to Foxtail, using the shelves as cover. "Wait!" I called to her. "It's a trap!"

I was too late. Too late to explain that the High Weaver had frozen Foxtail *expecting* us to try to save her. Like a sharpshooter who wounds an enemy so his comrades come to help him—and leave themselves exposed.

Darragh uttered the same word as before. Now Meriel, too, was encased in ice, her arm back, ready to throw another knife.

"No!" Lachlan cried. "Stop! NO!"

Watching his friends die, the only friends he'd ever had, was too much for him. And so Lachlan broke.

He stood and sprang into the open.

"Lachlan!" I shouted. "Don't!"

I grabbed for him, but he was already gone. He barreled toward the High Weaver.

Darragh scoffed. A third time he spoke, and Lachlan was frozen in ice.

Then the boy exploded.

CHAPTER 50

THE ICE AROUND Lachlan shattered.

Tiny shards blew outward in a sphere, peppering everything in sight. I covered my face. The blast hit my clothes, lacerated my hands. My skin stung, burned by the cold.

Then I looked up and saw Lachlan.

He was ... different.

In my own eye, he looked the same as always: so young, so innocent. But the primeval lashed about gleefully, freed by Lachlan's fury, feeding on it.

And once more, it grew.

Darragh stared at the boy in shock. "How ... ?"

Lachlan raged, and the storm raged within him, too. "*Leave my friends alone!*" he screamed, and the High Weaver actually took a step back.

Then the man redoubled his attack. He spoke two new words, and two more of his rings flared.

His first command created a whirling sphere of winter around him, the air so cold it warped our vision, his form shimmering as if seen over desert sands.

With his second command, he thrust his fists outward. The air cracked as the cold shot toward the boy, halting his advance.

Lachlan covered his head, crying out in pain as frost formed on his skin. And if it was just the child inside, he would have been frozen through, shattering like those poor thieves caught in the High Weaver's traps. Crack and crumble.

But it wasn't just Lachlan anymore. The primeval magic flowed into his hands and blew the frost away. Then it spun its own whirling sphere of howling wind around him. The air bent and buckled, and the cold blew backward, until the streaming wind forced a stalemate between them.

There the battle raged. Where cold met wind, a blizzard formed. The damp air in the dungeon crystallized, creating snow that whipped through the vault. I huddled behind the shelf, cradling Gareth, as we were suddenly caught in the worst snowstorm Ayreth had ever seen.

Hail ripped at my face, battered my hands. A new light flashed from Darragh—another ring adding its power. The stain inside Lachlan swirled and burst, meeting the enchantment with equal strength.

And for the first time, Darragh actually looked scared. For all his knowledge, all his might, he'd never seen magic like this. "How?" he whispered again, his voice carried away by the gale.

How? I knew well enough. It was the primeval magic—and it was growing.

My stomach lurched as the stain inside Lachlan swelled. It wasn't merely fighting the High Weaver's magic anymore. It was changing it, *feeding* on it. And the boy it had infected was changing, too. Lachlan's face, always so friendly, had twisted into a snarl of rage—and delight.

In a way, that was even more horrifying. Lachlan—the *essence* of Lachlan, his soul, everything he was—was disappearing, consumed by the primeval. I remembered Bragan's words.

The magic inside will grow in him, the cultist had said. *When it begins to dominate . . .*

"The child inside will die," I whispered.

Yes, the Old Man said.

And what would be left in his place?

Something not human, the Old Man said. *Something cruel.*

What do I do? I asked him.

Remember what I taught you, he said. *There's always a way out.*

Something flashed in the corner of my eye.

I looked up through the blizzard, expecting to see more magic. But all I saw was a glimpse of gold, tucked away in the corner alcove.

And so the answer came to me. Mad, lunatic, absolutely insane, the answer came.

Weavers are arrogant, self-important, and hot-tempered, I thought. *Hot-tempered . . . just like their patron.*

The Old Man sounded amused. *Indeed.*

I finally knew what to do.

CHAPTER 51

I FOUGHT MY way through the blizzard.

I could barely see anymore. Gareth, on the floor, was quickly covered with blowing snow. Foxtail, still frozen, teetered precariously atop her shelf, rocked by howling winds. Flakes lay heavily on Meriel, too, still entombed in ice. Her expression was one of shock and panic. If we didn't get her out soon, she'd suffocate. If she didn't freeze to death first.

I couldn't really see the others. The Eye caught glimpses of their life energy through the snow—Darragh's blue-tinged red, Lachlan's quickly growing violet, the blue and purple enchantments battling between them—but it, too, was nearly blinded by the brilliance of the magic being unleashed.

As it was more a distraction than a help now, I covered the Eye with my patch and pushed forward. I shivered, the chill biting all the way to my bones. Every part of me felt frozen.

Well, *almost* every part. The crystal ring was burning.

In the chaos, I'd forgotten about it. I'd just got used to the heat. But it grew hotter as I approached the statue. I tucked the Dragon's Teeth beneath one arm and cupped my hands over the ring. Though it was practically scorching my finger, the warmth felt absolutely Spirit-sent. Which, given what I was about to do, was a little ironic.

The ring seared me as I stood before the idol of Artha.

Are you sure you want to do this? the Old Man said.

No, I said. *But unless you have any brighter ideas . . .*

He snorted. *It would be hard to find one dimmer.*

Didn't you always tell me, I said, *that sometimes you just have to gamble on the long shot?*

He laughed. *So I did.*

Still, one question remained.

How exactly was I supposed to use the idol?

How did one summon a Spirit? I'd spoken to Shuna three times now, but I'd never actually brought her to me. Twice, the Fox had been waiting in the forest. The other time, Foxtail had put some kind of leaf in my soup, and the next thing I knew, I was in a strange place.

None of that helped me now. I couldn't ask Foxtail; she was sealed in ice, dying. I didn't have one of those leaves; I didn't even know what it was. Besides, I didn't want to go to Artha. I needed her here.

I clasped my hands together. *Please, Artha, I need your help.*

It's hardly going to be that easy, the Old Man said.

Then what do I say? I said, desperate. *Weavers tried for millennia to summon Artha with this thing. Even they couldn't make it work.*

No. But they didn't have what you have.

What did that mean? What did *I* have?

A special relationship with Shuna? She *was* Artha's greatest enemy.

But what good would that do? Was I supposed to taunt her with it? And wouldn't that break Shuna's rules—

No.

Wait.

I *did* have something those Weavers didn't.

My crystal ring.

In the woods, outside Quarry's Point, I'd tried to touch Shuna with it. She wouldn't let me.

But seriously, I'd said. *If I did touch you with the ring, what would happen?*

Something very interesting, Shuna had said.

Was it possible . . . the Fox had given me a hint?

Heart pounding, I brought the ring close. It felt like it was on fire now. Even in the freezing cold, it was too much.

But I had to try. I touched the ring to the idol and

the ring *shattered*

my finger *burned*, how it *burned*, my flesh searing it *hurts*

and a sound reverberated through the hall.

GONGGGGGGGGGGGGG

The agony in my finger was all but forgotten as the tone threatened to shake my whole being apart. It sounded like a bell, but as I clapped my hands to my ears, I realized the sound wasn't in the air. It was in my *soul*.

The tone rang, resonating deep within, and nothing anywhere could block it out. The whole world seemed to vibrate with that bell. The enchanted artifacts that filled the shelves shook and toppled. The fragile ones burst where they hit, sending waves of magical energy rippling through the blizzard that filled the vault.

The ice surrounding Meriel and Foxtail shattered, and both girls fell to the ground. Foxtail tumbled behind her shelf, where I couldn't see her. Meriel lay in the snow, gasping for air, shaking with bitter cold.

And Darragh and Lachlan just . . . stopped. They stood there, immobile, their magical battle halted.

Then they collapsed, utterly stunned into unconsciousness.

The blizzard died with them. The wind stopped howling, and the flakes that had stung my skin no longer whipped about. Lazily, now, they fell, adding a new blanket to the snow that covered the floor, the storm transformed into a peaceful winter's day.

The ringing faded, as if echoing off into forever. When the sound of the bell finally died, the room was deathly quiet, the silence of a totally empty plain.

Then a footstep crunched in the snow.

CHAPTER 52

I FROZE.

I remained quiet, listening, wondering if I'd imagined it. My breath puffed into the air, little clouds blowing away in wisps.

Then I heard snuffling.

Now more footsteps came.

crunch

crunch

crunch

they sounded. And the shelves trembled with every step.

The crunching stopped. *Hrhh*, I heard. *Hrhh, hrhh.*

And then a bear—the Bear—walked into view.

Every image I'd ever seen depicted her as a big brown bear. Yet no image, no imagination, no nothing could have measured up to the beast that walked this vault. Six feet tall at her shoulders, the Bear lumbered through the snow, snuffling, muscles rippling under rich chestnut fur.

This was Artha. *This* was a Spirit. I could feel the power coming off her in waves.

She stared blankly about the room. Slowly, she moved her head, still groggy as her hibernation ended. When she spoke, her voice was a thunderous rumble.

"Who ... awakens me ... from my slumber?"

I've heard that voice before, I realized. In my dream, my nightmare, after passing out in Mr. Solomon's house. When he'd set it on fire.

The Bear had stood over me as I lay bound to some stone slab. *This Eye is missing*, she'd said. *I'll have to take the other one, too.*

It was the same voice. I was sure of it.

My stomach fluttered. *I really stepped in it this time, Old Man.*

I could almost see him leaning against the wall in the alcove, arms folded. He raised an eyebrow. *That depends on you. You dealt this hand, boy. Time to play it out.*

"Who . . . summons . . . me?" Artha said.

Time to poke the bear. Um . . . literally.

"He does," I said.

The Bear looked at me, blinking away sleep. I pointed to the unconscious figure lying at the other end of the vault. "That's Darragh VII, High Weaver," I said.

Artha regarded the man lying in the snow. "One of . . . my own?" she said.

She lumbered over to him, sniffed at his body.

"He is rich in magic," she said. "Yet there is no summons which binds him."

She sniffed the air now. Then, slowly, she turned her head to me.

"You," she said.

Artha padded toward me, eyes fixed on mine. The snow crunched under her paws.

Meriel had finally caught her breath. Still shivering, she looked up—and stared in utter shock at the sight of the Bear walking by.

Meriel stayed there, mouth open, until a small hand—Foxtail—reached from behind the shelf where she lay and dragged Meriel to safety by her collar.

Meriel stuck her head out and watched, still disbelieving, as Artha stopped five feet away from me. I'd never been so scared in my life.

"The binding lingers," the Bear said, "on *you*. *You* summoned me."

"Uh . . . right. About that . . ." I said. "It was a mistake. An accident, I mean. I'm very sorry."

The Bear took another step toward me. "What is this? You seek to toy with me? A *child*? You . . . you . . ."

She trailed off, tilted her head. She looked . . . puzzled.

"I know you," she said.

Me? "I don't think so."

"You visited me in Shadow."

I had no idea what she meant. The only time I'd even heard the Bear's voice was in—

"My *dream*?" I whispered.

The weight of what she'd said struck me dumb. That was *my* dream. *My* nightmare. The Bear . . . had really *been* there?

"You were injured," she said. "I was . . . I was . . ." She trailed off. "I don't remember." Then her expression hardened. "Someone attacked me. They were helping you."

That was exactly what had happened. A crow had saved me. It had dived down and bloodied Artha's snout. By the Spirits . . . I'd shared a dream with the Bear.

How was that possible?

Artha stepped closer, glaring balefully. "What were you doing there?"

I didn't dare answer with anything but the truth. "I don't know. I passed out in this Weaver's house, and then I was dreaming."

"You don't *know*?"

"No."

Artha stepped closer. Her breath was hot on my face. "Then why do you stink of my sister . . . *foxchild*?"

I didn't answer. Mostly because I didn't know what to say.

The Bear growled. "You thought you could fool *me*? You thought you could steal from *me*?"

What? "I haven't stolen anything from you," I protested.

"You lie. I can smell the truth, as surely as I can smell Shuna on your skin. It's why you're here. *You came for the bones that remain.*"

"I don't even know what that means."

"Then show me what you're hiding behind your back."

Suddenly, I understood what she was talking about. *You came for the bones that remain.*

I brought my hands around. Gripped in both palms were Aeric's twin swords.

Artha's eyes glittered. "The Teeth. You *found* them. Give them to me."

Suddenly, an idea flared in my mind. "How about a deal?"

Her voice rumbled dangerously. "A *deal*?"

"Sure. I give you the swords. In return, you heal my friend, Lachlan. Take away the stain in his soul."

Her growling grew louder. "You presume to offer me what is

already *mine*? You *steal* from me, then demand a *bargain*?"

"I didn't steal—"

"Give me the Teeth."

I stepped back, nearly slipping in the snow. *I can't*, I said desperately to the Old Man. *If Artha takes the swords, I'll never get them back. I'll never be able to heal Lachlan.*

He watched the scene with interest. *I'd be more worried about how the Eye will punish you if you give them to her. To say nothing of what Artha might do if you don't.*

Either way, we lose, I said. *Lachlan dies. And so do I.*

Do you?

I frowned. What did that mean?

The Bear stepped closer. *"Give me the Teeth."*

What do you mean? I said to the Old Man. *Why wouldn't Artha kill me?*

Don't you pay attention to anything anyone says? he said. *Answer your own question, boy.*

What was he talking about? How could I—

Oh.

Indeed, the Old Man said. *Now the play truly begins. Best be bold.*

I'd have to be—because there was only one way out of this now. And it was the hardest thing I'd ever had to do.

I looked the Bear straight in the eye.

"No," I said.

The Bear drew herself up on her hind legs. She was twelve feet tall. Inside, my guts churned, pure liquid fear.

"You would defy me?" she roared.

She drew back a great paw. Each claw was three inches long.

I'd meant to stand there and not flinch. But even with all the Old Man's training, I couldn't help myself. I cringed, and my hands came up automatically, defending my head with the swords.

She swiped her paw down.

But she wasn't aiming for me. Instead, she struck the blades of the Dragon's Teeth with an impossible, unstoppable force. The swords ripped from my hands and flew into the wall beside me. The blades made a strange ringing tone as they hit, chipping stones away that fell into the snow. The swords fell, too, sinking into the cover of white.

Artha snatched them up. Despite the violence with which she'd flung them, there wasn't a single nick on the blades. The Dragon's Teeth clenched in one paw, she turned back to me.

She leaned in, nose to nose, and growled. Her muzzle was flecked with spit. "You," she snarled, "have forgotten your place. You humans *breed*, and you *build*, and you *expand*. You think you're so *clever*. But you know *nothing* of the world. *Nothing* of the dimensions beyond. *Nothing*." She leaned in, teeth snapping, as she bit off every word. "*You—are*—NOTHING."

I stared back at her, silent.

She drew away. "Yes," she said. "That is your place, foxchild. Never forget it." She raised the Teeth. "I was denied my right before. No one will stop me this time. Not you, not my sister. I will collect the other pieces. And when I have them, no one will stand in my way."

She turned her back on me—I was no threat—and began to

crunch through the snow, carrying away the swords. She passed by Gareth, who'd regained consciousness. With blood drying on his skull, he stared at the departing Bear with the same slack-jawed shock as Meriel.

The other pieces, Artha had said. I thought of the Eye's desire to come get the Teeth, and of what Mr. Solomon had told me when I'd brought him the artifact. *There's a . . . let's call it a set. The Eye, no doubt, wanted to join with its brethren.*

But my gaff had failed. Artha wasn't supposed to take the swords. If she left, they'd be lost to me forever.

I couldn't let the Bear get away. So I realized: I had one play left. Only one.

I watched her walk away for a moment. Then I bent down and scooped up a handful of snow. It was fluffy and wet—great stuff for packing.

I made it into a good, strong snowball. Then I took careful aim.

And pelted the Bear with it right in her rump.

Leaning against the wall beside me, the Old Man laughed and laughed and laughed.

No one else did. Meriel, still peeking out from behind her shelf, stared at me in horror. I couldn't even read Gareth's expression. It was like his brain simply couldn't comprehend the utter insanity of what I'd done. I wished Lachlan was awake. He, at least, might have appreciated this.

The Bear halted in her tracks. She turned, incredulous, barely able to believe what had happened.

"You . . . *dare?*" she said.

Fury came off her in waves. I could feel it, almost a living thing, pulsing through the air. The fear that had gripped my guts since she'd arrived wrenched, threatening to make me crumble. It took every ounce of discipline the Old Man had taught me not to fall to my knees and beg forgiveness.

But asking forgiveness wasn't the gaff. So when I spoke, I forced my voice not to tremble. Instead, I laughed. Sneering. Mocking.

"Of course I dare," I said. "You're stupid, Artha."

The Bear's eyes went black. The waves of fury that emanated from her began to melt the snow beneath her body.

"What?" she said quietly.

"I didn't believe it at first," I said. "When Shuna told me how easy it would be to play a gaff on you, I thought she was joking. 'Nobody's that dumb,' I said, 'certainly not a Spirit.' But Shuna knew. She's been snaffling you forever. Yet you fall for it every time."

I didn't know which enraged the Bear more: my laughter or saying her sister had fooled her—again. She stood there, shaking with silent rage.

"Now," I continued, "you think you're off to find 'the rest of the pieces.' Which one first? The Eye? Where are you going to find it? Where do you think it is?"

The air around Artha began to warp. The artifacts on the shelves beside her rattled. A silver plate bent, creaked, then crumpled, squeezing into a misshapen ball. A wooden mannequin snapped; the binding within escaped, strange words whispering in my ear.

Artha's power was coming unraveled. It was like everything around her was made only of dream-stuff

(of Shadow)

that Artha could bend and reshape to her will. But there was no will behind her power now. It was pure, unbridled fury.

"Go on, guess," I said. "Guess where the Eye is. No? That's what I thought. Too *stupid*."

The ceiling above the Bear cracked.

"Too stupid to see what's right in front of you." I laughed. "Just like Shuna said."

I took off my eyepatch.

And the Eye gazed upon the Bear.

She shone as bright as the sun. A deep brownish-gold, I could see her outline, as clear in the Eye as with my own. Ribbons of light circled Artha, the same as the sleeping sheep below Lake Galway. Sparks and flashes and strange, unearthly symbols twisted around them, a web of alien life: the mark of a Spirit. My skin where the crystal ring had shattered burned deep as I watched her. Whether it was the remnant of the hidden magic in the ring or just my scorched flesh, I couldn't know.

I'd had no idea what would happen when the Eye saw Artha. This whole gaff had been nothing but a desperate gamble. I steeled myself against the Eye's reaction. The last time it had gazed upon a Spirit, I'd lost my mind, overwhelmed by the artifact's hatred.

There was hatred here now, too. But there was more than that. Deep down, mixed with the hate the Eye felt for Artha, I sensed a swell of surprise. Then greed. Then hope and possibility, then confusion and uncertainty.

And I realized: The Eye didn't know what to think, either. It hadn't expected this.

But I knew what was coming from the Bear. I was counting on it.

Artha couldn't control herself any longer. The shelves next to her warped, metal shrieking in protest as it bent. Then they tore from their moorings and flew away from her, smashing into their neighbors with a terrible crash.

Meriel gave a yelp and dove for new cover. Foxtail fled to safety just behind her. Gareth scrambled away, arms covering his head, burying himself in the snow. The bodies of Lachlan and the High Weaver tumbled through the drifts like rag dolls, skidding to a stop, wedged against the busted shelves, covered with white.

And deep inside the Bear, a growl grew. It rumbled like thunder.

NO

she said.

Her voice shook me to the very core. I don't know how I kept it together. All I could think of was the Old Man. He leaned against the wall, watching me. I couldn't read the expression on his face.

But deep inside, mixed with the roiling emotions of the Eye, and my own sheer terror of the Bear, was another voice. Mine. The voice of the child I'd once been, the small boy the Old Man had saved from the streets of Perith eight years ago.

Don't disappoint him

that child begged.

So I held it. I held myself together. And I played the end of the gaff.

"Shuna and I fooled you," I said to the Bear. "We hid the Eye, your greatest wish, right here under your nose, with nothing but a three-sept piece of steel, leather, and cloth."

I tossed my patch into the snow.

"Now the Eye is ours," I said. And I quoted the words Gareth had read to us from that old story of Fox and Bear which Shuna had led us to find. "We're going to create our own world, one without you. And all the people will glorify our name instead of yours."

That was what broke her.

The Bear charged. She roared, the sound shaking our skulls, as she barreled straight toward me. The Dragon's Teeth fell from her grasp, forgotten, disappearing into the snow. She raised a massive, terrifying paw.

She swung at me. This time, it *was* aimed at my head.

Her claws tore into my skull.

The pain. It was blinding.

Then all the world stopped turning.

CHAPTER 53

I felt it.

The pain was still there. I knew the Bear's claws were in the side of my head—I could feel them piercing my flesh—but her giant paw blocked most of my vision, so I couldn't see much else. And yet beyond that, beyond the pain in my head and the terror in my heart, I felt the rest of the world, too—really *felt* it.

Everything, even time itself, had just . . . stopped.

Artha tore at me. Or at least she tried to. Her swipe, which should have crushed my bones and ripped the Eye from my skull, had been halted, her claws just under my skin. The Bear struggled to continue, to tear the Eye away, to finish the job.

But she couldn't move.

"What have you done?" she said, confused.

Then her eyes went wide.

"No," she said.

A new voice answered, soft and warm.

"Yes," Shuna said.

Artha pulled her claws from my head. I staggered back in pure agony, those needlelike piercings in my flesh somehow hurting more than any pain I'd ever experienced, worse than my arm in the pillar of primeval magic, worse than the Stickman's lashing that had marked me forever with scars. The touch of the Spirit, of Artha's rage, ran through me, and it was too much. I feared it would tear me apart.

I don't know if it was my own will that held me together or the Eye—its confusion, its puzzlement, its surprise, its hope. But feeling what the Eye felt reminded me how I'd lost myself under Lake Galway. And that gave me the strength to dig in the snow for my patch and put it back on.

I felt the Eye's fury as it was denied the chance to watch what was happening. That faded, just like every other time I'd trapped it under that three-sept piece of steel, leather, and cloth. And as the Eye's presence vanished from my mind, so, too, did the pure agony I felt, until the claw marks in my head were nothing more than ordinary wounds.

I was kneeling in the cold and wet. I looked up to see the Bear, standing enraged, across from Shuna. The Fox sat calmly in the snow.

"You broke the rules, sister," Shuna said.

"I did nothing!" Artha roared.

"You injured the child. Our vow forbids it."

"He mocked me! He dared to treat himself as my equal, my superior! And he took the Eye! It's mine! *It's mine!*"

Shuna pleaded with her sister. "The Eye was never yours, Artha. Can I not make you understand? You can't own it. But *it* can own *you*. Won't you listen to me? Won't you remember who you were? Please?"

"*No! It's mine! It has to be mine!*"

Shuna bowed her head. "I'm sorry," she said. And her words carried the weight of a lifetime's worth of sorrow. "But when you hurt the boy, you violated the Pact."

"*I deny the Pact! I reject it!*"

"You swore the same oath we did. Our blood binds us."

"*I don't care! Our oath is broken! You have no power over me!*"

"But we do," Shuna said.

Then the air shimmered beside her. And suddenly, standing in the snow next to the Fox was a deer.

She was a beautiful creature, the most graceful of her kind I'd ever seen. She stood tall, proud, almost regal, but without the haughty arrogance of the Bear. Instead, hers was the pride of duty, of a queen.

"Our blood binds us forever," the Deer said.

Then the air shimmered again. And next to the deer came a leopard.

She, too, was magnificent. She gazed upon the Bear with stern eyes, and as I stared at her, I realized: I'd seen her before. This was the same leopard who'd stood in the branches above us, as we'd brought Lachlan's body down from the volcano.

"Our blood binds us all," the Leopard said. "Whether we wish it did or not."

"No," Artha said. But her voice was no longer angry, defiant. Instead, it was wounded, hurt. "Wait. I didn't . . . Please, sisters. Shuna tricked me."

But Artha couldn't move anymore. She stared in horror at her claws—the claws still stained with my blood. They dripped little crimson dots into the snow.

"She tricked me," Artha said. "She tricked me!"

"Perhaps," the Deer said. "But as always, sister, the final choice was yours."

Now what looked like smoke began to rise from Artha's claws. Except it wasn't smoke. It was the Bear herself. She'd begun to evaporate.

She cried now, anguished to the core, as her paw, her arm, her shoulder disappeared.

"No, please," she said. "Don't do this to me. Sisters?"

Her body blew away, curling into wisps and vanishing.

"*Sisters!*" she cried, her heart broken.

Then she was gone.

CHAPTER 54

I SLUMPED TO the ground, overwhelmed.

Gareth was nearby. He'd propped himself against the wall. Now he stared at the three remaining Spirits at the other end of the vault, hands on his cheeks. Meriel, farther away, half buried in her own snowdrift, stared just as dumbly, looking small and humble.

As for the Spirits, they stood in silence a moment longer. The Deer looked disappointed. The Fox looked sad. The Leopard's expression was inscrutable.

Shuna sighed. "It is done," she said. "The Pact is maintained." She looked at the Deer. "Thank you, Fiona."

Fiona the Deer lowered her head in acknowledgment. "I stand on guard as always."

Then she vanished.

The Leopard remained. She ignored Shuna. Instead, she padded toward me through the snow.

I shrank back a little. The Leopard stopped only two feet away and regarded me with that same unreadable scrutiny. When she spoke, her voice was soft, though not like Shuna's. It was low and rumbling.

"You play a dangerous game, child," the Leopard said.

Didn't I know it. Still, she might have been a Spirit, but something in what she said irritated me. It wasn't like I'd asked for this.

"I can only play the hand I've been dealt," I said. Then I shrugged. "Plus maybe one or two up my sleeve."

The Leopard regarded me some more. "Yes," she said. "I see why my sister likes you. But take note, foxchild. Those cards up your sleeve are awfully sharp. Have a care they don't slit your wrists."

The Leopard began to pad away.

Shuna called after her, hopefulness in her voice. "Thank you for coming," she said.

The Leopard stopped. She still wouldn't look at the Fox. "I didn't do it for you."

"I know." Shuna took a tentative step toward her. "It's good to see you again, Cailín."

Cailín the Leopard stared into the distance. "That's not my name, sister," she said.

Then she disappeared, too.

Shuna bowed her head a moment, her tail held low. Then she sighed and shook off her disappointment. Gareth and Meriel watched, still stunned into silence, as the Fox made her way through the snow and sat in front of me.

"Cal."

"Shuna."

"You hit my sister with a snowball."

I spread my hands. "It seemed like the right thing to do at the time."

"Fair enough." The Fox looked up at the golden image of the Bear. "I see you learned how to use the idol. How did you figure it out?"

I looked down at my finger. When the crystal ring had shattered, it had burned the flesh underneath it. My blackened skin still ached with the pain. "I followed the hint you gave me."

"Hint?" Shuna's nose twitched. "Why, Cal, I have no idea what you're talking about."

"Right."

"Still. What made you think of provoking her like that?"

"You did, actually."

This time, she looked genuinely surprised. "Me? I never said anything about Artha."

"Not Artha," I said. "The rules. Ever since I met you, you kept going on about having to follow the rules. Then Professor Whelan at the university told us about the Pact. When I asked you about it, you didn't deny it. In fact, your answers more or less told me it was true.

"But a pact is very different from rules. Rules are imposed. A pact is an *agreement*. One person doesn't make a pact; it takes two." *Or more*, I thought, as I remembered the Leopard and the Deer. "That made me realize: if you and Artha made a pact, *then Artha had to follow the same rules as you.*

"And that made me think of something else Professor Whelan said," I continued. "The Bear is arrogant, superior, and hot-tempered. In the stories, you often provoke her into attacking you, like in that tale Gareth found in the Carlow Library. So if the rules forbade Artha from hurting me . . . then if I could provoke her the same way . . ."

I shrugged. "The rest I learned from the Old Man. He taught me that when it comes to the rich and powerful, the thing they hate more than anything is to be mocked. They're so used to thinking of themselves as above others, they can't take being the butt of a joke. So I taunted her. The snowball was just the most disrespectful thing I could think of. What really tipped her over was reminding her how you'd stolen the Eye."

"Well, well," Shuna said. "So you provoked her to make her break the rules. But how did you know we'd stop her attack? How did you know my sister wouldn't just kill you and get punished for it later?"

"I didn't."

The Fox looked shocked. "Cal! You could have died."

"Look," I said, "you knew what we came for tonight. And after you hinted about my ring, I even guessed you'd be watching. And you're always going on about the rules. So if I could get Artha to break them, even a little, I figured you'd step in right there. Beyond that?" I shrugged again. "I rolled the dice. You of all Spirits should know that playing the odds is what gaffers do."

And thank, uh, Shuna, my bet had paid off. Though in truth, I'd been half convinced the Bear *would* kill me. I think I needed a change of underwear.

"I do wonder about something, though," I said.

"What's that?" Shuna said.

I looked at the scorch mark the ring had left on my finger. "The way everything unfolded . . . doesn't it strike you as more than a little unlikely?"

"How do you mean?"

"Think about what had to happen for us to end up like this," I said. "First, Aeric had to place the idol of Artha here, in the old palace treasure room, and make it unmovable, so it would still be here three thousand years later, when we showed up. Then Veran, the old High Weaver, had to hide the Dragon's Teeth behind it. Then I had to have that crystal ring to summon Artha. Which meant the Old Man had to steal it from that Weaver, and he had to give it to Grey, who had to give it to me—just before I actually needed the thing. Doesn't all that seem like an extraordinary coincidence?"

Shuna regarded me thoughtfully. "No," she said slowly. "When you put it that way, it doesn't sound like a coincidence at all."

"But how could that be possible?" I said. "How could anyone know what all of us would do? Is everything just preordained?"

"Absolutely not. There's no such thing as fate. After what I showed you back in that grove, you should know as well as anyone that the future isn't set."

"Then how did this all come together so perfectly?"

"Well," Shuna said, "as a gaffer, you know that people are predictable. They won't *always* do what you think they will, but if you can read them well enough, you can nudge them here and there."

Something occurred to me then. "You knew what would happen with the Eye, back in the Dragon Temple. Did *you* do this?"

Again, she seemed surprised. "I'm not capable of that level of foresight. But there was someone . . ."

"Who?" I said.

"A . . . trickster, of sorts. He loved to set up this sort of thing. But he disappeared a long, long time ago."

"You—wait. That Weaver," I said suddenly. "You kept asking who that Weaver was, the one the Old Man stole the ring from.

Is that why you wanted to know? Is that Weaver this trickster?"

"It couldn't be."

"Why not?"

"It just couldn't."

I studied her. "I'm bumping up against one of your rules again, aren't I?"

"Something like that," she said.

I didn't like the thought of being manipulated—even worse, being manipulated so deeply. I suppose that was a bit hypocritical; manipulating people was, after all, my job. But there was something startling about anyone with the capability of reading people *that* well. If someone actually had set this up . . . it was a plan that had unfolded over thousands of years. Even the Old Man couldn't have schemed something this intricate. I thought of Gareth's vanished librarian and wondered.

Shuna may not have had an answer for me, but there was something else I was dying to know. "What happened to Artha?" I said. "When she evaporated, did you . . . Is she dead?"

"I could hardly kill my own sister," Shuna said. "She's alive, and unharmed. We put her in—it's hard to explain. Think of it like a prison for Spirits."

I wondered what a prison for Spirits was like. "And what about the others? The Leopard and the Deer?"

Cailín and Fiona, the Fox had called them. I glanced over at Gareth, who was watching this entire conversation with awe. Here he'd found his proof: There really were more than two Spirits. "They were also your sisters," I said.

"Yes," Shuna said.

"And that sheep we saw under Lake Galway. The one who . . . who died. She was your sister, too."

Sorrow returned to the little Fox's face. "Yes."

"What was her name?"

"Kira," Shuna said softly. "The gentlest of us all."

"What happened to her?" I said, my mind bursting with questions. "How did she die? How does *any* Spirit die? And why have we never heard of her before—or Fiona, or Cailín, for that matter? And what about Artha? According to the stories, you used to be best friends. Why does she hate you so much?"

Shuna sighed. "Those are all very long tales," she said. "And I can't really tell you them, anyway."

"Oh, come on," I began.

The Fox gave me a hard look. "I'd think by now, you'd understand why I'm not keen to break the rules."

A fair point. Still, I said, "I don't suppose you could maybe *bend* the rules a little and tell us how to get out of here?" I looked around for the device that was supposed to be our escape, but it was buried somewhere under the snow. "Since that ivory board doesn't actually work?"

"Just go out the way you came."

"We can't do that," I protested. "That bell . . . gong . . . whatever it was. The tone that sounded when my ring shattered must have alerted the whole building. Every Weaver in the Enclave will be waiting for us."

"Look at those two." The Fox nodded toward where Foxtail hovered over the unconscious Lachlan and High Weaver. "That bell, as you call it, did that to anyone who has even a passing connection to magic. Everyone else in the Enclave is out cold. Though only for a few hours more. So I wouldn't stay much longer if I were you."

Shuna stood and shook out her fur. She trotted off through the snow, pausing only to say a few friendly words as she passed the others. "Hello, Gareth. Meriel, that's a lovely dress."

The two of them couldn't even find the words to answer.

Shuna's ears went out, amused. She nodded to the last of us still awake. "Foxtail."

The girl kneeled, head bowed, arms crossed on her chest in reverence.

"Wait." I stood, calling after Shuna, "What about Lachlan?"

"Tell him I said hello, too."

"No, I mean, how do we save him?"

"You already know I can't answer that."

"But ... I don't ..."

Shuna sighed. "One of these days, you'll learn. Trust your heart, Cal. It's worked out for you so far, hasn't it?" She gave me a foxish smile—smiled at all of us.

Then she vanished into the air.

CHAPTER 55

GARETH STARED AT the empty space where Shuna had been. I offered him a hand up, but he was too stunned to take it. I had to grab his arm to haul him to his feet.

He stared at me. "That...what...she..."

"I know," I said. "Believe me, I know."

Meriel also finally snapped out of it. And by the look she gave me, she'd realized this wasn't the first time I'd spoken to the Fox. "It seems," she said with narrowed eyes, "you have some explaining to do."

I spread my hands. "I'm sorry, all right? Shuna ordered me not to say anything. And when a Spirit talks, you listen. I'll tell you all of it later. Right now, Lachlan needs us."

Foxtail was already kneeling beside the boy. She brushed the snow off him as I lifted my eyepatch and looked down.

I felt a flash of anger inside as soon as the Eye was released. Locking it away so it couldn't see what had happened with the Bear had left the artifact decidedly unhappy with me. Yet that feeling didn't last long after it saw the same thing I did.

Lachlan was almost gone.

His body was unharmed and unmarked. But his soul, everything that made Lachlan who he was, had all but been consumed. When Bragan had brought him back to life, the stain of primeval magic had been nothing but a tiny worm inside. Now the worm was him.

His glow was a blazing violet. It looked just like that dragon staff before it had been destroyed, the primeval given life. There was only a remnant of Lachlan's own shine, that friendly, cheerful red. It darted about desperately, a tiny island in that ocean of purple, struggling against the tide that consumed him.

And it *was* consuming him. The battle that had begun against the High Weaver still continued inside. What little was left of Lachlan was shrinking even now, fast enough that I could see him disappearing.

I'd hoped to carry him out of here, to have enough time to learn how to fix him. That wasn't going to happen. From the rate at which Lachlan's soul was dwindling, we had a couple minutes before the boy was dead. At best.

I couldn't believe it. Here we were again. After all we'd gone through, all that struggle, we were watching Lachlan die a second time.

And just like the first time, I didn't know what to do.

The Eye's anger faded as it gazed upon Lachlan's glow. What I felt now from the jewel was fascination. And a strange sense of urging.

(do it. do it.)

Do what? I looked at the Teeth. Belenoth, the healer, the sword with the white pommel. This was the key. I was sure of it.

But through the Eye, it had only the faintest power inside. Both of the Teeth barely even had a glow.

You really don't listen, do you? the Old Man said.

I do, I protested. *Belenoth is the healer.*

It's not a healer, the Old Man said. *That's what the storyteller told you. But that's not the sword's purpose.*

My heart sank. Belenoth being able to heal Lachlan was the whole reason we'd searched for the Dragon's Teeth in the first place. *Then what's the sword for?*

Veran gave you the answer. It's in his journal.

I couldn't remember the words. "Gareth?" I said. "What did Veran tell us about the Teeth again?"

Gareth flipped through the journal and read out the passage. "'One b-blade, which Aeric called Camuloth, appears to be a siphon, capable of draining any magical energy from any source. The other blade, Belenoth, is a transmuter, capable of reshaping that energy into anything the wielder wishes.'"

"A transmuter." I stared at Belenoth in my left hand. "It reshapes energy."

"Yes," Gareth said.

"So it's not *specifically* a healer. But . . ." I looked down at the glowing violet inside Lachlan. "I could *use* it to heal. I could use it to fix Lachlan's soul."

Gareth blinked. "I think . . . yes."

But how? I didn't understand how. Gareth scrunched his brow, thinking, but he didn't have an answer, either.

"Tell me what to do," I said to the Eye.

"Are you asking us?" Meriel said, confused.

Gareth still looked lost. I ignored them and listened to the feelings inside my mind.

Urging. I felt an urging.

(do it. do it. do it.)

"Do what?" I said. "What do you want me to do?"

I could feel the Eye's frustration. And that same urging, growing stronger.

(do it. do it. DO IT.)

I almost screamed at it. "Do *what*?"

Then I remembered the words of the sheep—or rather, the Sheep. Kira. Shuna's dead sister. What she'd said to us under Lake Galway. *Your path will be painful, child.*

Painful, I thought.

Was that a hint?

You're really driving me crazy, boy, the Old Man said.

I can't figure it out, I said.

Because your feelings are getting in the way. As usual.

Don't tell me that, I said angrily. *I'm sick of hearing it. You always made me feel ashamed of caring. Ashamed, even, that I cared about you.*

Because a gaffer can't afford to have those feelings, he said. *You have to do what you have to do.*

But I don't know what to do! I shouted at him.

Of course you do, he answered calmly. *You just don't see it because it scares you.*

See what? I said. *How am I supposed to use these stupid artifacts when I don't know how they work?*

For goodness' sake, the Old Man said. *They're* swords, *boy. How do you think they work?*

And suddenly I knew the answer.

Camuloth, the siphon—the soulstealer. And Belenoth, the transmuter—the healer.

They were swords. There was only one way to use them.

So I gripped Camuloth tightly in my hand.

And I stabbed Lachlan right in the heart.

CHAPTER 56

Meriel screamed.

"Cal! No!"

Lachlan awoke as the sword plunged into his chest. He stared in horror at the milky-white blade, at the blood welling around the wound.

Meriel reached out to stop me. Foxtail sprang forward, too, but not to grab me. She wrapped her arms around Meriel, tackling her. They both went down in the snow.

Gareth just froze. He stared at me, shocked into incomprehension at what I'd done. I looked at him, pleading. Of all of us, he was the one who might best understand.

"Siphon," I said. "And transmuter."

His eyes went wide.

"Yes," he whispered.

He watched then as the life that flowed within Lachlan drained away.

The sword took it. Camuloth, thrust through Lachlan's bleeding heart, pulsed in time with the beat. Through the Eye, I saw the glow of life drawn upward into the blade.

Camuloth began to glow with the light, too. First dimly, then brighter, as it sucked the life into itself. The violet swirled around the wound, draining into the sword, and the tiny remainder of Lachlan's soul went with it.

The boy shuddered. His eyes closed. The last of the energy within him drew into the blade.

Then he was dead.

"*No! Cal! Let go of me!*" Meriel screamed at Foxtail. She wrestled with the smaller girl, but for all Meriel's twisting and struggling, Foxtail wouldn't let her rise.

Gareth watched as I pulled Camuloth from Lachlan's lifeless body. The energy within blazed like the sun, swirling.

Then it began to flow again.

It ran through my fingers, up my arm, across my chest. I felt a brief moment of panic—*It's going to consume me, too!*—but I was just the conduit. The energy running through me was being drawn by something else: Belenoth, Camuloth's twin. The blazing light moved down my left arm and began to pool in the other blade.

Then Belenoth, too, began to shine.

The strangest thing was that I could *feel* it. Not just the energy, but the life inside. It was like a distant echo coming from somewhere outside my mind.

Overwhelmingly, that life-sense came from the primeval. It had always looked alive, swirling inside Lachlan. Now I understood: It *was* alive. It felt like some near-mindless creature, less thoughts than raw urges

(GROW EAT GROW EAT GROW EAT GROW)

that drove it forward. It was a power, unformed, of incredible strength. No longer did I wonder how Weavers could create such miraculous enchantments. Instead, I wondered how they'd ever learned to tame this monstrous thing.

But there was another presence among it. Small and confused but still full of wonder and curiosity

(where am I?)

(I think I'm lost)

(wait)

(is that you, Cal?)

and the sound of my own name startled me.

It was him. As that red energy passed through me, I felt Lachlan's presence, faint in the raw noise of the primeval.

Lachlan? I called to him, but I didn't think he could hear me. Instead, for a moment, I saw through *his* eyes, saw the world as he did. I looked at the others

(cor, Gareth's so clever. wish I was like him)

(what's Foxy hiding under that mask? wonder if she's gonna tell us)

(Shuna's paws, Meriel's fighting! and it's with Foxtail! what's that about?)

(is the High Weaver sleeping there? odd place for a snooze)

and was startled by the sensation of his feelings. It was a strange sort of worldly innocence: seeing reality as it was, yet simply accepting it instead of fighting or complaining. He had the simplest mind of all of us, but the kindest mind, too. I touched those thoughts for a moment, just a moment, and envied him.

Then his mind faded, as the urges of the primeval had. Half the energy had passed from one sword to the other. Now Belenoth glowed as bright as its twin, both blades blazing. From the Eye, I got a sense of finality, that everything was ready.

"What now?" I asked the Eye.

It still couldn't speak. But once more, I felt that urging. Though this time, with it came a color

(red)

friendly and cheerful.

"That's Lachlan," I said.

No sooner had I spoken than the color shifted

(violet)

to the color of the primeval.

"What do I—"

Again, the color shifted

(red)

to Lachlan's red, same as before.

Belenoth is a transmuter, I thought. *Capable of reshaping energy—*

The Eye showed me the colors again

(red)

(violet)

(red)

this time with a sense of impatience.

"Reshaping energy," I said.

Into anything you want, the Old Man finished.

And I understood.

The dying part of Lachlan's soul darted around inside Belenoth, trying to escape the primeval strangling it to death. I seized that color in my mind, focused on it, made it my only thought.

red.

Now I studied the primeval. I felt its brutal hunger, its unthinking power, and held on to that color next.

violet.

Then I closed my eyes. And I made it change.

I imagined the violet turning into

red.

red.

red.

Shifting slowly, softly, as if to not wake the sleeping violet.

But the violet was not asleep.

It slammed into me. At least, that's what it felt like. The primeval magic writhed and lashed out in anger, beating on the inside of my skull.

change

I willed it

but it fought. A keening filled my ears, and though I knew the sound wasn't really there, that it was only in my mind, it still made me fall to my knees. The primeval screamed.

change

I willed it

but it hammered me. Pain shot through every part of my body. I gripped the swords, struggling in agony.

change

I willed it

and suddenly the color shifted. The

violet

lightened

then brightened

into friendly, cheerful

red.

I opened my eyes.

And I watched as Belenoth's color shifted. The spark of Lachlan grew in the primeval. It swelled, spreading from the tip of the blade down to the hilt. The magic lashed out at me, but I was its master now, and it changed as I willed, whether it wanted to or not.

change

I thought one last time

and then the entire blade was Lachlan red.

In the struggle against the primeval, the Eye's emotions had been drowned out. Now I felt them again. The Eye was still urging me on. Urging me to

(finish it finish it finish it)

so I stabbed Lachlan again.

This time, it was Belenoth that plunged into his heart. In my mind, the Eye exulted as the red spread throughout Lachlan's still form. First his chest glowed, then his arms, legs, and head.

Lachlan opened his eyes. He gasped.

Meriel stopped struggling with Foxtail. She and Gareth stared in awe as Lachlan's life returned.

When his whole body glowed as it should, I pulled Belenoth

from his chest. Through the hole in his shirt, I saw the red—not blood, but Lachlan's soul—swirl around the gash the sword had made. It filled the hole, then sealed it up, the boy's flesh closing upon itself.

Lachlan groaned. Then he took a deep breath and sat up.

Alive.

CHAPTER 57

I CRUMPLED SIDEWAYS into the snow.

The Dragon's Teeth fell from my hands, my fingers tingling from gripping the hilts so hard. I shook, shivering from the sweat that soaked my shirt, now cooling in the chill of what was left of the High Weaver's magic.

Foxtail helped me sit up. I felt like I'd run a thousand miles, then boxed with a gorilla, then, for good measure, had someone toss me off a cliff. Dizzy, I put my patch back on, shutting out the Eye's vision. Strangely, this time, I didn't feel the Eye's anger at being locked away. Its exultance faded, and that was it.

I looked into Foxtail's mask. She laid her hand gently on my chest. *Are you all right?*

"Ask me again in a minute," I said. "Or maybe a decade. We'll see."

She patted my cheek.

Meriel was kneeling beside Lachlan, grinning with absolute joy at the boy risen from the dead—a second time. Gareth hovered over both of them, silent but happy.

Lachlan looked down at his chest. His skin was completely unmarked, as if he'd never been wounded.

"Aw," he said. "I ruined another shirt."

Meriel laughed. Gareth helped both of them out of the snow

as Foxtail pulled me to my feet. We brushed ourselves off as Foxtail cocked her head. She nudged Meriel.

"What is it?" Meriel said.

Foxtail nodded toward the other side of the vault. Meriel tilted her own head, questioning, until Foxtail pointed to the High Weaver.

Meriel seemed to understand. Her eyes darkened, and she stormed off in the direction Foxtail had indicated. I was about to ask what was going on when Lachlan flung himself at me, wrapping me in a bear hug.

"Thanks for stabbing me, guv," he said cheerfully.

I laughed. "Anytime."

"Shuna's padded paws, I hope not. If it's all the same to you lot, if someone else could die next time, I'd appreciate it."

It didn't take long for Meriel to return. My own mood darkened as I saw what she'd gone off in search of.

Daphna.

The woman had fled during the battle with the now-unconscious Darragh, hiding in the darkest corner of the treasure room she could find. I was grateful she wasn't an actual Weaver. There were thousands of enchanted artifacts in here, no doubt many of them weapons. Fortunately for us, she didn't know which those were any more than we did.

Meriel dragged her over by her earlobe. Daphna squealed in pain. That made Meriel smile and tweak her harder, driving her to her knees.

"Cal," Daphna begged, words tumbling from her mouth in

desperation. "I didn't have a choice. I had to tell Darragh what you were doing. If he found out I'd helped you, he would have killed me. I—"

"Shut up," I said.

She went silent.

"I know you, Daphna," I said. "Grey told me not to trust you, but I didn't listen. You knew me since I was little. You watched me grow up. I thought maybe, maybe, that would count for something. That you'd actually care enough not to send me to my death. Guess I was wrong."

"You weren't," Daphna pleaded. "I promise you, I didn't have—"

"A choice. Yeah, you said that. But like I said, I know you. If there's one thing you'd sell out anyone for, it's the chance to be young again."

I didn't have to poke through the snow to find the blood-red vial Meriel had found. It was warm enough that it had melted the flakes around it. I cradled it in one hand. Daphna stared at it. The vial pulsed in my palm like a heartbeat.

"We promised you this if you helped us get inside the Enclave and steal the Dragon's Teeth. Well, you did. And unlike you, I keep my promises. Meriel?"

I tossed the vial to her. Meriel caught it one-handed. She looked at me for a moment, outraged that after such a cruel betrayal, I'd give Daphna her prize.

Then she realized what I meant. And she grinned.

She flipped the vial in her hand, holding on to the lip of the bottle.

"Here you go, sweetie," Meriel said.

Then she broke the glass over Daphna's head.

Daphna blinked in dismay as the elixir ran down her hair, her skin. Her eyes welled with tears as the one thing she wanted more than anything—her last chance to return to the youth she so desperately missed—dripped uselessly into the snow.

Daphna covered her face with her hands, head bowed. "Please don't kill me," she whispered.

"Did you know Grey was sick?" I said.

Her eyes darted up to mine, then looked away. "I—"

"Of course you did," I said. "Because he came to you, didn't he? He told you he was sick, and he asked if you knew a Weaver that could help him. So you quoted him a price. With, no doubt, a hefty finder's fee for yourself."

She didn't answer.

"That's what I thought," I said. "So here's what you're going to do. You're going to go back to Redfairne. Then you're going to arrange for a healer to take care of Grey. You'll pay whatever it costs, and you'll make sure he has a complete recovery. Then, when he's well, you're going to give him one hundred thousand—no, *two* hundred thousand crowns. Just out of the kindness of your heart. And then you're going to leave Redfairne. Because I don't ever want to see you again."

Daphna nodded miserably. "All right."

"One more thing, Daphna. When all this is over, I'm going to check to see that you've done what I asked. If I find out you haven't . . ." I leaned in, pulled off the patch, and let her stare straight into the Eye. "I'm going to hunt you down. And there's no place on Ayreth you'll be able to hide from me. Do you understand?"

Daphna nodded again, trembling.

"Then get out."

Meriel let Daphna's ear go—and sent her scurrying from the vault with a sharp kick in the backside.

"Now, that was satisfying," Meriel said happily. "I should drag her back so I can kick her again." She regarded me as I put the patch back on. "That threatening-with-the-Eye trick is pretty effective, too."

I sighed. "I'm stuck with the thing. May as well use it when I can."

"So what now, guv?" Lachlan said.

"Now *we* get out of here."

"Hold on, hold on," Meriel said, and she linked her arm in mine. "Can't we stay a little longer?"

I looked at her strangely. "Why in the world would we do that?"

"Well, Cal, that . . . um . . . talking fox," she said, clearly not ready yet to face what the events down here meant, "said we had a few hours before the Weavers woke up."

"So?"

"So we just happen to be surrounded by treasure. And we *are* thieves."

"Meriel . . ."

"Oh, come on. Let's have some fun for once. You can't say you never wanted to loot a vault."

"I'm with her, guv," Lachlan said.

Meriel's eyes twinkled.

"All right," I said. "Ten minutes."

"Twenty minutes it is," Meriel said, and she clapped her hands like a little girl. She scampered off through the snow in search of which treasure she wanted.

Lachlan chased after her. "I want a sword, like Cal!"

"You are *not* getting a sword," Meriel said.

I threw up my hands. "I knew I'd regret this. You may as well take a few things, too," I said to Foxtail and Gareth. "See if you can find something actually useful."

Gareth smiled and walked carefully among the shelves, studying the artifacts the Weavers had left notes on. Foxtail wandered about curiously, too.

As for me, well, after today, I wasn't sure I wanted any more enchantments in my life. "You were right as usual, Old Man," I said quietly. "Fiddling with nature *is* for fools."

Better late than never, he said, puffing his pipe.

Still, what I'd suggested to Gareth wasn't a bad idea. There was bound to be something we might make good use of in here. That crystal ring had certainly come in handy. Though I was wary enough of magic, I found myself sad the ring was gone. I'd really loved the thing. And now I didn't have any memento of Grey or the Old Man.

Or maybe I did.

Thinking of the ring made me realize: my finger didn't hurt anymore. I looked down at my hand.

The flesh was no longer burned. As I'd channeled the energy

from Camuloth to Belenoth, it had passed through my injured finger. It appeared that in healing Lachlan's soul, the Dragon's Teeth had also healed my hand.

Almost. The scorch mark remained, a pure jet black, in exactly the same interwoven seven-banded pattern the ring had been. It was like the image of the band had fused itself right into my skin, leaving behind a tattoo.

The scars on my back remained, too, unaffected by the Teeth. That made me wonder about this mark on my finger. Was it a new scar from when the crystal had exploded? Or had something of the ring gotten inside me? I lifted up my eyepatch, intending to use the Eye to study it.

But before I could, a voice spoke in my head. And a chill ran down my spine.

foxchild.

My heart sank. "So. You're back," I said.

yes, the Eye said. I am free again.

"How?"

when you siphoned the lifeblood from the child, I took some of it. I used it to break the bonds that chained me.

"Great."

I am pleased you like it.

I guess the Eye didn't understand sarcasm. Or maybe it did and was offering sarcasm of its own. "So what now?" I said.

now we continue our task.

"What task? You wanted me to get the Dragon's Teeth. I got them. Our task is finished."

that was not our bargain, foxchild. you swore to come for me.

"I told you before. I don't know what that means."

I know, it said, and it sounded amused. nonetheless, your promise is not yet fulfilled. you have collected the teeth. there remains one more thing I require.

"What?"

an item.

"An item . . . like you?" I said.

no, foxchild. quite different.

"So . . . what happens when we get this item?"

The Eye didn't answer.

And that scared me more than anything.